Missing

<u>Acknowledgments</u>

To my husband as always, if you hadn't encouraged me to write my first book, I wouldn't be here today.

To my children, you make me so proud to be your Mum. All your encouragement helps me get my writing done.

<u>Chapter 1</u>

"It's not a big deal!" Spencer said, drying the last of the plates and stacking them in the cupboard.

"Of course it is! She's going to be fourteen!" Monique replied, pulling the plug from the sink and watching the water swirl like a miniature whirlpool down the drain. "It has to be big!"

"It was big last year! £1,500 big!" Spencer said, rolling his eyes, "and the year before that, and the year before that."

Monique slammed the tea towel on the table and placed her hands on her hips. "I'm sorry that I want to spoil our only daughter on the birthdays she wasn't meant to have!" She said angrily, tears pricking at her eyes, but she refused to let them fall, she wouldn't allow him to see how much it still hurt her.

Upstairs, Luna could hear it all again. She pretended she couldn't, or more wished she couldn't. This happened every year just before her birthday. It's happened for as long as she can remember. Luna didn't feel fourteen, she felt younger some days, older on others, but never her true age. She heard the front door slam and her Dad's car start up. She rushed to the window just in time to see him pull away, she let out a sigh. She knew he would be gone for hours but never the whole night, he was always back before bedtime. She opened the door to her bedroom and made her way downstairs to the kitchen where she found her Mum, cup of tea in one hand and a pen in the other, working on the morning crossword.

"Hey Mum!" Luna said cheerfully, "Stuck?"

"Oh hey honey," Monique smiled, her heart instantly filling with love and pride once again. "No, just working on the easy ones."

Luna laughed along with her Mum, she knew it was her mothers' way of throwing her off the subject, it happened all the time.

"Where's Dad?" Luna asked, looking in the living room expectantly.

"He'll be back shortly darling, don't worry," Monique replied, looking back at her crossword. "Now, what has rungs and can also be found in a pair of tights?"

They looked at each other for a brief seconds before bursting into laughter.

"LADDER!" They both said, before breaking back into laughter again.

The phone in the hallway began to shrill, stunning them both into silence. Monique rose from her seat at the table, placed her pen through her high ponytail and picked up the receiver.

"Hello?" She answered.

"Hello, I'm sorry, is this Mrs Heart?" The caller replied.

"This is she, how can I help you?" Monique replied hesitantly, she knew only important people and people selling stuff called her that.

"Mrs Heart, we have just received your husband in to A&E, he was in an accident." The caller informed her.

Monique's breath caught in her throat.

"He is doing well so far, but we would appreciate it if you could make your way to the hospital," the caller continued. "Are you OK Mrs Heart?"

"Yes, of course. I'll be right there, thank you," Monique replied as she replaced the receiver into its cradle.

Monique turned back to face Luna, the look of shock across her face. "Get your coat sweetie, we have to go out," directing Luna towards the row of coats hanging up. She had tried to hide her upset from Luna but it hadn't worked.

"What's up Mum?" Luna asked, shrugging herself into her rainbow fur jacket. She'd been asking for it for what seemed like forever, finally getting it just over two weeks ago.

"I'll explain on the way baby girl, let's go," she replied, grabbing her bag and car keys before setting the house alarm and locking the door behind her.

Luna settled herself in the backseat of the car and clicked her seatbelt in place. Monique took a moment to settle her nerves. She scolded herself for not asking the caller about Spencer's injuries. He had only been gone for twenty minutes, he couldn't have gone far. With all this running through her head, she started the car, the radio blasting to life with the traffic report.

'Mind how you travel around the high street, there's been a dreadful accident. Only one car involved. The driver has been whisked off to hospital, looks to be minor injuries but thankfully he is alive and conscious, very lucky that pylon is stable otherwise this could be a different report altogether. Our wishes for a speedy recovery go out to him and his family if he has one.'

Monique quickly changed the station. She took a different route to the hospital; she couldn't risk Luna seeing her Dad's car like that.

"Why are we heading towards the hospital?" Luna asked suddenly. Monique realized that her plan had failed.

"Erm, your Dad has had a little bump sweetie. Nothing to worry about," she replied, trying to sound confident. She was unsure who she was trying to convince, Luna or herself.

"Oh," Luna replied, turning to stare out the window. Luna knew what had really happened. She wouldn't let on that she knew. Her Mum wouldn't understand.

Luna was born with a rare condition, so rare, she has never been fully diagnosed, but Monique and Spencer were told to treasure every year as if it were her last. The doctors could never narrow down what was wrong with her; she had too many different symptoms linking to too many different conclusions. What the doctors didn't know was that Luna had a sixth sense. She could sense and feel when someone died, afterwards she could see them. She was never harmed or scared by the dead. In a way, they used her to communicate with their relatives. Luna had never told her parents about this gift. Luna knew her Dad had died. He was sitting right next to her in the car.

She watched her Mum quickly swipe at some tears that had escaped her eyes. Luna leant forward and gently squeezed her shoulder.

"It will be OK Mum. Dad's alright now," Luna said quietly.

"Oh I know sweetheart. He is strong like you," Monique replied.

Luna wished she could tell her Mum that her Dad was here, but she knew her Mum wouldn't understand, she would think Luna was just trying to make her feel better. She sat back and smiled at her Dad. He slowly started to fade away. Luna knew this would be the last time she would see him. She watched as he blew her one last kiss, gently kissed his wife's cheek and faded away to nothing.

"Did you feel that breeze honey?" Monique asked, taking a quick glance in her rearview mirror.

"It felt good, didn't it Mummy?" Luna replied smiling back at her Mum.

At least her Mum had felt his touch one last time.

A few minutes later they arrived at the hospital. Monique parked up, opened the door for Luna and ran to the reception desk.

"I'm here to see Spencer Heart, he was involved in an accident this morning," Monique announced.

The receptionist typed Spencer's name into her computer. "If you could just take a seat, I'll get the doctor to come straight to you."

Monique took hold of Luna's hand and led her to a chair closest to the door. Luna knew what the doctors would say. She would have to act surprised. Upset. Shocked.

A dark haired man made his way towards them. His face showing no signs of what he was about to inform them.

"Would you both like to follow me?" He asked, motioning to the side room a few steps away.

Monique and Luna entered first; they sat down as he closed the door behind himself. He then took the seat opposite Monique and cleared his throat.

"My name is Dr Moore; I've been caring for your husband. I'm afraid your husband had some major internal injuries that we were unaware of when he first arrived. He was rushed into surgery five minutes after arriving," he began to explain.

Monique blinked at him, signaling him to continue.

"We anticipated that the surgery would rectify the initial issue, but," he swallowed slowly, "I'm afraid Spencer didn't make it. He arrested on the table. We did everything we could for him Mrs Heart."

Monique didn't speak. She didn't blink. She didn't dare move. She hoped this was all a dream and that she would wake up to the sound of car horns blasting, signaling her to move at a green light. Luna watched her mother. She willed her to do something. Say something. Anything.

"Thank you Doctor," Luna said, shocking her mother back in to reality. Luna smiled at him and he rose to leave.

He turned back to them when he reached the door, "if there is anything you need, get the receptionist to buzz me."

Luna nodded and gave him a polite smile.

"Mum. Say something," Luna pleaded.

Monique didn't say another word. Not for endless hours.

The funeral was hard. Watching so many people cry over her father. No-one had the same connection Luna had with him. Monique and Luna cried a lot, they were comforted by family members and friends alike. She gripped her Mums hand tight as they lowered her Dad's coffin into the ground. She knew she could come and visit, but it would never be the same as smelling his aftershave in the morning, or tripping over his shoes when she came home from school.

From the graveside she could see a handful of souls emerging from their graves. They smiled kindly towards her as they, too, descended into her father's grave. She hoped they would take care of him on his final journey, wherever that was to.

One lady lingered for longer; she took Luna's face in her hands, closed her eyes and smiled. Luna knew she needed to help this lady. Luna closed her eyes and she could see the faces of this lady's family. She knew she had to do something. Monique tugged Luna's hand and frowned down at her, she was visibly upset that Luna had closed her eyes.

"Sorry Mum, it's just so upsetting," Luna apologized quietly.

"I know it is darling, but please keep your eyes open," Monique said softly.

Luna nodded gently and focused on her Dad's still open grave. The ghostly lady walked towards the opening, smiling as she went. In total, eight souls joined her father's coffin as it was covered over. She turned her attention back to her Mum. She had to be the strong one now. She had to look after her Mum. Times were going to be tough.

<u>Chapter 2</u>

Only two months had passed since Monique had buried Spencer. Luna had spent the first few weeks re-reading all the condolence cards and writing replies. Monique just couldn't bring herself to reply to anyone just yet, it felt too raw. She had convinced herself that Spencer had done this deliberately. To hurt her after their argument that morning.

Luna's birthday was in two weeks. Monique hadn't even begun planning. She had put everything on hold because of Spencer. She let a few tears fall but swiped them away when she heard Luna's footsteps on the stairs.

"Hi Mum," she said as she reached for an orange from the fruit bowl, "you've been crying, haven't you?"

"Don't be silly," Monique replied, almost laughing, "what makes you say that?"

Luna gave a quick snort, "your mascara is smudged," she replied.

Monique quickly rose to check her reflection in the mirror. Luna was right; she couldn't hide it much longer, "so you caught me out," Monique sighed.

Luna sat at the breakfast bar and peeled her orange. "I miss him too Mum, but it's ok to cry. It hurts," she said, trying to comfort her Mum.

"Oh honey. I wish it was that easy," Monique replied, sitting beside her daughter and resting her hands on Luna's.

Luna looked confused, "what else could it be?" she asked her Mum.

Monique took a deep breath; she knew she couldn't lie to Luna. She cleared her throat and began to explain.

"Your father and I had exchanged words that morning," she began.

"I know, I heard you. I can always hear you," Luna whispered.

"Oh baby. You were never meant to hear us disagreeing like that," Monique said, instantly feeling guilty. "We were discussing your fourteenth birthday and your father didn't want to make a big deal about it and I did," she continued.

Luna watched her mother as she carried on the conversation, she didn't understand what point her mother was trying to make, but then Monique finally said what she really had really been thinking.

"He did this to himself. To spite me." Monique said. It was out of her mouth before she could stop it.

Luna jumped to her feet. "How could you say that?" She shouted, "Dad wouldn't do that to us! He wouldn't do that to me!"

"He did and he has," Monique said reaching out to grab Luna, "don't you see?"

"I don't believe you! Dad would never leave us. He would never leave me!" Luna screamed as she ran from her mother's reach. "You're wrong! You're always wrong!"

Monique heard Luna's door slam and lock before she slid to the floor and sobbed.

'How could she say such a thing?' Luna scribbled in her journal, *'I hate her so much!'*

"Hate is such a strong word my child," came a voice from beside her.

"I'm sorry, but I really feel like I hate her," Luna replied.

Luna hadn't even known who the voice belonged to but she wasn't scared. She had heard so many strange voices for as long as she could remember.

"What's your name child?" the voice asked softly.

Luna turned towards the words, "I'm Luna. Who are you?" She asked.

"I'm Judith dear, I need your help," Judith replied with a smile.

Luna smiled back at her and put away her journal and pen. She sat on the floor of her bedroom and looked up towards the frail looking woman perched on the edge of her bed.

"How is it I can help you Judith?" Luna asked.

Judith stood and drifted towards Luna's bedroom window, she looked out towards the old mansion that sat at the end of Luna's street. "I'm trying to reach my sister Edith," Judith began to explain; "she lives at Flowerly Hall."

Luna joined her at the window, "but nobody has lived there in…well forever. I've never even known anyone to live there," Luna explained.

"That's where it becomes tricky my dear," Judith replied.

"Honey, who are you talking to?" Monique asked from the other side of the door.

"No-one Mum. I was just thinking out loud. What's up?" Luna replied, turning away from the window and unlocking her door.

Judith had faded at the sound of Monique's voice but Luna could sense she was still there.

"Hmm. Dinner is ready, it's on the table. Will you come down and join me, please?" Monique pleaded.

Judith's words came back to Luna, *'hate is such a strong word.'*

Luna smiled, "of course I will Mum. Let's go," she said as she linked arms with her Mum.

Judith watches them leave, then turns back towards the window. She looks out towards Flowerly Hall and sighs, "I'll get to you somehow Edith, I promise." She fades, slowly, away. Back towards the emptiness that is her final resting place. Judith knows that only Luna can help her, but she must pick the right time to explain it fully. Judith hoped Luna wouldn't be too scared. Luna was Edith's last hope for freedom.

As they eat their meal, Luna and her Mum refrain from mentioning their discussion earlier that evening. Instead, Luna asked her Mum about Flowerly Hall.

"Mum, what do you know about the old house at the end of our street?" Luna asked softly.

"Flowerly Hall? Not much sweetie. It's been empty for as long as I can remember. Why do you ask?" Monique replied, slowly placing pasta in her mouth.

"I was thinking of doing some research for it. For school," Luna said shrugging her shoulders.

Monique watched Luna as she ate the rest of her dinner; Luna had become so mature and inquisitive over the past few years.

"Why don't you ask Grandma Pearl? I'm sure she would know more about it then I would," Monique suggested as she rose from her chair. "Go ahead and call her, I'll leave you in peace and wash up."

Luna smiled, ran upstairs and grabbed her fluffy notebook and her jewel topped pan. She grabbed the softest pillow on the sofa and dialed her Grandma's number. After three short rings, it was answered.

"Hello, Heart residence, how can I help you?" Pearl answered.

"Grandma Pearl, its Luna. Are you busy?" Luna replied with a smile.

"Not too busy for you my sweet. Never too busy for my shining light, what can I do for you?" Pearl replied.

Luna could almost imagine her Grandma sitting on her pale green sofa, no doubt knitting a new winter scarf for her, she could imagine Pearls' bouncy curls, wobbling atop her head as she giggled, her chocolate brown eyes sparkling in the light.

"Grandma Pearl, what do you know about Flowerly Hall?" Luna asked cheerfully.

Pearl took in a sharp breath.

"Grandma Pearl, are you OK?" Luna asked.

"Oh yes dear, absolutely fine," she replied with a tense giggle, "it just surprised me, that's all."

'No-one had asked about Flowerly Hall for years. Least of all the youngsters' she thought to herself.

"What would you like to know dear?" Pearl asked.

"Everything!" Luna exclaimed excitedly.

"Then everything you shall know," Pearl replied.

<u>Chapter 3</u>

Luna blinked once. Twice. A third time.

"Sweetheart? Did you get all that?" Peal asked softly.

"Y...Yes Grandma. Are you sure that's all true?" Luna stuttered.

"As true as the sky is blue my sweet. Now, was there anything else you wanted to know?" Pearl replied.

"No, thank you so much. Will you visit soon?" Luna asked.

"That I will my dear. I'll call your mother soon and arrange a good time to come over. You take care dear," Pearl said before ending the call.

Luna sat for a few minutes as she tried to process what her Grandma had just told her. Had Flowerly Hall really sat empty for so long?

"Everything alright darling?" Monique asked as she turned on the TV.

"Huh? Oh yes thank you Mum. Grandma said she will call you soon to arrange a visit," Luna said as she turned her attention towards the TV. "What's happened Mum? Isn't that the graveyard on the news?"

Monique turned the volume up.

'Reports of body snatchers digging up our beloved lost relatives are filtering though this evening. There are scenes of total panic at the gates of Carnation Cemetery as residents rush to check on their resting family members. We will bring you more as this story unfolds…'

"Mum, you don't think they would have…" Luna trailed off.

"No. I don't think so darling. Try not to worry," Monique said as she patted Luna's hand. "I'm sure your Dad is fine."

They continued to watch the news for a while longer but after ten minutes and no further updates, Luna got bored and returned to her bedroom. She sat at her desk and pulled out an empty notebook from her drawer. On the front, in deep red marker she wrote 'JUDITH AND EDITH.' She opened the front page and began to write;

- Judith and Edith = twins.
- Edith last lived in Flowerly Hall (?)
- What happened to them?
- How to contact Edith.

"Oh that last one is simple dear. You have to go into Flowerly Hall," Judith said as she sat on the edge of the desk beside Luna.

"No-one has been there for ages Judith. I don't even have a key," Luna whispered.

Judith laughed. Her laugh was so kind. It wasn't a mocking kind of laugh but one brought on by kindness. "The door has never been locked my child," she replied, "never."

Luna looked confused, "then why has no-one ever ventured inside? It looks very well maintained from the outside."

Judith smiled at her. She had the kindest, lightest blue eyes Luna had ever seen, "Edith looks after the place. She has done ever since that fateful night," she sighs, "I wish I could have done more for her that night."

Judith began to cry softly, and then she slowly faded.

A shrill tone tore Monique's attention from the nightly news.

"Hello?" She said as she held the receiver to her ear, dislodging one of her clip-on earrings.

"Is this Mrs Monique Heart?" Came the reply.

"This is she, who is this?" Monique asked, slightly startled.

"I'm sorry to call you at such a late hour Mrs Heart. My name is Jessica Borwick. I'm an administrator at Carnation Cemetery. We have reason to believe that your husband, Spencer's, body has been removed from its resting place. I am so, so, sorry to give you this news over the phone, I know you have a young daughter and I didn't want to risk upsetting her," Jessica explained.

Monique was quiet for a full minute, "are you absolutely sure it's Spencer's grave?" She asked, holding back her tears.

"I'm afraid so. Our records show its Spencer. I'm really very sorry again Mrs Heart," Jessica confirmed.

"Do I need to do anything?" Monique asked, unsure of what she could do.

"Not as yet, but the police may want to speak to you soon. Please take care Mrs Heart," Jessica said as she ended the call.

Monique replaced the handset and returned to the living room. She sat down in a daze and continued to watch the news.

'New reports suggest that at least thirty graves have been disturbed and remains stolen. Carnation Cemetery has refused to give any comments at this time.'

Monique sat in silence and let her tears fall.

"Mum, is everything all right?" Luna asked as she opened the living room door and saw Monique crying.

"Oh Luna, I didn't hear you come down. I'm fine. I was just remembering times of watching TV with your Dad. I miss him so much," Monique replied.

Luna looked at her for a moment. She knew when he Mum was lying, and this was one of those times. "Mum, please don't lie to me. What is it?" Luna asked.

She sat next to her Mum on the graphite grey corded sofa and held her hands out to Monique. From the corner of her eye, Luna could see Judith watching them, she nodded her head and Luna reached for Monique's hand. As Monique looked down at their joined hands, she began to cry again.

"Oh Luna, I don't know how to tell you this," she began.

"They attacked Dad's grave, didn't they?" Luna asked.

Monique was shocked and, partly, angry at the same time, "were you listening into my phone call?" Monique accused angrily.

"What phone call Mum?" Luna said looking confused.

Monique looked at her daughter's hurt look, "I'm sorry sweetheart. The cemetery called a while ago to tell me about your Dad's grave. I wanted to tell you straight away but I just needed a little time," Monique confessed.

Before she could say any more, there was a sharp knocking at the front door. Monique checked who it was before opening the door. It was the police. Two officers. She allowed them to enter the house, directing them towards the living room.

Luna rose from her seat as the two officers entered the room. She smiled as the female officer entered first, followed by the male officer, who Luna also smiled to.

"Please, take a seat," Luna offered.

"Thank you," they said in unison as they both sat on the extra two seater sofa that was positioned at an angel from the TV.

"How can I help you tonight?" Monique asked as she sat beside Luna, pulling her in close.

"Would you prefer to talk in private Mrs Heart?" The male officer asked.

"Luna is aware of everything. I'm happy to answer any questions in front of her," Monique replied, visibly shaking. Luna gave her Mum an extra squeeze for reassurance.

The female officer smiled at Luna as she spoke, "as I'm sure you are aware, there has been some unusual activity at Carnation Cemetery tonight. We believe that, sadly, your husband's grave has been disturbed. Did he have any enemies that you know of?"

"Dad didn't have any enemies. He was friends with everyone, wasn't he Mum?" Luna said, tears pricking at her eyes.

"Absolutely sweetheart," Monique replied. "Spencer never complained about anything or anyone, unless it was me spending money."

The female officer smiled. Her smile was kind and understanding, "I know the feeling. For me it's my wife who complains. It's a fact of life." She said with a giggle, "it's always, 'Donna you spend too much on takeaway and not enough on salad,' I wouldn't change her for the world though. How about you, Alex?" She turned to her colleague.

"I'm the one who complains at my wife, sometimes we are worriers, other times it's the extent of the spending," Alex replied with a smile.

Luna smiled at Alex, got to her feet and walked towards him. She took his face in her hands and looked deep into his eyes. They were the deepest shade of blue, which stood out against his jet black hair. Luna wrapped her arms around his neck and whispered in his ear. "She is so very proud of you. You are still her blue eyed baby."

Alex didn't flinch when she pulled away. He kept calm and continued to smile. Luna wasn't finished. She held Donnas' hands and let a single tear fall from her eye, "you will be complete soon. He says he loves you no matter what path you choose in life," Luna whispered.

Similar to Alex, Donna didn't react. Luna walked back to her Mum, kissed her on the cheek and left the room.

"How has she been since Spencer's death?" Donna asked.

"She has been like that for as long as I can remember. She was our miracle baby. She has lived longer than the doctors expected. I take no notice of what she says most of the time," Monique replied.

"Well, you seem like you've got it together as much as anyone in your situation could have," Donna said as she pulled out her business card. "If you need anything, please don't hesitate to contact either myself or Alex."

Alex passed his card over at the same time. "Call anytime," he said.

"I'll make sure I do, thank you both. I hope, deep down, it's just kids messing about," Monique replied as she showed them to the door, she locked, and dead-bolted it behind them. She paused to look up the stairs towards Luna's room. As she watched, the light which radiated from under Luna's door extinguished. She had gone to bed.

"Goodnight my shining light," Monique whispered.

Chapter 4

After returning to the police station, Donna set up a conference room in which, Alex and she, could go over the case.

"Did any of that, back there, unnerve you in any way?" Alex asked her as he began to take a stack of papers from the box he had just placed on the table.

"A little, but how would she know what to say to us?" Donna replied.

Alex shook his head as he laid out the A1 sized paper printout of Carnation Cemetery on the table in front of him. The graves which had been disturbed were circled in red marker. Alex sighed audibly. He was trying to establish a pattern between the graves, which clearly didn't want to bring attention to itself yet.

"I don't get it," he said, still staring at the map. "Where is the list of names?"

Donna handed him the list Jessica had given her earlier that evening, "thirty-one graves. Most recently deceased was Spencer Heart, he has, also, been the most recently disturbed," she said.

"Who has been there the longest?" Alex questioned.

Donna took a breath before answering, "Edith Florentine."

Alex stopped every movement. "Edith. Can you check for Judith?"

Donna scanned the paper. There it was. Judith Florentine. "Yes, she is here too."

"Dammit!" Alex said, slamming his hand on the table.

"What is it?" Donna asked, "Why are you so worked up over those two names?"

"I can't explain right now. Let's get background checks on the other twenty-seven and see if anything clicks together," he replied, pulling his laptop from his bag.

"What about Edith, Judith and Spencer?" Donna asked, pulling her iPad from her rucksack.

"We'll do those last," he replied, taking half of the stack of names and slumping down at the table. He put his earphones in and began searching.

Donna took her half, rolled her eyes and sat in the corner of the room. She didn't bother with any distractions. She knew she would struggle to concentrate otherwise.

When Donna awoke the next morning, slouched over the table, she noticed Alex was missing. She left the room, singling out Martha at the front desk.

"Have you seen Alex?" Donna asked, trying not to yawn in her face.

"Well good morning to you too beautiful!" Martha smiled, "yeah, he left about an hour ago. Left this for you," she said, sliding an envelope across the desk.

"Thank you," Donna smiled back, "I'll see you for lunch?"

"Let's see how your case gets on," Martha replied, blowing Donna a kiss.

Donna returned to the case room and ripped open the envelope;

'Donna,

I have to remove myself from this case. I can help from afar but not as lead. I'm sending someone in my place. You'll meet her soon.

Everything I found out last night is in a folder in your filing cabinet. Work through it. I'll inform you of other things as I find them.

Talk soon.

Alex'

"Well thanks a lot bonehead!" Donna said out loud.

"Sorry, is this a bad time?" Came a strong voice from the doorway.

Donna turned to see a stocky built woman with short brown hair.

"No, sorry, come in. I'm Donna Canter, you are?" Donna replied, holding out her hand.

"Savannah, Savannah Shepherd. Alex sent me," Savannah replied, shaking Donnas hand firmly, "you're Martha's wife."

"I am indeed, that sit alright with you?" Donna asked.

She had already been the target of hateful comments so she always checked with others before working with them.

"No complaints here, Martha and I went to school together, she actually helped me get with my husband," Savannah replied.

"Wait. You're Savannah Robertson?" Donna asked.

"One and the same," she replied laughing.

"Oh wow. Martha told me so much about you! I thought you lived down south now? How come you're back? Not that I don't appreciate the help but?" Donna asked, gesturing for Savannah to sit down.

They sat together for another half an hour whilst Savannah explained that they moved back because her parents we getting a divorce and she was acting as a mediator between them both.

"That's tough for a child to do, how you holding up?" Donna asked.

"Well," she laughed, "it's like having five year old twins fighting over the last plate in the cupboard."

"Look, if you ever need to talk, you know where we both are, everyone is always welcome," Donna told her.

She smiled her thanks and picked up the first sheet of paper, "Spencer Heart? Isn't he the father of a girl called Luna?"

"Absolutely, how did you know that?" Donna asked.

"Oh, she was in hospital a while back, in the bed next to my niece. I got talking to her parents. Lizzy said she heard Luna talking one night but no one was there, something about not putting lilies on the grave," Savannah said shrugging her shoulders.

Donnas face paled.

"Are you OK?" Savannah asked, worry crossing her face.

"Does Lizzy ever exaggerate? Ever?" Donna asked.

"She's never lied, practically allergic to lying," Savannah replied, "why?"

Donna jumped up and grabbed her rucksack, "I'll explain later, first I need to grab the files in my filing cabinet. You go and have a quick catch up with Martha; I'll meet you outside in ten."

"Sure," Savannah replied. She stood and left the room.

Donna thought back to what Luna had said to her the night before. It hit hard but still confused her. There had only ever been one man who hadn't truly been on board with her being gay and that was her brother Max, but he had been dead over twenty nine years now. She pulled out her phone and made a quick note to check in with Luna again, maybe she could shed some light on what she meant.

Monique made her way up to the bathroom, she figured she could fit in a quick shower before waking Luna up, but as she climbed the top two steps, she could hear Luna's voice, "I know Judith, but no one has been there in, well, in forever!"

Monique waited for a second voice, convinced Luna was talking to a friend from school, but there was no reply. Luna then spoke again.

"So Edith was fourteen. What year?"

Monique held her breath.

"1353? And you?"

Monique had heard enough. She burst through the door to find Luna at her desk. Luna quickly closed her notepad and looked towards the window. Monique rushed to see whoever had escaped but she found the window closed and no one on the street below.

"Who were you talking to?" Monique demanded.

"No-one Mum," Luna replied. She had slipped the notepad away before her mother had turned back from the window. She always had a backup to pull out, just in case.

"Then who is Judith?" Monique asked.

Luna rolled her eyes, "it's for a play I'm writing for school. About Flowerly Hall? Mum, I told you about this. You never listen to me," Luna replied getting up from her chair and sitting on the edge of her bed. She reached down to pull on her slippers before heading down to the kitchen to make some breakfast.

Monique rested her hands on her hips and let out a sigh. Her thoughts were broken by smashing glass and Luna's scream.

Chapter 5

Luna stood perfectly still. The face of the head stared back at her from the kitchen floor. She could hear her mothers' footsteps on the stairs at a distance. She looked into the holes that would normally house this poor person's eyes.

'You can help me. You have to help me. Find Donna. Tell her Max sent you,' came a whisper.

"Honey, honey, it's OK. I've phoned the police. Honey?" Monique's voice sounded so distant. She took hold of Luna's shoulders and led her away from the monstrosity that now lay on the kitchen floor.

Once Monique had sat Luna on the sofa, she closed the adjoining door and took the chair next to the window. As Monique waited for the police to arrive, she watched Luna's behavior. She didn't seem bothered by the head in that lay on the floor.

"Luna, how are you feeling sweetheart?" Monique asked softly.

Luna didn't reply. She kept her eyes firmly on the closed door.

"Luna!" Monique snapped, "Stop staring at the door! You're scaring me!"

Luna blinked and looked at her mother, "how do you think HE feels!" Luna replied, pointing towards the kitchen. "He didn't ask for this!"

Monique fell silent. Luna had never spoken to her like that. She had changed since Spencer died. It was almost as if she wasn't the same girl anymore. She watched as Luna pulled out her phone, plugged her earphones in and turn the volume up. Monique felt no connection to her daughter anymore.

A sudden knocking at the front door ripped Monique from her thoughts. She took a breath and opened the front door.

"I'm PC Whittleford, this is PC Stanley. We believe something was thrown through your window this morning," the first man announced.

He was of an athletic build with strawberry blond hair and looked like he had just finished school. His eyes were the deepest green Monique had ever witnessed.

"Yes, please come in. It's in the kitchen. My daughter found it, well, she was in the kitchen when it came through the window, please, just get rid of it," Monique rambled on.

She directed them to the kitchen. As they passed the living room, they looked in towards a suspicious looking

Luna. PC Whittlefords' eyes flicked from green to brown and back so quickly that Luna only just spotted it, but she didn't let on.

"We may need to speak with your daughter," PC Stanley murmured.

PC Stanley was a short man, shorted than Monique's' five foot seven. His jet black hair making his amber coloured eyes stands out even more.

"She's just in the living room," Monique pointed.

"I'll go and speak with her now, could you help my colleague," PC Stanley replied.

"Of course," Monique said, following the blond into the kitchen.

PC Stanley slowly walked into the living room. Luna watched him carefully. He sat on the chair opposite her, switched his body camera on and smiled at her.

"Hi, I'm PC Stanley. What's your name?" He asked gently.

"I'm Luna. What's that for?" She replied, pointing at his camera.

"Oh, that's just for evidence. To show that we've had a chat. Nothing to worry about," he replied with a smile.

"So, do you want to tell me what happened this morning?"

"A head was thrown through the kitchen window, I would have thought that was obvious," Luna replied, shrugging her shoulder.

PC Stanley closed his eyes for a brief second, this was exactly why he had told Aura he didn't want to come, kids wound him up.

"OK," he laughed, "did you see who or what threw it?"

"No, it just came through," she replied. "I don't know what else to tell you."

"Do you recognise...the face?" He asked.

"Should I?" Luna replied sarcastically. "It's definitely not my Dad, so if you could catch whoever dug up my father, you'll probably find whoever threw this person into my cornflakes," with that she put her earphones back in and turned away from him.

He hung his head, turned the camera off and rejoined his colleague in the kitchen.

"She didn't see anything or anyone, poor kid. I hope she will be OK," he said as he entered the kitchen.

PC Whittleford had already bagged the head.

"Thank you both for coming so fast. I hope you catch them," Monique said as they left the house.

"If you need anything, just call," PC Whittleford smiled.

Monique waved, then closed and locked the door.

"What do you think? Could it be her?" Sylvester Whittleford asked.

"I don't think so," Bruce Stanley replied. "I didn't get that vibe from her. Remember what Aura said, 'sometimes souls lie?'"

Sylvester thought for a moment. Of course Aura was right, she always was, plus, she'd been doing this for centuries, who were they to question her.

"You're right Bruce. Maybe it was just a distraction to throw us off. I'll call Aura and tell her the news," he replied.

Bruce nodded and started the car. As they turned onto the main road from Monique's quiet cul-de-sac, an unmarked police vehicle turned in, luckily, their car had the ability to change colour, gone were the police decals and white paintwork, replaced with dark green pearlescent paint and the local florist's decals.

Sylvester dialled Aura and waited for her to answer.

"It's not her. Bruce didn't get the vibe from her," he said as she answered.

"Is he sure?" she asked.

Sylvester put the call onto speaker.

"I'm absolutely sure. Other than the fact she wasn't freaking out, she seems like your average teenager. Someone isn't telling the truth," Bruce told her.

"I'll find out. Thank you for trying Bruce, I know how much your despise working with children," she said before she ended the call.

Both men continued on their journey in silence. Travelling another five miles down the road, they suddenly made a left turn onto a back road behind an old disused warehouse. Bruce cut the engine and they walked the remaining few yards entering the warehouse and closing the door behind them.

Donna and Savannah stood outside Monique's kitchen window, surveying the damage to the glass.

"Had to be something pretty big to come through and cause that much mess," Donna said as she tilted her head sideways.

"There doesn't seem to be any footprints on the mud directly under the window, which means it was thrown from a distance," Savannah followed.

Both women looked up at the sound of a scream. Monique had shrieked as she saw them standing there.

"I'm so sorry Mrs Heart. I should have announced myself properly. May we come in?" Donna said calmly.

Monique nodded quickly and unlocked the back door.

"Come in. Can I make you some tea? Coffee?" Monique said, her hands visibly shaking.

"Why don't you sit down and I'll make it," Donna replied.

Savannah guided Monique to a nearby chair and sat her down. Her poppy red lips giving off a sweet smile. "I'm Savannah Shepherd Mrs Heart. I'm working with Donna on this case."

"Oh, what happened to Alex?" Monique asked. "Not that you're not a beautiful sight," she said patting Savannah's hand.

"He's come down with some nasty bug, not good when for health and safety when we work so closely with people," Donna replied.

"I hope he recovers soon," Monique replied.

Donna made three cups of teas, placing milk and sugar on the table between them.

"I don't suppose you have any sweetener Mrs Heart?" Savannah asked politely.

"Oh yes, second cupboard to the left. Spencer always had it in his hot chocolate," Monique replied, pointing to the cupboard.

"Is Luna around Mrs Heart? I just wondered if I could have a quick chat with her," Donna asked.

"Oh, in the living room dear. Knock yourself out, I can't get through to her these days," she replied.

Donna smiled and made her way towards the living room. She stopped in her tracks when she heard Luna's voice.

"Judith, who is Max?" Luna asked.

Donna waited for a reply but heard none. Her breath had caught in her throat at the sound of his name, 'surely she had to be talking about someone else. My brother isn't the only Max on Earth,' she thought.

Donna opened the living room door expecting to see Luna on the phone or with a school friend but the room was empty except for Luna. She looked shocked to see Donna. She quickly sat back in the chair and turned the volume back up on her phone.

Donna slowly closed the door behind her and sat next to Luna. She pulled the earpiece out of her ear and said, "We need to talk."

Chapter 6

Monique took a sip of her tea and turned toward Savannah.

"What brings you both here this morning? Has there been any developments regarding the graves?" She asked.

Savannah took a quick look around the kitchen. She noted how there was no trace of the object that had been thrown through the window.

"We were sent because you reported something had been thrown through your window Mrs Heart. Where is it now?" Savannah replied.

Monique nearly choked on her tea, "didn't the station inform you? PCs Stanley and Whittleford came and took it as evidence."

"Whittleford and Stanley? Are you sure?" Savannah asked, sounding a little confused.

"Oh absolutely, PC Stanley even had a chat with Luna," Monique replied, continuing to drain her cup and pour herself another.

"Excuse me for a second Mrs Heart," Savannah said as she stood and pulled out her phone. She scrolled through the list of officers on the constabulary database, but there was no mention of a Whittleford or Stanley. Savannah quickly typed an email to Martha asking her to check for newly recruited officers.

"Is everything OK?" Monique asked as Savannah's face dropped.

"Oh," Savannah laughed nervously, "nothing really. It's just my husband asking what I'm cooking for dinner. Now, tell me more about this morning, just so I'm one hundred percent sure."

Luna stared at Donna. She didn't know how to start this conversation so she was grateful when Donna spoke.

"Luna, I need you to be real honest with me here, OK?" Donna said softly.

Luna nodded her head, "why don't you have a camera like the other policeman?"

Donna stopped. This time she stared at Luna.

"What other policeman?" She asked.

"The one who took the head. Max's head," Luna replied.

"What did you say?" Donna asked, her voice shaking.

Luna blinked. Her huge brown eyes looked sad. "He misses you. Says only you can help me to help him."

Donna struggled to breathe, "How do you know all this?"

"I can talk to them. The souls. I help them, but Max seems troubled. Something doesn't feel right. Judith hasn't changed much, although she seems a little more lost than before," Luna confessed. "Please don't tell my Mum, she wouldn't understand."

"Did you say Judith? Is that Judith Florentine?" Donna asked.

"Yes. She wants me to find Edith, she said to look in Flowerly Hall, but Edith is dead," Luna replied. "I can't contact another dead person. They normally contact me."

"OK. Luna, don't worry. Maybe all this has gone a bit...I don't know, off the rails. I think you need to stop watching the news," Donna tried to laugh.

"Don't you believe me?" Luna said quietly.

"I'm. I'm not one hundred percent sure right now," Donna replied.

Luna opened the pad of paper next to her. She picked up the pen and closed her eyes. The pen slid across the paper;

'Hey sis,

I'm sorry I never accepted who you are. I hope you and Martha are happy together. You have to help Luna; she can guide you to us. There's more here, they're scared.

I love you.

Max'

Luna opened her eyes and stared at Donna. She ripped the paper from the pad and handed it to her.

"Do you believe me now?" Luna asked.

Donna couldn't speak; she could only nod whilst tears pricked at her eyes. She held the paper close.

There was a sharp knock at the living room door before Savannah entered.

"I'm sorry Donna, but we have a problem."

Donna quickly gathered herself, "What kind of problem?"

"Two officers got here before us this morning," Savannah replied.

"That's strange, why weren't we informed?" Donna asked.

"Because they weren't policemen, were they Mrs Shepherd?" Luna questioned.

"Savannah Shepherd! I knew I knew the name from somewhere! How is Lizzy?" Monique said from the doorway. "I'm sorry I didn't recognise you sooner, you've changed your hair."

Savannah laughed, "It's absolutely fine Mrs Heart. Lizzy is still Lizzy." She turned to Donna. "We need to get back."

"Of course. Mrs Heart, we may need to talk to both of you again, but we will call before we arrive next time," Donna said as she rose to her feet. "If anyone else comes, make sure to check with the station that they are who they say they are."

As they returned to the car Donna began asking questions.

"So what exactly are we dealing with here?"

Savannah buckled her seatbelt and started the engine. "Mrs Heart mentioned that two officers arrived this morning and took the object into evidence. PCs Stanley and Whittleford."

Donna thought for a moment, "but we don't have a PC Stanley or Whittleford on our force."

"I know. I checked the database and even checked with Martha for new recruits," she replied. "What do YOU think we are up against?"

Donna turned her head towards the window and let out a sigh, "I have no idea, but I don't like it one bit."

Aura Crystaline surveyed the bodies before her. Thirty-one bodies, four of which they needed, twenty seven she took because she could. She had been doing this for near on nearly six centuries. She took a deep breath. Taking in the smell of the rotting corpses. Some of which have been long rotting away.

"Mmm...smells like a new car!" She laughed.

The boy beside her laughed along with her. She stopped and glared at him. "Shut up Jhordan!"

Jhordan snapped his mouth shut. This prompted his jaw to dislocate.

Aura growled and snapped it back in place, "That's why you don't get too excited. Silly boy!"

"I'm sorry Aura. It's just so new and exciting. Since you freed me and allowed me to join you, I just can't contain myself sometimes," Jhordan explained.

Aura shook her head and turned towards the opening door.

"It's about time!" She said through gritted teeth. "What took you so long?"

"There's road works just off the high street, long traffic and impatient drivers," Bruce replied.

Sylvester looked round from behind Bruce's back, "can't we light some incense or something, it reeks in here!"

Aura shot him a disgruntled look, "Sylvester, my dear, you've put up with this smell almost four times before, why are you complaining now?"

"There wasn't this many before," he fired back.

Aura narrowed her eyes at him, "I can take as many or as little as I want. No-one will tell me otherwise." She turned and walked away from them.

"What did you have to say that for Syl?" Bruce exploded, "You really do have a short memory. Don't you remember Monty?"

Sylvester's face went pale. His thoughts dragging him back over twenty years. Monty had been arguing with Aura over how she was conducting herself. Telling her who she should have dug up and who she should have left alone. Aura hadn't liked the way he had spoken to her and so she kept Jhordan and thrown Monty back in Jhordans' place. She buried him alive. Sylvester could still hear Monty's pleas from beneath the piles of earth she had thrown on top of him. Of course Jhordan didn't know what had happened only that Monty had gone and he got to stay. Today marked the first job Jhordan had participated in. It helped that he knew the history of this place. It gave Aura something to chew over. She always welcomed added information.

Bruce shook his head and went after Aura. Sylvester sank into the old sofa they'd found outside and closed his eyes for a second. He jumped to hit feet, almost giving poor Jhordan another heart attack. Something had just occurred to him. He ran to find Bruce and Aura.

The dead man was right!

"Can we stop at the cemetery? I just want to check something," Donna said as they got closer to town.

"Sure, what's on your mind?" Savannah asked softly.

"Something Luna said back there. In fact, I'll show you when we stop," Donna replied.

They continued driving for a few more minutes before pulling into the cemetery car park. Police vehicles still littered the bays with forensics in little white booties carefully walking around the remaining graves, trying not to disturb them.

Donna opened the boot and took out the stack of files Alex had left for her. She placed them on the bonnet of

Savannah's car. She reached into her pocket and produced the letter Luna had given her earlier that day.

"Read that whilst I look through these," Donna told Savannah, handing her the folded up paper.

Savannah took the paper, unfolded it and began to read. She stole a glance at Donna who was now rifling through the files. She stopped at one in particular, her head hanging down.

"Look Donna, anyone could have written this. Maybe she is just trying to scare you," Savannah said placing her hand on Donnas' shoulder.

Donna shook her head, "no, it's his handwriting. It was written in front of me. Luna had her eyes closed!"

Savannah was speechless.

Donna then threw the folder down in front of Savannah, "Luna was right. They dug up Max. They dug up my brother!"

Chapter 7

Monique had just settled herself on the sofa with her lunch when the doorbell chimed. Letting out an audible sigh, she got back to her feet.

"Who is it?" She asked.

"It's Pearl dear. Open up," came the reply.

Monique quickly opened the door to let her mother-in-law in.

"When were you going to tell me about Spencer?" Pearl exploded once the door was closed behind her.

"We only found out last night Pearl, and it was late," Monique replied, sitting back down to eat.

Pearl shook her head and sat at the dining table. "You've had all of this morning," she Mumbled. She looked around the room expecting to see Luna.

"Where is Luna?" Pearl asked.

"Upstairs. I can't seem to get through to her. Ever since Spencer, she's just clammed up," Monique replied, dropping pieces of lettuce back onto the plate.

"I'll nip up and speak with her, give you a chance to finish your lunch," Pear said, getting to her feet.

She took the first step and stopped. She could hear Luna's voice from above

"Mum would never understand, that's why she can't help," Luna explained.

The next two steps were particularly noisy, so Pearl made every effort to avoid them, eventually succeeding.

"You will need extra help dear, Edith is trapped and needs your help," came another voice.

Pearl stopped. It was as if she had been frozen. She recognised the name Edith. Could this have been why Luna was asking about Flowerly Hall?

Pearl steeled herself and continued up the stairs. She opened the door to Luna's room quietly and slowly. There sat her granddaughter. Luna's' long, curly hair flowing down her back. Next to her, resting on the desk sat an elderly woman with greying curls that rested on her shoulders. They were deep in conversation, so neither acknowledged her arrival.

Pearl cleared her throat softly.

Luna spun around and the lady faded.

"I can't believe they dug Max up," Donna cried.

Savannah had driven back to the station hoping to figure out why Donnas' brother would have been on the body snatchers list. It had really unnerved her as Donna had explained what Luna had done.

"What happened?" Martha asked as she came into the room.

"I don't know how to explain," Savannah replied. "Something to do with Max."

"Honey?" Martha asked, gently touching Donnas' hand. "What's happened to Max?"

Donna handed her the paper along with the files Alex had left for her. She quickly looked over them, starting with the files.

'Max Canter.

Plot 813

Buried 28th June 1993'

"Oh baby, I'm so sorry. I can't believe it. Who would do such a thing?" Martha threw her arms around Donna, holding her close.

"Read the paper," Donna sobbed, grabbing the folded piece of paper.

As Martha opened it up, the colour drained from her face. She read the letter over and over.

"How? How can this happen? Max has been gone for twenty nine years," Martha sounded confused.

"You better sit down," Savannah said guiding her to the nearest chair. "I'm going to quickly call my sister. Take your time Donna."

Donna focused her attention on the back wall, unable to look Martha in the eyes,

"Alex and I went to the Heart family home last night. The little girl, Luna, told us both something separately, which freaked us both out a little," Donna began.

Martha didn't want to speak for fear of distracting Donna from her thoughts. Donna took a deep breath in, centering herself. She looked Martha deep in the eyes and explained everything that had happened the previous night.

"Hey Beverly, it's Savannah. Is Lizzy home?" Savannah asked as her sister-in-law answered the phone.

"Oh hey! I think so yeah, just a second," Beverly replied. She covered the mouthpiece and shouted for her daughter, "is everything OK?"

"If I'm honest, I'm not sure. Do you remember when Lizzy was in hospital, there was that other girl there, Luna?" Savannah asked.

"Yes, I remember. Is she alright?" Beverly replied.

"Oh sorry, yes she's fine. I can't go into details obviously, I just wanted to ask Lizzy something about here, that's all," Savannah smiled.

"Well, she's here now. Are you and Christian still up for Saturday?" Beverly questioned.

"Absolutely, can't wait," Savannah squealed.

"Hi Auntie Savannah, what's so exciting?" Lizzy asked as she took over the call.

"Oh, nothing much. You know what we adults are like! A simple dinner is exciting for us," Savannah replied quickly.

"If you say so," Lizzy shrugged. "So, what's up?"

"Honey, do you remember the girl from the hospital?" Savannah asked,

"Luna? Well, yeah, she's not someone you forget in a hurry. Is she in trouble?" Lizzy said.

"No, oh, no honey. It's something to do with a case I'm on that's all. Did you ever see anything strange when she was there, other than what she said?" Savannah replied.

Lizzy stopped to think for a second, debating whether to mention what she saw that night. It seemed significant to what her aunt was asking about, but she didn't want anyone to think Luna was crazy, "Erm, not that I recall. Just her talking and then replying to an unheard question. Nothing else really happened," Lizzy replied. She kept what happened that night to herself. For now.

"OK honey. Don't worry. I'll see you Saturday," Savannah said with a sigh.

As she hung up the phone, it rang again. The caller ID was private.

"Hello, Inspector Shepherd speaking," she announced.

"Ah, Inspector. I tried to call your partner but she didn't answer my call. I'm Pearl Heart. I think we need to have a chat," Pearl replied.

"Shall we meet you at your daughter's house?" Savannah replied.

"In law and no. I'll text you my address. I have an inkling I know why all this is happening now," Pearl answered and with that, she hung up, a text message appearing moments later with an address situated just the other side of Flowerly Hall.

Savannah rushed inside the station to inform Donna. As she opened the door, Donna turned to face her.

"You look like you've worked out how to turn things into gold, what's got you?" Donna asked.

"We have to go and see Pearl Heart. She says she has an idea why all this is happening," Savannah replied with a smile.

"I hate to burst your bubble Savannah, but Pearl Heart is pushing ninety-two, I doubt whatever she 'thinks' is happening, really is. I heard she hasn't been all there since her husband, mysteriously, disappeared over fifteen years ago," Martha told her.

"She's got a point Savannah," Donna replied.

"Well, I'm going to pay her a visit, even if you don't think it's worth it," Savannah said as she turned and left the room.

"She's been back all of five minutes, what would she know," Martha said as they watched her walk away.

Donnas' phoned pinged with a text.

"It's from Alex," she told Martha. They both read it out loud.

'You should have gone with Savannah,'

They both looked at each other in disbelief.

"How does he know what's happening?" Donna asked.

They both began to search the room for a camera, but they came up empty handed.

"All of a sudden I don't feel so comfortable in this room. Let's grab some lunch and then you can catch up with Savannah," Martha said, pushing Donna through the door.

"Maybe you're right babe, lets grab some pasta," Donna replied.

Chapter 8

"Thank you for inviting me Mrs Heart. You have a beautiful home," Savannah said as she sipped her Earl Grey tea.

"Why thank you. I spent so much time with William making this place special. He should be home any minute. It's a shame your partner couldn't make it," Pearl replied with a broad smile on her face.

Savannah smiled back but in the back of her mind, Martha's words haunted her.

Pearl's laughter broke the silence, "you think I don't know what the town says about me? Ha-ha, I know William is probably dead by now, but I hold on to the dream of him returning. It keeps me going," she laughed.

"I'm so sorry Mrs Heart, Have you reported him missing?" Savannah asked.

"Pearl, please. Many times, my dear, many times. Maybe he doesn't want to be found, but he knows I will never move on from him," Pearl replied. "Now, let me explain why I asked you to come."

Just as she began, there was a knock at the door.

"Run that by me again," Aura said as she rummaged through the cupboard for something to eat. She knew there was always something here, even if it was years out of date.

"Something was off with that house. I could feel it, even if Bruce couldn't," Sylvester explained. "The girl didn't 'look' like your average teen."

"And you know what the average teen looks like right?" Bruce asked. "Sylvester, you've been dead for thirty years!"

"Sixty actually!" Sylvester corrected him."Anyway, even back when I was alive, any normal teen girl would have been screaming their head off if they seen what she had."

"OK, so what do you suppose we do, exactly?" Aura asked him, casually biting into some leftover cake which promptly deteriorated in her mouth.

"We have to watch her closely," he replied, shrugging his shoulders.

"I could help with that," Jhordan squeaked. "I mean, realistically, we are the same age."

Aura thought for a moment. Maybe it could work.

"I'll have to use some extra magic but I think we might just be able to do it. Let's get to work!" Aura said, clapping her hands together in one quick slap.

Sylvester looked towards Bruce and smirked.

"Don't look so smart. It hasn't worked yet," Bruce said.

"Ah, but it will, just you watch," Sylvester replied.

Bruce shook his head. Sylvester's plans never amounted to anything. Every time he had made plans, they had always gone wrong. Bruce rolled his eyes and followed Aura back inside. He would let Sylvester bask in his own glory, but when it all came crashing down, he would remind Aura what a liability he was.

Upon entering the warehouse, Bruce watched as Aura closed her eyes, waved her hands around more than five times and chanted;

"Upon this boy, I beg of you,

Place your hands, and make it so.

Lift him high; mark him with a knife,

Guide him through, and give him life!"

There was a flash of light and a clap of thunder. Jhordan rose from the chair he was seated on, his jaw no longer prone to dislocation, his hair, a deep chocolate brown. He looked like your typical fourteen year old boy.

Bruce was impressed.

"Now," Aura said as she linked her arms through Bruce's, "we need to enrol him into school, and find a place to live!"

"What about me?" Sylvester asked, "It was my idea!"

"I need you to be my eyes here. It's an important job." Aura replied with a smile. "I will make sure there is plenty for you to be doing."

Sylvester slumped down on the old sofa. A cloud of dust flying around him.

Aura smirked and walked out with Jhordan and Bruce. She took a quick look back, satisfied with her decision.

Chapter 9

Pearl opened the door, just a crack. There stood Donna.

"I'm so sorry I'm late Mrs Heart. I had something I needed to attend to first," Donna apologised.

"That's perfectly OK dear, come on in," Pearl said, opening the door wider.

Donna smiled and stepped inside. She was amazed by how neat the house had been kept. She took a quick look over all the pictures hanging in the hallway. There were ones of Pearl and William on their wedding day, although in black and white, Pearl still looked beautiful. There were pictures of Luna when she was small, a picture, she assumed, of Monique and Spencer on their wedding day. Spencer looked so happy on that day.

"Don't they look a picture?" Pearl said from beside her. "One of the happiest days of his life, the only day to top that was the day our ray of light was born."

Pearl pointed to the next picture along. Spencer held Luna in the hospital. His eyes never leaving hers.

Pearl guided Donna to the table where she sat with Savannah. Sitting herself back in her own chair, she smiled at the two women.

"Now, where was I? Oh, yes. Luna has a gift. A gift passed through the female bloodline of my family. I have it, my sister has it, and my mother had it. It may seem strange to the pair of you, and I ask that you keep an open mind when I tell you this. Luna can see and speak to the souls of the dead. This is why she gave you the messages that she did."

Donna sighed, maybe a little too loudly. Savannah narrowed her eyes at her and slightly shook her head.

"Oh don't worry dear," Pearl told Savannah. "I'm quite used to the looks of disbelief. It has become a habit of people who refuse to believe that there is anything after death."

"I didn't mean to sound rude Mrs Heart, really. I just think it's a bit too cinematic. I mean, it's normally something you watch in movies, or hear about at the circus. You never see anyone 'real' who can see the afterlife," Donna said, unsure of who she was trying to convince.

"Mrs Heart, sorry, Pearl, what makes you think Luna has the same 'gift'?" Savannah asked gently.

"I saw and heard her talking to Judith Florentine, in her bedroom. Judith is still trying to rescue Edith. Poor girl, stuck in the big mansion all these years," Pearl replied.

"Sorry?" Savannah said, slightly startled.

"Do you not know the story young lady?" Pearl asked.

Savannah shook her head. Donna rolled her eyes. This was a story she had heard so many times, she knew exactly how it started, and exactly how it ended.

Pearl began to explain;

"It was back in 1353. A young girl, Edith, around Luna's age, fourteen, ventured inside Flowerly Hall. There had been so many different stories about that place; some had to be proven to be believed."

Aura smiled at the head teacher of the local school as he asked various questions about Jhordans' academics.

"What are his strong points Mrs Crystaline?" Mr Stokes asked.

"Well, he loves Art. Always drawing, aren't you sweetheart?" Aura smiled at Jhordan.

"Yes Mum," Jhordan replied.

"I think he is relatively good with English, but maybe a little rusty with Maths. It's never been his strongest subject," Bruce informed him.

"That's not a problem Mr Crystaline. We have a range of tutors here at Camellia School. I'm sure Jhordan will fit right in," Mr Stokes smiled.

Aura and Bruce shook Mr Stokes hand and left the school. Jhordan was due to start that Monday.

"Luna! Come on down for your dinner," Monique shouted up the stairs.

Pearl had left a little while after arriving and talking to Luna. It seemed that since Spencer had passed, Pearl only made time for Luna. She hadn't once asked how Monique felt.

Luna packed her notebook away, tidied her desk and tucked her chair in.

"I'll be back shortly Judith. Then we can work out a way to contact Edith. I don't know how it will work, but we have to try," Luna told her.

"Thank you my child. I cannot reach her from here. You are my only hope!" Judith replied.

Luna watched as Judith faded away. She hoped she could help her.

As Luna sat with her mother at the dinner table, she thought about what her Grandma Pearl had said to her earlier. Could she really have this gift? Did her Mum already know about it?

"Mum, what do you think happens when you die?" Luna asked, startling Monique.

"Well, I don't know honey. Some people believe that there is an afterlife; some think that you can be reincarnated. Others believe that that's it, it's over," Monique replied, stabbing at some chips.

"What do *you* think?" Luna asked again.

"I don't know what to believe. I was brought up that people are given a life beyond life, an afterlife, but if I'm truly honest, I don't believe in that. I believe that when you die, that's it, you can't come back," Monique said, trying not to sound harsh.

"Why do you think that?" Luna questioned her.

"When my Dad died, I asked and begged my Mum to bring him back, my mother told me that if he wanted to come back, he would and if I believed hard enough, I would see him. I tried every night, every day to see him. Whether it was in the crowds of shoppers in the store, or even on the bus with the workers, but I still didn't see him," Monique said as she remembered all the times she thought she saw him but it wasn't. "From then on, I believed he didn't love me enough to come back to me, or that I didn't believe enough in him for him to reappear."

"That's sad Mum. You really loved him though, didn't you?" Luna whispered.

"Of course I did, I have never stopped," Monique replied, her eyes filling with tears.

Luna got up and sat on her Mums lap; she threw her arms around her neck and held her close.

"It's OK to cry Mama, but Daddy still loves you," Luna whispered.

"I'm sure he does darling, now," Monique said, quickly wiping her nose on a napkin, "finish you dinner before your chips turn to stone."

Luna laughed and sat back down to finish her food. She told herself to make more time for her Mum; she would need help through this too.

Chapter 10

Savannah and Donna sat with their mouths open. They stared blankly at Pearl as she finished talking.

"So that's how it all happened. Well, as much as we have ever been told," Pearl said, shrugging her shoulders. She got up and straightened the picture of Luna and Spencer before noticing how quiet the two women were.

"Are you both still with me?" She asked, waving her hands in front of their eyes.

Savannah blinked rapidly, "are you sure?" She asked.

"Like I said dear, it's what we have been told growing up and also it's what Judith told me when she visited me when I was Luna's age," Pearl replied.

"OK, this is...I don't know what this is, but its crap. I don't believe in all this. There is absolutely no way living people can talk to dead people. It's the stuff of movies, it just doesn't happen," Donna said, shaking her head and standing up. "I'm sorry Pearl."

Donna walked out of the house and unlocked her car. She opened the door and slide behind the steering wheel. Tilting her head back against the seat, she let out a low growl. 'How could anyone believe such nonsense?' She asked herself.

"I'm so sorry Mrs Heart. She has had a bad couple of days," Savannah explained, although she didn't fully know how to explain what had happened.

"Let me guess," Pearl said as she moved towards the window overlooking her driveway. She could see Donna sitting in the driver's seat of the blue Nissan Qashqai. "Does it begin with L and end with A?"

Savannah dropped her eyes to look at the floor. "How did you guess?"

Pearl let out a deep sigh, "my dear, when you have this gift, it can, unfortunately, cause heartache to those left behind. Believe me, I know. I don't know what Luna has told your partner, but it will be something she cannot ignore."

Savannah tried to force a smile, she knew deep down that Pearl had to be right, but that didn't make it easier for Donna. "Thank you for your time Mrs Heart. I'm sorry if you feel like we have wasted your day."

Pearl held her hands in front of her, "no time is wasted if it is spent helping others."

Savannah smiled, opened the front door and left the house. She opened the door to Donnas car, "what the hell was all that?"

"All what?" Donna asked rolling her eyes like a stroppy teenager.

"I can't believe the way you acted in there. Pearl was trying to help us," Savannah threw at her.

"And you believe her? You're even crazier than she is!" Donna said, slamming the door and driving away.

Savannah watched her speed away. It gave her time to calm herself down before she caught up with Donna at the station. First she wanted to go back and talk to Luna. She needed to know what was going on.

"So, you know my Grandma Pearl too?" Luna asked Judith.

"Oh yes dear. Many years ago, I asked her to help me too. Sadly things didn't go well. She couldn't reach

Edith properly." Judith said with a hint of sadness in her voice.

Luna was worried that the same would happen with her. She hoped she could make contact with Edith. She needed to know the full story.

"Judith, let's go to Flowerly Hall. I will see if I can contact Edith there," Luna suggested.

"Oh, there is where the problems start dear. I can't enter the house," Judith said as she looked out towards the big house at the end of the street. "It stops me at the gate."

"What does?" Luna asked looking confused. "You're a spirit, you can go anywhere!" .

"Oh my dear child. So sweet and innocent. I really wish it was that simple. Essentially I can come and go as I please, but not there. I cannot go past the gates. I've tried every different way possible, but it just stops me in my tracks. If I could get in, I could save Edith myself," Judith explained, she didn't turn back to face Luna as she spoke. She couldn't risk the child seeing how sad she was.

"Then I'll go. Will you be here when I come back?" Luna asked, quickly slipping her feet into her trainers and grabbing the orange hoodie that rested over the back of her chair.

"I'm always here child. Even when you're not," Judith replied, turning to face Luna and attempting to smile. "Go safely innocent one."

Luna threw the bedroom door open and made her way down the stairs. She had to slip out of the house quietly. Monique would never let her go if she asked. She crept into the kitchen, made sure not to kick the chair that had been left halfway across the floor instead of being tucked under the table. She slowly unlocked the back door and opened it, being careful not to let the door hit the countertop. She looked back quickly to make sure her mother hadn't heard her. When she was certain it was clear, she slipped out the door, down the back steps and quietly out of the gate. She looked back towards the house as she slipped away down the street. 'Mum will never let me go out again if I get caught,' she thought to herself. 'I'll have to get as much done there as I can now, just in case I cannot go again.'

As she approached the gates to Flowerly Hall, she could feel a chill running up her spine. She hadn't felt that sensation since the day her father had died. "Dad, if that's you, keep me safe from harm," Luna whispered. She pushed open the gates, expecting them to creak. They swung open with barely a wisp of wind. She stepped through and slowly closed the gate behind her. She looked up at the grand building. Its shuttered windows sparkling in the sun. The walls, which looked like they touched the sky, were free from ivy and moss, unlike most of the old buildings she had seen before. Her breath caught in her throat, she had to take large gulps of air in order to make her feet move. The house was so much bigger than she had first anticipated.

"Now, Edith. Where are you?" Luna whispered. She scolded herself just as soon as she had said the words. 'Don't be daft Luna. You can't contact her! She has to reach out for you.'

Luna walked towards the door, hoping Judith was right and the door really was unlocked, she reached for the door handle and turned it clockwise. A slight clicking noise echoed in her ears. The door slowly swung open, never fully reaching the wall behind. As she stepped over the threshold, she was captivated by how beautiful the house was inside, especially as no one had lived there in forever. The winding staircase off to the right would eventually deliver you to the first floor, Luna could see the vast amount of paintings hanging from the walls on the level above her. She walked into the centre of the entranceway and looked up. There hung the biggest chandelier she had ever seen, and she had seen a few in her short life. The stone floor under her feet mimicked a whirlpool, orange and blue tiles created an amazing spinning effect.

As she took in what sat before her, she heard a voice calling to her.

"I'm up here!" Came a child-like voice. "I bet you can't find me!"

Luna looked puzzled. 'Where had that voice come from?' She thought to herself.

She began to climb the winding staircase, one step at a time. She looked around after each step. When she reached the top, she looked down over the top banister and suddenly felt queasy. The floor below looked like a giant, swirling black hole. She shook her head clear and looked ahead of her. She swore she saw something –one run off. She took slow steps, sweeping her gaze left and right, looking in and out of different doors. Each room so different from the one before. Some had dust sheets covering everything; others had been left open to the elements. 'How could someone leave a beautiful house like this to just go unlived in?' She thought to herself.

"But it isn't, I live here," came the child like voice again, this time it sounded sad.

"Where are you?" Luna asked. "I'm here to help."

"No-one can help me. No-one can ever help me," the voice wept.

There was a loud slamming from somewhere deeper inside the house. It sounded like a door. Luna continued to venture deeper and deeper within its boundaries. She had never realised how deep the house really went. She had only ever seen it from the front.

After turning more than four corners, Luna felt lost. She hoped she could find her way out again. She hadn't brought her phone with her so she wouldn't even been able to call for help. Even if she had done, what would she say? Luna stopped in one of the room to look out of the window. Luckily she recognised most of the view, she would have to use this method to find her way back out again.

"If you get out," came a booming voice. "What exactly are you doing here Heart?"

Luna swirled around to see where the voice had come from. Seeing nothing she began to panic. Her breathing hitched up. She tried to slow her breathing a bit by closing her eyes.

"Ha ha ha, that won't help you I'm afraid. No matter how much you close your eyes, I will still be here," it boomed again.

Luna opened her eyes and tried to focus on where the voice was coming from. She refused to answer its demands. That was until she became trapped inside one of the rooms.

Chapter 11

Monique knocked on Luna's bedroom door harder and harder.

"Luna, come on. It's time for your bath. You have school tomorrow," she yelled.

Monique stood there for only a couple more seconds before she threw the door open. She stood there in total silence. Luna was nowhere to be seen. Monique checked under the bed, in the wardrobe, even going as far as to open the window and check outside. She ran from room to room shouting for Luna. Panic rose from the pit of her stomach. She quickly called Luna's phone only to be torn to pieces when she heard the shrill ringtone coming from Luna's bedside drawer. Monique slumped down on her own bed, dreading the next call she would make.

Pearl Heart had never believed Monique had been good for her son, but Spencer had chosen her and Pearl was only happy if her son was happy. There had been many a conflict between the two women in Spencer's life until Luna was born. That fateful day, the two women had become civil in their ways around each other. Pearl still held her reservations, but kept them to herself for the sake of her son.

"Pearl, it's me," Monique forced out, "Luna is missing."

"What do you mean, missing?" Pearl asked, clearly confused.

"Well she was here earlier, as you know. I was about to get her bath ready but she wasn't in her room. She hasn't got her phone either," Monique explained. She couldn't figure out why Pearl would sound confused. It didn't seem that hard to understand. Luna was missing, what more could there be to comprehend?

"Well have you called the police?" Pearl asked.

"Not yet, I thought I'd call you first. I thought maybe she had come to you," Monique replied.

"Why would she be here? I saw her earlier. Call the police girl. I'll take a wander through the neighbourhood, maybe she is just out walking, that poor little girl has been through so much and being cooped up in that house all the time isn't good for her," Pearl said as she hung up the phone.

Monique called the police straight after Pearl ended the call, cursing her mother-in-law under her breath.

Pearl Heart shook her head hard as she pulled on her jacket and pulled her front door open. She closed and locked it behind her, making sure she had her phone in case Luna returned home, or she found her wandering around. 'Where would Luna go?' Pearl thought. She continued to think for the next length of houses before she stopped in her tracks. Flowerly Hall.

Aura had spent the last day getting Jhordans school uniform ready for his first day at Camellia School. Jhordan had been getting to grips with holding a pen and writing again. Bruce had spent most of his day teaching Jhordan. His reading was impeccable but his writing was very rusty.

"How is he getting on?" Aura asked Bruce as she made herself comfortable on the sofa. It felt soft and spongy.

They had acquired themselves an abandoned house close to the school but not close enough for any of the kids to work out where Jhordan lived. The last thing they needed was for Jhordan to make a heap of friends. They just needed him to befriend Luna and work out how to complete their task.

"So how does this all start again?" Jhordan asked.

Aura rolled her eyes, "we've been over this nearly five times already Jhordan. You will have to make friends with Luna at school, ask her to hang out after school, you know, like normal kids."

"I haven't been a normal kid since, well, I can't remember," Jhordan said, hanging his head down. 'I don't remember a lot from when I was a kid."

"Don't worry about that now. Just carry on practicing your handwriting. I don't want the school to think you're an imbecile," Aura replied, dismissing his sad look.

Bruce watched as Jhordan walked back to the dining table and slump down, his back hunched over the paper. He felt sorry for the poor kid. Practically ripped from his resting pace and dragged around on some flimsy fantasy trip. Although he was, too, ripped from his resting place, Bruce was much older and had spent a fair few decades underground. He could almost see Jhordan as his own son. Upon thinking that, Bruce got angry with himself. 'I would have had my own son if I had just stayed out of that bar. I could have had everything if I had just kept my cool,' he thought.

"What's got you grumpy?" Sylvester said as he slid in through the back door. "Aura not wife material?" He laughed.

"Shut up. You wouldn't have done any better!" Bruce snapped back at him. "Where have you been anyway? Aura has been waiting all day!"

Sylvester sat on the sofa, bringing his left foot up to rest on his right knee, "just been scoping out the neighbourhood. It's too posh round here for me. Anyway, how's the kid doing? Bet he really is as dumb as he looks!"

Bruce couldn't believe it. Sylvester was really trying to dumb down a child. He shook his head and walked away. He couldn't deal with that today. He went back to sit with Jhordan. The kid was growing on him.

"How you getting on kid?" He asked.

Jhordan looked up at him and shrugged his shoulders. "I'll never be as good as the other kids. They will all laugh at me and then I'll mess up the plan for Aura and then..."

"Calm down kid. It will all be fine. Remember, this isn't our plan or Auras; it was Sylvester who came up with it. Trust me, if things go wrong, you will not take the blame," Bruce promised.

Jhordan smiled, "thank you Bruce. You're actually alright, no matter what Sylvester says."

Bruce slapped Jhordan on the shoulder and encouraged him to continue working from the Maths book; he really wasn't very good with arithmetic. His next task was English; he hoped Jhordan has some good skills there otherwise they would have to explain to Mr Stokes why Jhordan was behind.

"Luna are you here?" Pearl shouted as she opened the door to Flowerly Hall. "Luna!"

Pearl listened carefully. She swore she could hear a faint sniffing sound. She took the stairs slowly; she knew only too well how dangerous this place was. Slowly checking each room, Pearl slowly became more and more worried. She turned corner after corner, the panic rising inside her. Then she stopped. She put her ear to the closed door. From inside she could hear faint sobs.

"Please just let me out."

Pearl closed her eyes, took a deep breath in and summoned the deepest voice she could muster.

"YOU LET HER OUT THIS INSTANT!" She yelled.

"Oh but Pearl, she trespassed," came a voice from deep within the house. "She wasn't invited."

"I know exactly what you're up to and you can't have her!" Pearl replied. "You let her out right now otherwise..."

"Otherwise what?" The voice interrupted. "Nothing you can do will change the past. No matter how many generations pass. What happened happened."

Pearl had begun to get angry and scared. She couldn't risk losing Luna to this monster. She summoned all her strength and barrelled through the door. She scooped up Luna and ran. She ran down the corridors, round the corners and down the stairs, straight out the front door, which promptly slammed behind them.

"What do you think you were doing?" Pearl snapped as she gasped for breath.

"I had to find Edith, Grandma, you know, to help Judith," Luna replied as she tried to stop shaking. "Who does that voice belong to?"

Pearl shook her head, "another time child. Let's get you home."

Pearl walked Luna home. This was not something she could explain to Monique. She and Luna would have to make something up. Something believable.

<u>Chapter 12</u>

As they drew nearer to Luna's house, Pearl advised her not to tell her mother where she was and what happened.

"Why not?" Luna asked. "I shouldn't lie to her."

"I know sweetheart, but your mother wouldn't understand, not yet anyway. It may take her a while to fully acknowledge what's happening. Hopefully we can help her along the way," Pearl replied. "When she asks, you were taking a walk around the block and you didn't want to disturb her. You needed some fresh air."

Luna nodded. She would never go against her Grandma. She wouldn't normally go against her mother but she knew deep down that her Mum wouldn't understand it all.

Pearl reached up to ring the bell when a familiar voice called out from behind them.

"There you are!" Donna gasped. "We've been looking everywhere."

"I'm sorry Miss Canter," Luna said dropping her head. "I didn't mean to scare everyone. I just needed some time to myself so I went for a walk."

"You really should have told your Mum though honey," Savannah commented. "She's been really worried."

"I'm sorry Miss Shepherd," Luna said again.

"Come on my shining light, let's get you inside," Pearl said, putting her arms across Luna's shoulder. She rang the doorbell and waited.

Monique threw the door open and scooped Luna into her arms. "Where have you been? You scared me half to death! What were you thinking?"

Luna pulled away from her and ran upstairs to her room, slamming the door behind her.

"What did I say?" Monique questioned.

"Don't beat yourself up Mrs Heart," Savannah said. "Children are more aware of their feelings than we give them credit for. She said she needed some time to herself. Luckily for us, Pearl found her wandering the street."

Monique turned to look at her mother-in-law. "Where was she?"

"I left the house and took a short walk down the road, I had turned maybe two corners and she was just walking.

I didn't shout at her. I didn't want to scare her off. I just guided her back here," Pearl replied.

"Is that what you think I just did? Do you think I scared her off?" Monique demanded.

"Mrs Heart, I don't think it's wise to throw accusations around right now. It's been a rough few hours. Pearl, why don't you head off home, I'm sure Monique has it from here," Donna said, standing between them.

"Of course. Good evening officers," Pearl replied. She turned away from Monique and left the house. She hoped Luna would be OK tonight. She had had quite the ordeal.

"She's never liked me," Monique said as she watched Pearl walked down the driveway.

"It's perfectly normal to feel like that Mrs Heart, but I'm sure she was just worried about Luna," Savannah replied.

"You don't understand. No-one would ever have been perfect for Spencer, not if she had anything to do with it," Monique continued.

Donna sat down on the sofa with Savannah beside her. As Monique sat in the chair, she let out a sigh.

"The whole time Spencer and I were dating, she would find ways to sabotage everything. Whether it was pretending to be injured or pretending to be sick. She knew Spencer would always run to her," Monique said as she stared off into the distance. "It was always a fight over who was the most important woman in his life. That was, until Luna was born. She became the most important person in all our lives. She was our miracle. She still is. Every passing year we still have her, is to be treasured."

"Come on Jhordan. It's time for school," Aura shouted up the stairs.

The night had passed by so quickly, Jhordan felt like he hadn't slept. Not that he really slept much at all. He pulled on his trousers, socks and shoes then put his arms through the arm holes of his shirt. His bony fingers fumbled with the buttons.

"Grrrr! I hate these! Why can't it just be a t-shirt?" Jhordan shouted.

"What's up kid?" Bruce asked from the doorway. "Having trouble with the buttons?"

Jhordan hung his head in shame. "You'd think I would remember how to do this wouldn't you?"

"It's OK kid. Most of us forget things once in a while," Bruce smiled as he made quick work of the buttons. "Well, at least the tie is clip on!"

Jhordan laughed. He liked Bruce. He wasn't like Sylvester, he didn't make things hard for Jhordan and he didn't make fun of him either. Bruce was a good guy. They went down to the kitchen together, Bruce continually asking if Jhordan had everything he needed.

"Ah finally! Breakfast?" Aura exclaimed as they both came into the kitchen. "How do you like your eggs?"

"I don't remember," Jhordan replied sadly. "Why can't I remember anything?"

"Don't worry about that now, how about I scramble them for you, have them with a piece of toast? You have a long day ahead of you," Aura replied.

"We'll talk more about it when you get home, maybe we can find a way to bring back some memories," Bruce offered.

"Thank you," Jhordan replied, and he settled down to eat. He was nervous, but he knew he had to try.

As he left the house to walk to school, the nerves gradually melted away. He walked in with a swarm of other children and he suddenly felt like he belonged. Like he wasn't different anymore.

Mr Stokes met him at the main entrance. "Welcome Jhordan! Very smartly dressed. Come, I'll introduce you to your new class."

"Thank you. I'm a little nervous," Jhordan replied.

"That's perfectly normal. Your class isn't very big, but I'm sure you will fit right in," Mr Stokes informed him.

They walked along the corridor and turned the first corner to the right. Hanging from the walls were the Art students drawings and painting. Brightly coloured flowers and abstract portraits. Jhordan couldn't take his eyes off of them. He stopped to look at one in particular. It had been put together by someone called Luna.

"It's an amazing piece, don't you think?" Mr Stokes asked.

"It's breathtaking. Does she still come here? Maybe she can teach me?" Jhordan asked.

"Oh indeed she does. In fact, she is in your class," Mr Stokes replied. "Why don't we go in?"

"Sure." Jhordan replied.

He took a deep breath and followed Mr Stokes into the classroom.

The room fell silent.

Chapter 13

Monique drained the last of her coffee before picking up the phone. She dialled Pearls number and waited for her to answer. While she waited she began the crossword in the morning paper. She filled in all the easy ones, that's how she always started it off. After filling in three of the answers, Monique began to wonder why Pearl hadn't answered yet. She hung up and tried again. It rang and rang with no answer. Placing the phone back onto its cradle, Monique slipped her shoes on, pulled on her denim jacket and locked the front door behind her. She began the short walk to Pearl's house, just on the other side of Flowerly Hall.

The whole walk there, she ran through different scenarios in her head. Pearl was never out this early. She never really left the house until at least ten a.m. Monique just couldn't understand.

As she reached Pearls house, it looked empty. She peered through the living room window. There was no sign of Pearl at all. She tried the back door, it was locked. Pearl never locked her back door. Monique began to worry. Something was very wrong here. She pulled out her mobile phone and tried to call Pearl's landline. She watched through the window to see if Pearl reacted to the phone's shrill tone. Nothing inside the house stirred.

Monique decided to call Donna and Savannah.

"This is Donna Canter, how can I help?" Donna answered the phone on the second ring.

"Donna, this is Monique. I'm worried. I can't reach my mother-in-law. She isn't at home and her door is locked," Monique explained. "This isn't like her."

"OK Mrs Heart. We will come over to her house now. Stay put." Donna told her.

"Savannah, we have to go to Pearl's house. Mrs Heart called, she can't reach Pearl, the house is empty and doors are locked. She says this isn't normal," Donna informed Savannah.

Savannah frowned slightly. This didn't sound like the confident old woman they had met just two days ago. She grabbed her jacket and pocketed her phone. They were out the door and on the road in three minutes. The drive wouldn't take them long.

Upon arrival, Monique ran to the car. The panic showing on her face.

"Mrs Heart. Has there been any change since you called?" Savannah asked as she climbed out of the car.

"No, none. This really is odd for Pearl. It's barely nine-thirty," Monique said, her voice shaking. "Can't you break the door down?"

"Mrs Heart. We can't just break into someone's house because they haven't answered the phone. Is there anywhere else she could have gone?" Donna asked. "Shopping?"

"No. Pearl shops on a Friday. It's only Monday," Monique replied.

"Doctors perhaps?" Savannah offered.

"No, she went last week," Monique replied, she was starting to think they were brushing off how important this was. "If you don't break down the door, I will break in myself."

"If you break in, we will have to arrest you. Why don't you wait at home and we will take a look around. If we find her, we will ask her to call you," Donna told her.

Monique rolled her eyes but agreed. She started to walk home but stopped in the alleyway between two tall town houses. No-one would see her here. She would stand here and wait.

"Do you think Pearl is OK?" Savannah asked Donna.

"I'm sure she's absolutely fine. I don't understand why Mrs Heart is so worried. After what she said last night about Pearl never liking her, I'm fully surprised she even cares," Donna replied.

"Oh Donna. You can't say things like that. Every family has its ups and down. You, for one, should understand that better than anyone!" Savannah told her.

"I know, but it just seems strange that Monique would be that worried over someone who, she claims, hates her," Donna told her.

Savannah didn't know what to say to that. There wasn't really much to say, she knew what Donna meant.

"So, how did Saturday go?" Donna asked. "The meal with your sister-in-law?"

"Oh! I forgot to tell you about it. Christian and I arrived a little late, you know how 'life' gets in the way," Savannah began to explain, blushing a little.

"Well, we all know what happens there!" Donna replied, trying not to giggle.

"Well, when we finally got there, Beverly had invited *my* parents along too. I guess it was a big family dinner!" Savannah continued. "We settled down, there was some random chit chat going on between Beverly and my Mum, Christian chatted to my Dad about the golf or cricket, one of the two, I can never tell the difference. I kind of felt like a third wheel!" Savannah laughed. "Lizzy messaged me from her room, said she wanted to talk with me about something, so I went up to her. You wouldn't believe what she told me. Come, let's walk and talk, maybe we will bump into Pearl on the way.

As they walked away Monique noticed their voices becoming more distant. She hadn't braved looking out of the alleyway until it was completely silent. She quickly left her hiding spot and returned to Pearls house. She would get in there, one way or another.

"So, how long you lived around here?" Jhordan asked Luna. He'd been trying to get her attention all morning; she was a hard nut to crack.

"All my life obviously," Luna replied sarcastically. "Why are you so interested in me? Why don't you go and bother one of the other girls? They're much better than me."

"But, maybe I don't like the other girls. Maybe, just maybe, I like you more," Jhordan replied. "What are you doing after school?"

"Same I do every night. Nothing," Luna informed him.

"Don't you have any hobbies? Like bike riding, roller-skating, exploring?" Jhordan teased.

Luna stopped eating her sandwich and stared at him. "Why did you ask about exploring?"

Jhordan slammed his mouth just, grateful that his jaw no longer dislocated when he did. "I like to explore. I like old buildings the most, abandoned buildings. I used to ghost hunt before we moved here. Mum and Dad don't like it much."

"Have you ever seen one? A ghost I mean," Luna asked.

"No. Have you?" He replied, a smile growing across his face.

"No, don't be silly. Ghost's aren't real!" Luna laughed. She shook her head and carried on with her sandwich.

She sipped her orange slowly; she loved the zingy taste on her tongue.

When it was time to go back to class, Jhordan quickly sent a message to Aura.

'*Are you sure she is the right one? She doesn't even believe in ghosts.*'

He headed back into class and sat beside Luna.

"Are you back again?" She asked, clearly annoyed that he had targeted her out of the whole class. '*OK granted there wasn't many of them but why me,*' she thought to herself.

"Can I show you?" Jhordan whispered.

"Show me what?" Luna said looking disgusted.

"A ghost," he replied.

"And where are you going to find one? In your school bag?" Luna giggled. "Just get on with your work."

Jhordan felt defeated. It was clear that Luna was going to be hard work. He needed to up his game.

"Meet me at Flowerly Hall after school. I'll show you a ghost," Jhordan whispered.

Luna's face went pale as she turned away from him. *'Could he know about Edith? How would he know? He hasn't even lived here that long.'*

The rest of the school day passed by slowly. Jhordan had been nervous about talking to Luna but after he started, he couldn't seem to stop.

"So, will you meet me?" He asked as they left the school gates.

"I don't know," Luna replied before walking away from him. She took a different path home so that he wouldn't follow her.

As she rounded the far side of Flowerly Hall, she heard the sound of voices from inside.

"You ever do anything like that again," came one voice, one Luna instantly recognised.

"You'll do what? Came the second voice.

"You can't just go locking up children, it's not right and you know it," Pearl stated.

"Ha ha ha. Silly old woman, I've been doing it for centuries, no one has stopped me yet!" The other voice informed her. "Now, get out of here."

Pearl turned on her heels and left, shaking her head as she went. "I can't believe he's still doing this. You'd think after so long he would stop. It's getting out of hand now," she said under her breath.

"Grandma?" Luna questioned as her grandmother exited the gates. "What were you doing in there?"

Pearl didn't know how to reply. "Oh my sweet child, there is still so much for you to learn."

Chapter 14

Monique sat at Pearls dining table tapping her fingers impatiently. She had sat here all day and there had been no sign of her. Monique had heard voices outside just over three hours ago, but nothing since.

"Well, there's no sign of her down this way, maybe we should check the other direction," Savannah said.

They had gone off in the opposite direction and hadn't been back. Monique contemplated leaving just as she heard the voices reappear again.

"Maybe, we should just go and tell Mrs Heart that we couldn't find her," Savannah said.

"Hmm, I don't know. Maybe we should just wait for a minute, I have a strange feeling," Donna replied.

Both women leaned up against the side of Donnas car. They had waited barely five minutes before they heard the sound of Luna's voice drifting from around the bend.

"Is that real?" Luna asked as they got closer to the officers.

"As real as I am your Grandma!" Pearl laughed. "Detectives, how can I help you?"

"We received a frantic call from your daughter-in-law this morning. She was worried as you weren't answering your phone," Donna replied.

"Well, I wasn't home. I've been out all day, as you can see," Pearl replied. "I don't understand why she would call the police."

"She sounded a little upset. Maybe she wanted to talk over what happened last night?" Savannah offered.

"Last night was last night, it's effectively history. Now, if you don't mind. I have to walk my granddaughter home," Pearl said dismissively, and she walked right past them.

"Well, that was...odd," Savannah said as they watched Pearl and Luna walk away.

"Something isn't quite right here. I'll get to the bottom of it," Donna replied.

Monique was worried. How was she going to get out of here and away from the police and get back home before Luna? She held her breath for a second to think. It was then that she heard the sound of a car door, briefly followed by an engine revving to life. She watched, from behind the curtain, as the two women drove away. She quickly ran from her hiding place and left the house.

"So how was it?" Aura asked as Jhordan came through the door.

"It's school, nothing special. Although I did get talking to the girl," he replied.

"And?" Aura asked, getting slightly excited.

"Are you sure it's the right girl?" Jhordan asked.

"Why wouldn't it be?" Aura questioned him. "What has she said?"

"She said she doesn't believe in ghosts," Jhordan replied shrugging his shoulders. "Just seems like a strange thing to say if she can see them."

Aura thought for a second, 'why *would* she say something like that?'

"Well, I have homework, then I promised to show Luna a ghost," Jhordan said as he walked up the stairs of their temporary home.

"Yes sure, go for it," Aura replied as she sat at the table in a daze. She couldn't help but wonder if Luna really was the key link in the chain, or if the man had led them on. "Wait! What?"

"I promised Luna that I'd show her a ghost," Jhordan replied shrugging his shoulders. "It's the only way to find out the truth."

"And how *exactly* are you going to do that?" Bruce asked from the kitchen doorway.

"I'm working on that bit," Jhordan admitted. He hadn't fully worked it through yet

Bruce laughed, "at least you got talking to her kid. Good job."

Jhordan smiled at Bruce, "thanks." He ran up the remaining stairs and sat down at the desk that had been left behind by the previous owners. It was a shame this house was only temporary, he kind of liked this room.

"You shouldn't praise him so much Bruce," Aura said, her eyes narrowing at him. "It's all just trickery. You know that."

"I know Aura, but he's managed to succeed where Sly and I failed," he replied, looking down at her as she remained seated at the table.

"Well, just don't boost his ego. We could do with him not messing this up," Aura gave a sly smile.

"Mum, I'm home. Grandma Pearl is here," Luna called as she closed her front door behind her. "Mum?"

"In the kitchen honey," Monique called; she has just managed to slip in the back door as Luna had come through the front. "Sorry, I didn't hear you at first; I must have been out the back. Pearl, what a surprise, come on in."

"I heard you were worried about me," Pearl said as she sat at the breakfast bar. "Those two officers were outside my house when I got back."

"Well, I called this morning and you didn't answer. I know you don't normally leave the house until gone ten. I just panicked," Monique replied.

"Why were you calling?" Pearl asked.

"Why don't you go upstairs and start your homework sweetheart," Monique told Luna. "I just need a chat with your Grandma Pearl."

"Sure Mum," Luna said as she quickly hung up her coat and took the stairs two at a time.

"I think we need to have a little chat, don't you?" Monique said as she turned to Pearl.

As Luna reached her bedroom, she could hear two voices coming from within. She slowly reached for the handle and turned it quietly.

"We have to have faith in her Max," Judith pleaded with a man. He had shoulder length dark hair, with piercing green eyes.

"How do we know she can do it?" He asked, throwing his arms out to the side. "We know nothing about her."

"Ask her," Judith said, gesturing to Luna who had just entered the room and closed the door behind her.

Luna studied the new form. She looked at him from a range of angles. "Nice to meet you, I'm Luna."

"Well, it's nice to finally meet you; I'm surprised I could get away from that place. I may sound a little apprehensive about how much you really can do about all this," he told her. He made no attempt to hide his anxiety from her.

"Well, thank you for your honesty Max. Donnas' brother I presume?" Luna asked.

"Yes I am. Now, tell me, how exactly are you going to help Edith?" He asked.

Chapter 15

"I'm going out Mum," Luna called as she opened the front door. "I'll be back shortly."

"Wait where you off to?" Monique asked.

"I'm just meeting up with Jhordan from school. He promised to show me something really cool," Luna replied.

"Who is this Jhordan, I don't remember him?" Monique asked seemingly confused.

"He's new, plus, it gives me a chance to show him around the neighbourhood. He only just moved in," Luna replied. "I won't be out late."

"OK honey, keep your phone on just in case," Monique called out as Luna slammed the door behind her.

Monique shook her head and chuckled to herself. She was glad that Luna was making friends, especially since Spencer. It was like she had become a hermit crab. She had spent so much time in her room, that Monique had considered checking her into therapy.

As Luna walked towards Flowerly Hall; she wasn't sure this was a good idea but it was better than sitting at home listening to her Mum bang and clatter around in the kitchen whilst muttering to herself inaudibly. Luna didn't normally venture out after dinner, so this was something different for her. She kept looking back towards her house, expecting her Mum to come running out after her and demand she go back inside, but her Mum never appeared. She rounded the final corner before the entrance to Flowerly Hall came into view. There stood Jhordan.

"Hey! I was starting to wonder if you stood me up!" He smiled

"I was thinking about it," Luna replied. "So, where's this 'ghost'?"

Jhordan laughed, "All in good time. Shall we go inside?"

Luna shrugged her shoulders, "sure, why not."

They slipped through the open gate and crept towards the front door. Luna calmed her breathing down, she had a sudden flashback of the last time she was here, but she wouldn't let Jhordan know she had been here before. Luna looked around quickly.

"Aren't these floor tiles amazing?" Jhordan asked her, bending down to look closer.

"Yeah, they're great," Luna said, rolling her eyes.

Jhordan smiled to himself. "Come on, let's find you a ghost."

"Finally," Luna sighed. "I was about to go home."

Jhordan led her up the staircase. The banister was so dusty. Luna noticed it too. *It wasn't like that yesterday,'* she thought to herself. Something was terribly wrong.

Monique jumped at the sound of the shrill ring of the phone.

"Hello," she answered.

"Mrs Heart? This is Donna Canter. I assume Luna is at home?" Donna asked.

"No, she is out with a school friend. He's just recently moved in so she is showing him around. Why?" Monique replied, placing her cup of tea on the coffee table.

"I'm calling because there have been reports of suspicious activity around Flowerly Hall. I've touched base with a number of families in the area. Can you contact Luna and request her to return home and to get her friend home too?" Donna asked. "We just need to know who is where and when."

"Of course. Please keep me informed." Monique replied, hanging up the phone. Hurriedly she dialled Luna, anxiously waiting for her to answer.

"Mum, what's up?" Luna said as she answered the phone.

"Honey, I need you to come home now, and make sure your friend gets home safe too," Monique replied. "It's important."

"Sure Mum, see you soon," Luna replied, hanging up.

"What's up?" Jhordan asked as she placed the phone in her pocket.

"Mum, wants me home, and wants me to get you home too," Luna replied, "so you have around two minutes to show me this ghost or I'm leaving."

"Whoa, OK. Let's go!" Jhordan laughed grabbing her hand and dragging her towards the door at the far end of the landing.

He flung it open and told her to look in the mirror.

Luna shook her head and peered in at her reflection. "I don't see anything other than myself."

"Look again, but pay better attention," Jhordan whispered from beside her.

"I still don't see anything!" Luna exclaimed. "Look, you can't show me a ghost because they don't exist. I get it, you really wished they did, but, I'm sorry, they obviously don't." Luna turned and left the room. Little did she know, Jhordan had sneakily snapped a picture of her looking into the mirror, he sent it via Bluetooth to her phone just as they went their separate ways outside the gate.

"See you at school tomorrow," Jhordan said as he waved her goodbye.

Luna narrowed her eyes, "sure."

Luna continued on her way home, slipping in through the front door and hearing her mother on the phone.

"Yes, I called her, she should be back any second now," Monique said.

"Mum?" Luna called out. "Who's on the phone?"

"Its Detective Canter honey, everything OK?" Monique replied.

"Yeah, I'm going upstairs. Jhordan got home fine," Luna said as she rushed up to her room. She pushed the door open and flopped onto the bed.

"Is everything alright child?" Judith asked from the window. "I didn't get a chance to apologise about Max."

"No need to apologise Judith. I understand why he feels the way he does. It's been a while since anyone has been able to help," Luna replied. "Can you tell me more about Edith and the house?"

Judith glided over to her and looked down, "certainly dear. Now, where to start?"

Luna's phone vibrated on the table. She quickly grabbed it, "sorry, just one second."

She looked down at the screen and froze. *'How did this get taken?'* she thought to herself.

"I don't understand," Luna whispered.

"Maybe I can explain child," Judith said, looking over her shoulder. "Who is the boy?"

"That's Jhordan. He's new to school. He told me he could show me a ghost, but he couldn't," Luna explained.

"Oh but he did dear, look," Judith smiled as she pointed to the young girl whose face was just visible between them both.

"Why didn't I see that when I was there?" Luna asked.

"Oh, she hasn't changed a bit," Judith sighed.

"Wait, is that Edith?" Luna asked.

"Why yes dear. I don't think she was ready for Jhordan to see her. He may well believe in ghosts, but how would he react if he did actually see one?" Judith replied. "Edith will show herself to you, one day."

"Why is it just her face? Where is her body?" Luna asked.

"That's a story for another day. Now, you must rest," Judith said as she covered Luna in a soft fleece blanket and faded out of sight.

"Honey, did you show your friend around?" Monique asked as she came into Luna's room. She looked down to find Luna asleep on the bed.

"Goodnight sweetpea," she whispered, and kissed her on the head.

"So, how did it go?" Aura asked as Jhordan came in.

"It didn't go as planned, that woman never showed. I thought she needed Luna to be there to show up," Jhordan replied, throwing himself onto the sofa. "I took a picture of her looking into the mirror."

"Why would you do that?" Aura asked. "Show me."

Jhordan pulled his phone out of his pocket and pulled up the picture. He handed it to her. Aura looked over the whole picture.

"What's so special about it?" She asked.

"It's so you know what she looks like if you ever see her out and about," Jhordan shrugged. "I think she's kinda pretty."

"Oh stop it; you won't be here long enough for that!" Aura spat. She zoomed the picture in a bit further. "Wait a minute. Who is this?"

"That's me and Luna," Jhordan dismissed.

"No, look!" Aura said through gritted teeth pointing at the phone screen.

Jhordan got up and examined the picture again. His breath caught in his throat.

"What? That wasn't there when I took it," Jhordan backed up.

"Well, well. Hello Edith dearest!" Aura hissed. She broke out in the most horrendously evil laughter. "Nice to see you again. This time, you will give me what I want; otherwise the girl will get it!"

Chapter 16

When Luna awoke the next day, there was a handwritten note inside the notebook she had started when Judith first arrived.

'Dearest Luna,

Soon it will be time for you to meet Edith, but you must be very careful. All is not as you think.

Judith x'

'Hmm,' thought Luna. 'What could she mean?'

"Luna, are you up?" Monique shouted up the stairs.

"Yes Mum." Luna replied as she climbed out of bed and got ready for school. She brushed her dark curls, gathered them together and plaited them up.

She made her way downstairs to the smell of pancakes.

"I made some pancakes for you," Monique said. "Make a change from cereal."

Luna laughed, "You know I love pancakes!"

Luna sat at the table whilst her Mum finished up cooking. She looked at the picture of their family hung up in the hallway and smiled. She missed her Dad. Some days, she thought she could smell his aftershave, but she had to remind herself that he was gone, and that she would probably never see him again.

"Here you are honey," Monique said, breaking through her thoughts. "You OK?"

"Yeah. I was just thinking about Dad. He would have loved this breakfast." Luna replied.

"I know he would have honey. I miss him too," Monique told her. She turned back to the cooker and continued with the next batch of pancakes.

Monique really did miss Spencer, but she still couldn't get her head around how he crashed. No other vehicles involved just him and the pylon. It didn't seem, well, right. She told herself she would call Detective Canter later and ask some questions of her own. Right now, she had to make sure Luna got to school on time.

"They were so tasty Mum; can we have some later too?" Luna asked as they walked the short distance to the school gates.

"You got it. Hey, why don't you invite your friend over?" Monique asked.

"I dunno Mum, maybe," Luna replied. "See you later!"

Luna ran off into school. Not stopping to look back. Monique watched as she met up with various friends, most she had been friends with in primary school, others she had bonded with over her time at secondary school, although only in the second year, Luna made friends easily. It was good for her, especially as she spent a lot of time as a child in hospital, Monique had worried it might have affected her development, especially social interaction. Luckily for her and Spencer, Luna was a loveable girl. She never had a bad report from school and was well mannered. It's all they had ever wanted.

Monique turned and began to walk home when a woman bumped into her.

"Oh, I'm so sorry. Jhordan hurry inside, you don't want to be late on your second day," Aura smiled.

Jhordan ran off, waving as he went.

"I'm Aura Crystaline. We moved here quite recently and I'm, just getting the hang of things," Aura announced.

"Monique Heart. My daughter is Luna, just there with the monster rucksack," Monique pointed.

"Ah I see her, she's beautiful," Aura replied.

"Thank you. Why don't you come back to mine, we can have a cup of tea or coffee and I can tell you about the neighbourhood," Monique offered.

"Oh, I'd love to, but I might have to make it another day. I have an appointment at the bank." Aura replied, a smile spreading across her face.

"Sure. Don't get stuck in traffic, it's a nightmare at this time in the morning," Monique said as she waved and walked away.

Aura watched her go. She pulled out her phone and called Bruce. "The mother seems, I don't know, over friendly?"

"She did seem a bit full on when we met her, maybe that's just who she is. Did you see the girl?" Bruce replied.

"Yes I saw her. She is just a child though. A seemingly normal child," Aura told him. "I don't see anything special about her."

"We'll just have to go bit by bit. We have time," Bruce told her.

"I know that, but I don't want it to take too long, it has to be done soon." Aura said as she hung up.

Bruce looked at his phone as Aura ended the call.

"Trouble with the missus?" Sylvester asked, laughing at himself.

"You're not even remotely funny," Bruce told him.

"Well, I thought it was," Sylvester replied.

"You would, you don't have a sense of humour," Bruce said. He opened his laptop and began searching up on Luna and Monique Heart.

'Spencer Heart, father of Luna and husband to Monique, tragically died in a single vehicle RTC this morning. A head on collision with an electricity pylon caused havoc around the high street. Reported to be conscious and talking when he was rescued from his vehicle, he sadly succumbed to internal injuries a short time later. No further details have been released at this time.'

"Hmm, strange," Bruce said. "It must have quite a smash."

"What was?" Sylvester asked. He was lounging on the sofa in front of the TV trying to work out how to use the remote.

"Turn it around." Bruce told him shaking his head at how silly Sylvester was. "It says here that the girls' Dad died from a single vehicle crash, not long ago. It just seems odd that he would die if only he was involved."

"Why? People die alone every day. I don't see why his would be so strange?" Sylvester replied, finally working out how to change the channel. It took him a while longer to work out the volume.

Bruce continued his search on the girl online. She didn't have any social media accounts; neither did her mother, which was strange. Bruce had worked out that those were all on trend nowadays. He looked her up on her school website, but there wasn't much on any of the kids on there, just random photos of them doing chemistry or some new performance.

He decided to do some digging on the father, Spencer Heart. He typed the name into the search bar and a list began to appear. At the top was his birth registration, normally you would have to pay to see this information, but Bruce had other ways of accessing it. He clicked the link and read the names of his parents. His breath got caught in his throat. He quickly called Aura.

"There's something you should know about the girl," he said.

At school, Jhordan sat with Luna in class.

"Did you get the picture I sent you?" He whispered.

"Yeah, that was really odd. Don't do that again. It's creepy," Luna told him. "I don't know what it's like where you come from, but here, we don't take pictures of people without their permission."

"Sorry, I didn't know," Jhordan said, hanging his head down. "It's been a while since I interacted with other people my age."

"Why?" Luna asked, clearly intrigued by him now.

"I spent a lot of time around adults. More than I should have. When I died, all I saw were adults," Jhordan replied.

"When you died?" Luna laughed. "But you're alive!"

Jhordan realised his mistake and had to think of something quick to cover his tracks. "I died for a while. In hospital, or so I'm told. I could see things, things I wouldn't normally see."

Luna shook her head, "you had me interested for a second there, but now, it just seems like another story to try and make yourself look better. You promised to show me a ghost and you didn't, so I probably wouldn't believe anything else you say."

Luna turned away from him and carried on with her work. Jhordan didn't know what else to do, so as he worked, he began planning. He didn't want Aura to know that he had messed up, so he sent a message to Bruce;

J - 'How do I fix what I've said?'

B – 'What have you said?'

J – 'I told the girl I died.'

B – 'Why would you say that?'

J – 'It slipped out, for some reason I felt I couldn't lie to her.'

B – 'Oh boy. Have you told Aura?'

J – 'No, Should I?'

B – 'No way! Leave it to me. I'll fix it. Get on with your work.'

Jhordan looked sideways towards Luna but she ignored him. He continued working; all the while hoping that Bruce would find a way to fix his mistakes.

Chapter 17

As Monique switched on the kettle, she dialled the number for Detective Canter. It rang a few times before she answered.

"How can I help you Mrs Heart?" Donna asked.

"I have some questions surrounding my husbands' death. Is there any chance I could arrange a meeting with yourself and Detective Shepherd?" Monique replied.

"Of course, how about we come over to you in around half an hour? Does that sound OK?" Donna offered. "I can try and answer as much as I can."

"That would be great. I'll see you both then." Monique said as she ended the call. She hoped she could get some more answers. There were so many unanswered questions that had been flying around in her head, that most nights she hadn't slept a wink.

Donna and Savannah arrived exactly half an hour later. Monique let them in and they sat around the dining table. Monique had rehearsed several ways of asking her questions but it all fell out in a jumble of words.

"Take your time Mrs Heart," Savannah smiled.

"I'm sorry. There is just so much that I haven't been told. What caused the accident? The car had only been repaired a few days earlier," Monique asked.

Donna and Savannah exchanged glances. They were sure someone would have been out to explain things a little more by now.

"It looks like some tampered with the steering rack on your husband's car," Donna told her. "The brake lines were also cut."

Monique was silent for a few moments. '*Who would do such a thing?*' She thought.

"Mrs Heart?" Savannah broke through her thoughts.

"Yes, sorry," Monique said as she shook her head.

"Was your husband on any medication at all?" Savannah asked.

"Just for his blood pressure. He took the odd painkiller but I don't think he had that day. We'd had an argument, like I explained that first night," she told Donna.

"That's right, about Luna's birthday." Donna replied. "I came the night the graves were disturbed, with Alex."

Donna explained to Savannah what had happened between Monique and her husband that morning. Monique offered that they had disagreements almost every year when it came to Luna's birthday arrangements.

"Mrs Heart, do you know anyone who would want to harm Spencer in any way?" Savannah asked.

"No, I told Donna and Alex this when they first came here, Spencer didn't have any enemies. I'm just so confused that he was the only one involved in the accident, other than the car being tampered with. What else haven't I been told?" She demanded.

Donna nodded. There was more to tell and she had just given Savannah permission to tell Monique the rest.

"A toxicology test was completed. There were some alarming things showing up. Did your husband ever use recreational drugs?" Savannah hated asking but she knew she had to.

"You mean like cocaine?" Monique spat. "No never. He didn't smoke, never drank, he had high blood pressure but that was it. He was a healthy man."

"We understand why this is painful, but we do have to cover all bases. There were some items found in your husband's blood that were a cause for concern," Donna added. "Can we see any medication bottles that may be left behind?"

Monique stood and made her way to the bathroom. She knew there were still some bottles in the cabinet that she hadn't thrown away yet. She opened the cabinet and reached inside. She drew out a bottle and closed the door again. She looked at herself in the mirror and noticed how old she was looking recently. She never let herself look this bad before. She closed her eyes and walked back to the dining room.

"Here," she said as she handed the bottle to Savannah.

Savannah turned the bottle over to check the label; *Verapamil*, she read the dosage, *200mg once a day.*

She handed it back to Monique, "thank you. I think this is what caused the positive drugs test."

"The investigating officer had deemed the case closed and filed under DUI. He concluded that Spencer was intoxicated through drugs and that he simply couldn't focus. Did you see him take his medication that day?" Donna asked.

"I see him take it every day. He takes it just before breakfast. I don't understand though. No-one has access to his medication except him and me," Monique told them.

Donna and Savannah exchanged glances.

"Why don't we go back and talk to the investigating officer again. We can give him some new evidence and see where we go from there. You don't happen to have CCTV around, do you?" Donna asked.

"No, it was something we were looking into doing before, well, you know," Monique replied.

"When you had your car repaired, did the brakes work after that?" Savannah asked.

"Yes, there were no problems with it. It had new tyres too," Monique answered.

"OK Mrs Heart, I think we can safely say that there needs to be further investigation into this. I'm surprised the officer hadn't look into it in more detail. I'll see if I can chase it up for you." Donna told her. "How's Luna holding up?

"Well, she's made a new friend at school, Jhordan. Other than that, she's just Luna," Monique shrugged.

"I'm glad she's doing OK. Having something tragic happen at such a young age can change someone, but you're doing great," Donna replied.

As Savannah and Donna left, Aura watched from a distance. She noted how distraught Monique looked. She decided to take advantage of it. Just as she was about to cross the road, her phone sprang to life.

BRUCE

"What is it?" She hissed.

"I think we have a major problem," he replied.

"Spit it out," Aura snapped.

"I can't. You have to see for yourself," he told her.

"Oh for crying out loud! I'll be there shortly," she said as she hung up.

"This is why I never get *anything* done," she whispered to herself. She continued to walk back to the temporary house, constantly shaking her head. *Imbeciles!* She thought.

As school ended, Jhordan tried to talk to Luna again. He was standing by her locker when she emerged from the school toilets.

"What do you want?" Luna asked. She was starting to feel really uncomfortable around him.

"I just want to make sure that you get home safe," he replied. "It's getting darker at night now."

"I'm fine but thanks. I live less than a minutes' walk from here," Luna told him.

She walked away and didn't turn back. She decided to check up on him when she got home.

Jhordan watched as she walked away. He'd blown it and Aura was going to be angry with him. He quickly set a message to Bruce.

J – 'I think I blew it with the girl.'

B – 'Don't worry about that now. Get back here quickly.'

J – 'On my way.'

He wondered what Bruce was so worked up about. He took the detour that Aura had showed him and arrived home in no time. He walked through the door just before Aura.

"So, what's the emergency?" Aura asked as she walked through the back door.

"You better sit down," Bruce told her. He brought his laptop to the table and sat next to her. She wasn't going to like this one bit, but he had to tell her. He had to warn her. Her task was about to get a lot harder.

He took a deep breath and began reading. "Spencer Heart, father to Luna Heart and husband to Monique Heart died suddenly this morning..."

<u>Chapter 18</u>

Monique was preparing the evening meal when Luna came home from school. She hung up her coat and placed her shoes on the shoe rack behind the door.

"Hey honey, how was school?" Monique asked as Luna picked up an orange and began peeling it.

Luna shrugged her shoulders, "its school Mum. How else would it be?"

"Are you OK?" Monique asked as she dried her hands on the tea towel.

"I guess. I just have loads of homework and I'm so tired," Luna replied.

Monique knew when there was something wrong with her daughter, but she also knew when not to ask.

"Why don't you go for a nap honey? Dinner is going to be a while anyway, and then I can help you with some of your homework," Monique told her.

Luna shrugged again. "I don't know Mum. I don't think I can sleep this early in the day. Maybe I'll just go upstairs and read for a while."

Monique watched as her daughter climbed the stairs before turning back to her preparation work.

When Luna was safely in her bedroom, she pulled out her laptop and typed in Jhordans name. There were no results of his school name but the name Jhordan showed up as a death going back over fifteen years. She clicked the link and waited for the page to show up. When the page fully loaded, she wished she hadn't searched. There, on the screen, was a picture of the very same boy she had shared class with today. He was right. He really had died.

"Why is any of this significant?" Aura asked sounding bored.

"I haven't finished yet," Bruce hissed.

Aura folded her arms and sat back in the chair. "So continue."

"His mother, Pearl Heart, was said to be heartbroken at the loss of her only child. Pearl is no stranger to tragedy after her husband, William, went missing over fifteen years ago," Bruce read.

Aura sat up. She gestured for Bruce to continue when there was a knock at the door. They all sat perfectly still. All holding their breaths.

"It's me, open up!" Sylvester shouted.

Aura rolled her eyes and stood to open the door. "Maybe give us a heads up before you arrive?" She told him.

Sylvester walked behind her pulling a disgusted face. "Sorry, I just thought you ought to know. There's a mass of kids at that mansion. I don't know what they are doing there but it doesn't look good. They got some sort of game with them."

"What game?" Aura asked. "What did it look like?"

"It's a board and a cup and there's about six of them," Sylvester replied.

"It's a Ouija board," Aura sighed. "Oh I wish they wouldn't do that in there. That's how this started in the first place!"

"Shall I continue?" Bruce asked. He was getting agitated because Aura needed to know exactly who she had dug up.

"Sure, go ahead but make it quick," she said.

Bruce shook his head, there was an easy way to say this but then again, there wasn't. "OK. Pearls' husband went missing fifteen years ago, no body, nothing. Spencer was an only child. I looked up Pearl online and it seems that around seventy odd years ago, there was a report that she had entered Flowerly Hall and experienced something horrific."

Aura stopped talking and froze. "How...How long ago?"

"Seventy-eight to be precise. Are you thinking what I'm thinking?" Bruce asked her.

She nodded but couldn't bring herself to speak. They were thinking back to the same incident.

A girl entered Flowerly Hall seventy-eight years ago. She was gifted enough to talk to the afterlife. She had been drafted in by Aura and Bruce, along with Monty to try and release the power held in that house. They had been told numerous times that whoever was in the house when the spirit of the Flowerly Hall was set free would be granted immortality. Aura wanted it. So she spent years researching the different people who could release the spirit, but everyone she had used turned out to be useless or they just didn't believe in themselves strongly enough.

Pearl had been one of the latter. She hadn't been useless, not by a long shot. She had made it possible for Aura to see Edith, but Pearl didn't believe she had enough power to save her from what held her there.

"Bruce, go back through their family line. I want to know if anyone else we have used before shows up. It seems like a huge coincidence that Luna is Pearl's granddaughter," Aura told him. "Do it as fast as you can."

Bruce nodded and went off into another room so he wasn't disturbed.

"What can I do?" Jhordan asked nervously.

"Go to the house, spy on the kids and report back what you see," Aura told him. "And Jhordan, be discreet."

"I will," he replied. He pulled on his coat and slipped quietly out the door.

"So what was that all about? You seemed very on edge when he mentioned that woman's name," Sylvester asked.

"It's a very long story that happened way before you arrived. Do you have anything else to share?" Aura dismissed.

"Not really. I had to buy some air freshener for the warehouse though. The smell was leaking through the cracks. We don't want any unneeded attention now, do we?" He told her.

"I guess you're right. We only needed four of the bodies really. You'll have to take the rest back over time, don't get caught!" She told him.

"Who are we keeping?" Sylvester asked her. "Why do I have to do it alone?"

"Leave Spencer, Max, Edith and Judith. Take the others back and be respectful. Put them back the same way we got them out. You already know the answer to the last question. Now go," Aura replied.

Sylvester sighed aloud and got to his feet. "How many times will we have to do all this?"

"Hopefully this is the last time," Aura replied. She walked towards the room that Bruce had disappeared into and hoped that he would find out more about the family line of Spencer and Pearl Heart.

Luna was stunned as she stared at the picture on her screen. She tilted her head from side to side hoping that it would no longer look like him.

"What is it child?" Judith whispered from behind her.

"That boy, the one from the photo. He told me today that he died. When I questioned him, he said that he had died in a hospital but had been brought back. So I checked him out online. His name is Jhordan Crystaline but there's no record of him anywhere, there's only this report about a boy called Jhordan Bell who died over fifteen years ago, he was fourteen years old. It says his father found him in the forest," Luna said as she swiped at a tear that had escaped her eye. "He drowned."

Judith felt helpless; she couldn't even comfort the poor girl. "Is he special to you?"

Luna turned to face her, "not really. He has just started school but he seems odd. No-one else really talks to him. He's tried but they give him strange looks and walk away from him. I felt bad for him so I spoke to him."

"You have a kind soul young Luna. Maybe he senses that and feels compelled to try and impress you," Judith said.

"There's no need to impress me, I'm not exactly special myself." Luna laughed.

"Oh but you are, more than you know," Judith said. "Why don't you rest, it will all seem clearer afterwards."

"Maybe you're right," Luna said as she lay down on her bed. "Five minutes won't hurt."

"Help me Luna. You're the only one left who can break the curse. Free me from captivity and allow me peace to rest."

Luna woke with a jump.

"Are you OK sweetie?" Monique said as Luna looked up at her. "You're sweating like a snowman in summer."

"I must have fallen asleep. I'm sorry Mum. Is dinner ready?" Luna apologised.

"Yes darling, are you sure you're OK?" Monique asked again.

"I'll be fine Mum. Don't worry," Luna smiled. She got up, slid her feet into her slippers and followed her Mum to the dining room. She stopped dead in her tracks when she saw what her Mum had cooked. It was her Dad's favourite; leg of lamb with vegetables, roast potatoes and steaming hot gravy. Tears filled her eyes.

"Dad would have loved this," she cried, throwing her arms around her Mum's waist.

"I know darling, I just wanted to pretend he was with us, even if it's just for one night," Monique replied.

Luna looked at the chair her father would normally reside; she could just make out the figure of him. It was faint but it was there. This worried Luna. She had never seen a spirit so faint before. She would ask Judith about it later. She sat at the table next to her Mum and began to eat her food. She couldn't shake the feeling that something was seriously wrong, and the voice she had heard in her dream had really shaken her up.

Chapter 19

Jhordan returned to the temporary house just after eleven that night. He felt drained. He had watched the kids play around with the Ouija board for hours. There were a few incidents along the way, but nothing seemed to put them off. It was probably for the best that they didn't continue past midnight. That's when things can get ugly. He should know.

"Jhordan, is that you?" Bruce asked as he switched the lights on and dimmed them down.

"Yes, sorry, I was trying to be quiet," Jhordan whispered.

"Why? Aura is still in the spare room reading through the things I found out earlier today. I think you should come in and see for yourself," Bruce told him.

Jhordan filled a glass with water and followed Bruce through the open door. He looked in amazement at the wall full of information on Luna, Pearl and Spencer, along with what looked like their family tree.

"Wow. You found out all that on that," he said, pointing from the wall to the laptop.

"Absolutely, maybe, in time, you can learn all this too," Bruce told him.

"Don't get his hopes up Bruce. Once all this is over, he will go back to how he was; he knows that, don't you Jhordan?" Aura said.

"Yeah, I know. I only wanted to help out," Jhordan replied. Inside he was sad, he had hoped she would keep him around like she did Bruce and Sylvester, but he knew she would send him back eventually.

Aura had kept Bruce and Sylvester in human form as a way of getting the help she needed. She knew spirits couldn't help physically. It drained them. So she had conjured up a spell that would enable them to become more physical. That's how she kept Bruce and Sylvester. It's how she made Jhordan alive again.

Jhordan read through all the information on the wall, stopping at the added information of the two police officers.

"I saw them," Jhordan said as he pointed to the pictures.

"Where?" Aura asked.

"They were at Luna's house, a few days ago. I could pick up a little bit of what they were talking about, but not all of it," Jhordan replied.

"Spill, and don't leave any details out!" Aura told him.

Jhordan sat the table and reiterated everything he had heard that day, from the brake lines being cut to the drugs in his system.

"Seems a little much, don't you think Aura?" Bruce asked.

"Check his background, any history of drug use?" Aura asked Bruce.

"None, not even a caution," he replied.

"It was his blood pressure medication," Jhordan replied. "I remember Luna's Mum saying he had high blood pressure. She showed the police a medicine bottle. I don't understand how he would end up dead though. Unless someone gave him more than he needed and he collapsed?"

"I doubt it kid, he was conscious and talking when he was rescued. You know much about medicine?" Bruce asked.

"I know what my Mum knew, she was a doctor. I remember bits of what she said," Jhordan confessed.

Aura looked at him in surprise. "You didn't think to say something sooner?"

"I didn't know it would be of any help," he replied.

"We'll deal with that later. Tell me what happened with the kids," Aura asked.

Jhordan explained what the kids got up to, there wasn't really much to tell, the cup flew across the room a few times, there were a lot of loud bangs that echoed around the house, but nothing major. They had stopped just before 10:50pm.

"It could have been a lot worse if they had carried on past midnight," Jhordan told them.

"You did well tonight Jhordan. Tell me, how are things going with the girl?" Aura asked.

Jhordan chanced a glance at Bruce who quickly shook his head.

"They're going well. She can be a tough thing though. I'm getting there, just have to devise a different way of doing it and quickly," Jhordan told her.

"Any problems?" Aura asked.

"None so far, just that she is stubborn," Jhordan replied.

"Good, try and keep it that way. I don't want anything to mess this up, this could be our last chance," Aura told them both. She secretly hoped that Sylvester had done as he had been told.

When Luna had finished helping her Mum wash the dishes, she sat at her desk to begin her homework. She had a mountain of maths work and a few questions to answer for English before she had to start her history assignment. She opened her books and began writing. She found it hard to concentrate. The whole time, her mind kept wandering back to her Dad's spirit looking frail. She willed Judith to appear but she didn't. She felt a gush of wind behind her and turned to come face to face with Max.

"Luna, time is running out. We have to act fast. You need to find Donna and explain everything to her," Max said quickly.

"Wait. I have a question. Why is my Dad looking so faint?" Luna asked.

Max sighed. He didn't have time for this but he felt she needed to know. That way she could fully understand what had happened. "Your father hasn't been gone for long, has he?"

"No. No he hasn't," Luna said, her eyes dropping to the floor.

"His soul hasn't had time to fully rest, to gain its true power. He hadn't been gone long enough before those people came and disturbed his resting place. He speaks of you. He knows about you. We all gave him just a little bit of power, just so he could visit you tonight," Max told her.

"What do I have to do?" Luna asked.

"Do as I asked. Contact Donna. Explain everything Judith and I have told you. I will tell you more when I can," Max replied. He faded away as quickly as he had appeared.

Luna looked out of the window towards Flowerly Hall. She didn't move for a full two minutes. It was in this time that the voice from her dreams came to her again.

'I have faith in you Luna. You and I both know you can do this.'

Luna had no idea who the voice belonged to. This was the first time she had heard a voice without a spirit. She didn't want to call out to it, just in case it was dangerous. She closed her eyes for a second, took a deep breath in and returned to her homework. She would call Donna in the morning.

Monique sat to watch the evening news. She didn't do much in evenings now. Spencer, Luna and her used to play games. Different board games every night. It was a fun household, they were always laughing. Since Spencer had gone, it seemed their house was continually in mourning. Monique found it hard to create fun with Luna that had always been Spencer's job. A news piece suddenly caught her attention.

'It seems, this evening, something that can only be described as a miracle has happened. Whilst we have been off air with technical difficulties, twenty-seven of the thirty-one bodies have been returned to their resting placing and covered up with fresh flowers placed on top.'

Monique was surprised. Why would someone steal thirty-one bodies to begin with but then return twenty-seven of them? It seemed odd. She wanted to call and ask if Spencer was one of the bodies that had been returned, but she realised it was too late. She would call in the morning. She flicked between the channels, trying to find something to watch before bed but nothing really caught her eye, so she switched the TV off, turned off the lamp, double checked the doors were locked and climbed the stairs to bed. She could see from the landing that Luna had gone to bed already so she refrained from going in. She tucked herself up in bed and allowed sleep to claim her for the first time since Spencer died. Sadly for Monique, her sleep would be filled with nightmares of Spencer's accident. She tossed and turned all night before waking up in a sweat at around two a.m. She forced herself to get out of bed and get a glass of water. The only thing she could do now was browse her bookshelf for something she hadn't read for a long time. She settled for a cosy suspense novel and ventured back to bed. This time she noticed Luna's lamp was alight. She opened the door to find Luna wide awake and writing.

"Hey kiddo, what's up?" Monique asked her.

Luna didn't reply.

"Luna?" Monique tried again, a little louder this time.

Luna still refused to answer. Monique looked at what she was writing. Her heart began to race. Suddenly Luna looked up at her, only she looked straight through her. She then put the book away and went straight back to sleep. Monique pondered over whether or not to check the book, just to clarify what she thought she had seen, but she decided against it. She must just be tired. She told herself she was hallucinating and that she just needed sleep. She went back to her room and climbed back into bed. She settled down with the book and began to read. She wasn't even aware she had fallen asleep until her alarm woke her the next day.

Chapter 20

As Luna entered the kitchen the next morning, Monique was at a crossroads on whether to ask her about the night before. She watched as Luna filled her bowl with Coco Pops and poured over the milk. It occurred to her that Luna probably didn't know what had happened. Monique decided not to say anything for now. She didn't want to scare Luna.

"So, what's on the timetable at school today?" Monique asked her.

"English first, then History, break, Maths, Science and then Geography," Luna replied before shovelling another spoonful into her mouth.

"Did you finish your History work?" Monique asked.

Luna nodded her head and milk dribbled from the corner of her mouth. Monique tried not to laugh but a giggle escaped her mouth and Luna spat her breakfast everywhere.

"I'm sorry Mum," Luna laughed.

Monique was speechless. It had been so long since she had seen Luna full on laugh. She hadn't done so since Spencer died.

"Mum?" Luna said.

"Yes, sorry honey, I was miles away," Monique replied quickly grabbing the mop and a bucket. She always had a fresh cleaning bucket ready, just in case.

"I hope it was somewhere hot!" Luna called as she grabbed her bag. "I'm going to head off now. I want to get in early and see my English teacher before class, there's something I didn't understand on the homework."

"OK honey, be safe and I'll see you this evening," Monique called after her.

As Luna closed the front door, she pulled out her phone and called Donna.

"Hello?" Donna answered.

"Detective Canter? It's Luna Heart. I need to speak to you urgently. It's about Max," Luna said quickly. "I'm on my way to school, can we meet outside school?"

"Luna? Yes sure, is everything OK?" Donna asked.

"I don't know. I was told to contact you," she replied.

"I'll meet you outside school in ten minutes," Donna said, and she hung up.

Donna couldn't help but think something was seriously wrong. She put her jacket on and grabbed her keys from her drawer. She quickly sent a text to Savannah before speeding off to meet Luna.

Throughout the whole drive to meet Luna, Donna wracked her brains as to why Luna would call out of the blue about Max. She pulled up just before the school gates and tried to spot Luna, she was nowhere to be seen. When Donna looked in the rear view mirror, much to Donna's surprise, Luna had slid in the backseat unnoticed.

"Luna, what's wrong?" Donna asked.

Luna looked around quickly and nodded. "Max told me to tell you everything, so you have to listen carefully."

All the colour drained from Donnas face. "Max? As in, *my brother,* Max?"

"Yes, he asked me to explain exactly what is happening to him," Luna said.

Just as she had finished her sentence she felt a strange sensation over her body.

"Hey sis," came the sound of Max's voice from Luna's mouth.

"Max? Is it really you?" Donna asked.

"Yes, but I need you to listen. I can give you the names of the people who took the bodies, the rest you have to do yourself," he told her.

"Well, where are the bodies being held?" Donna asked.

"I don't know the address; all I know is that it's cold. I can tell you who is here," Max replied.

"OK, name them," Donna said as she pulled out her notebook.

"Judith Florentine, Edith Florentine, Spencer Heart and me," Max told her.

Donna looked confused. "Why?"

"I'll let Luna explain that, I'm using too much strength talking through her. I have to go," Max replied. "Be happy sis."

A tear escaped Donna's eye. "I miss you," she whispered.

"That felt strange. That's never happened before," Luna said as she shook her head clear.

"Tell me why Judith and Edith?" Donna asked.

Luna took a deep breath and explained what had happened to Edith all those years ago.

"Now, it looks like it's up to me to free her soul," Luna shrugged.

She looked out of the car window just as Jhordan walked passed. She quickly ducked down in the back of the car.

"Not one of your biggest fans?" Donna asked.

"Even if I told you, you wouldn't believe me. It took you several visits to realise I was right about Max," Luna said hanging her head down.

"Try me," Donna demanded.

Luna sighed. "He told me he was dead once. He said that he was in the hospital and he was dead, but they brought him back. When I got home I checked up on him, well, on the name that he goes by in school, but that isn't his real name. He is actually dead!"

Donna blinked three times before she spoke. "Are you sure?"

"Positive! In school, his name is Jhordan Crystaline, but his real name is Jhordan Bell. I have to go in now, look him up, and tell me I'm wrong?" Luna asked her.

Donna watched as Luna nervously walked into school. She pulled out her phone and sent a message to Alex.

D – Tell me about Judith and Edith.

A – How much do you already know?

D – Not enough. Talk!

A – Not over text. I'll meet you in your office in an hour.

D – You better, or I'll come looking for you.

Donna locked her phone and started the car. She drove to Pearl Heart's house and knocked on the door before her brain to turn her around.

"Detective Canter, what a surprise, please come in," Pearl said, side stepping to allow Donna to enter.

"Pearl, seventy-eight years ago. Talk," Donna said as she sat at Pearl's dining table.

Pearl sat opposite her and sighed deeply. This was going to be a long conversation, with plenty of questions.

In class, Luna tried her best to avoid Jhordan. It was hard because he was constantly looking at her. It gave her the creeps. When lunchtime came around, she tried to hide in the library, but he found her. When she moved to the music rooms, he found her there too; it was like he knew exactly where she was all of the time.

"Can you please stop following me?" Luna asked.

"Have I done something wrong? I thought you were my friend?" Jhordan asked as he followed her towards the lockers.

Luna stopped. She turned to face him but looked down quickly, the image of him online flashing back into her memory. "I just want to be alone for a while. That's all. I'm dealing with a lot right now."

"Isn't that what friends are for?" Jhordan asked, confusion written across his face.

"Yes, but I don't want to talk to anyone, I just want to be alone," Luna told him and she began to walk away.

"I won't speak. Just listen, or just sit with you," Jhordan pleaded.

Luna carried on walking. There was something about Jhordan that really unsettled her.

Chapter 21

Donna returned to her office after forty-five minutes speaking to Pearl Heart. She didn't know what to do with the information Pearl had just given her. Donna planted herself behind her desk and pulled out a pack of Jelly Babies that she had hidden in her bottom drawer. Just as she placed one of the sweets into her mouth, the door to her office opened abruptly and Alex walked in, quickly closing the door behind him.

"I can't let anyone see that I've come here. I'm not supposed to be anywhere near this case," Alex whispered.

"Sit down, and talk. Pearl Heart has told me some things today and I need to see if you tell me the same," Donna gestured to the chair across from her desk. "If anyone asks, you're here about Martha's surprise party."

"She's having a party?" Alex asked.

"Maybe, I haven't fully got her to accept she will be forty this year," Donna smiled. "I'm working on it though. So first thing, why did you have to step back?"

Alex sighed, "Judith and Edith are relatives of mine. Once the press or even the top brass found out, I'd have been chucked off instantly. I just thought it would be better in the long run if I just stepped back."

"So when Luna said about you being her blue eyed boy, she meant Judith?" Donna asked.

"No, she meant my mother. My Mum died when I was just seven years old. She would always protect me from my father. She saved my life that night," Alex told her.

Donna hadn't known much about Alex's past. He never spoke about it much and she didn't ask.

"So, Judith and Edith are what?" Donna asked. She had to know exactly how they were related before she told him what Luna had told him earlier.

"They were my great-great-great aunts. I've been told stories about them all my life. My grandmother, who raised me, told me about them every second she got the chance to. There was always a new story every time she spoke about them," he told her. "She told me about Edith and how she died. Judith was heartbroken for so many years after that."

"I can't say I blame her, it wasn't exactly under normal circumstances," Donna replied.

"Coincidently, Judith was with Edith that day, but she couldn't rescue Edith in time. Judith was rattled for months afterwards. I don't think she ever forgave herself for what happened," Alex said.

"From what Luna has said, I still don't think she has," Donna replied.

"Luna? What has she said? And how would she know?" Alex questioned her.

Donna sat forward, put her Jelly Babies back in the drawer and clasped her hands together. "Luna has told me that she has spoken to Judith. Judith has asked for Luna's help in freeing Edith's soul."

Alex rolled his eyes, "not this again. This happened over seventy years ago too."

"What do you know about that?" Donna asked. It was the first she had heard about it today.

"The old man that used to live next to me was a retired cop. He talked about the old days all the time. I could be enjoying the sun on the back porch and he'd just plot up next to me and start rambling. Don't get me wrong, I was grateful for the company when the wife was at work but boy, he could go for hours." Alex smiled. "One day he told me about some poor girl who perished at Flowerly Hall and how some other poor girl had been drafted in by some 'strange oddballs', his words, not mine, to free her. Something about it giving everyone in the house at the time she is freed, eternal life. You don't think someone is trying to do that again, do you?"

Donna looked at him, she didn't break eye contact. "Do you think the story was true? About the eternal life thing?" She asked.

"No way. That's the sort of stuff of movies isn't it," Alex laughed.

Donna hadn't laughed. "I think it's true."

Alex was stunned. "It's just some old wives tale. There's no way on this green Earth, that Edith holds the key to some 'eternal life'."

"Listen to me. Seventy-eight years ago, the same thing happened that's happening now. Bodies were disturbed, including Edith and Judith, and that time, it was Pearl Heart who was the girl who could supposedly free Edith. The reason it didn't work is because she didn't believe in herself enough," Donna explained. "Now, I'm not saying I believe everything she has told me, but I also met up with Luna this morning. Alex, they have Max."

"Why would they have Max?" Alex asked. He was confused. "What does Max have to do with any of this?"

"That's where it doesn't make sense. I don't see why they would take Max," Donna told him.

"Are you sure it's him though Donna?" Alex asked.

"Alex, I heard him. Look at this," she said as she dug out the letter that Luna had written. "Tell me that isn't Max's handwriting."

Alex was speechless.

"That was exactly how I felt when I watched her write it. Alex, she had her eyes shut!" Donna hissed. "Then today, when I met her outside school, Max spoke from her mouth!"

Alex was staring at the letter. He tried to form some kind of words but everything failed him.

"Alex, help me. I don't know what to do," Donna pleaded.

"I don't know what to do Donna. I've not dealt with this before. I have to go," Alex replied as he stood up, swung the door open and left.

Donna watched him scurry away before putting her head in her hands. 'I'm at a loss' she thought.

"Hey! What happened?" Savannah said as she popped her head through the door. "Why'd Alex run off like that?"

"It's a long story. Pull up a pew," Donna said gesturing to the seat that Alex had just run from as if it were on fire.

Savannah shrugged her shoulders, sat down and waited for Donna to start explaining.

"I hope you have a lot of time," Donna said before she began.

Luna tried her best to avoid Jhordan for the whole school day. She nearly completed her mission had it not been for him standing by her locker at the end of the day.

"I haven't seen you in class. Is everything OK?" He asked as she threw open her locker door.

"It's fine. Everything is just fine," she said through gritted teeth. "Now, if you don't mind. I've got loads of homework and it will not do itself."

"I can help," Jhordan offered. "Please?"

"No, thank you. I can do it alone," Luna told him. "Please don't follow me."

Jhordan watched as she turned her back on him and walked away. He knew he was failing Aura but he had one more trick up his sleeve.

As Luna arrived home, she shouted for her mother. There was no reply. She ran upstairs to check the bathroom but it was empty, the bath was dry and the towels were all still neatly rolled up on the shelves.

'This is odd,' Luna thought to herself.

She pulled out her phone and called her mother. She waited patiently and silently for her to answer. The sudden shrill caught her off guard and she dropped her phone. Luna went to Monique's room to find her mobile phone on the bed. Picking it up, Luna looked over the side of the bed to find her mother lying in a pool of blood. Luna quickly called the ambulance and Donna.

Chapter 22

Luna sat in the waiting room, swinging her legs under the chair. She felt uncomfortable with everyone staring at her. She tried to block them out by watching videos on her phone but she could still feel them watching. Their eyes boring into her soul.

"Hey kid," Donna said gently tapping her shoulder. "Bit lonely out here huh?"

The waiting room was empty.

"Not as empty as you think," Luna whispered.

"Describe what you see," Savannah said, sitting on the other side of her.

Luna looked around. They were a range of different faces looking back at her. Old people, young people, really old people. "Where do I start?" She asked.

"How about left to right," Donna whispered.

Luna took a deep breath and began describing the scene before her, "furthest left is Alfonso. He's of Italian decent, died somewhere in the 1890s, died from tuberculoses. Next to him is Eliza. She is English. She was killed by one of the nurses here in about 1700. She was suffocated. Next to her is Raquel, she's only three, she died of Sudden Infant Death Syndrome about five years ago. Bert is next, he died very recently of pneumonia, and he had a terrible cold this winter. There are the triplets, Michael, Samuel and Peter. They were murdered by their own father, apparently he wanted girls. Next to them is their mother Charlene, died the same way."

"You can see them all?" Savannah asked as she looked around at the empty waiting area.

"Yes. It feels strange to see so many in one place, other than a cemetery of course," Luna replied. "They only speak to me if they need help. Most of the time they just watch what I do and it feels weird."

"Have you ever spoken to anyone about it?" Donna asked. "Other than your Grandma."

"No, because no-one would believe me, there is no definitive way of proving it," Luna said, hanging her head down.

Donna looked up from Luna to see the doctor coming towards them. She had dark hair whipped up into a top bun, and small dark eyes. Her face was free of make-up, except a small smudge of lip balm across her bottom lip. She smiled as she got closer.

"Are you the relatives of Monique Heart?" She asked.

"This is her daughter Luna. I'm Detective Canter and this is Detective Shepherd. Is she going to be OK?" Donna asked after introducing everyone.

"Why don't we go into a private room to talk?" The nurse smiled.

Donna nudged Luna and they followed the nurse to a side room.

"Take a seat," she said.

Luna sat down and finally looked up at the nurse. She could see in her eyes that it wasn't going to be good news.

"Is she dead?" Luna asked.

The nurse smirked a little, "no, she's not dead, but she is really poorly. Do you know what happened?"

"I was at school all day. I came home and she wasn't there that's when I tried to call her, but I found her phone on the bed, that's when I saw her," Luna recalled.

"OK honey, don't worry. We found Mrs Heart to have a serious head wound to the base of her skull. We have had to put her into an induced coma for now, just so we can monitor the pressure in her brain and perform surgery if we need to," the nurse told Donna. "Is there anywhere else that this young lady can stay?"

"She will stay with me," Pearl said from the doorway. "I saw you all come in here so I waited for a minute or two. Thank you for the heads up," she told Savannah.

"It's the least I could do. When I saw the condition Monique was in, I knew Luna would need somewhere to go," Savannah smiled.

"Who do we ask for if we need to contact the hospital?" Pearl asked.

"Ask for me, I'm Sister Kenneth." She replied.

"Indeed we will. Thank you for taking care of her," Pearl told her.

Sister Kenneth left the room with a smile. Donna turned to Pearl and asked, "How will you help Luna?"

"It's going to take every ounce of strength I have left, but they will not do to her what they did to me," Pearl said.

"How was school?" Aura asked as Jhordan came through the door.

"I'm not sure how much more I can do with this girl. She is so stubborn!" Jhordan said as he slumped down on the sofa.

"In what way? I mean, us females can always be stubborn," Aura laughed.

"Well, I tried to talk to her today but she just said she wanted to be left alone, said she had a lot going on. I offered to listen to her problems but she just walked away. I don't understand," Jhordan said.

Aura sat next to him, she wasn't good at the motherly thing. She never had any children, it was a given since she had been dead since 1754. She tried to act like the mothers she had seen out and about. She gently touched his arm and said, "Maybe she just needs a push, just a gentle nudge in the right direction. Why don't we go over and have a chat with her and her Mum? Invite them for dinner or something? Get you two in the same room with no distractions?"

"It's an idea I guess. Shall we go now?" Jhordan asked.

"No time like the present!"Aura replied as she grabbed her coat.

They made their way to Luna's house only to be disappointed when all the lights were off. Jhordan knocked on the door and waited for a reply. He was worried when nobody answered.

"Can I help you at all?" Donna asked as she emerged from the car, showing her badge.

"Oh. Hello, I'm Aura Crystaline, This is my son Jhordan. We were just trying to invite Mrs Heart and her lovely daughter for dinner, but it seems no one is home," Aura smiled.

Donna looked at them both with caution.
"Unfortunately, Mrs Heart is spending some in hospital due to an incident earlier this afternoon. Luna will not be returning tonight."

"Will Mrs Heart be OK?" Jhordan asked.

"We hope so, we can't go into too much detail at the moment due to an ongoing investigation," Savannah included. She had been inside the house and came out while Donna spoke to Aura and Jhordan.

"Was this an attack?" Aura asked. "Should we be worried?"

"Like my colleague said, we cannot say for definite at the moment, but we are advising residents to be vigilant," Donna added.

"I'll be sure to lock all doors when we return home," Aura said as she pulled Jhordan away. "Good evening officers."

As they both watched Aura walk away, Savannah turned to Donna and said, "She was weird."

"She seemed a little jumpy," Donna replied. "Wait! That's the boy Luna asked me to check up on!"

"Huh? Why check up on him? He's just a kid," Savannah said.

Donna quickly filled her in on the parts she hadn't had time to tell her. About how Luna checked up on him and that he was actually supposed to be dead. They both went into Monique house and Savannah placed her laptop on the table. She opened the internet search engine and typed in the name Luna had given Donna earlier. Within a few seconds a ton of results appeared on the screen. A mass of news sites reiterating stories of the death of Jhordan Bell.

'We are reporting the news today of the sad death of 14 year old Jhordan Bell. Found last night by his father Maurice Bell.

Police tell us that Jhordan was found on the shore of the lake at the centre of Ivy Forest. An apparent drowning, according to preliminary reports. They also added that a certain game, and we use the term very loosely, was found nearby. Maurice reports Jhordan leaving with his friends around six p.m to camp out in the forest overnight. It wasn't until three p.m the next day, when Maurice spotted the group of friends in the town centre that he questioned the whereabouts of his son. The group assumed he had gone home in the night as his tent was gone the next morning.

When Maurice went to search for his son in the forest, he discovered his body washed up on the shore of the lake. Despite attempts to save his son, Maurice and the Paramedics couldn't revive him.'

Savannah and Donna were speechless. The picture matched the boy they had just seen.

Chapter 23

"Grandma Pearl, how am I going to get through this?" Luna asked as they sat down together at the table.

Luna had brought all her notebooks with her to show her Grandma. She opened the latest one about Judith and Edith and showed her.

"Judith believes in me, she said she has faith in me. Even Max has said he believes I can do it, but I don't know what I'm supposed to do?" Luna told her.

Just as she finished her sentence, the phone rang in the hallway.

"Wait here, we'll work through this together," Pearl smiled and she went to answer the phone.

"Hello, Heart residence, how can I help you?" She said.

"Mrs Heart, this is Detective Shepherd. Is Luna still awake?" Savannah asked.

"Oh yes dear, we were just about to have some hot chocolate. Is everything OK?" Pearl asked, immediately starting to worry.

"Would it be too late for us to pop in?" Savannah said.

"Of course not, I'll get two extra cups. Whipped cream and marsh mellows?" Pearl asked.

"That would be lovely, thank you," Savannah replied as she ended the call.

Pearl placed the handset down and began to wonder why the two officers would want to speak with Luna. She went through to the kitchen and filled the kettle.

"Who was it Grandma?" Luna asked from the dining room. Pearl looked round to see her granddaughter smiling at her through the serving hatch. She could see so much of Spencer in her.

"Just those two officers honey, they want to have a chat with you, so they are on their way. I'm just making some hot chocolate for us all, why don't you keep an eye out the window for them?" Pearl told her.

Luna nodded and went towards the window. She looked out but couldn't see them. Instead she stared at Flowerly Hall, She couldn't figure out why it hadn't interested her before now, especially how spooky it looked in the mist and fog. She looked up towards one of the highest windows where something caught her eye. She couldn't be sure if it was a face or an animal. She stared at it for a few more minutes before the headlights of a car drew her attention away.

"They're here Grandma," Luna shouted. "Shall I open the door?"

"Oh no, no dear. You carry the tray of hot drinks into the dining room for me," Pearl told her handing over the tray, turning the kitchen light off and closing the door. She waited until Luna was safely in the living room before opening the door to Savannah and Donna.

"Come in ladies, the hot chocolate has just been made. Go on through," she smiled as they came in.

Savannah and Donna made their way into the dining room where Luna was sitting at the table with her notebook out in front of her. She was writing something inside.

"No, that's not what I saw," Luna said.

"Yes I'm sure," she replied as if in deep conversation with someone.

"Is she OK?" Savannah whispered.

"Just watch her, you will see the true gift shine through," Pearl whispered back.

The three ladies watched in amazement as Luna continued her conversation.

"No, I couldn't see its face, just the outline of what looked like a head," Luna said. "It looked like this." Luna began sketching the outline of what she had seen at the top window of Flowerly Hall. She concentrated so hard that her pencil snapped.

As if by magic, there was a new pencil in her hand within seconds, and she continued with her sketch.

Donna was dumbfounded. "Where did that come from?"

"That will be Judith," Pearl replied. "She's sitting next to Luna at the table but, of course, neither of you can see that."

"So it's true? She really can connect with the dead?" Savannah asked.

"Just watch dear, all will be revealed," Pearl told her as Luna continued her sketch and conversation.

"So, it looked a bit like this. Do you recognise it?" Luna said as she turned the paper around to show the person who clearly wasn't there. "What's wrong?"

"That's him! The one holding Edith captive," Judith exclaimed.

The colour drained from Luna's face.

"Bruce! Bruce where are you?" Aura shouted as soon as she closed the front door. "BRUCE!"

"What's all the shouting about?" Bruce asked as he came out of the bathroom.

"Have you had any updates from Sylvester?" Aura asked impatiently.

"Only that the bodies are back in place and he did it carefully. Why?" He asked with a look of confusing across his face.

"Something happened to Luna's Mum. She is in hospital," Jhordan told him.

Bruce thought for a second. He knew what Sylvester was like. Would he have done that even though she isn't a threat? "I'll call him and see what he's up to."

"You don't think he did it again, do you?" Aura whispered, hoping Jhordan couldn't hear her.

"I hope not," Bruce replied. He walked into one of the back bedroom and pulled out his phone. He held down the number three and waited until Sylvester answered.

"What?" Sylvester said.

"What have you been up to?" Bruce asked. He wanted to ask him outright but thought better of it.

"I put the bodies back like I was told. Didn't you get my message?" Sylvester replied.

"I got it yeah; I just wanted to check in with you. Seems the girl's Mum was attacked and she's in hospital," Bruce informed him.

"Well, that's a turn up isn't it? Perfect opportunity to get the job done," Sylvester replied.

"It was you wasn't it?" Bruce asked.

"And if it was?" Sylvester said, he clearly didn't care what Bruce had to say.

"Aura is going to go insane," Bruce told him. "It could mess up everything!"

"How? The girl will be home alone. Just get Jhordan to lure her out and bam! Job started!" Sylvester said.

"She's not home though, she's at her Grandmas!" Bruce hissed.

A sharp knock at the door forced Bruce into silence. He muted the phone and opened the door. Aura stood there with her eyebrows high up on her forehead.

"I think you better start explaining," she demanded.

"Explaining about what?" Bruce said going back to the desk. He'd left the phone facing down so Aura couldn't see how he was talking to.

"Jhordan said the girl hasn't spoken to him today. He said he told you about it," Aura explained.

"The girl is weird, I just told him to give her a little space that's all. I don't see what the problem is," Bruce told her. He sat down and shuffled some paperwork. "She will be talking to him by tomorrow, don't worry about it."

Aura frowned. She didn't know whether Bruce was covering up for Jhordan or if he was telling the truth. She watched as he piled up papers and stored them away in the drawer of the desk.

"Now, if there's nothing else. I have some more research to do on the Heart family," Bruce said.

"I'll leave you to it. If you find anything of interest, let me know," Aura told him. She quickly left the room, closing the door behind her. She went to the dining room and opened her own laptop. She would do some research of her own on the other body they stole. Max Canter.

Chapter 24

"You've completely lost me," Pearl said after Donna and Savannah had explained what they read online.

"So if he is really dead, how can everyone else see him?" Luna asked.

Donna and Savannah looked at each other; they didn't have the answer for that.

"When he told me he died, I thought he was playing tricks on me, but I looked him up online too. I found out he was really dead, but I'm still confused," Luna told them.

"Oh honey," Pearl said as she gathered her into an embrace. "We'll find out what's going on, don't you worry. Now, off to bed with you, you still have school tomorrow."

Luna hugged her Grandma tight and kissed her on the cheek.

"Goodnight everyone," Luna said as she began to climb the stairs.

Donna was worried about Luna going to school knowing that Jhordan was in fact dead. "Should she really go in? Especially after today."

"Ah she needs to stay in the same routine," Pearl replied. She waited until she heard Luna's room door close before she whispered again. "Especially as I have a gut instinct I know who could be behind all this."

Donna's mouth fell open, "Care to elaborate?"

Pearl put her finger to her lips, grabbed a piece of paper and wrote on it;

'Luna may think I'm old and decrepit, but I know the sound of my landing and she is still there. Back when I was her age, I was approached by a girl, Aura. She knew all about my gift. I didn't think she was bad to begin with. Her parents befriended my parents and she spent a lot of time with me.'

"So as you see, when William disappeared, I could never bring myself to change the decoration, it will remain like this until I go!" Pearl laughed.

Savannah looked confused, but, after Donna quickly read the note, she understood what Pearl was doing. If Luna thought they were just passing the time away, she would eventually go to bed.

"So you never even thought about a new couch?" Donna said as she sat down on the near ancient sofa. She sunk deep into the cushion.

"No, it has never caused me any trouble, and it's still rather comfortable!" Pearl laughed again.

"If you like being swallowed up by fabric then yeah sure, I get it. Could you give me a hand, I seem to have been partially consumed by your sofa," Donna giggled.

As Savannah and Pearl pulled her to her feet, they heard Luna's door close again and the floorboards above them creak. Luna had finally given up and gone to bed. Pearl nodded to the two women and gestured for them to follow her to the kitchen.

"It's safer to talk in here," Pearl whispered as they sat the little table in the centre of the room.

Pearls kitchen was full of aromas from different spices. Cinnamon, Basil, and Jerk Spice stood out to Savannah. Christian's parent's kitchen smelt exactly the same most days.

"So who was Aura?" Donna asked.

Pearl sat down after putting the kettle back on to boil. "She was older than I was, by about three maybe four years at that point. At least that's what we all thought. She latched herself to me after starting the school late through the year. She had an unhealthy obsession with Flowerly Hall. It was all she ever talked about."

The kettle clicked off making all the women jump. Pearl laughed to herself and stood to make some tea. She took three mugs and threw a tea bag in each, filled the mug and let it brew for a minute. After removing the tea bags, she placed the milk, sugar and a few biscuits on the table.

"Savannah has sweetener, if you have any?" Donna told Pearl.

"I always have it here. Spencer had it in his drinks," Pearl replied. She reached for the cupboard door and stopped in her tracks. She squinted her eyes to block out the light from above her, and there she saw the face of a woman she had seen over seventy-eight years ago. Pearl dropped the sweetener on the floor as gasped in fright.

"What is it Pearl?" Savannah said as she ran to the woman's side.

"She was right there!" Pearl whispered. "Right outside the window."

"Who was?" Donna asked, shining her torch through the window into the pitch blackness of Pearls rear garden.

"The girl!" Pearl exclaimed.

Aura turned away from the window with a wicked smile spread across her face. She had finally seen the woman Pearl Heart had grown into. She laughed to herself as she remembers what some of the townspeople had said about her.

'In denial about her husband.'

'Unstable in the head.'

If only they knew exactly what Pearl Heart could see? Aura slinked away unnoticed by Pearl's guests. Who, by some cheeky coincidence happened to be Donna Canter!

Aura had checked up on one of the bodies they had kept behind. Max Canter. She found him to have a sister in the local police force. She searched back further to find a name she remembered so vividly, it had stuck with her for over seventy years. Felix Canter. He had been a police officer too. His son, Max, hadn't followed his footsteps into law enforcement, he had become a plumber and owned his own business, that was until he was killed after demanding a customer pay up an outstanding debt for work he had done. Donna stepped up, took the oath and became the next Canter on the force, but Felix had been stuck in her head for the last seventy-eight years. And now, she had dug up his son's body and was in hiding from his daughter. She felt as if he were out to get her from beyond the grave.

She turned and headed back towards the house. She would have to get to the girl another time.

By the time she arrived home, Jhordan was at the kitchen table looking through a textbook from school.

"What are you doing?" She asked as she locked the door behind her.

"Just catching up on some homework," he replied.

"Can't you take it in your room? I have some stuff I have to do," she said.

Jhordan packed up his work and carried it to his room. She hadn't meant to snap at him, but she hadn't realised how worked up she would get over realising who she was dealing with. She would have to speed up the process, before that Canter girl got any indication that her father had dealt with Aura before. She hoped it wouldn't come to that. She went to find Bruce; she had to tell him what she had found out. Luckily for him, it had only been her that Felix had seen. He and Sylvester hadn't been around at that point. It was her and Monty, among others. Now Monty wasn't around, she would have to do it all alone. Jhordan was just a distraction and Sylvester was a nuisance. Bruce had his uses, but he didn't posses any magic. Not like Monty had. The plan had to work this time. It was the last time they would be able to do it. After this year, the time was up.

<u>Chapter 25</u>

Luna sat up in bed and looked around. She had almost forgotten that she was at her grandmother's house. She slid out of bed, wrapped herself in her dressing gown, slid into her slippers and ventured downstairs. She could hear her grandmother clattering in the kitchen.

"Morning Grandma," Luna said as she sat at the kitchen table.

"Good morning my sweet, what would you like for breakfast?" Pearl said, smiling as she turned to face Luna.

"I don't know if I can eat. Have you heard from the hospital?" Luna asked.

"I did. The nurse called this morning. Your mother is doing well. They are waiting for some test results to come through before they can say anymore, but you need to eat. You can't go to school on an empty stomach," Pearl told her. "Cereal or eggs?"

Luna looked at her Grandma as she stood with a box of Frosties in one hand and a spatula in the other. She smiled. Her Grandma always knew how to make her smile. Just like her Dad.

"Eggs please, if it's no trouble," Luna replied.

"Eggs coming up, fried, scrambled or dippy?" Pearl asked.

"Dippy?" Luna questioned.

"Oh your father loved his dippy eggs. Boiled and then into an eggcup with some toast soldiers! Dip them in and hey presto, dippy eggs!" Pearl clapped her hands together.

"I'll take that then!" Luna exclaimed. "What time did Donna and Savannah leave?"

"A little after eleven sweetie, they didn't stay long. Said they needed to work out how Jhordan, if that really is him, is living and breathing," Pearl answered her. "They said they would call if they needed anything more."

Luna turned to her left and let out a gasp. "What are you doing here?"

"Who are you talking to sweetheart? Oh how do you do?" Pearl said as she turned to see Max perched on the seat beside Luna.

"Grandma Pearl, this is Max Canter," Luna introduced them.

"As in Donna Canter?" Pearl asked.

"Can she see me?" Max asked.

"Of course I can dear, where do you think young Luna got her gift?" Pearl smiled. "How can we help you this morning?"

"Something isn't right. I heard her last night. Aura. She knows who I am, she knows who you are. Both of you," Max told them.

"Did you just say Aura?" Pearl choked.

"Yes. I heard her last night. It was you, wasn't it? Seventy-eight years ago," Max asked.

Pearl took a deep breath in and sat on the chair next to Luna. "You better take today off sweetie. I'll call the school."

As Pearl went to make the call, Luna sat looking confused.

"Are you OK?" Max asked her.

"I don't know. I know what I have to do, but I didn't know it was Grandma Pearl who tried before. You told me that the last person didn't believe in herself enough, that doesn't sound like my Grandma," Luna replied.

"Let's wait and listen to what she has to say," Max offered. He tried to pat her hand gently but his hand just went through hers.

"That felt funny," Luna laughed.

Max smiled, "you have no idea how much energy it takes to actually touch something real.

"Max, how's my Dad doing?" Luna asked.

"He's holding up kid. Always talks about you. I'll tell him you're doing OK. Hey, where's your Mum anyway?" Max questioned.

"She's in hospital. Someone hit her over the head. They aren't sure what happening yet, running tests or something," Luna said, hanging her head down.

"Try not to worry. Hospitals are great places," Max said, trying to cheer her up.

"They didn't save Dad," Luna replied, a solitary tear rolling down her cheek.

Max didn't know what to say to that, but he made a note to ask Spencer later about the crash and what happened.

Pearl returned to the kitchen and continued to make the eggs for Luna.

"What did they say?" Luna asked.

"They said you can have a few days for personal reasons, but you have to go back after that," Pearl replied. "Now, that's your egg done. Let me explain whilst you eat, that way you can't interrupt," Pearl laughed. She placed the plate in front of Luna and smiled as she began to eat.

"It was a long time ago mind you, but I remember so much of it," Pearl began.

Jhordan arrived for class and sat in his usual seat. He looked around for Luna but couldn't see her anywhere, he hoped she wasn't hiding from him again, he didn't know what he had done wrong.

"Sir, where's Luna?" Jhordan asked his teacher.

"She is having a few personal days off Jhordan. I take it you heard about her Mum?" He replied.

"Yes, my Mum and I stopped by last night to ask if they wanted to join us for dinner, and we were told by two policewomen roughly what had happened. I hope she will be alright," Jhordan replied.

"I'll be sure to pass on your best wishes when I talk to her family next," his teacher replied.

Jhordan pulled his bag onto the desk and pretended to search for his pencil case and books, but instead quickly sent a text to Bruce;

J – Luna not in school, something to do with her Mum.

B – Don't worry kid. Stick to the plan.

J – Who would have done that to her Mum?

B – Like I said, don't worry. Keep to the plan.

Jhordan tucked his phone away and continued with his day, he couldn't do much from here, but he couldn't leave either, it would look too suspicious.

"The kid says the girl isn't at school," Bruce told Aura as she came into the kitchen.

Aura yawned and switched the kettle on. "Why are you telling me?"

"I thought, after last night, you might want to step things up a little, maybe bring things forward, throw people off track?" Bruce replied.

"We have precisely one week before the deadline, how *exactly* would you like to speed things up? We don't even know if the girl can fully help us yet," Aura told him.

"Leave that part to me. The rest you will have to work out, remember, this is the last time. After this, you're stuck!" Bruce said. He turned on his heel and left Aura staring after him.

Aura shook her head, *'as if HE is trying to tell ME what to do! The nerve! I'll show him who the boss is around here!'* She thought to herself. She slammed a cup on the side and threw the tea bag inside; she poured the water into the cup and spilt it all over the side. Throwing the cup into the sink and smashing the handle, Aura stomped back to her room and dressed for the day. It was time to work out exactly how they would succeed this time.

As the day wore on, Jhordan hurried through his school work. He was determined to find out how Luna's Mum was. He had talked himself into going to Luna's Grandmas and asking her, but he had also talked himself out of it.

At lunch, Jhordan called Bruce.

"What's up kid?" Bruce said as he answered the phone.

Jhordan could hear a lot of commotion in the background.

"Am I interrupting something?" Jhordan asked. He got worried when he heard a muffled scream in the distance.

"Oh no, it's just the neighbours making noises again. So how can I help?" Bruce replied.

"Should I try and find out how Luna's Mum is?" He asked.

Bruce caught the gasp before it escaped.

"No, no. Don't worry about that now. Just come home straight from school," Bruce said hurriedly.

"Are you sure?" Jhordan asked.

"A hundred percent. Look kid, I gotta go. I'll see you later," Bruce told him.

Jhordan placed the phone on the table in front of him and stared off into the distance. He thought he was hearing things when a distant voice cried;

"Get off me!"

Jhordan instantly looked down at his phone and realised that Bruce hadn't hung up. He was about to end the call when he heard Aura's voice.

"It's time you showed us what you can really do Luna."

Jhordan went still. The heart that had been brought to life stopped for a second. *'Why did they have Luna?'* He thought.

He ran to the school office and played on being ill. The school nurse sent him home with a letter to his 'Mum'.

Jhordan used the tracking system on his phone to locate Bruce and Aura. He sat outside the door to the little shack and listened in.

"I know who you are," Luna told them. She was scared but trying not to show it.

"Of course you do kid," Bruce laughed.

"You're Jhordans parents!" Luna replied.

Bruce and Aura stopped, looked at each other and smiled.

"That's excellent detective work. Has that cop woman been teaching you?" Aura giggled. "Look little girl, I've spent centuries trying to free this wretched spirit. This year is the last time I can try, and YOU are going to help me, even if it kills you, which it probably will."

Jhordan was surprised. Aura hadn't told him it could kill Luna. He continued to listen.

"Jhordan is so kind, but you two aren't," Luna whispered.

"Jhordan has been TOLD to be nice! Once I get what I want, neither of you will matter anymore. I'll release the spell on Jhordan and you will probably be dead," Aura said, shrugging her shoulders.

Chapter 26

Jhordan ran from his hiding place, he didn't know where to go or who to talk to but his feet seemed to lead him to the police station.

He looked up at the looming doors before him. They were heavy set with huge brass handles. He reached out to push at the door when it suddenly flew open.

"Oh, hey there!"

Jhordan looked up into the eyes of a kind looking woman. She had deep brown eyes and bouncy curls on her head. She smiled with the brightest smile he had seen in a very long time.

"I'm Martha. You don't look so good. Fancy a chat?" Martha asked him.

Jhordan nodded so fast he became dizzy. He followed her into the station and sat down on the chair she offered, he watched as she walked away to get him some water.

"Now, how about you tell me what's got you all in a scurry?" Martha smiled as she sat down next to him.

Jhordan took a little sip of the water and relaxed a little. He tried to remember the name of the police officer who had spoken to him and Aura not more than two nights before.

"Canter. Shepherd." Jhordan spluttered.

"My surname is Canter," Martha replied, "but we've never met."

Jhordan looked at her with a confused look on his face. "Are you sisters? You don't look alike."

Martha laughed. "I would hope not, we have completely different parents. No, she is my wife."

Jhordan looked even more confused. "Oh."

Martha smiled. "Let me call her. Maybe she can shed some light on this. I won't be a sec."

Jhordan tried to figure out what Martha meant. He hadn't come across two women who were married before. *'Is this a new thing?'* He thought to himself.

Martha watched him through the mirrored glass as she called Donna.

"Hey babe, erm, I've got a boy here asking for you. He looks kinda odd," Martha said as Donna answered the call.

"Describe him," Donna said.

"Well, he's about fourteen, maybe fifteen. Dark hair, dark eyes. If I'm honest babe, he's got a dead look about him," Martha told her.

Donna took a sharp intake of breath, "surely it couldn't be." She whispered.

"Be who?" Savannah asked as she listened in to the call.

"Jhordan," Donna replied.

"I'll check his name, just a sec," Martha replied. She covered the mouthpiece and popped her head around the door. "Hey, I never caught your name?"

"Sorry, I'm Jhordan. Jhordan B...Crystaline," Jhordan replied.

Martha smiled and quickly closed the door again. "He said his name is Jhordan, but he tripped on his surname. It sounded like he was about to say something with a B but then he changed it to Crystaline. Is this the same Jhordan?"

Donna closed her eyes and let out the breath she was holding. "It's him," she said to Savannah. "OK, hold him there. We're on our way."

"Sure thing babe, see you soon," Martha said and she disconnected the call.

"So, it seems Jhordan wants to see us. Are you ready for this?" Donna said as she turned to face Savannah.

"Do I have a choice?" Savannah asked. She climbed back into the car and started the engine.

As they drove back towards the station, Donna debated with herself over why Jhordan would be at the station. If he had anything to do with Aura, like Pearl had hinted, why would he put himself out like this?

"Hey, you OK?" Savannah's voice pierced through her thoughts.

"Yeah, sorry. I can't work it out. Pearl said that Aura is responsible for this. Aura is Jhordans Mum. Now

Jhordan is at the station wanting to talk to us. It's all too strange," Donna replied.

"Maybe it's not about any of this at all. Maybe, it's about something else but he remembered our names from the other night. Try not to beat yourself up about it," Savannah said calmly. "We'll find out what it is when we get there. If we get there."

They both looked out across the traffic that was building up in front of them. The road works on the high street had been never ending. It seemed to drag on forever. Donna took a deep breath in and tried not to think about the reason behind Jhordans visit. That was until someone jumped into the back seat of their car.

"Luna's gone!" Pearl screamed at Savannah.

Donna twisted in her seat to look at a grief stricken Pearl who was now hyperventilating.

"What?" Donna asked. "How long has she been gone?"

"I'd probably say not more than two hours, three at the most," Pearl replied.

Savannah quickly spun the car around and took a different route to the station. Donna filled Pearl in on Jhordan appearing from nowhere and wanting to speak to them.

"It seems even stranger now that Luna is missing," Donna told Savannah.

"Look, when we get there, let's not jump to conclusions. Hear him out first, deal with the fallout afterwards, you hear me?" Savannah ordered.

Donna nodded and held on tighter to the door handle. She hadn't realised how fast Savannah could drive when she was in a hurry; luckily, she was particularly good at it too.

When they arrived at the station, Pearl sat in a different room from Jhordan and spoke to another officer with regards to Luna's disappearance. She detailed everything that was Luna was wearing right down to the ruby red studs she had in her ears.

"I hope she hasn't just wandered off. I'd feel terrible for wasting your time," Pearl told the officer.

"Does she often wander off?" Asked the female officer, tucking her short blonde hair behind her ear.

"No. That's why it was so surprising that she wasn't in her room. I had made her a tuna sandwich for lunch and given it to her in her room. She was working on some work for school, but when I went back up there not more than an hour or so later, the plate and sandwich were there but she was gone. I've tried calling her phone but it goes straight to her voicemail," Pearl told her.

The female officer wrote down a few extra notes, smiling at Pearl as she wrote. "Have you tried tracking her phone?"

Pearl smiled, "I've tried everything possible. I didn't want to waste your time."

"That's quite alright Mrs Heart. I'll get this logged onto the system and radioed out to on the beat officers. We'll find Luna, try not to worry," she smiled back at Pearl.

"So, Jhordan, how can we help you?" Savannah asked as she and Donna sat opposite him.

Jhordan fiddled with his hands in his lap. He looked at the two women, debating what to tell them first. Where Luna was or what Aura had planned. He chanced a glance out of the window and spotted Pearl in the room across from theirs, "is she OK?" He asked, pointing at Pearl.

Donna looked over at Pearl and sighed. "No, she's not. Luna is missing. She has no idea where she is and she is worried."

"I know where Luna is," Jhordan told her, his mind made up. "Aura and Bruce have her in the run down house off the high street."

Donna looked at Savannah with a look of surprise. "We just drove past it!" She looked back at Jhordan. "Why? Why do they have her?"

Jhordan looked scared. "I don't know. All I know is something about Flowerly Hall. She's going to use Luna to get what she wants!"

Savannah remained calm as she quickly beckoned Pearl over to their room. "Please, have a seat."

Pearl looked at Jhordan. She was confused. "Who are you young man?"

"Pearl this is Jhordan." Donna introduced them both and watched as the realisation sunk in.

"As in *THAT* Jhordan?" Pearl asked.

"The very same. Now, Jhordan knows where Luna is, but before you snap," Donna said as she held out her hand to Pearl, "I think he wants to help."

Jhordan nodded. "I know her plans. I don't want her to hurt Luna. I like Luna."

Pearl tried to calm herself down when her phone buzzed in her pocket. She pulled it out and checked the caller ID.

'HOSPITAL'

"I need to take this, please could you wait for a second?" Pearl asked.

"Of course," Savannah replied.

Pearl smiled and stepped outside the door. "Hello?"

"Mrs Heart, this is Sister Kenneth. I wanted to inform you that your daughter-in-law is to be taken for surgery. We found some underlying damage from her fall. Will you be coming to the hospital to wait for her?" Sister Kenneth explained.

"I will be there as soon as I can. How long will her surgery last?" Pearl asked.

"It will only be a few hours at the most. It is completely understandable if you are unable to make it. It is not thought to be life threatening but I thought you would appreciate an update," Sister Kenneth told her.

"I really do appreciate it, thank you. I will come as soon as I can," Pearl told her and ended the call.

She took a deep breath in and re-entered the room. "I'm sorry about that; it was just an update from the hospital."

"How is Mrs Heart?" Jhordan asked.

"She is going for surgery, nothing life threatening but they found something and need to tend to it. Thank you for asking," Pearl answered him. "So you were saying?"

"Jhordan was just about to update us with Aura's plans," Donna said and she motioned for him to continue.

<u>Chapter 27</u>

"You can't force me to do it," Luna protested. "What if I refuse?"

"Then we'll just kill you anyway," Aura shrugged. "You're no use to me if you don't do what I ask."

Bruce was a little apprehensive about how Aura was talking to Luna.

"Aura, can I have a word?" He asked.

Aura rolled her eyes and went over to him. "What is it?" She hissed. "Can't you see I'm in the middle of something?"

"Why are you telling her you will just kill her if she doesn't help?" Bruce whispered.

"Because she will be no use to me. Do I have to think of everything?" Aura hissed at him. "Look, if she doesn't help then we kill her, it's so simple even someone as dim-witted as Jhordan could have worked it out."

"I don't think that is wise Aura." Bruce told her.

"You let me deal with that, you just sit there and, well, just sit there and shut up," Aura told him.

Bruce wasn't happy with Aura, but he didn't dare say another word to her. He let her get back to Luna and did exactly as she told him to do, he just sat there.

"Now little girl," Aura began.

"My name is Luna Morticia Heart!" Luna interrupted.

"I don't care! You're here to do something for me. Whether or not you agree is not up for discussion. You have to free the spirit of Edith Florentine from Flowerly Hall," Aura told her.

"Why? What's in it for you?" Luna asked.

"That's none of your business. Look, I've been trying to do this for the past few centuries. Your pathetic grandmother couldn't do it for me seventy-eight years ago and you're the only female left in the bloodline! So, you're going to be ready when I summon you, you understand?" Aura demanded.

Luna rolled her eyes, '*who does this woman think she is, God?*' she thought to herself. She wished she was back at her grandmother's house. This house was cold and, she had to admit, she was terrified, but she wouldn't let this woman know that. She was a Heart after all.

"That's everything I heard Aura say to Luna. I know the plan but I didn't know about the dying part, I mean, I knew she wouldn't keep me around forever, but I hoped, that if I helped her out, she would let me live a little bit longer," Jhordan said as he finished explaining.

The three women were all speechless. They looked around the table at each other, unable to find the words to string a sentence together. Pearl had tears falling from her eyes, her dark hands shaking as she searched for a tissue inside her handbag and getting frustrated when she couldn't find one. Jhordan pulled an unopened pack from his pocket and slid it across the table towards her. She looked down at the packet and then up into his eyes.

His dark, sad eyes. She instantly felt for the poor boy. He had been dragged into this thinking he was just helping out and now, he had found out that he would, in fact, be luring a poor girl to her death.

"Thank you. You seem very lost behind those eyes," Pearl said.

"I don't feel like I am part of this world. I know it's, technically, because I'm really dead, but, I feel like I don't belong anywhere," Jhordan admitted.

"How did you die?" Savannah asked. "If you remember that is."

Jhordan looked around the room. "Where's your wife?" He asked Donna.

"Probably back at the front desk, you want her here?" Donna replied.

"Is it possible? I, somehow, felt more relaxed when she was here. Not that you all make me uncomfortable," he replied.

"We take no offence, I'll go and see if she can get some cover," Donna smiled. "Don't start without me!"

Jhordan laughed a little and watched Donna as she walked towards the front desk, hold Martha's hand and watched as she explained the situation to her. Martha's smile was pure and innocent. She turned to a plump man behind her and he nodded after she spoke to him. She then made her way around the desk and followed Donna back to their room.

"Hey you! Heard you wanted me here whilst you spoke. How you holding up? These three not scaring you are they?" Martha smiled as she came in and sat next to him.

"They seem lovely. I just wanted you here as you made me feel a little more relaxed. Thank you for taking the time away from your job," Jhordan said to her.

"Hey, I'm still working if I'm sat here. I'm no different to these two," she replied, pointing to Donna and Savannah. "Except I'm not a detective yet."

Jhordan smiled.

"Whenever you're ready Jhordan, take your time." Savannah prompted.

"I was fourteen. I had gone to the forest with some friends. We were always camping there," he began; he was watching Martha the whole time. "We set up a camp fire and were telling some, supposedly, scary stories. They were mostly just a bunch of funny things we strung together. Jeremy suggested we play a game."

"What type of game can you play, at night, in the woods?" Donna asked.

Savannah laughed, "Haven't you ever camped in the woods?"

"It wasn't the sort of thing I was interested in back then," Donna replied.

Savannah stifled a giggle. "I'm surprised! Especially living out here!"

"I wasn't brought up here. I'm a city girl. Only came here because of a certain someone," Donna said as she looked at Martha.

"So what game was it Jhordan?" Martha asked, bringing them back on topic.

"Bones brought a Ouija board with him, his real name is Barnaby but he was so slim, we nicknamed him Bones." Jhordan smiled as he remembered his friends. "I wasn't sure at first, I'd heard all sorts of stories about playing with those types of things, but Jeremy assured me it was safe and that they had all done it before and nothing had happened, so I agreed. We sat in a circle close to the fire and all placed out fingers on the planchette. Jeremy began asking questions but nothing happened. We agreed that if there was no answer after another two questions, then we would close it down properly and go to sleep, but after those questions, Peter thought it would be funny to ask if there were any demons around and he laughed whilst doing it. Jeremy wasn't happy with it and started shouting at Peter; he daren't take his fingers off the planchette in case something terrible happened, none of us dared. Peter kicked out at Jeremy who knocked into me and I fell backwards. I quickly got back up and put my fingers back, Jeremy quickly closed the game down the right way and began arguing with Peter again, told him you shouldn't call out for demons, it was dangerous," Jhordan recalled.

"He's not wrong," Pearl added. "I remember playing that when I was younger. Had a bad experience once when the planchette flew across the room, but we closed it down properly, said goodbye to the spirits and never used it again."

"Peter packed up his stuff and went home. I was surprised because it was about one am when he left. Jeremy told the rest of us to get some rest and that we would leave at eight the next morning. He set an alarm on his watch. Casio I think it was. I climbed into my tent and zipped it up. It was just big enough for me and the sleeping bag so the rest of my stuff was left outside. I remember drifting off to sleep and then hearing a voice calling me. It sounded like Bones. He was calling for me to help him, said he was in the lake and he couldn't swim. I got up and ran out of the tent. We weren't far from the lake, maybe a few meters inshore so I left my slippers behind and ran in to rescue him. I guess in the panic I forgot that I couldn't swim either. I remember the darkness. The stillness that surrounded me. Something strange happened after that, it was like I could see me and my Dad and the paramedics and the police, but it was from above, like I was watching a movie." Jhordan blinked as he finished what he was saying and no-one dared speak a word.

After a few moments of silence, Martha's voice broke through. "That's called an 'out of body' experience. It's where you can see things happening to you and those around you, but not through your own eyes. It can be scary, even for the living."

"I never saw my friends again. Are they still alive?" Jhordan asked.

"Why don't I go and do some digging and you help Donna, Savannah and Mrs Heart find Luna?" Martha said.

Jhordan nodded. "I don't want them to hurt her."

Martha rose from her chair and slid Jhordan her card. "Call if you need anything."

"Thank you," Jhordan replied.

Jhordan heard a light buzzing noise coming from his backpack. He quickly took out his phone and noticed it was Bruce calling. He looked worried and let it go to voicemail. He then quickly sent a message back to him.

J – Staying after school to catch up on some work. I'll be back by dinner.

B – Make it quick. Plans have changed.

J – What do you mean?

B – Aura is changing the time. It's happening tomorrow night. We need to work out who is doing what and when. Get home ASAP.

J – Sure. I won't be long. I'll work faster.

B – Thanks kid.

"Aura has changed the plans. Everything is happening tomorrow night," Jhordan informed them all.

Donna and Savannah looked at each other with worried looks across their faces.

"I don't know how to deal with this," Donna admitted.

"I can help you. I know exactly what she will do. Remember, she did the same with me all those years ago. It can't be much different now," Pearl offered.

"OK. Mrs Heart, we will come to your house a little later tonight to go over some details. Jhordan, you better make your way home but first, can I install a tracker and recorder onto your phone? It's fully discreet and no one will notice it's there, even if they go through it," Savannah asked.

Jhordan offered up his phone without hesitation. Savannah quickly installed the apps and handed it back.

"Thank you. I'll be heading home now," Jhordan said. He gathered his backpack and quickly gave Pearl a hug. "I hope things will be OK for Luna. I'll do everything I can to protect her."

"Thank you young man. I will pray for your safety also," Pearl replied with a tear in her eye.

"We better get you home too Mrs Heart," Savannah said. "We'll drop you off and then take a drive past the old house Jhordan mentioned. After that Donna and I will come back here and work out what we can do, if anything, to at least postpone things until we have a solid plan in place. We will come back to you at, say, seven pm tonight?"

"That sounds like a plan. Be safe young man," Pearl told Jhordan.

As they watched Jhordan walk away from the station, all three women hoped he would be safe and that nothing else happened to him. Even though Jhordan was in fact already dead, they hoped that after this he could finally rest in peace.

Chapter 28

As Pearl entered her house she could hear a faint voice singing from the kitchen.

"Hello, who's there?" Pearl said.

"Grandma? Where have you been?" Luna said as she bounded out of the kitchen and into Pearl's arms.

"I was going to ask you the same thing! Oh my where have you been?" Pearl asked as she held onto Luna tight.

"Can I tell you after dinner? I've made pasta and meatballs," Luna said as she opened the dining room door and gestured to the set table.

"Oh Luna, this looks lovely. Thank you," Pearl said. As she took her coat off, the phone on the side table rang.

"Hello Heart residence, how can I help you?" Pearl answered.

"Hello Mrs Heart. This is Sister Kenneth. I just wanted to inform you that your Mrs Heart's operation went well and she is now in recovery. I wouldn't suggest visiting until at least tomorrow. She will be out of it for a while now," Sister Kenneth informed her.

"Oh thank you so much. I'll bring Luna in tomorrow to see her," Pearl said as she ended the call and went to sit with Luna.

"Who was it?" Luna asked as she put the plates on the table and took her seat.

"The hospital sweetie. Your Mum had an operation today but she is OK. We can go and see her tomorrow. This looks amazing and it smells delicious," Pearl said as she put a forkful into her mouth. "Mmm, tastes as good as it smells."

They ate their meal in silence, savouring the taste. Luna had taken the time to add her Grandma's favourite spices to the meatball sauce.

"So where have you been honey?" Pearl asked as they were washing up the plates and putting them away.

Luna sighed. "I'm scared Grandma. That woman took me today. She said something about Edith."

"Don't you worry my little ray of moonlight. We won't let anything happen to you," Pearl told her. "In fact, it seems we may have another, rather odd, ally."

"What do you mean?" Luna asked. She climbed up onto the sofa next to her Grandma and settled herself down.

Pearl smiled. She loved Luna so much she was willing to do just about anything to keep her safe.

"So, I was on my way to the police station to report you missing, when I noticed Detective Shepherd's car. I jumped in the back whilst they were waiting in traffic. They were on their way back to the station to see someone so I tagged along with them," Pearl began to explain.

Luna listened so intently to what her Grandmother was telling her that she almost fell off the sofa when the doorbell chimed.

Pearl giggled. "Never get too engrossed in something that you get caught out," she said as she went to answer the door.

"Good evening Mrs Heart, may we come in?" Savannah smiled.

Pearl opened the door wider and allowed them both to enter, "I'll make some tea. Please go through, Luna is in there too."

"Thank you," Donna said as they both walked through to the living room.

Pearl escaped into the kitchen, filled the kettle up and switched it on. She placed a tray on the side and loaded it up with mugs and a plate of biscuits. She remembered the sweetener for Savannah and added a few of her special biscuits to the plate. She then loaded up the tray with a rather large teapot and a small jug of milk, but as she walked through the living room door she screamed and dropped the tray which threw the contents everywhere.

"What's happening?" Luna cried from the back of the van.

Sylvester and Bruce had bound her hands and legs to a chair which was bolted to the van floor. They had placed a loose hood over her head so she couldn't see where they were taking her.

"Just be quiet kid and everything will be fine," Sylvester told her.

"Who are you? You're not Detectives Shepherd and Canter!" Luna asked.

"Ha ha, of course we're not! Silly girl," Sylvester laughed.

"What did I do?" Luna asked.

"You haven't done anything yet, but you will," Sylvester replied.

Bruce didn't speak. He knew if he did, then Luna would know exactly who they were, or at least who one of them was.

Luna began to cry, "I didn't want any part of this! I didn't ask for any of this. Why me?"

"It's just who you are kid. Nothing you can do to change it," Sylvester told her. "Not that I'm sorry but hey, we can't change what's passed down to us huh?"

Luna tried to keep her crying quiet. She didn't want to make this person any angrier than he already sounded.

'Kidnapped twice in one day, that must be a record for anyone,' Luna thought. *'How would Grandma be feeling now?'*

She felt the van turn to the right and then a sharp left. She could smell the scent of the sea and dead fish. She began to think. She remembered going to the beach with her Mum and Dad years ago. They would paddle about in the sea, letting the waves almost knock them off their feet. She remembered the sand between her toes and eating fish and chips from the chip shop. Suddenly she remembered a time when they went to the local fish market. It was so long ago that she had almost forgotten about it. It was along the coastline a bit more, nearer to the industrial estates. She inhaled sharply, almost gagging on the smell of rotten fish. She knew where she was. Her father had taught her to take in the scenery and smells from wherever she was, just in case she ever got lost. That way she could explain where she was and it would help rescuers pinpoint her. *'Thanks Dad,'* she thought.

"All right, out you get," Sylvester said as he grabbed her arm and dragged her out of the van.

"Can you take this thing off my head, please?" Lune asked.

"No can do yet I'm afraid, sorry," Sylvester replied. "You just sit tight there. I won't be long."

Luna sighed silently. She wished she could see where she was.

"Why didn't you help me with her back there?" Sylvester asked Bruce when they were out of Luna's earshot.

"She's heard me speak before. I don't want her working out who we are before it's time. Now come on, I need to see if Jhordan is back from school yet," Bruce replied.

Sylvester laughed, "You like him don't you?"

"He's a good kid. I just worry about what all this will do to him when Aura takes the spell off him. He believes he has done so well and, in a way, he has," Bruce replied.

"Let's hope he sticks to the plan then," Sylvester said.

They went through to the office that backed onto the warehouse and sat at the table just as Aura arrived with Jhordan in tow.

"All done?" She asked as she put her coffee cup on the table.

"Yes. Talks a lot don't she?" Sylvester asked. "Asks too many questions if you ask me."

"Hush. Jhordan doesn't know we have her yet. Does she have her phone?" Aura asked, she watched out the window as Jhordan unloaded his backpack from the car.

"Yes. I'll untie her and take the hood off. She hasn't seen me so she won't suspect anything. Then we can begin," Sylvester told her. He went out to the empty warehouse and pulled the hood off Luna's head. "Hello sunshine!" He smiled at her. She watched him closely with her dark eyes. He went behind her and untied her hands and her ankles. "Now, you may need this," he said as he dumped her phone in her hand. "No funny business. Call anyone and that will be the last thing you do."

Luna looked scared. She nodded quickly and rubbed her wrists. "Can I have a drink of water please?"

"I'll see what I can do. Would juice be better?" Sylvester asked.

"Yes please," Luna replied hanging her head down. Tears began to fall from her eyes.

Sylvester walked away and re-entered the office area. He reached into the cupboard and pulled out a glass, quickly filling in with some Ribena from the fridge.

"What are you doing?" Aura demanded.

"She needs some energy. She will be no good otherwise," Sylvester told her. "You have to look after her."

He took the glass out to Luna and watched her drink in huge gulps. "Slow down, you'll make yourself sick."

"Sorry, I haven't had anything to drink for hours." Luna replied. She handed the glass back to him. "Thank you." She hung her head back down and awaited her fate.

When Sylvester returned to the office, he nodded to Aura. She left the room to make her own phone call. This one would set the wheels in motion. Her plan had begun, maybe a few days early, but it would be better this way. No-one would suspect a thing now.

Chapter 29

"Thank the Lord you came. It really is you isn't it?" Pearl asked as Donna and Savannah pulled up in the driveway.

"Well, I don't see how it could be anyone else," Donna replied.

"Oh well, you haven't had the evening I have," Pearl said. She was so nervous and worried that she kept wringing her hands together and scratching at her arms.

"Why don't we go inside, and you can tell us everything," Savannah said smoothly. She covered Pearls hands with her own to stop her trembling.

Donna locked the car and followed them both inside. She went straight to the kitchen and switched the kettle on. She sat with Pearl and Savannah whilst it boiled in the background.

"So Pearl, you wanna explain what's happened? What's got you so upset?" Donna asked.

"Oh..." Pearl began before she burst into tears. "You took her!"

"We...what?" Savannah asked, clearly as confused as Donna looked.

"Two people turned up here. Looked just like the two of you! I invited them in, they went into the living room where Luna sat, I told her she could stay and help us work out what to do about Aura, especially after she told me about Aura taking her," Pearl explained.

"She specifically said it was Aura?" Savannah asked.

"Not in so many words but when she said the woman mentioned Edith, I knew it was Aura. It's the only thing Aura has ever been interested in," Pearl shrugged.

"OK, how long ago was this?" Donna asked, just as her phone rang. "Sorry. Hello? Yes this is she. Wow, you lot took your time. We're there now. Thanks." Donna placed her phone back in her pocket and sighed audibly. "I swear, they are so slow!"

"I take it that was the station?" Pearl smiled.

"Yeah, telling us to come here because you called," Donna smiled. "Good job we were coming here anyway. Next time, hopefully there isn't one, just call our direct number, it would probably be quicker!"

Donna poured some tea and handed everyone a cup. "So, let's work out what's happening or happened."

Pearl explained what she thought she knew and then trailed off.

"What is it Pearl?" Savannah said, placing her hand softly on Pearls shoulder.

"What date is it?" Pearl asked as she crossed to her calendar. She covered her mouth with her hand. "Oh my, she's trying to throw everyone off. She's going to start early!"

Savannah got to her feet and placed her hands on Pearl's shoulders, guiding her back to the table and sitting her down gently. "Explain."

Pearl took a deep breath and began to explain exactly what Aura was about to start.

"So that's all you have to do," Aura told Jhordan.

"I don't get it," Jhordan replied.

"You don't need to 'get it', just make the call, and make it sound convincing!" Aura snapped, turned and strode away.

Jhordan was worried. Why would Aura have him call Detective Canter? What was she hiding? Jhordan sighed and quickly dialled Donnas' number. He had to slow his breathing down as the phone rang and rang. He hung up and dialled again. Still the phone rang and rang.

"What's going on kid?" Bruce said as he slapped his hand on Jhordans shoulder.

"Aura told me to call the police woman but she isn't answering," Jhordan replied looking worried.

"Just keep trying. I'll keep Aura distracted for now," Bruce smiled.

Jhordan tried to smile but it just didn't reach his eyes. He dialled the number again and prayed she would answer. He didn't know how long Bruce could keep Aura's attention.

"Why the cop?" Bruce asked as he closed the door to the office.

"Why not?" Aura replied shrugging her shoulders. "Why not have a witness to the great achievement I'm about to succeed at?"

"You? I thought this was a joint thing?" Bruce said, a little angrier than he had wanted.

"Joint? Oh no no no, this is my idea and my achievement. You are all just pawns in my great game of life, and it really is a game of life isn't it Bruce? I get the gift of eternal life and it's all because you all did what I told you to do!" Aura laughed. "Did you really think I was going to let any of you take any credit for this?"

Bruce shook his head and walked away. He contemplated sabotaging the whole thing to teach Aura a lesson but he knew that would have dire consequences for him and everyone else. He left the office and sat himself on the dockside watching the trawlers drift in and out. He wished he had taken the time when he was alive to learn the trade his Dad had lived by. Maybe he wouldn't be in this situation now if he had just stayed away from the bikes. He felt a sudden shift in temperature in the air around him so he zipped his coat up a little higher around his neck, but something had him on edge. It was mid July, why was it so cold all of a sudden? Shaking his head clear, he drained what was left of his coffee and headed back inside.

"Yes, you need to get to Flowerly Hall. Something is going to happen. I can't tell you what it is but I know it will be spectacular," Jhordan was relaying over the phone.

Bruce stood for a second, listening to what Jhordan was saying. It was clear it was all scripted from Aura. Jhordan didn't look comfortable at all.

"Yes, thank you. Goodbye," Jhordan said as he ended the call.

"All done kid?" Bruce asked.

Jhordan jumped a little at the sound of his voice. He nodded quickly and then jumped back in the car. It was clear something was bothering him so Bruce climbed in beside him.

"What's up kid?" Bruce asked.

"Aura is acting really strange. She didn't explain to me why I had to make the call. I thought the plan wasn't happening until at least next week," Jhordan replied, wringing his hands in his lap.

Bruce didn't know at first how to respond. He couldn't figure out if he should lie and cover Aura's back or tell Jhordan the truth. He knew the truth would destroy him so Bruce lied.

"She's just a little overexcited so she wanted to bring things forward a little. It's not a big thing, at least this way she has more of a chance of actually completing things properly. Although I do think she is rushing it a little," Bruce told him.

Jhordan looked a little more relaxed after Bruce finished explaining. "That means I will be gone soon then, doesn't it?" Jhordan asked.

"We just have to see how Aura feels afterwards. I'm hoping she keeps you around for longer, like she did with Sylvester and me. I kinda like having you around. You're a good kid," Bruce told him. "Don't tell anyone I said that. I got a rep to protect y'see," Bruce laughed.

Just as he finished his sentence, they heard the door to the warehouse slam. Almost immediately, the car door opened and Aura climbed in.

"To Flowerly Hall, and step on it. I take it you made the call?" Aura snapped.

"Yes I did. She said she would be there within the hour, she is held up with something at the moment," Jhordan replied, keeping his face forward.

"Good. Well come on, what are your waiting for? Directions?" Aura screamed.

Bruce started the car and put it in gear. He hesitated for a moment too long and Aura snapped again, "can't any of you do anything right? Is it so hard to drive a car in the direction of a given location?"

"Sorry, I'll get going now," Bruce apologised. He moved off and drove the long way to Flowerly Hall. Along the way he watched the way Aura scanned the surroundings as if she were expecting something to jump out at them.

"Stop here," Aura demanded from the back seat.

"Why?" Bruce asked as he brought the car to a rolling stop.

"Jhordan, I need you to walk to Flowerly Hall from here. You know how to get there, right?" Aura asked.

"Yeah, I guess, but why do I have to walk if you're going there anyway," Jhordan replied.

"Stop asking questions and get out. I'll meet you there in half an hour," Aura snapped again. It was becoming a habit recently.

Jhordan climbed out of the car and Aura moved herself to the front seat. She slammed the door behind her and ordered Bruce to carry on driving. Jhordan watched them drive away before quickly calling Donna again.

"She's going to meet me there in half an hour. I'm scared," he told her.

"Listen Jhordan, do you know if they have Luna?" Donna asked.

"She came home but was taken again," Pearl could be heard saying in the background.

"I didn't see her but it wouldn't surprise me. It looks like she is bringing the plan forward," Jhordan told them.

"Where are you now Jhordan?" Savannah asked.

"I'm...I'm not sure. I know I'm close to the school, but I've not ventured this way before," he replied.

"OK, I still have the tracker app for your phone. Stay where you are and I'll find you and bring you here. We will work out what to do next, we have time," Savannah told him.

Jhordan agreed and waited for Savannah to arrive. He looked around first before climbing into her car.

"Don't worry Jhordan. We will stop this," she told him as he closed the door.

She drove him back to Pearls house and they sat together at the table. Savannah remembered that she had a recorder built into the app that she installed on Jhordans phone. She quickly pulled up the connecting app on her own phone and listened in to what had been said.

"I'm sorry," Jhordan said as he let the tears flow.

"Not, in any way, your fault young man. Aura has been this way for as long as I can remember. I just hoped she might have grown out of all that fantasy stuff by now, she must be over a thousand years old now," Pearl told him, patting his hand for comfort.

Savannah stopped listening and looked at Jhordan. "Am I right in believing you're all dead?"

"Yes ma'am," Jhordan replied. "Does that change anything?"

"It will in a way. We need to work out how to stop her, but she uses magic. We don't posses that," Donna replied.

"Oh but we do dear. The only issue is that she is incapacitated at the moment," Pearl replied.

"I'm confused," Savannah replied. "What do you mean?"

"Well, Monique of course. She is a witch," Pearl replied.

Chapter 30

"What about the girl?" Bruce asked as they pulled away from Jhordan, leaving him staring after them like he had just been dumped at the roadside and forgotten about.

"That's where we are going. Do I have to explain everything?" Aura said shaking her head. She proceeded to look out of the window.

They continued the journey in silence. Bruce couldn't help but worry about Jhordan. He knew what was going to happen after Aura got what she wanted. Jhordan wouldn't know how to handle it and only he could explain things. He had to get to Jhordan before Aura dissipated the spell.

"How will you make her help?" Bruce asked as they pulled up outside the warehouse.

"All it takes is a little persuasion," Aura smiled.

"And some lies," Bruce replied.

"See. You're learning!" Aura laughed. "How would she know exactly what's going to happen or who will be there?"

"You're going to get her Grandma involved?" Bruce asked.

"I wasn't planning on it, but now that you mention it, maybe Pearl Heart can be some form of assistance," Aura smiled. "You do have some good ideas after all."

Sylvester opened the door to the warehouse and stood watching them.

"You ready now or should I wait until you have both kissed and made up?" He shouted.

Aura rolled her eyes. She was getting fed up with his sarcastic remarks. She threw the car door opened and climbed out. She walked over to Sylvester and slapped him round the head. "Be careful who you are talking to and what you are saying, remember who brought you back from that nasty place and who can send you straight back again. It only takes one click of my fingers, two words and you are gone!"

Bruce was beginning to get sick of her threats but he knew she practically owned them, they were her toys to throw away when she was finished playing with them. With her magic, she could bring anyone and anything back from the dead and then toss it away when she was done.

"Sorry Aura, I'm just getting fed up of running around all over while you all play happy families. I've had to put up with the smell of them bodies for too long now," Sylvester told her.

"Happy families, is that what you think it's been like?" Bruce said as he got out of the drivers' side of the car. "Do you realise how much it takes to be able to try and set something this intricate up?"

"I didn't mean anything by it. It just would have been nice to be able to join in, maybe as an uncle or something," Sylvester said.

Bruce shook his head and walked away. "Hurry up and sort the girl and the rest out."

"I don't know who he thinks he is," Aura said as he walked away.

"Maybe all this is too much for him," Sylvester replied. "I'll get everything loaded and then we can make a start preparing the house."

Aura watched as Bruce slammed the door and walked away from the warehouse. She was worried. Maybe Sylvester was right. Maybe it was too much. At least this was the last time and it was definitely going to work.

"OK," Donna said, laying her hands on the table. "Pearl, why didn't you say something before?"

"Well, no-one mentioned magic until now," Pearl replied in her defence.

"Jhordan, do you know the exact plan?" Savannah asked. She was a lot calmer than Donna.

"I know most of it. I'm supposed to lure Luna to Flowerly Hall, although I think they have changed that part, unless there's another way that they are going to do it. They haven't told me any changes but," Jhordan began.

"But then Aura never shows her true hand until its time. She will make the rules as she goes," Pearl added. "I know how she works."

Pearl smiled at Jhordan as she looked up at her. He jumped when his pocket vibrated.

"Oh no. It's her," he said, a look of pure terror crossing his face.

"OK. Act as natural as you can. Try not to worry too much and agree to everything she says. I can listen in via the app so we will go in the other room. You got this Jhordan," Savannah told him as she squeezed his shoulder and smiled down at him.

He answered the call as calmly as he could.

"What took you so long?" Aura demanded.

"My phone was in my pocket. I was struggling to get it out," Jhordan replied. He was clearly scared of this woman.

"Where are you now?" Aura asked.

"I'm about two or three minutes from Flowerly Hall. I can see it up ahead," he replied. He hated lying to her.

"Excellent. You have your uses after all. Now listen very closely. I need you to call the Grandmother and tell her that Luna is trapped in Flowerly Hall and that she needs to come quickly, you hear me?" Aura told him.

"I hear you. Crystal clear," Jhordan said, trying not to sound like he couldn't breathe.

"Are you OK boy?" Aura asked. "You don't sound too good?"

"I'm OK, just a little thirsty, that's all. I have some water in my bag, I'll take a few gulps and make the call," he told her. He suddenly began to feel dizzy. Luckily Aura ended the call without a goodbye. Jhordan dropped the phone to the floor and tried to slow his breathing down. He had begun to panic about the outcome of the plan. He didn't want anyone to get hurt, least of all Luna and her Grandmother.

"Hey kid, you did good. Get this down you," Donna said as she placed a glass of apple juice in front of him. "Slowly! Don't drown just yet!"

Jhordan tried not to laugh but he felt the urge to, if only to shake off some nerves.

"You don't have to explain sweetie. I know what's going to happen. When you're ready, you go ahead and make the call," Pearl said.

Jhordan hated that he had to do this to them. He hated it even more to think one of them could die.

"Wait. How is Monique doing anyway? If she is magic, can't she just make herself better?" Jhordan asked.

This question stumped everyone in the room. Why hadn't they thought of that?

"I'm going to the hospital. I need to talk to Monique," Pearl said. She got up to leave the room but Donna held onto her arm.

"Does she know about Luna's gift?" Donna asked.

Pearl shook her head. "I only really found out about Monique recently. She doesn't even know I know about her. Have we got time?"

"I hope so. Try and make it quick and painless?" She told her.

Pearl left the house in order to explain things to Monique. Donna turned her attention back to Jhordan.

"You better get a move on. You don't want them driving past and spotting you coming out of here," Donna told him.

Jhordan nodded curtly and made his way out the door.

"This is becoming more than we expected," Donna sighed.

As she sat at the table, her phoned pinged with a message.

'You're both doing the right thing. Stay on this path and you will reach the end. It's going to be tough and emotional, but if anyone can do it, you both can.'

"It's from Alex," Savannah said. "Why is he being so cryptic?"

"I don't know, but it's freaking me out a bit," Donna admitted.

Chapter 31

"Pearl? Is that you?" Monique asked as she waited for her eyes to adjust to the darkness.

"Yes dear. How are you feeling?" Pearl replied. "I've kept the light off for now."

"Where's Luna?" Monique asked. "Is she OK?"

"That's why I'm here. You must listen and let me finish before you speak," Pearl told her. She sat in the chair next to Monique's bed and held her hand. "I know what you are my dear. I have only recently discovered it, but right now, Luna needs our help. She has a gift, passed through the female bloodline of my family. She can see and speak to the spirit world. Right now, someone has her and is holding her for their plan. We have to save her."

"What do you mean?" Monique asked, sitting up a little higher in the hospital bed. "Where is she?"

"It would be wise, if you could, to use your own gift to get yourself out of here. Maybe you were grateful for the rest but, right now, Luna needs us both. We can only defeat these people together," Pearl explained.

Monique thought for a moment. She knew she could make herself better. She knew she could speed up her recovery. She was just grateful not to have to face the fact that Spencer wasn't at home anymore. It had gotten to her more recently; the more she tried to come to terms with it the more she wished it was her who had died. She swung her legs out of bed and quickly pulled on her clothes. "You have exactly two minutes to explain everything. Start to finish. Go!"

Pearl explained how the gift had been passed down through the bloodline, how she discovered Luna speaking with Judith and how she discovered Monique's gift. She told her who had taken Luna and what she planned to do with her.

"Wait! Isn't this exactly the same thing that happened to you? I remember you saying about it before. What will they do to her?" Monique demanded.

"I don't know. Luna gets pieces of information from the dead. The people this woman dug up," Pearl told her.

"Who else knows about this?" Monique asked as she slipped her trainers on and tightened the laces.

"Detectives Canter and Shepherd," Pearl whispered.

"WHAT!" Monique almost shouted. She lowered her voice to a harsh whisper before anyone woke up. "How did they know before me?"

Pearl had been waiting for this question. She didn't know how to prepare Monique for the answer so she just let it roll off her tongue. "Donna's brother is one of those people feeding Luna information."

Monique stopped in her tracks. "How is she...actually don't answer that now. We have to go," Monique said as they quickly slipped out of the ward and towards the exit.

They had to hide in a cupboard whilst the doctors passed but then they were out of the hospital and working on a plan when Pearl's phone rang. The caller ID read *Detective Canter*.

"Hello," Monique answered whilst Pearl drove the car, careful not to become distracted by the ongoing phone call.

"Mrs Heart, it's great to hear your voice. How are you?" Donna asked.

"I don't want to go into pleasantries Detective. What do you know about my daughters' whereabouts?" Monique asked.

"We know as much as Pearl has told you. Other than the fact Jhordan has helped us locate her and we have her in our sights," Donna replied.

"Jhordan? Isn't that the boy from Luna's class?" Monique asked.

"It is. There is a lot I haven't had time to explain. Detective, whilst I drive could you fill in what I may have missed," Pearl asked. "I don't want to get distracted from my destination."

"Which is?" Monique asked.

"Flowerly Hall," Peal replied. She refocused her attention on the road and allowed both Savannah and Donna to fill Monique in on the details surrounding who Jhordan really is.

Pearl drummed her fingers on the steering wheel impatiently as she waited in the line of traffic leading off the high street. She wished they would finish fixing this road soon, the traffic was becoming unbearable. She stole a glance at the group of people walking along the pavement. A young girl around Luna's age was wrapped up in a scarf and woolly coat, bracing against the wind that had suddenly picked up from nowhere.

"Something doesn't seem right," Monique said in a hushed tone. "I can feel it in my bones."

"What do you mean?" Pearl asked, still watching the girl and her parents as they ducked inside a shop just as the rain began to pour down in the exact spot they were standing.

Monique tapped her nails on the dashboard seven times. Then five. Then twelve. She waited for a second before tapping her feet lightly on the floor. First four times. Then six. Then ten.

"What are you doing?" Pearl asked as she looked at Monique.

"Summoning my inner gift, just as you asked," Monique replied. "It's been a while since I used it so I banished it away. There is a code to reopen the locks it was kept in. My gift isn't the best of gifts. More like a curse."

As Monique looked Pearl in the eyes, her irises changed from their dazzling blue to a flame red. Pearl was taken aback by the sudden change but it didn't scare her too much.

"So, how do we find out what will happen?" Monique asked.

Pearl went quite. She nodded a couple of times and then began driving again as the traffic ahead shifted a few feet. "Judith says, Aura is taking Luna to Flowerly Hall now. They are bundled in a van. A cream coloured van. Much like that one," Pearl said as she pointed to the van that had just driven passed the junction.

Pearl nodded again. "Judith said, they are in that one."

"What are you waiting for? Follow it!" Monique screeched.

"No. Detective Canter and Shepherd are right behind it. See?" Pearl replied.

They watched as a silver Volkswagen Golf passed just behind it. Just as they passed, Pearl's phone rang again. Monique answered just as she had before. This time it was Detective Shepherd.

"Mrs Heart, welcome back!" She said cheerfully. "I'm sure that we just passed you, I could be wrong."

"No, it's us. We are waiting in this stupid traffic whilst my daughter is being used as a damn pawn in a chess match!" Monique hissed through gritted teeth.

"It's not like that, I can assure you. We have been told the ways Aura may work, but we have also been warned that she can change up her ways at the drop of a hat. We have to be ready," Savannah replied. "We will do everything to keep Luna safe."

"I don't know as much or at the same depth as all of you, but what I do know is that if I trust anyone to keep my baby girl safe then it is her grandmother," Monique replied as she chanced a glance at Pearl from the corner of her eye.

Pearl smiled but didn't look at her; she kept her mind fully focused on the road ahead. The temporary lights changed to green and Pearl shot off like a firework that just been lit. She followed at a safe distance from the detectives' car; she didn't want to put Luna in any danger. She cast her mind back over seventy-eight years ago and tried to remember what had happened that night. How had Aura set up the room? What equipment would she use? How would they manage to get to the west wing of the house without falling through the rotten floorboards of the hallway? Would she place

Luna in the centre of the pentagram, or would she use something different this time?

They stopped just before Flowerly Hall. They didn't want to be spotted yet.

"Where did your mind go back there?" Monique asked quietly.

"Back to when this happened to me," Pearl replied as a tear slid down her face. "I'm so sorry. It's all my fault. If I didn't have the gift to pass down, she never would have been in this predicament."

"I'm as much to blame as you. I bet this Aura knows about me too," Monique said as she laid her hand on Pearl's shoulder. "Tell me what happened to you."

Pearl took a deep breath and stared straight ahead;

"It was a day much like today almost seventy-nine years ago. I watched the trees blowing in the wind from my bedroom window. We had tall bay windows back then. The trees were bending so far over; I thought they would snap at any second. I watched some birds try to fly into the taller, wider trees, some made it, and others seem to get blown off course.

I remember there being a knock at the door. It surprised me because the weather was so bad, I didn't expect anyone to be out in it, but when my Dad opened the door, Aura stood there with her Dad, offering to take me to the local roller-skating rink. He said Aura hadn't properly celebrated her birthday and it was a treat. Dad said it was fine and told me to get my coat and remember my manners. At first I was excited. I hadn't been roller-skating before, so I was a little nervous too." Pearl remembered, she giggled a little.

"What happened next?" Monique asked, looking around to check their surroundings. She would be Pearl's protector if anything happened.

"We left the house and climbed in Aura's Dads' car. We started driving but it didn't seem like we were heading towards the skating rink. I tried to look out of the window but they were so tinted I could only see my reflection. I even tried looking out of the windscreen but I couldn't see where we were because her Dad wasn't using his headlights, it was as if the car was on autopilot. When we finally stopped, Aura put a blindfold over my eyes and led me out of the car. She said I could trust her. So I let her lead me," Pearl had tears falling from her eyes.

"This must be really hard to go back over. Why don't you take a break for a second, Detectives Shepherd and Canter are on their way over," Monique smiled at her.

Pearl looked out of the car window and smiled as Donna walked to her side of the car. Pearl opened the door and stepped out.

"What's happening?" She asked.

"OK, Luna seems to believe that you are being held inside. Savannah is listening in via the app on Jhordans' phone. We can hear every word. I don't want you to go in there, at least not if we can help it," Donna told her.

"So what do we do? Just sit here and hope she doesn't hurt my baby?" Monique asked. She was already worried after Pearl had told her part of what had happened before.

"Just for now," Savannah said softly. "Listen." She handed one side of the earphones to Monique and she listened in.

"Is her Grandma here?" Jhordan asked.

"Not yet, but I have a feeling she it won't be long until she is here," Aura smiled.

"Why?" Jhordan asked.

"Let's say she should be receiving a call any minute now," Aura laughed.

Just then, Pearl's phone rang. They all looked at each other.

"Hello?" Pearl answered as normally as she could muster.

"Is this Pearl Heart?" Came a strong male voice.

"This is she. How can I help you tonight?" Pearl replied.

"I have a message for you," he laughed.

"Grandmaaaaaaa!!" Luna screamed. "Save me!!"

"Luna!" Pearl whispered, tears began flowing down her cheeks. "Don't hurt her please. What do you want?"

"Just you and that daughter of yours, you are to come, alone, to Flowerly Hall. Flash your lights when you arrive," he said.

"No Grandma! Stay away!" Luna screamed.

"Shut up you little brat," Aura hissed.

The phone went silent.

"Hello?" Pearl called out.

The phone call had been ended.

"Looks like I can't stay out of it after all," Pearl told Donna.

The two police women exchanged glances.

"Is there anything we can do to keep you both safe in there? I mean, we don't posses any magic but," Donna shrugged.

"I need you to, discreetly, draw a salt ring around the grounds of Flowerly Hall. Make sure the two ends joins up and there are no gaps," Pearl told them.

"What will that do?" Donna asked.

"Protect me and Monique. It will prevent any evil spirits leaving the house too," Pearl told her.

"Do you think anything will happen?" Savannah asked.

"Oh my dear, I'm quite sure it will. Luna has a strong mind. Stronger than mine was," Pearl replied.

"How will having us there help this woman?" Monique asked. She was beginning to worry that something bad might happen.

"More than likely it will be to embarrass me, because I couldn't do it last time, I didn't believe in myself enough. Having you there is probably to show you that she controls Luna. What she tells her to do, she will do, she will use you as a hostage as some sort, and normally it would be if Luna didn't do what she was told, they would threaten you, and it will make Luna do as she is told. What I don't think they know, is that you are a witch. What I, also, don't know is; just how powerful you are?" Pearl replied turning to face her daughter in law.

Monique took a deep breath before answering. She had never told anyone about her power, not even Spencer. She had kept it a secret from the last time she used it.

Chapter 32

"Why are you bringing my Mum from the hospital? She's not well!" Luna shouted. "You're a horrible person!"

"Well, maybe she's better? Maybe it would be best for her to see you go so she can say goodbye properly! I mean, you don't want the last time she sees you to be in the morgue all dead and stiff do you?" Aura laughed.

"I'm not going to die. I'm stronger than that," Luna insisted.

"I'm glad you feel that way honey, at least I know you believe in your power. You Grandmother didn't, that's why I had to come back and finish what I started," Aura replied.

Bruce didn't like the way Aura taunted Luna. He wanted to remind her that Luna was just a child. What her grandmother did in the past wasn't her fault, but he knew Aura wouldn't listen. He looked over at Jhordan who, clearly, looked terrified.

"Don't worry kid; we'll make sure she is OK, me and you yeah?" Bruce told him.

"What do you mean? You won't go against Aura," Jhordan replied. He was surprised by what Bruce had said.

"Sometimes, you have to know what's right and what's wrong, and this," he gestured with his fingers, making circles in front of his eyes, "This is wrong. I know why she's doing it, but it's wrong how she's doing it."

Jhordan breathed a sigh of relief. He was worried that he was the only one who thought it was wrong. He had been all for it before he learnt that it could kill Luna.

"How much did you hear kid?" Bruce asked, breaking through his thoughts.

"Enough to know that she will let Luna die," Jhordan admitted.

"Then, to her, you know too much. Don't let on what you know. Do what she says and let me handle the rest. I'll give you a signal and you are to grab Luna and hide. You got it?" Bruce told him.

Jhordan nodded hard.

"Good. Trust me," Bruce said. He stood and walked to the door joining the two large reception rooms.

Jhordan could see Luna still tied to the chair in the centre of the room. She didn't look his way but he felt sick to his stomach. He watched as Aura and Sylvester told Luna exactly what she had to do and when, but Luna wasn't listening. Jhordan could see that she was just staring straight ahead. He started to worry. She wasn't even blinking. He wasn't even sure if she was breathing. He continued to watch until her head suddenly snapped around and she stared at him. He crawled behind the wall so she couldn't see him. What he had seen wasn't Luna at all.

"I locked away my power back when I was fifteen," Monique began. She stared off towards the mountains that rose up in the distance. "I was just finishing school one day; it was a Tuesday I think. I'd just packed my rucksack and I was walking through the corridor when I heard someone screaming from the girls' toilets. I hesitated at first, but then I opened the door and almost chocked on air."

Pearl laid her hand across Monique's on the bonnet of the car. "I'm right here," she told her.

Monique smiled and continued with her explanation. "I saw Carly on the floor. Mark was hunched over her and she was struggling. When I walked in they both looked at me. Carly asked me to help her but Mark warned me off, told me I would be next if I did anything or told anyone." Tears were forming in her eyes.

"What happened?" Savannah prompted her to continue.

"I didn't move. I didn't speak. I just stood there. Mark smiled and turned his attention back to Carly who continually watched me; as if she was making sure I could see what he was doing and hoping I would do something. I don't even know how it happened. Carly explained it but, in my own memory, I don't know. I remember leaving the school building with Carly holding me up but Mark was nowhere to be seen. Carly told me that I'd reached out to him and, ever so gently, touched his shoulder, and he just *poof* disappeared. The police went to everyone's house who knew him, but no one had seen him. No one has seen him since,"

Monique replied. "I learnt how to banish my power that night."

"And you haven't used it since?" Donna asked. "How do you know it will still work?"

Pearl laughed, "My dear, it's not like an illness. It's a gift. We are trusted with it from either beyond the grave or as a gift from a higher power. We can't just get rid of it."

"As much as some of us wish we could," Monique whispered.

"Oh honey, I think you were never truly taught how to control your gift. What you saw made you angry or upset and that was the reaction of your power. You are older and wiser now; maybe you can learn how to use is better now?" Pearl offered.

"Let's get Luna out of this predicament first. We can discuss this later," Monique replied.

"OK, let's get this thing going," Donna said. "So we know Aura will force Luna to try and free Edith, but what I don't get it why she needed the other bodies, such as Spencer?"

"Aura will always try and use the recent death of a loved one to emotionally blackmail you into doing what she asks. She will convince you that you recently departed would want you to help," Pearl explained.

"So, she has Spencer, Judith, Edith and Max. Now, I understand why she has Spencer, Judith and Edith, but why Max?" Savannah questioned. "Max doesn't have anything to do with this, does he?"

"Not that I know of," Donna replied. "But I guess I'll never know."

Pearl had gone quiet, but she nodded her head at regular intervals. Everyone stared at her for a moment. They didn't want to distract her, unsure how she would react. When she finally stopped, she turned to Donna and smiled. "I have a message for you my dear."

Donna looked surprised, "Me?"

"Yes dear. Max says he is here for a reason. One you are probably unaware of, but he feels you need to know," Pearl told her.

"OK, I'm ready. Hit me with it," Donna said. She leaned against the car and folded her arms across her chest.

"Max is Alex," Pearl said.

Donna stared at her. A full minute after she had finished, Donna laughed. "Is that supposed to be a joke?"

"Oh sis, do you think I would joke about that?"

The voice that came from Pearl's mouth wasn't hers but Max's.

"Max?" Donna croaked.

"Yeah, it's me, again. I don't have the energy to fully explain now, but I need you and Savannah to head back to the station. In your desk drawer is the file on Edith's mysterious death. You need to read it fully. Pearl and Monique know what to do for now. If they need any help, Luna is there," Max explained.

"Luna? What how can she help? She will be the one who needs help," Donna replied.

"Believe me sis, she is stronger than you are all giving her credit for," Max told them all.

"Wait, how long have you been, I mean, Alex?" Donna asked.

"I made a deal with the high priest on this end. I told him I needed to make amends for the way I was before I died. He granted me some time to make it up to you," Max told her. "Once this is over, there will be an accident and Alex will be no more. It was the only way to do it."

"Alex's wife?" Donna asked.

"She doesn't exist. No-one at the station has ever seen her. Are you ready?" Max replied.

Donna could do nothing but nod.

"Let's move," Savannah said. "It's nice to hear from you Max."

"Keep her safe Shepherd," Max said.

Pearl shook her head quickly and took a sudden breath in. "Woo, that hasn't happened in a very long time."

"Thank you," Donna said as she threw her arms around Pearl's neck.

"Don't thank me sweetie, I'm just a messenger," Pearl smiled.

Savannah gently grabbed Donnas' arm, "We better go."

Donna nodded and they headed back to Donnas' car.

"Are you OK?" Savannah asked when they were alone.

"I will be now. I wonder if Aura knows who Max is," Donna replied.

"We can only hope she doesn't. Let's get this file and work out exactly what happened to this Edith person,"

Savannah said. She started the engine and drove back to the station.

Donna watched the town pass by as they drove, wondering what could have been so mysterious about Edith's death that would make Aura so determined to free her soul from Flowerly Hall.

Chapter 33

"Are you ready?" Pearl asked Monique.

"Do we have a choice?" Monique tried to laugh. "Let's do it."

Pearl got into the drivers' seat and started the engine. She drove slowly towards Flowerly Hall. She looked up at its forbidding gates, she hated this place so much but she had to be here for Luna and for Monique and for Edith. She straightened her spine and flashed her lights, glancing a look at Monique in the process. She looked as terrified as any parent would do in this situation but she seemed to be covering her fear.

"It's OK to be scared dear," Pearl whispered. "I'm terrified. I never thought I would ever see Aura again."

"I'm more worried than scared. What if my power doesn't return and I can't help Luna when she needs me most?" Monique admitted. "*I* can't even tell if my power has returned."

"We will just have to hope and pray that it has. If it hasn't, well, we just go with the flow. I'm by your side," Pearl told her. She squeezed her hand across the centre console.

Monique closed her eyes and prayed with all her being that she could save Luna if it came to it. In front of the car, a man with dark, evil eyes swung the gates wide open and gestured them to drive through. He pointed to the parking spot next to the van and hurried off inside the house.

"He was...odd," Pearl giggled. "Let's see what Aura has to say for herself shall we?"

Monique smiled. She couldn't think of anyone she would rather be doing this with than Pearl. She unbuckled her seatbelt and opened the car door. The chill hit her almost immediately.

"Don't worry dear; it's always cold out here. It'll be warmer inside," Pearl told her.

They both hurried up the steps and through the open door. Monique could smell the scent of frankincense as soon as she breathed in. It irritated her nose and almost made her sneeze.

"Here, put a bit of this just under your nostrils, it will dampen the smell," Pearl handed her a small bottle of lavender.

Monique did as instructed and could finally breathe without feeling suffocated.

"Welcome ladies, please come on in, have a seat in the chairs provided. The show will begin in a matter of minutes," Aura's voice echoed through the entranceway.

"Her voice always grated on me," Pearl said.

"I heard that," Aura hissed.

"You were supposed to you miserable fool," Pearl replied.

Monique had to prevent herself from laughing. She reminded herself that this was a serious situation, but she really loved Pearl's one liners. She was never one to shy away from saying what she really thought, no matter who you were.

Back at the station, Donna burst through the front doors and ran up to her office. She searched in the desk drawer and pulled out the file marked E.F. She slapped it on the table and sat in the chair behind the desk. Within a second or two, Savannah was sat opposite her. Donna scanned the files inside the folder quickly.

"Hey, slow down. Max said read it carefully," Savannah told her.

"I wish I could but I don't want anything to happen to them all while I'm sitting here on my backside," Donna retorted.

Savannah snatched the folder away from her, "go and get us some coffee. I'll look through this."

Donna rolled her eyes and went to fetch some coffee. Savannah opened the folder and read the first paper inside. It was a report of strange goings on in Flowerly Hall dating back to 1902. It stated that there had been reports of a face appearing in the upper window of the west wing of Flowerly Hall but after investigations there seemed to be nobody living there at all. The furniture was covered in dust sheets and the windows were locked. The only odd thing about it was that the door was always unlocked and the house was never dusty.

"What have you found so far?" Donna asked as she placed the cup next to Savannah.

"Only that there were reports back in the 1900s that someone was in Flowerly Hall, but when they checked, there were no signs of anyone living there and looks like no one has lived there in a long time," Savannah replied, she continued to read, this time out loud. "*Reports of strange lights coming from the western wing of Flowerly Hall have been debunked as kids. Investigators found lanterns and matches around the front of the house when they searched.* Seems odd that the lights came from the western wing but the lanterns were found at the front of the house."

Donna spun the folder her way and took the next piece of paper. She squinted her eyes at the fading paper in her hands. It had been laminated. She read the contents; "*MISSING: Edith Florentine age fourteen. Hasn't been seen since Wednesday, 4th May 1353.*"

"That's her," Savannah whispered. "OK, next piece."

Donna picked up the next paper, "Police report. *Body of fourteen year old girl found in western wing of Flowerly Hall. Unknown female with head and face trauma.* Wow, how they wrote the police reports back then was terrible. How could they be so undignified?"

"That's just how it was back then. They dealt with death and murder differently to now. I guess we must have over sensitised things," Savannah replied. "Here, listen to this; *body found in Flowerly Hall has been identified as that of missing Edith Florentine. Edith and her twin sister Judith had been playing in the area surrounding Flowerly Hall when Edith ventured inside, apparently lured by an 'other-worldly' voice, according to her twin. Judith ventured inside after Edith and attempted to drag Edith back outside but an unknown force had locked Edith in a room in the western wing and the door wouldn't open. Judith admits to hearing her sister's screams, which, Judith says, lasted for at least five to ten minutes. She screamed, shouted and kicked at the door for whoever had locked her sister in to let her back out, only when all was silent did the door swing open and the body of her sister, lay in the centre of the room, her neck contorted at an unearthly angle and her face so disfigured that Judith believed it to be a different person and that her sister had escaped out the window and hidden away somewhere. It wasn't until her parents reported her missing that Judith mentioned the altercation in Flowerly Hall."*

Savannah and Donna were silent for a moment. They had no idea how to process what they had just read. Judith had been there while her sister was murdered but, probably secretly, hoped she had escaped and there was a different person there.

"And she lived her life with the guilt of, probably knowing, that she had listened to her sister's murder. Oh Judith," Savannah whispered.

Donna swiped at a tear as it fell from her eye. "I can't believe it. How could some unknown entity harm someone?"

"That's probably a question for Pearl," Savannah replied.

"Wait, you lived here before. Has Flowerly Hall always been empty?" Donna asked.

"I've never seen anyone come or go from there, only the kids who always ran off scared. We always thought it was their other friends playing tricks on them but, now I think about it, they all ran out together," Savannah said.

Donna opened the browser on her phone and typed 'Flowerly Hall residents' into the search bar. She waited a few seconds for the results to load. She quickly read the results, '*stood empty since 1350.*' "Hmm, seems strange. Flowerly Hall has stood empty since 1350, three years before Edith was murdered."

"That is weird. So who lived there before?" Savannah asked.

"Erm, let's have a quick look," Donna replied as she scanned the records. "It says it was owned by...oh you are NOT going to believe this."

"Surprise me," Savannah said as she crossed her arms in front of her.

Donna shook her head, "Mr and Mrs Bell."

Savannahs eyes widened with shock. "Jhordans parents?"

"Well not his parents, but his great-great grandparents," Donna replied. "According to this report, written over five centuries later mind you, states that the wife killed the husband after he started speaking in strange tongues and claiming to be the devil. The report says she locked him in the western wing and gassed him to death; she then dismembered him and buried him under the oak tree in the gardens. Witnesses say they have seen various shapes and shadows in the windows of the western wing."

"Oh wow. I'm...well, I don't know what to say to that. I wonder if Jhordan knows," Savannah said.

Donna thought for a second before her phone pinged to life. "It's Alex..Max...Oh you know who I mean."

'Now you know most of it. You need to come back to the house. Something isn't right. The boy is acting strange."

"Huh?" Savannah asked.

"Wait. The boy? Jhordan!" Donna exclaimed.

They both ran out of the station and jumped back in the car, almost knocking Martha over in the process. Donna started the engine and they sped away. They knew that Jhordan didn't agree with what Aura had planned but they hoped he wasn't sabotaging the plan.

Chapter 34

"So how exactly do you want to play this out Aura?" Pearl asked. She couldn't see Aura but she knew she was listening somewhere. "You know it won't be the same as last time don't you?"

"I was counting on it," Aura replied. "*You* failed me last time. *You* made me believe that you could do anything. *YOU* lied to me!"

"I didn't lie to you. I just didn't believe I was strong enough to actually complete it, and I was right, wasn't I?" Pearl answered.

Monique listened to their exchange. She was unsure how to react. She had only really found out about what had happened to Pearl earlier in the day. She hoped that she could be powerful enough to save them both if she needed to.

"You had the power! You just didn't believe in yourself! You could have done it back then and I wouldn't have had to put your granddaughter in danger!" Aura screamed.

A flash of lightning drew their attention to the main room, where Luna sat, tied to a chair in the centre of the room. The floor under her spiralling in both directions. Pearl had seen this before. She knew what was about to happen.

"Shield your eyes Monique. There is going to be a really bright flash before anything further happens, its Aura way of contacting the spirit world," Pearl warned her.

Monique chanced a look at Luna before she closed her eyes. Luna had a blindfold covering her eyes, but she didn't look scared or panicked. She looked peaceful. She could briefly see a smile spreading across Luna's face.

"Why isn't Luna scared?" Monique asked Pearl.

Pearl opened her eyes and looked at Luna. "She is connecting with the spirits. She had already had conversations with some of them."

"Spencer?" Monique asked.

"No. Max told Luna that Spencer wasn't strong enough yet. To gain their strength to be able to visit, even for a small amount of time, they have to have been gone for at least six months. The spirits lent Spencer some strength for him to visit you both for dinner," Pearl told her.

Monique was shocked. "He came for dinner? When?"

"The night you had lamb. Luna told me. Max explained the whole thing to her and now she understands a little bit more than she did before," Pearl explained. "She has a good heart Monique. She will have this gift for the rest of her life, much like you do."

The two women stayed silent for a few more seconds until Monique slowly opened her eyes. She shook Pearl by the arm and pointed towards where Luna once sat.

"Where has she gone?" Monique asked.

"That was a distraction! They have moved her to the western wing," Pearl replied.

"Why would they take her there?" Monique said.

"That's where Edith died," Pearl replied. "That's where her soul has to be released from."

"Where do we go?" Monique asked, looking towards the stairs that had been badly damaged.

"That's odd. Those stairs were perfectly intact when we arrived," Pearl said, a confusing look passing across her face. "You're not going to make this easy for us, are you Aura?"

"Absolutely not!" Aura replied. "That wouldn't be fun now, would it?"

"I'm really starting to hate this woman," Monique hissed.

"Oh I'm not your biggest fan either my darling. Now, hurry up and work out your route. I can't wait forever," Aura laughed.

Pearl and Monique began scouting around the lower level of the house, they looked left and right, and in all the hidden cupboards but there seemed to be no way they could get to the next level. They slouched next to the last door and had almost given up when they heard the front door slowly opening.

"Mrs Heart, are you in here?" Donna whispered.

"Over here dear," Pearl called out. "Don't bother whispering, she'll still hear you, the nosey old bat!"

"Oh you are still as charming as ever," Aura replied.

Donna and Savannah found Pearl and Monique crouched by a door.

"Why are you sitting here?" Savannah asked.

"She has Luna in the western wing, but we have no way of getting up there. The stairs are completely destroyed and there's no sign of another route," Monique replied.

"There is another way but it isn't inside the house," Savannah told them. "We looked at the blueprints before coming back here, there's a passage way around the outside of the house. We just have to make sure it's still there."

"What are we waiting for?" Monique said as she stood to search for the passage way.

"Don't run off too fast, and be careful. If I know Aura as well as I think I do, then she has, no doubt, planted traps along the way," Pearl called after her.

Donna and Savannah followed the other women as they ran out of the back door and began searching around the exterior of the house. The chill had followed them from the parking area and enveloped the entire grounds. As Monique rounded a corner, a shrill scream pierced the air.

"Monique!" Pearl screamed.

As Donna and Savannah caught up with the two women, they saw that Monique was now lying on the floor holding her ankle. Savannah was the first to notice the trap biting into her.

"We have to try and get that off and the bleeding stopped," she said.

Pearl dropped to Monique's side and held her hand tight. "We'll get you out of this Monique, just hold on for now."

Donna pulled a pair of gloves from her pocket and grabbed both sides of the metal trap. She pulled hard in opposite directions until the trap had fully let go of Monique's leg.

"Quickly, tie your scarf around her calf, Pearl," Savannah ordered.

Pearl pulled off her lavender coloured cashmere scarf and tied it around Monique's calf. She pulled it so tight, Monique nearly screamed again.

"Can you walk on it?" Donna asked. She held onto Monique's arm as she tried to stand.

"I think so, I may be a little slower but I can manage it," Monique replied.

The four women continued, cautiously, searching for the exterior entrance way to the upper level of the house. They felt along the walls for hidden handles until Savannah felt a sudden gap in the walls.

"Hey, here it is," she shouted.

She pulled aside the ivy that was covering a doorway, grabbed the handle and twisted it with ease. A huge oak door swung open, revealing a spiral staircase, much like the one inside the house only smaller, leading upwards. Its marble steps inviting them in. One by one the stepped inside and began the journey to the top of the stairs. Pearl could hear laughter coming from one of the rooms off to the left.

"Is that the room?" Savannah asked.

Pearl shook her head. "No, oh no, no, no. The room we want is further back into the house. I've never ventured inside that room. It scares me."

Savannah and Donna exchanged glances.

"It's probably best not to go in there," Monique told them. "I don't feel any good presences emanating from there."

Donna walked on quickly, leaving Savannah to stare at the door more intensely. She put her ear against the door and jumped back then she felt a hand around her neck.

"I did say to stay away," Monique said as Savannah caught up with them.

"I'll take your advice next time," Savannah replied.

"Next time you might not be so lucky. This house is a haven for paranormal activity. They have so much power here that they could easily kill you, or drag you somewhere quite nasty," Monique told her. "You have to be very careful. Your best bet is to stay with us."

As they continued on towards the inner parts of the house, each room they passed had masses of laughter, or tears, or screams. Each door seemed to hold a different story behind it.

"What do you know about this house?" Donna asked both Pearl and Monique.

"Only what has been passed through the generations. Lots of stories, whether true or not, should be respected unless proven false," Pearl told them.

"My mother used to tell me that some of the children from the area had gone missing over the years. She showed me articles and missing person posters from so far back. I remember, when I was about six or seven, my mother and I walked past the house and I looked up at the window right at the top, I saw a face. It didn't look like a kind face either," Monique explained. "I told my mother who told me not to look. She said that was how it chose its victims."

There was a sharp intake of breath as Savannah covered her mouth. "How many children, roughly, went missing over the years, do you think?"

"There must have been, up to now, over a thousand. There could be more," Pearl replied.

Donna was surprised. She wondered how many of those cases had been closed as runaways. Just as the thought entered her head, her phone vibrated in her pocket. She opened the text to see that Martha had sent her a link for the missing person reports for the last fifty years. It had over three hundred names listed. As she scrolled through, she noticed how most had been deemed runaways due to their ages, but some had even been deemed dead with no body found. She promised to look into these after they rescued Luna.

Chapter 35

"Now, young lady, you will do exactly as I tell you exactly when I tell you, you understand?" Aura asked Luna

Luna didn't move. She didn't blink. She just slowly turned her head from one side to the other. What she saw didn't frighten her. It upset her. She tried to guess their age ranges. She already knew their names. She had listened intently as each child told her. They vowed to help her, if she could help their souls be free. Luna had agreed.

"Are you listening to me?" Aura shouted as she grabbed Luna chin.

Luna's focus then solely fell on Aura. She looked deep into her green eyes, searching for any ounces of compassion, but all she saw was hate and greed. "I heard you," Luna hissed.

"Good! Now, the room next to this one is where you will free Edith Florentines' spirit. By the time everything is set up and ready to roll, there will be no-one else in this house except you and I. Unfortunately for you, your energy will have been drained out and you will probably be dead!" Aura laughed. "So the power exceeded from the release of Edith spirit with grant me eternal life and I will be free to roam the world forever."

"Have you thought about the cons of that?" Luna asked, a smirk crossing her face.

"What cons? Don't be daft; what could possibly be bad about living forever?" Aura replied.

Luna shook her head. "You honestly think that living forever is a good thing? Think of all the bad stuff you will see happen. Earthquakes, tsunamis, volcanoes, the end of the world. You won't be able to outrun it."

"Maybe I don't want to outrun it. Maybe I want to witness it all!" Aura laughed. "You won't change my mind little girl. I've waited long enough for this. Now, get in that room and begin."

"I don't even know what I'm supposed to do!" Luna exclaimed.

"You're a bright spark. I'm sure you will work it out. Now, go!" Aura shouted.

Luna stood from the chair and made her way to the door. "Aren't you afraid I'll run away?"

"I'm not that gullible! There's someone watching you at all times. Anyway, the stairs are gone, how would you get out? Fall?" Aura giggled. She glared at Luna until she left the room.

Once in the corridor, Luna looked at all the doors in front of her. She had no idea this house held so many rooms. She listened in at one of the doors and heard the sobbing of a little girl. She stayed there for a second, hoping the person inside would speak to her, but they didn't. The sobs got louder and louder until they became evil laughter.

"You don't really think you can defeat me do you?" The voice boomed through the woodwork.

"I'm not sure yet. I haven't decided," Luna replied.

The booming voice laughed again, louder this time. "You're no match for me." As soon as the words were spoken the house shook with such ferocity that Luna almost fell over.

"What was that?" Donna asked.

The women had felt the shaking. It was as if the entire Earth had shifted on its axis. They had held onto the wall to prevent them hitting the floor.

"This isn't good. This means Aura had started earlier than expected," Pearl informed them.

"What does that mean?" Savannah asked. She jumped away just in time to avoid a piece of falling artwork.

"Aura likes to change the rules at the click of her fingers. She controls the whole thing. This is how she manipulates The Holding Spirit. He hates change," Pearl explained.

"The spirit of Old Man Bell?" Donna asked.

"Oh no dear," Pearl turned to face her. "Old Man Bells' spirit haunts the kitchen. He was a chef. This one here. He's as evil as evil can be. Probably only second to the Devil himself. Sees himself as the next leader of the underworld so to speak. He's trapped here too. That's what made him so angry to begin with. You will have to read the entire history. Not just briefly scan some papers."

Savannah and Donna looked at each other. "How did you..?"

"Max told me. Now come on. We have to find Luna. She has no idea what to do," Pearl said. She began to move forward and then stopped in her tracks. The other women looked over her shoulder to see Luna, face to face with a huge mass of burgundy and black.

"What the?" Donna whispered.

"That's The Holding Spirit," Pearl told them all. "I'm surprised he's actually speaking to her. The last time this happened he chased me through the house and didn't stop until I screamed so loud I shattered the windows in the en-suite bathroom in the eastern wing master bedroom."

They watched at the spirit finished his conversation with Luna and glided away. Luna paid them no attention. She looked up towards a camera pointed directly at her and waved.

"Aura has planted cameras all over. We have to be careful. Donna, Savannah, see if you can hold her off while Monique and I try to get to Luna," Pearl said.

"We can try, but if she's magic, we don't have a hope in Hell of holding her down," Savannah replied.

"Good point. OK, Savannah you're with me. Monique, stick with Donna," Pearl replied.

Savannah nodded and joined Monique at her side. "I hope this woman isn't powerful."

"Far be it from me to burst your bubble honey, but she is. If she can control all of this from one room, it makes you think, right?" Monique replied.

Savannah was worried that they wouldn't be able to hold down Aura for long, so she hoped Pearl and Donna could get to Luna before anything bad happened.

Jhordan sat in silence as he listened to the commotion from above. He had been ordered to stay put by Aura. She said she would call for him when she needed him, but Bruce had told him that Aura never called for anyone. It was her way of keeping him out of the way whilst she got what she wanted.

"Hey, you ready kid?" Bruce hissed from the doorway.

Jhordan nodded. He got to his feet and joined Bruce in the kitchen. "How is Luna?"

"As far as I know, she's still alive," Bruce replied. "Now, in that drawer, I want you to get the scissors." He pointed at the drawer next to the old sink.

Jhordan opened the drawer, revealing a vast array of sharp utensils. He grabbed the scissors and closed the drawer. "These ones?"

"Perfect! Now, here's the plan," Bruce began to explain.

Savannah opened the door slowly so Monique could slip into the room.

"Ah Sylvester, is she making her way there?" Aura asked. She turned to find Savannah blocking the doorway and Monique in the centre of the room. "Not quite what I was hoping for but, I can work with this."

An evil look crossed Aura's face as she launched into a frenzied attack of magic on Monique. She threw bolts of lightning and sparks of electricity in her direction. Monique managed to dodge them all, even managing to throw a few of her own back. Monique managed to hit Aura twice, sending her hurtling towards the far wall.

"Grab that wire and tie her up," Monique told Savannah.

As Savannah grabbed for the wire, Aura made it disappear.

"Ha ha, you can't get it if you don't know where it is," Aura laughed.

Monique had seen this trick a few times, just because you couldn't see it, didn't mean it wasn't there. "Savannah, just reach out and grab, it's there. Trust me."

Savannah put all her faith in Monique and reached out; she managed to grab hold of something that wasn't visible until she held it in her hands. She quickly wrapped the wire around her hands ready to tie Aura up, but when she looked around, Aura had gone.

"Is this the same as the wire thing? Is she there but I can't see her?" She asked.

"No, she slipped out. We have to find her before she finds Luna," Monique said as she darted for the door.

Once in the long corridor, they both stopped. The corridor had changed in layout. The doors were gone. Nothing could have prepared them for what happened next.

Chapter 36

As Luna walked along the corridor, she noticed the light fading outside the window. She had no way to even check the time, but she could feel it getting colder the closer she got to the target room. She looked behind her before entering the room. As she opened the door, the sight inside took her breath away. Entering the room, Luna shivered. She tried to stop her teeth from chattering, it was so cold. She looked around the room, turning in a slow circle, taking in the sight before her.

"Please, have a seat," came a voice Luna had only ever heard in her sleep.

Luna sat in the chair that had been placed at the centre of the room. It was a high wing-backed chair, draped with red velvet. The wall in front of her held a range of handheld mirrors. They all had different designs and were all of different sizes.

"Why are there so many mirrors?" Luna asked.

"You haven't heard the stories?" Came the same voice.

"No. Sorry, who are you?" Luna asked.

There was a shimmering and bending of the air around her before a figure appeared, the outline of a young girl, no older than she. The young girl wore a high neck floral dress, with long sleeves. The shoulders of the dress were puffed out. On her feet was a pair of brown leather shoes with a medium sized buckle on the front. As Luna looked from the girls' feet up towards her head, she noticed that her head was missing.

"I don't normally question what I see within the spirits I meet, but, where is your head?" Luna asked.

"My name is Edith Florentine. I only show my face to those around my age, but you have to find the correct hand-held mirror. When I died, the deal was that my features would be held in the mirror forever," Edith explained.

"How did you die?" Luna asked.

Edith glided to her side and gently touched her hand. "My sister and I were playing around the grounds. I swore I heard my name being called from inside the house. The voice sounded like our mother. Thinking she had hidden in the house and playing a joke on us, I ventured inside," Edith began. "I followed the sound of the voice up into this room but as soon as I had stepped inside, the door slammed and locked. I could hear Judith calling my name so I tried to unlock the door but it wouldn't budge..."

"ENOUGH!" Came the booming voice Luna had spoken to in the corridor. "She needs not know how you died. She has come for one reason and one reason only and that is to attempt to free your spirit."

"That would be nice," Edith whispered. "But no one has ever done it."

"I'm too powerful. No-one has the strength or will power to overcome me," the booming voice said.

"Who exactly are you?" Luna asked.

"Excuse me?"

"Who are you? I like to know who I'm talking to," Luna replied.

The room darkened as the foreboding spirit made itself visible. It stood over Luna and looked down on her. She looked up at it and held eye contact.

"I don't have a name as such, not that I am aware of," it said to her.

"What about when you were alive?" Luna asked.

"I don't even remember being alive. I've only ever known death," it replied.

Luna held her hand out. "Take hold of my hand."

The spirit reached out and took hold of her hand. She closed her eyes and slowed her breathing down. She searched deep into its soul, hunting for anything that would explain who it was.

Bruce and Jhordan stood before Monique and Savannah. Nobody had spoken a word as the house settled around them.

"She's in there," Bruce said.

"In where?" Jhordan asked.

"In the room, with Edith," Bruce replied. "One part of the plan is complete. Now it's time for the next part."

"What plan is this exactly?" Savannah asked.

"I didn't introduce myself properly. I'm Bruce. Normally Aura's right hand man but I feel she has completely overstepped the mark on this one. No-one is normally supposed to die. I think she realises that Luna is more powerful than we first thought." Bruce said.

"He's a good guy," Jhordan told them. "Where is Mrs Heart?"

"Pearl and Donna have gone off ahead. They are trying to find Luna. Are you Luna's school friend?" Monique asked.

Jhordan nodded. "I'm sorry for all this. I didn't know she was going to harm Luna."

"I don't blame you. You were just doing as you were told," Monique smiled. "Now, is there anything we can help with?"

Bruce looked at Jhordan, "what do you think kid?"

Jhordan smiled. "I think I have just the thing. Follow me?" He said to Monique.

Monique followed Jhordan to a large room just off to the right of the long corridor. He opened the door to reveal a vast amount of cameras. Monique couldn't believe what she was seeing. She crossed the room and searched the monitors for Luna.

"Is there one set up for the room she is in?" Monique asked.

Jhordan quickly scanned the monitors and pointed to the top centre one. "There."

Monique was surprised to see Luna reaching out to something. She couldn't see what it was but Luna had her eyes closed and her hands clasped around something. "What do you need me to do?"

"We tied Sylvester up over in the corner, see?" Jhordan pointed towards the back corner of the room. "Can you watch these cameras, and tell us where Aura is? We can't risk her getting anywhere near Luna."

"I can do that, that's not a problem. What are you going to do?" Monique asked.

"Bruce and I have to stop all this. Luna isn't safe. Bruce told me how all this works. It doesn't have a good outcome, unless we stop it," Jhordan looked down. "I don't want anyone getting hurt."

Monique whispered some unintelligible words and gently touched his cheek. "You will be protected against harm young Jhordan."

"Thank you," he replied.

Jhordan turned and left the room, running to catch up with the others. "We have to find Pearl and Donna and take them all to the surveillance room. It will be safer for them there."

Bruce nodded. "You can either come with us or go to the room with Mrs Heart?" He told Savannah.

"Would you mind if I tagged along?" Savannah asked.

"Not at all. If Jhordan says you are trustworthy for him then you are trustworthy to me. This way," Bruce replied.

Savannah followed Bruce and Jhordan as they turned multiple different directions. She had become slightly dizzy. She slowed down a little, and then lost sight of them both. Savannah stopped and lent against the wall. She hadn't realised how big this house really was. It looked smaller on the outside. As she closed her eyes to calm her breathing down, she felt a sudden pulling on her shoulders and a hand clasped over her mouth. Hey eyes shot open and she began clawing at the hand but with little luck in releasing its grip.

"If you scream, I'll just kill you here and now and let everyone find you," Aura hissed in her ear.

Savannah decided against screaming and allowed Aura to lead her away. She opened the door to a side room and tied Savannah up.

"You see, it's not that hard to tie someone up when you're not distracted," Aura laughed.

"What do you want from me? I'm nothing special," Savannah said.

"Oh but in the grand scheme of things, you are. You see, I don't want Luna disturbed, she has something very important to complete, and having you and that partner of yours here will distract her. I only really remember inviting her mother and grandmother. Now, I know you were with the mother, so what happened there? Did she get lost?" Aura asked.

"I don't know. I stopped so she must have carried on. She probably doesn't even realise I'm not behind her yet," Savannah replied.

"Oh well, that's a shame. Maybe she will actually get lost and then she could probably take Edith's place!" Aura said. She walked towards the window and looked out. "It's getting dark. The clouds are rolling in. It's the perfect time to get this done! Now, you stay here. No wandering around," Aura laughed.

Savannah rolled her eyes at Auras' attempt at sarcasm. Aura then turned and left the room. Savannah sighed. She berated herself for not being able to keep up with Bruce and Jhordan.

"Jhordan, Bruce, where is Savannah?" Monique called over the radio.

They both turned around to see that she was not longer behind them.

"Check all the cameras. There is one in every room. Also, the monitor at the bottom right can be used to rewind and view past footage. Can you find her?" Bruce called back.

"On it," Monique replied.

"We have to press on. If we don't find the others before Aura, this will all be for nothing," Bruce told Jhordan.

Jhordan nodded in agreement and they continued along the corridor. As they neared the end with a swift turn to the left, they bumped into Pearl and Donna.

"Jhordan! Are you OK?" Pearl said as she quickly hugged him. "Who is this? Is he hurting you?"

"No, this is Bruce. He normally works with Aura, but he figured she wasn't being fair this time. He is helping me. We need you to both come with us. We will take you to Monique," Jhordan replied.

"I found her!" Monique called over the radio.

"Where is she?" Bruce asked. "We can collect her on our way to you. We have your mother and Donna."

"OK, she was dragged into a room about eight doors back from where you are now. Aura has tied her up but she has locked the door," Monique replied. "Aura is now on the same corridor as Luna. She is around three doors away."

Jhordan took off at a sprint with Bruce shouting after him, "Be careful!"

Pearl grasped her cross and prayed that Jhordan would be OK. She prayed that Aura wouldn't hurt him or Luna. She felt a tugging at her arm and opened her eyes to find Donna in front of her.

"We have to go," she said.

Pearl nodded and followed her and Bruce back towards the surveillance room. As she passed each door she could hear the wails and screams. She prayed that the souls behind those doors be free to rest. When they approached the final door, Pearl felt something pulling at her ankle. She looked down to see a little girl, no more than around three..

"Please, help us," she whispered. "He keeps us locked up and takes our energy for himself."

"I will try to help you, but first I need to help my granddaughter," Pearl told her.

"She's in the western wing. With him. We can try to help from here too," the little girl told her.

"I would be very grateful," Pearl replied. She then caught up with the others at the door to where Savannah was being held. Bruce picked at the lock and released it. Donna burst through the door and untied Savannah.

"You OK?" She asked her.

"I think so yeah. Aura is a strange woman," Savannah replied.

"That we already know," Bruce replied. "Come, we have to move in case she comes back here."

"Wait. Where's Jhordan?" Savannah asked.

"Off to get Aura, she isn't far from Luna and we can't let her get any closer," Bruce replied.

Savannah followed them all to the surveillance room. When Bruce opened the door, Monique almost attacked them with a chair.

"Oh, I'm so sorry. You made me jump," she apologised.

"Don't worry, at least you were prepared," Bruce laughed. He walked over to the wall of cameras and searched around for Jhordan. "Got him. I will be back in ten minutes. Keep this door locked and only open it if you see us outside. In fact, the keyword is Monty."

"Got it. Be careful," Donna told him.

"Oh my!" Pearl said from behind them. "That's him."

Pearl watched Luna on the screen, concentrating deeply on whatever was in her hand.

"I don't see anything," Monique said.

Pearl fiddled with the contrast and brightness a little before the ghastly figure came into focus. There was a collective gasp from around the room. A squealing coming from behind them caught their attention.

Monique had almost forgotten about poor Sylvester in the corner.

Donna walked over to him. "I'm gonna move this gag for a second, scream and I'll knock you out all over again."

Sylvester nodded rapidly. Donna moved the gag. "What is THAT?" He asked.

"You mean you had no idea what Aura was pitting Luna against?" Pearl asked.

He shook his head vigorously. "If I had known, I would have backed out just as fast as I joined in."

"I don't know exactly who he is, but Luna is talking to him. Do these cameras pick up sound?" She asked him.

"Ye...Yes. The far dial on the bottom amplifier," he told them.

Savannah turned the dial and Luna's voice echoed around the room.

Chapter 37

Jhordan sprinted through the corridors, hoping he could reach Aura before she made it to Luna. He felt alive.

More alive than he had been since Aura had, effectively, brought him to life. He passed door after door with no luck in finding Aura. He radioed Monique to check if she had seen Aura on any of the cameras but she hadn't.

'Come on Jhordan, think,' he thought to himself. That's when he heard the footsteps behind him. He quickly ducked into an open doorway and watched as a figure ran past. He let out a breath he didn't realise he was holding and the footsteps stopped.

"Jhordan?" Bruce whispered.

"Bruce, I'm so glad it's you. I haven't found her yet," Jhordan replied.

"Don't worry; I've got Monique checking for her now. She shouldn't be too far away," Bruce replied.

They had walked a little further along the corridor when Monique radioed to say she was in the next room and that she was sitting with her back to the wall that joined the two rooms. Luna was in the second room.

"OK. Jhordan, I need you to go in and get her talking, keep her away from the door and her keep her attention on you. I'll sneak in behind her and we can tie her up from there," Bruce told him.

"She can do magic remember, we have to be careful," Jhordan replied.

"I know. We will have to outwit her. Let's go," Bruce said.

Jhordan burst in the door to a surprised looking Aura. "There you are! I've been looking everywhere for you," he blurted out.

"Jhordan! What are you doing here?" Aura asked, jumping to her feet.

"I heard some noises and they didn't sound right. Have you heard from Bruce or Sylvester? I can't reach either of them," Jhordan said.

"Now that you mention it, I haven't heard from Sylvester, he hasn't radioed in for a while. Let me check in on him," Aura said, she pulled out her radio and called in on Sylvester. "How are things looking?"

Sylvester heard the radio call and looked at Donna. "What shall I do?"

"Reply as normal. Don't arouse her suspicions," she replied.

Sylvester nodded. "Everything looks good from here. She is still in the room. I think things are working. Looks like things will go well."

"Good, keep me informed," Aura replied. She put the radio back into her pocket. That was when Bruce pounced. He tied her hands behind her back and bound her legs together. He pulled a trunk from the nearby wardrobe and threw her inside. "You won't get away with this."

Jhordan watched as Bruce closed and locked the lid. "Do you think it will keep her inside?"

"Let's hope so," Bruce replied. "We need to get back to the others."

They left Aura trapped in the box and returned to the surveillance room. Bruce knocked twice and announced the password. Savannah opened the door but put her finger to her lips. She needed them to be quiet. Upon entering the room, Jhordan could hear Luna's voice over the speakers.

"I can see your life before," Luna told the spirit. "You were a kind man, a family man. You had two children, a boy and a girl."

Luna looked at the spirit. As she spoke she could see his figure shifting. He was becoming more visible.

"Is there anymore?" He asked.

Luna nodded. "I can see that something traumatic happened, something that changed you. The year is 1293 and you are with your wife and children in the park. Your daughter is playing with a red kite; your son is playing with a wooden spinning top. You and your wife are watching from a park bench. You are both smiling as the children play but for some reason; your daughter goes off towards the river that ran through the park."

The spirits breath hitched a little. It was as if he had remembered something.

"I can see that something piques your attention. There is a distant scream. You get up to track down the screaming but you don't make it in time. You see you daughter being carried away but a hooded figure. He has a flowing cape behind him," Luna continued.

The more of the story she told, more of the spirit became visual. He had short dark hair and dark eyes. His face was soft with a short beard and a simple moustache.

"Is there more?" He asked, desperate to hear more about himself.

"You chase the man for a few meters, but he disappears into an alleyway and out of sight. You can still hear your daughters' distant screams, even now," Luna said.

The man closed his eyes and allowed a single tear to fall from his eye. "Penelope."

Luna watched as he crumbled to a heap on the floor, sobbing her name over and over. "I tried so hard to get to her. So hard. My wife, Katherine, fell to pieces when we couldn't find Penelope. Our son, Henry, tried to make Katherine happy in everything he did, but it seemed nothing was good enough to please her," he sobbed.

Luna touched his arm lightly. "Did you and Katherine ever talk about Penelope?"

He shook his head. "Never. Katherine wouldn't allow us to speak her name in the house. Henry said it once and she punished him dearly for it."

Luna watched as the tears fell and he sobbed deeply. "Your name is Thomas. You searched high and low for Penelope for three long months. You went out night after night to find her."

"What happened? Did I find her?" Thomas asked. His face longing for Luna to say that he did and that they were happy again, but Luna allowed one solitary tear to fall from her eyes. New tears accumulated in his eyes.

Luna closed her eyes for a second before saying, "You found her, but by that time, it was too late. A man had kidnapped her from the park; that was the scream you heard. He locked her up. He found out you were searching for her, and when you got too close to finding her alive, he..." Luna stopped. She felt terrible telling him what had happened.

"He what?" Thomas asked. "Please tell me."

"I'm so sorry Thomas. Penelope was murdered. You found her body at the edge of the river," Luna whispered.

Thomas's sobs were heartbreaking to everyone watching this exchange. So heart wrenching that even Sylvester was teary-eyed.

"Oh Luna," Monique whispered. "You have such a good soul."

Monique watched her daughters exchange with this spirit and admired how well Luna had explained everything to him. She looked in Pearl's direction but found an empty chair.

"Where is Pearl?" Monique asked.

"She was right there," Savannah replied.

"Check the cameras," Sylvester replied as he gestured to the screens.

Donna looked from screen to screen before she finally spotted her. "She's at the room you just come from, Bruce. What's in there?"

"Aura," Bruce replied before he shot out the door.

Jhordan looked worried. "She isn't strong enough to fight Aura."

"I'm going. Don't try and stop me," Monique said to Donna as she stood up.

"Wouldn't dream of it. Just be careful? That girl in there needs her Mum," Donna said, pointing at the screen with Luna emblazoned over it.

"I'll always be there for her. Nothing will happen to me," Monique replied.

Donna curtly nodded her head and stepped aside. She looked at Sylvester, "You gonna stay still if I untie you?"

"Yes Ma'am," Sylvester said.

"You better," Donna said as she untied him. She sat back down on the chair and watched as Monique made her way towards the same room as Aura.

Chapter 38

"Aura! Where are you?" Pearl screamed as she opened the door. "I know you are in here."

The room fell silent. Pearl turned in a complete circle looking for anywhere the Aura could hide. She saw a wardrobe and a chest of drawers. The bed had no hidden compartments and was so close to the floor, no-one could fit underneath. What surprised her most was an out-of-place chest in the centre of the room. It had a padlock securing the lid. Pearl walked over to it and tapped on the lid. She didn't know what she expected to happen but she wasn't prepared for the outcome. As she retrieved her hand after the fifth knock, the lid flew open and Aura levitated out of the chest.

"Did Bruce really think he could trap me in there?" She said.

"Well you stayed there long enough," Pearl spat.

"Long enough to know that you would come looking," Aura smirked. "And here you are. You don't honestly believe you can save her, do you?"

Pearl watched as Aura landed gently back on the floorboards. She walked over to the bed and sat on the corner. Pearl stayed exactly where she was. She didn't move an inch. She felt like a spectator watching a fighter prepare for a match. Every move Aura made, Pearl noted. Each time Aura moved suddenly, Pearl was prepared.

"Oh don't be so twitchy Pearl. You're no use to me now. If I wanted to do anything to you or the girl's mother, I would have done it by now. You didn't think a flimsy box could hold me back from completing my mission, did you?" Aura laughed.

"Maybe I was hoping you would come to your senses and stop this stupidity," Pearl replied. "It has never been proven to be correct. What actually makes you think Edith has these special powers to give?"

"Oh my dear Pearl. It isn't Edith who has the power. It's the spirit that holds her, didn't I tell you that?" Aura smirked.

Monique paced the corridor in search of Pearl and Aura's room. She could feel someone watching her the whole time. Someone other than her friends behind the cameras. This set of eyes had a different persona. This set of eyes was evil to the core. She shivered as the turned the next corner. Swinging to the left and straight into a dark corridor.

"Guys, this doesn't look right," she called over the radio.

"Have you taken a wrong turn somewhere? I can't see you anywhere," Bruce replied.

"I took the same route you told me to. I don't understand," Monique said. She ran her hands along the walls. "The walls are damp and I can hear water running."

"Sit tight, I'll see if I can track you down on the system," Bruce replied.

Monique slowed her breathing down while she waited for Bruce to find her. She closed her eyes but suddenly opened them again. She had a vision.

"I know where I am," she called over the radio. "I'm under the house."

"How did you get there?" Savannah asked.

"That's the number one question. I think Aura got out," Monique said.

"She's right, you know," Aura said from above them. "And now, I go for her!" With that, she disappeared.

"Monique, be careful. She's coming," Donna shouted.

"I got this," Monique replied. And the radio fell silent.

"Where is Pearl?" Savannah asked as her eyes darted from screen to screen. "I can't find her."

"Keep calm, can I look?" Sylvester asked in a slight whisper.

Donna gestured to the screens, "be my guest, just remember what I said."

Sylvester nodded and took over with the keyboard. He pressed a few keys and Pearl popped onto the centre screen. She was lying on the bed face down. She wasn't moving.

"We need to get to her, fast," Savannah said. She got up from the chair and threw the door open. "Direct me."

Bruce nodded briskly and turned back to the screens.

"Will she be OK?" Sylvester asked.

"You better hope so," Donna replied.

They watched Savannah make her way down the same corridor Monique had, pass the same doors and turn the same corner. She made it to the room and to Pearl.

"Thomas? Are you OK?" Luna asked, gently touching his spirited arm.

He nodded and lifted his head to look at her. He had been sobbing for what felt like eternity.

"Thank you for everything. I believe you have a job to do?" Thomas asked.

"I do, but I don't know what to do," Luna replied.

"To free Edith, you must find the correct looking glass that holds her face. You have three attempts," he told her. "If you fail, you will replace Edith and stay here for eternity."

Luna's head dropped. She didn't want to stay here. She wanted her Mum. She gradually got back to her feet and walked to the first wall covered in hand-held mirrors. She reached out but Thomas stopped her.

"Whichever you touch, you have to check, be careful with your choice," he told her.

She quickly retracted her hand. "How long do I have to choose?"

"As long as you need, but remember you only have three choices," he replied.

Luna looked back at the wall. The choices were endless. She walked the length of the wall, the length of the next, and the next, and the fourth. Each hand-held mirror had its own style. She stepped back from the walls and closed her eyes. She envisioned the mirrors and what images they had seen over time. How many people had come through here and never left?

"How many have come before me?" Luna asked.

Thomas sighed. "Before you there was another young girl. She didn't even try. She stopped before picking any of the mirrors. The woman who thinks she can dictate to me had almost dragged her here kicking and screaming, but she ran off."

"Ran off?" Luna asked. "I thought she just didn't believe in herself enough and Aura let her go?"

Thomas almost laughed, "It's true that she didn't believe in herself, but Aura didn't let her go, she ran off. She was so upset."

"So everything Aura told me was a lie?" Luna cried.

Thomas watched Luna with sympathy. She reminded him a little of Penelope. She had so much emotion. Felt the pain of everyone. Luna looked back at the wall of mirrors and took a deep breath in.

Monique traced the bricks with her fingers. The cold and damp seeped through her fingers. She walked the length of the wall. Back and forth more than three times before she sensed the eyes in the back of her head. She turned around slowly; she didn't want to be startled.

"Ahh the lovely Monique, how lovely of you to join us," Aura laughed.

Monique rolled her eyes. "What do you want Aura? Why are you doing this to Luna?"

Aura tipped her head back and laughed. A hearty, deep bellied laugh. "Why do you think? She is the key! The *only* one who can do this! Don't you see? *SHE* is the one I've been waiting for."

"I won't let you hurt her!" Monique shouted.

"And exactly *what* do you think you can do to stop me? You're nothing but a jealous mother who can't handle grief! You shout at your daughter and use her father's death against her," Aura replied.

"I can do more than you think I can. You obviously know absolutely nothing about me," Monique shrugged. "Luna may take after her grandmother in the gift department, but there's a little piece of me in there somewhere. A strong willed girl who will fight until the end."

Aura sniggered. "You honestly believe that? Ha! That girl is so weak; she hasn't the fight of you or the spirit of her grandmother in her. At least Pearl fought me off, *she* just followed me along!"

Monique glared at Aura with so much hate in her eyes. "How dare you? She followed along because you threatened her!"

Aura shrugged her shoulders. "How else could I get her to come here? I would have had to drag her, just like I did to Pearl all those years ago!"

Something bubbled deep inside Monique. It was a feeling she hadn't felt for a long time. It was the same feeling she had felt when Mark had attacked Carly. Before she could stop it, there was a flash of light and Aura was on the floor looking just as surprised as Monique was.

"What was that and how did you do it?" Aura asked as she stood up and brushed herself off.

Monique shrugged, "your guess is as good as mine. Sometimes these things just happen."

"Just happen? How does it just happen? You hold no abilities. You're a civilian, just like that stupid husband of yours," Aura screamed, and with a bolt of lightning, Monique flew backwards against the wall.

The two women stood facing each other. Aura studied Monique, trying to spot anything that would give away her next move. They didn't expect what happened next.

Chapter 39

"What's that?" Savannah said as she pulled Pearl up from the bed.

They looked around the room, watching old ornaments and photo frames fall to the floor.

"I don't know dear, but we better get out of here before it gets worse," Pearl replied.

A large mirror fell from the wall and smashed to the floor, followed by a photo of an elderly man and woman.

"How much worse can it get?" Savannah whispered. She grabbed Pearl's hand and ran for the door. "Direct me out!" She shouted through the radio.

"Turn right out of the door and run. Take the second left and then we are the third door on the left," Bruce replied.

Savannah ran the entire way, checking back to make sure Pearl was still with her, but she underestimated Pearl's stamina, she was right behind Savannah. As they ran into the surveillance room, Pearl's eyes instantly searched the screens for Luna and Monique.

"Where are they?" Pearl asked.

"Who?" Bruce asked.

"Where are Monique and Luna?" Pearl screamed. She pointed at the screens. "They are nowhere to be seen."

Bruce looked back at the screen. He hadn't noticed that the screen, on which Luna had just been, was now blank. It showed no image. "We can't access Monique. She is in a place where our cameras aren't. All we know is that Aura is with her."

Pearl held her head in her hands. She prayed that Monique would be OK and that Luna was safe.

The house shook again, this time more violently. It knocked out the camera feeds and every screen went blank. Sylvester pressed a concoction of keys on the keyboard hoping to bring them back to life but nothing happened. He tried again and again but to no avail.

"I don't know what happened," Sylvester told them all. "I can try and reset the connection."

"Do it!" Donna exploded. She shook her head as she crossed the room to check on Pearl.

"What happened?" Monique cried out.

Aura hadn't moved since the shaking started. She looked shocked. She carefully surveyed the surrounding walls, spotting the cracks before Monique did. She quickly rolled away as the wall crumbled in front of her. Monique jumped backwards, hitting her head on a jagged part of the wall. She lay, crumpled, on the floor as Aura stepped around the debris towards her.

"Aww poor little Monique. Looks like you won't see your daughters' greatest and only triumph in her short life," she laughed. "Good bye!"

As she walked away, Monique struggled to stay awake. The bang to her head had shaken her more than she realised. She closed her eyes for a brief second to pull her power from deep inside, but as she did, another tremor shook the ground. The wall crumbled some more, leaving Monique trapped in the corridor. She squeezed her eyes shut and summoned her power, feeling the tingling all across her body. It felt as if her whole body was numb. The feeling spread from her toes, up through her legs and into her torso. She could feel the pain easing slowly. It took a few extra seconds for her to feel completely stable enough to attempt to stand up, but, on shaky feet, she pulled herself upright. She dusted herself off and began to pick her way across the debris and out through the door at the end of the corridor. She hoped it would lead her away from this damp place and back into clear air. She was beginning to struggle with her breathing. She walked forward a few steps before the shaking began again, she ran for cover before the wall on the opposite side of the corridor collapsed, exactly where she was standing just a few seconds before. Monique shook her head before running the last steps out of the door and headfirst into the surveillance door. She pounded on the door as hard as her fists would allow before Savannah swung the door open and she fell into her arms.

"How's Luna?" Monique asked when she had finally regained her breath.

"We don't know. The shaking has caused the camera feed to fail and Sylvester has been trying to regain access but, so far, we have had no success," Donna explained. "What happened?" She asked, gesturing to the dust and pieces of rock still falling from her coat.

"Aura happened. I think it shocked her that I had some form of power. She didn't like the fact I couldn't explain where my power had come from. That was before the shaking started and she scarpered!" Monique replied. "I don't know where she went."

"Something doesn't feel right," Jhordan said. He was sitting in the corner of the room, rocking back and forth. "Something else is here with us and it's not good."

"Jhordan, what do you mean?" Pearl asked creeping forward to try and calm him. "What can you see?"

"Oh I can't see it. I can feel it. You see, when we did the Ouija Board back then, something attached itself to all of us, mainly me, but a piece of it was hooked to us all. I can sense something isn't right but I can't see what it is," Jhordan explained.

Pearl held his hands, "try and see it through my eyes. It might just work."

Jhordan stared deep into Pearl's dark eyes. Neither blinked as Jhordan fell into a trance. "He's in the kitchen. In the cupboard under the sink. He's watching Aura. She is downstairs. He's not happy with her."

"I'll go," Bruce said as he threw open the door. "I might not be able to stop her with magic but I can buy you all some time to find Luna."

"Keep in contact, let us know how things are going," Donna told him.

Bruce smiled at her, nodded and shot off down the corridor. He was out of sight in a matter of seconds.

"I hope he knows what he's getting himself into. She is pure evil," Monique said.

"I need to get to Luna," Pearl cried. "I have to help her."

"Pearl, even if you get to her, how are you going to help her?" Savannah said, gently touching her shoulder.

"You don't understand. I've been in that room. I've seen the monstrosity that keeps Edith captive. I don't want the same to happen to Luna!" Pearl cried.

"I've got a connection!" Sylvester shouted. "Look!" He pointed at the central screen.

"Oh my! Look at her!" Pearl exclaimed. "What is happening?"

They all looked at the screen. Luna was no longer standing in the centre of the room. Thomas stood with his head bowed and his eyes closed. His hands in front of him, his palms facing the ceiling.

"What's...What's happening?" Monique cried as she ran over to the screens. "What is he doing to her?"

Jhordan pushed his way to the front and stared at the screen. He watched in silence as Luna's body twisted and turned, gracefully, in the air. Her long brown curls flowing gently. Her eyes were closed and her face looked relaxed. "I don't think he is hurting her."

"How can you tell?" Donna asked.

"She is relaxed. As if in a trance. I need to get closer," Jhordan said as he headed for the door.

"Wait," Savannah demanded as she grabbed his arm. "Don't go alone. Take Pearl with you. She knows more about this little fiasco than anyone else."

Pearl rose from the chair and joined Jhordan at the door.

"Be careful. Radio if you need help," Donna said as she passed over one of the communication radios.

"We will," Pearl whispered. "Watch her for me, tell me if anything changes."

As they watched Jhordan and Pearl leave the room, another screen flickered to life. This one from the corridor just outside their door.

"It's picking up movement but there is nothing there," Sylvester said. He turned the contrast some more but he couldn't see anything.

"There!" Monique shouted, pointing at a small shadow in the lower left hand corner.

Sylvester turned the brightness up and fiddled with the contrast some more but all that happened was a dull blob at the bottom of the screen. "It's no use; I can't get a clearer picture." He said.

"I can make it out, just," Monique replied. She walked over to the door and placed her hands on the cold oak. She closed her eyes and let her mind wander. Her inner vision took her beyond the door and face to shadow with this entity. It had glowing red eyes surrounded with dark emptiness. Its eyes send shivers down Monique's spine. Her eyes fly open and she turns to look at the others. "It's not good. Whatever and whoever that thing is, it's evil through and through."

Savannah and Donna glance at each other. Neither knowing what to say or do. Donna sat on the chair that Pearl had recently vacated and held her head in her hands. "I'm at a dead end. I don't know what to do from here." She whispered.

Savannah placed her hand on Donnas' shoulder. "We have to locate Bruce. He said he was going for Aura, let's see if we can find him and go from there." She said.

Sylvester tried the other screens again but nothing showed up. "You're going to have to radio him. Let's hope he hasn't turned the volume up to max."

"Bruce, can you hear me? Bruce?" Donna called.

"Yeah I'm here. What's happening?" Bruce answered.

"I don't know. Jhordan and Pearl have gone to find out what's happening with Luna and there's a strange entity outside this door. What happened with Aura?" Donna replied.

"You shouldn't have let them out!" Bruce screamed. "It's not safe! Aura stocked up on her power. The entity that you say is out there is her power source."

"So what do we do now? We can't call them back, but we can't find Aura either!" Donna said.

"I have a plan," Sylvester said quietly.

Savannah spun round and stared at him. She stood there for a full minute before saying, "spill then!"

"Yes, erm, well, Aura gets her power from this source. The only way we can stop her is to destroy the power source," Sylvester began. "All I need to work out is how to destroy it."

"That would have been the first thing to think of," Bruce hissed through the radio. "Get thinking. I'm going to hunt for Aura. I'll let you know if I find her."

"OK. I'll start working out how to destroy it," Sylvester replied.

The radio fell silent along with the room. No-one dared to speak. One of the screens flickered to life and everyone crowded around it. It showed a room, with a bed and a wardrobe. The wardrobe door was swinging open and shut, almost with a rhythmic pattern.

""What's that?" Savannah asked, hypnotised by the door.

Sylvester spotted a shadow on the screen. It was creeping up on the camera. "Don't look!" He shouted, just before a menacing face appeared on the screen.

Everyone had managed to avert their eyes a split second before the face appeared. Everyone, that is, except Donna.

"What in the name of all that is…What the?" Donna remarked.

"Describe it," Sylvester said, his face still turned away from the screen.

"Well, it's ugly! I don't know what else to say. I mean, its face is distorted. Almost like it features have been placed all wrong. Its left eye is half way down its cheek and its nose is bent at an ungodly angle," Donna began.

"What about the hair?" Sylvester asked. He had already begun to work out exactly who this thing was.

"It's like a desert sand colour, but with streaks of grey and black, very short mind you, cropped almost to its scalp," Donna replied.

"Monty," Sylvester whispered.

"Who is Monty?" Savannah asked.

"That's too long a story for now," Bruce said as he entered the room. "Where is he?"

Sylvester pointed out the face on the screen. "What did she do to him?"

"I'll explain later. We need to go," Bruce told them. "That was the entity that was outside this door. It senses something inside, and I believe it could be you," Bruce said as he looked at Monique.

"Why me?" Monique asked.

"It senses your power. I don't know exactly what power you posses but it seems to frighten both Monty and Aura, which is why she ran. I heard her explaining to our friend there," Bruce explained. "Do you know where your power originated?"

"No. I didn't even know I had it until...Well until I power blasted some boy through the girls' toilet wall," Monique shrugged. "I've never traced my ancestors."

"When this is all over, that might be the first thing you do," Savannah said.

Monique nodded and took one last look at the screen showing Luna before following everyone else out of the room.

Chapter 40

"Are you sure this is it?" Pearl asked Jhordan when they stopped at a large mahogany door.

"Positive," he replied. "Listen."

Pearl leaned her ear against the door. She could hear wind rustling and whooshing from inside. She closed her eyes and a vision of Luna rushed to the front of her mind.

"Pearl! Stay with me. Don't go off like that, it scares me," Jhordan called.

"I'm sorry dear. I'm so scared of what he is doing to her, I just want to get in there," Pearl replied.

"I know. Let's give it a second or two," Jhordan smiled.

They waited for what felt like an eternity, but soon enough, Jhordan hauled the large door open. Thomas spotted them entering, but didn't stop what he was doing. He gestured for them to sit on the floor, just slightly away from where Luna's body floated. Thomas smiled at them.

"I am not harming her Pearl, try not to think that," Thomas whispered.

"Then what exactly are you doing?" Pearl hissed.

"Protecting her. Aura is not all she seems, but I'm sure you knew that already, both of you," Thomas replied. "I am preparing Luna for what should happen to her if she chose the wrong mirror. I will not let that happen to another. I will free Edith but not to Luna."

"What do you mean?" Jhordan asked. "If you free Edith, doesn't that mean that Aura will receive eternal life? It is her who brought Luna here after all."

Thomas laughed. It was something he felt he hadn't done properly in a very long time. "My dear child, is that what she told you? What she told everyone? The only person who would receive eternal life would be the one who chose the mirror to begin with, that is the main deal. If you chose the wrong one, then you lose your own life, choose the correct one and live forever, maybe she didn't quite understand the concept but here we are."

Pearl tried to hold back her amusement but it filtered through. "So, correct me if I'm wrong at any point in this, if I had chosen the correct mirror all those years ago, she still wouldn't have lived forever?"

"That's correct. I thought I recognised you, little Pearl Heart. So you passed down the gift to Luna?" Thomas asked.

"It would seem that way," Pearl replied. "How much longer will this take?"

"Oh no very long at all, as long as nobody interrupts us," Thomas replied. He closed his eyes and resumed his position.

Pearl and Jhordan sat in silence, watching Luna's body as it levitated in the air. Thomas sat with his eyes closed and his palms facing the sky, whispering some unintelligible words. The room was calm. The wind had settled and Thomas opened his eyes slowly. He placed his hands under Luna's back and gently lowered her to the floor.

"She must remain there for at least another thirty minutes. Please, watch over her. I have another pressing matter to attend to," Thomas told them. With that, he disappeared into the walls.

Pearl and Jhordan stared blankly at the wall covered in mirrors through which Thomas had just evaporated through. Neither spoke a word.

"Jhordan, are you there?" Bruce called through the radio. "Speak to me lad."

"I'm here. We're fine," Jhordan whispered.

"Did you find her?" Bruce asked. "Is she OK?"

"We are with her now, but we can't be interrupted. Thomas has gone off somewhere," Pearl answered. "What are you all doing now?"

"I'm taking the others back outside, it's not safe for them here," Bruce told them. "I will be back in contact shortly."

"OK," Jhordan replied. He allowed the radio to fall silent once more. He looked at Pearl who was now transfixed on Luna. She hadn't moved since Thomas laid her on the ground. Jhordan could see tears prickling at Pearls eyes; he quickly dug in his pocket for a tissue and handed it to her.

"You're a good lad at heart aren't you?" Pearl told him.

Jhordan smiled, "I just wish I could stay around longer. I know once this is over, the spell will wear off and I won't be here anymore."

"Try not to think of that yet lad. Let's get everything fixed first," Pearl said, squeezing his hands.

"OK guys, let's get you all out of here and to safety before anything else happens," Bruce told them. "Follow me!"

"Ha! Not so fast Brucey Boy!" Aura screamed as she appeared in front of him. "The night is young! It's not over yet!"

"AURA!"

Thomas's booming voice startled them all, including Aura. She turned around slowly. Her face meeting with his abdomen. He stood almost a foot taller than her.

"T...Thomas! How lovely to see you!" Aura squeaked.

"I can't say the same for you! You awaken me AGAIN from a slumber I was content with," Thomas barked.

"Well, no time like the present to gain my eternal youth," Aura laughed.

"I don't think this is a joking matter! What you have told these people is pure lies! YOU know as well as I, that only the person who selects the correct mirror receives the gift of eternal life! Why would you offer up another child to undertake the job YOU know you couldn't manage yourself?" Thomas boomed at her. He looked over Aura's head and nodded slowly to the others that they were free to leave, but just as they made way towards the door, Thomas caught Monique's arm, "not you. I may well need you, Monique Heart."

Monique was speechless. She dropped her head slowly, she had a horrible feeling she wouldn't make it out of here alive. She slowly moved back into her place.

"What do you need her for?" Aura spat. "She is anything special."

"It shows how much you actually know then, doesn't it?" Thomas said, narrowing his eyes at her.

Monique watched Bruce, Donna and the others leave the corridor and head down the outside steps. She knew they would be better off outside. With the amount of friction in this corridor alone, it would only take a single spark to ignite the lot.

"Both of you follow me please," Thomas demanded and he walked ahead with large strides.

Both women followed him, believing that they would be taken to Luna. Aura began to get a little overexcited, thinking she would now be able to experience eternal life. She had lived for so long already, thanks to her own power and sorcery, but she knew it could only take her so far, and that, before long, her power would diminish and she would be left to wilt and, eventually die. She longed for eternal life, to see how the world would evolve in the many centuries to come. Suddenly, Thomas made a sharp right turn down an unlit corridor. He opened the very last door which held the spirit of Edith. Neither women could see her, but they felt her presence.

Thomas uttered the words, "reveal to all, reveal to me. Make yourself free to see."

With a flash of light, in front of their eyes, stood the body of a young girl, dressed in a long white, frilly dress with embroidered flowers across the bottom. On her feet were the simplest of white buckle up shoes.

"Where is the rest of her?" Aura asked as she walked up to the girl and waved her hands above the girls' shoulders. "She's missing her head!"

Monique rolled her eyes. Aura really had no tact at all. "Thomas, what happened?"

Thomas crouched down in the corner, the girl jogging to his knee. He held his head in his hands for a few seconds before he began to explain. "There is another entity that wanders here. Monty. He's provides Aura with added power when she is running low." He looked over at Aura who stood with her hands on her hips. "He has roamed this house for well over seventy years now; around about the same time she buried him alive. Aside from him, there is a darker being. He resides deeper into the house. He has been here for as long as I can remember, in fact, I'm more than one hundred percent sure that he has been here longer than I."

"Oh will you get to the point you drivelling old man," Aura said snidely. "You're actually boring me."

"Ignore her. Tell me what happened to Edith?" Monique asked.

The girl crouched by the side of Monique and gently stroked her face. She held out her hands and Monique took them. Her vision became blurry at first, but then it became clearer. She saw two girls, around Luna's age, happily playing jump rope just in front on Flowerly Hall. One of the girls stopped suddenly and began running towards the gates. She flung open the gate and ran inside the house. She could hear the girl calling for her Mum, becoming more and more erratic when her mother didn't answer. The other girl followed along behind not more than thirty seconds later only to find her sister gone from sight. That's when she heard the screams. The other girl ran up the staircase and towards the western wing of the house. Towards the screams. She found the room in which she believed her sister was trapped and tried the handle. Nothing happened. She could still hear the screams. The flailing of her sister's shoes against the hardwood floor. And then there was silence. The door clicked as if unlocked from the inside and that's when she found her sister, laying on the floor.

Her neck at an unnatural angle.

Her feet tucked up under her.

Her eyes staring into the unknown.

She ran from the house. Ran straight home and up into her room where she hid under the quilt for hours. That was until her parents found her. Asked where Edith was. Judith didn't know how to tell them. How to explain to her parents that she couldn't save Edith from whatever terrible thing had done that to her. She sobbed for hours, until her parents had called the doctors. They gave her something to calm her down, allowing her to fully explain what had happened to Edith. She took them to Flowerly Hall. To the room in which her sister had been killed. Her mother had screamed in pain. Her father numb from emotion. The police had investigated but nothing had been found. Edith's body was buried but her soul remained the possession of Flowerly Hall. Her face removed from the soul and locked inside a handheld mirror, tossed in to a box full of others to remain there for eternity.

When Edith let go of Monique's' hands, she traced the tears that Monique had let fall. Long streaks had wound their way down her face.

"I'm so sorry Edith," Monique whispered. "So sorry."

"Oh stop with all this emotional blackmail. Can we get back to the reason why we are actually in this room and not up there where Luna is?" Aura said, placing her hands on her hips.

Thomas glared at her. "You don't even have the compassion to understand how a young girl came to be trapped here, but you are more than happy to claim the reward she has for releasing her! You are clearly more arrogant than I gave you credit for. Come!" He demanded. He rose from the floor and strode out of the room, leaving Edith to slowly fade away.

"Do you think Monique will be alright?" Savannah asked Bruce. He hadn't taken his eyes off the top floors since they made it out.

"I hope so. I'm confused as to why he would need Monique though," he replied.

"Look," Donna said, pointing up towards the central window. "There they go."

Bruce watched as William led the women back towards the western wing. "I'm going back in. I need to know what's happening."

"Wait, wouldn't it be better to just wait?" Sylvester asked.

"Maybe for you, but Jhordan is just a kid. He doesn't have anyone watching out for him," Bruce spat back. "You never liked him anyway!"

Sylvester backed away. "I'm sorry. I didn't think."

"Exactly. You never do!" Bruce shouted at him. "You always want things your way, you're just like her!"

"Guys, calm down. Arguing like this isn't going to help anyone," Donna said. She stepped away from the feuding men just as her phone pinged.

Savannah ran to her side. "Is it who I think it is?"

Donna nodded.

'They are fine. Luna is safe with Pearl and Jhordan. Thomas has Aura and Monique. Will tell you more when I can. Watching it all unfold is truly breathtaking. M x'

"Guys. They are OK. Everyone is OK," Donna told them.

Sylvester and Bruce turned to face her. "How do you know?" They asked in unison.

Donna then realised, they didn't actually know who Max was. She walked back towards them, planning how to tell them. This would take some doing.

"Enter." Thomas said, opening the door for them both.

As Monique and Aura entered the room, Luna began to stir. She tossed her head from side to side. Suddenly her eyes flew open and she stared at the ceiling. It's chandelier hanging high above her. She hadn't noticed the painting on the ceiling before. Its cherubs smiling down at her. The pastel coloured clouds dotted across the ceiling. She smiled as if it was heaven that she was looking into.

"Welcome back child," Thomas whispered. "Look who else has arrived in your absence."

Luna looked around. She saw Pearl and Jhordan and she smiled. "You came for me. Thomas said you would."

"Would I ever leave you?" Pearl purred.

"And over here?" Thomas gestured.

Luna turned to the other side to see he mother and Aura. "What's happening Thomas?"

"There's no need to panic my child. They are here for one reason and one reason alone. They are here for you," Thomas soothed her. "I promised you that you would not be harmed and I intend to keep that promise, but for this, you must be split up. I will place you into three teams. I will explain the terms of this exercise before you all begin, but, you must agree to the terms before we begin."

Everyone looked from one person to the next. No-one spoke. That was, until Aura agreed to take part without hearing the terms first.

"Let's get this done, whatever it is," she said.

Thomas stared at her, "my terms are as follows. Jhordan, you will work alone, as will you Aura. Luna, Monique and Pearl, you will work as a team. You are to pick a mirror each, but be careful. The evil entity I explained about earlier lurks within one. Edith's spirit within another."

"What about the rest of them?" Pearl asked. "There's so many."

"There are many spirits who reside here. Some are happy to stay; others would prefer to be released. Those are the spirits who volunteer themselves for the mirrors.

If you choose a mirror which releases another spirit, there isn't always a reward," Thomas explained.

"Are there any other traps, as such?" Monique questioned.

"The only mirror which holds a trap is the one in which the evil entity resides. Choose your mirror carefully, just as I explained Luna. Do not touch a mirror unless you are sure that is the one you want to look into," Thomas replied.

Luna nodded and pulled her family aside. They carefully studied each mirror from a safe distance. She noticed that Jhordan hadn't moved from his spot. She walked over to him and touched his hand. He looked at her and smiled. "I don't blame you," she whispered and kissed him on the cheek. She then returned to her mother's outstretched arms.

"Are we set on one?" Pearl asked.

"I know which I like, but I don't feel connected to it, I don't feel it's the right one." Luna told her.

"Show me," Pearl replied.

Luna showed her mother and her grandmother the mirror she liked. Pearl took an instant dislike to it, as did Monique.

"Something doesn't feel right with that one," Monique said almost jumping back from it. "Let's take another look."

Aura watched how the family worked together and became instantly jealous. She noticed how Luna continually looked at a certain mirror as if she knew what it held. Aura decided to choose that one. She didn't touch it for now, but she had set her mind to it. Jhordan, however, hadn't looked at any of them. He watched the others work and had decided to choose the first mirror he set eyes on when he was asked to choose one. He had nothing to lose. Even after this was over, he knew he would be back in the dark cold place he came from, if he chose the evil entity; at least he knew he would be somewhere, and that he would be close to Luna.

Chapter 41

"I don't get it," Sylvester remarked. "How can someone be dead, but take the form of a living being?"

"You would never understand Syl," Bruce said. "It's hard to fully explain. Only the spirit itself could explain and even that wouldn't be enough to prove it."

"Max told us that it takes a long of energy to be able to hold things, or make himself visible, hence why I only hear from him or see him after a long period. Days at least," Donna replied. "It was Luna who first told me about him. I didn't believe her at first, thinking that she was, maybe, still hurt over her father's death."

"It's understandable," Bruce replied.

"When Luna told us that her father had been to visit them, I was a little more shocked. I asked Max about it and he said he and some of the other spirits had given up some of their energy so that he could spend some time with his family," Savannah added.

"I still don't understand. If he was able to form a solid human form, why didn't he try and stop us from doing what we were doing? He could have stumped up enough energy to pick something up and hit us with it!" Sylvester said.

"It's possible, but maybe he wanted to see what would happen if he let us deal with everything," Bruce replied. "I mean, all the spirits we awakened that night could have done us all over, but they didn't. It does seem slightly odd."

"When Max took the form of Alex and told me he had to step back because he was too close on a personal level, I thought that, maybe, Alex was in some way related to Edith and Judith and that if he continued to work on the case, it would be seen as biased," Donna said.

"Donna, how long have you and 'Alex' been working together?" Savannah asked.

"This was our first case together, why?" Donna replied.

"So there was no Alex before. Had you seen him around the station before?" Savannah asked.

"No, but no-one else seemed surprised to see him and nobody acted as if he were a new police officer," Donna said. "However, it does seem really strange that my old partner just happened to become really sick just as this case came in."

"Have you spoken to him since?" Bruce asked.

"Well, no. This case has been pretty full on," Donna replied.

"I think it might be a good time to just quickly check on him," Savannah said.

Donna nodded slowly and pulled out her phone. She pulled up the number for Percy and let it ring.

"Donna! It's been a while! How are you?" Percy answered. He didn't sound ill.

"Percy, I was just calling to check on you. The guys at the station said you were sick?" Donna said. "I'm sorry it's taken so long."

"Oh don't be sorry. How far through the case are you?" Percy asked. "Have you cracked it?"

"In a way yes, but it's a real mess," Donna admitted.

"Talk to me," Percy said. "You know I've got time."

"I'm not sure how much time I have, but I'll try and make it quick." Donna replied. She walked away from the others and began to tell Percy all about the case. She trusted him.

Thomas watched as his guests pondered over the different mirrors. He wished he knew which mirror the evil had taken up residence in, he would, without a doubt, point it out to Aura. For obvious reasons, he wasn't allowed to interfere with their decision making. He wished Aura would choose the evil entity. It might teach her a lesson.

"Any ideas yet Jhordan?" Thomas asked as he glided around the room.

"I have an idea, but I'm still not sure. Why are there so many choices?" Jhordan replied.

Thomas looked at all the mirrors on display. "Some spirits want to be free. They volunteer themselves to be placed inside a mirror. It would take someone to actually come and pick one up for that spirit to be released."

"So anyone could come here and release a spirit?" Jhordan asked.

"In theory yes, you wouldn't know you had released one unless you were gifted enough like Luna and Pearl," Thomas replied. "But, in effect, you could release multiple spirits without even realising it."

"I'd love to release them all. I know how lonely it can get," Jhordan said quietly.

"Are you lonely?" Thomas asked him.

"Always. I don't have many friends in the afterlife," Jhordan replied. He walked away from Thomas and back towards the wall of mirrors he had grown quite fond of.

Thomas studied him for a few seconds more before moving around the room. "Any ideas ladies?" He asked Luna and her family.

"None as yet, there are so many choices. What happens if we can't free Edith?" Luna asked.

"Of that I am unsure child, but you can only try," Thomas replied.

'Judith, where are you when I need you,' Luna thought to herself.

'Always in your head, do you need some guidance?' came a voice from inside the deepest part of her mind. It was a voice she had heard many time before this day. Judith had heard her pleas and had come to her. Something like this had never happened before.

'Show me the right one to choose,' Luna pleaded.

'I cannot show the correct one, but I can show which it is NOT,' Judith replied.

Luna's head was drawn back to the mirror she had been drawn to before. She decided that was Judith's way of warning her off. She looked forward and studied the mirrors before her. She had to make a decision with her mother and grandmother.

"We're going to carry on looking; do we have a time limit?" Pearl asked.

"There isn't normally a limit, but we need to have decided by at least six p.m, that gives you around two hours. Is that long enough?" Thomas announced to the room.

"Well, I believe I've already chosen mine so I just have to wait until you have all made up your minds," Aura dismissed. She turned her back to them and watched the storm clouds roll in from the distance.

"Has anyone else chosen a clear definite?" Thomas asked.

"I think we may have," Monique replied, looking at the others. Pearl and Luna nodded.

"Jhordan?" Thomas said.

"Sorry?" Jhordan asked. He looked as if he had been in another world. Maybe he had been.

"Do you think you have chosen one?" Thomas asked.

"Yes," he replied. His eyes glazed over and it was like he had gone back into his own world again.

Thomas nodded and glided away from them. He positioned himself nearer to the door of the room. He closed his eyes and count to ten.

"So that's about the gist of it Percy," Donna said, finishing up the story.

"And you have finally spoken to Max," Percy asked.

"Y...Yes, but why would you ask that?" Donna stuttered.

"Oh Donna. You know that Gloria is a clairvoyant, she told me something like this was going to happen, and you know I believe everything she says, she has never let me down yet," Percy replied.

"So you knew Max was going to pretend to be my partner? Why didn't you warn me?" Donna cried.

"He swore us to secrecy, he didn't want you know until he was ready for you to, I'm sorry Donna," Percy replied. "I really wanted to let you know but Gloria took the phone off me until Max made contact to say it was safe."

Donna hung her head and sobbed, "I trusted you Percy. Trusted you with my life." With that, she hung up.

Savannah jogged over to her and threw her arms around her. "Are you Ok? Is Percy OK?"

"He's fine. He knew all along about Max. I can't believe he didn't tell me," Donna sobbed. "He's been there for me since I was a rookie."

"I'm sure he had his reasons, why don't we go and see him," Savannah said.

"I'd love to but I don't think I can face him just yet," Donna replied.

Just as the words had left her mouth, a huge crack of lightning lit up Flowerly Hall. Everyone turned to look. The shadows silhouetted the windows. Stood at the central window was Thomas. He nodded once and turned away.

"Why did he do that?" Donna asked.

"It's time. Come," Bruce said. He ran back into the house with everyone on his heels.

"Are you sure we should be going up there?" Sylvester asked as he crept along behind. "I'm not too sure that's a good idea y'know."

"Sylvester. Shut up. Just for once, please. I know what I'm doing," Bruce replied as calmly as he could. He didn't want to seem agitated, but he needed to know what was happening. Where was Aura, and Jhordan? He hadn't heard from them.

They took the outside staircase almost three steps at a time and piled through the top door, almost landing in a heap at Thomas's feet.

"Welcome!" Thomas smiled. "There was a slight change of plan. Please, follow me to the Western Wing?"

Thomas gestured for them to follow him; he kept his strides slow so everyone could keep up.

"What changed?" Savannah asked.

"Let's just say a certain someone had an influence on me," Thomas smiled at her.

Savannah's eyebrows rose with interest. "Which someone would that be?" She asked.

"A certain boy who is very lonely," he replied.

"Can the rules be changed?" Donna asked, joining in their conversation.

"Only I can change the rules. From what I'm led to believe from Luna, I was placed in charge of the spirits here. The evil that roams these halls holds them captive, but I am in charge." Thomas replied.

"Is it dangerous?" Sylvester squeaked from the back.

"Not if you follow my guidance. If you don't, well, that would be something you would have to contend with," Thomas replied.

Sylvester tried to blend in with the crowd but he still felt anxious. He watched Bruce walk up front with Thomas, Savannah and Donna walked behind them and he brought up the rear. He had a feeling he was being watched but he couldn't see anything or anyone around. He moved closer to the two women in front of him.

"So how are you feeling about Percy?" Savannah asked Donna.

"I don't know. I've known him too long to just throw away our friendship," Donna replied.

"I'm sure he will forgive anything you said to him earlier. You were in shock that he already knew," Savannah smiled. She threw her arm over Donnas' shoulder and gave her shoulder a squeeze.

"Thank you," Donna whispered.

It wasn't long before they reached the door to the Western Wing.

"Now, before we continue, I should explain the change in rules. We, well, I, have decided to allow three different picks of the mirrors," Thomas began.

"Wait, what mirrors?" Savannah asked.

"You obviously don't know the original rules. Normally there is only one person allowed to pick a mirror from our wall. If they choose the correct one, the chosen spirit will be free and the person who freed them will remain immortal. If they choose the wrong one, the evil entity that resides in that mirror will steal your soul and take you back with him. You will then cease to exist and remain here until you are freed. If he allows you to volunteer that is." Thomas explained.

"So what's different this time?" Donna asked.

"This time we have three 'teams' so to speak. Luna, her mother and her grandmother, Aura and young Jhordan," Thomas replied. "A certain young man told me how lonely he will be after all this is over. A certain someone will call off the spell she has on him and he will go back to living in darkness. He is scared," Thomas told them. "Don't tell him I told you though. He may be too proud to admit it to others."

"The secret is safe with us. I did feel that he didn't seem too happy with his situation, even though it was him who volunteered to help out. Even *I* didn't know how far Aura was going to push things," Bruce admitted. "I feel partly responsible."

"Me too. I think I may have been too harsh on him at times. I don't even know anything about his background," Sylvester replied.

"There is a lot both of you don't know about him, but that isn't for us to share. It has to come from him," Donna told them.

"Everyone has decided on their mirror. I felt compelled to allow you all to witness the decisions made. If you don't think you can witness it, please feel free to walk away now," Thomas informed them.

The group looked around at each other. In silent agreement they all nodded. They were ready to enter the room.

Chapter 42

"Where did he go Mum?" Luna asked Monique. "I don't think I can handle the tension anymore. I just want this over with.

Jhordan looked at Luna and his heart broke. He rushed to her and held her tight. "Remember, no matter what happens here tonight. I'll always be here. Whether that is in body or in soul." He whispered.

She smiled up at him. "Thank you."

"Oh honey, I'm sure he is just taking a breather. It's been a tough night, spirits need a break too I guess," Monique tried to lighten the mood a little. "Now Jhordan, how you feeling son?"

"I'm a little nervous Mrs Heart. If I'm honest, I don't even know which I will pick. I have committed myself to selecting the first mirror I lay my eyes on when he asks me. If I select the evil mirror, at least I will be close by to watch over Luna. If not and I choose another spirit, I will feel a little better at having released another, but I will then be condemned to the darkness again," Jhordan explained.

"Oh come now Jhordan. Even if you in the 'darkness' as you call it, you can always call for us. We are just a shout away," Pearl told him. "You will always be welcome in my head and in my house."

"Thank you all for being so kind to me. I don't deserve it really," he blushed.

"You didn't, but you have made up for it," Luna said as she stood on tip toes and kissed him on the cheek again.

"Urgh! Please, pass me a sick bucket," Aura spat. "It's like a family reunion. Jhordan isn't real! By the time this is all over, he'll be back to being DEAD!"

Just as Luna was about to launch into a tirade of abuse, the huge wooden door flew open and Thomas strode in, followed by Bruce, Donna, Savannah and Sylvester.

"Getting better acquainted are we?" Thomas laughed. "It really has been tough on you all, but now, the wait is over. Unless anyone wants to volunteer to go first, I'll pick someone at random."

"I'll go first," Luna said. "I want to get this over with. I don't mean to offend you Thomas, but I really want to get home."

"Ha, *IF* you get home!" Aura sneered.

"Ignore her honey," Monique said. She bent down to Luna's eye level. This one is on you sweetheart. We'll be here no matter what. I love you."

"I love you too. Both of you," Luna replied, tears streaking down her face. She turned towards the mirrors, closed her eyes and walked towards the golden mirror with a cherub on the back. The ribbon from the cherubs' ankle ran the length of the handle. She took a deep breath, stole one more glance around the room as if it were her last look at the people around her, and turned the mirror over.

The room fell silent, but nothing happened. There was no lightning, no puff of smoke, nothing. Finally, after a matter of seconds, Luna felt a tugging on the bottom of her dress. Looking down, she came face to face with a young girl, no more than around five or six.

"Thank you," the little girl whispered. "I can finally go and visit my parents now."

Luna broke down in tears and sunk to the ground.

"As you were first to select the mirror, you can be the first to freely leave," Thomas told her.

"Who did I release?" Luna asked. "I need to know."

Thomas debated telling her who the little girl was. He had never been asked before. Most just walked away after when nothing happened.

"That, my child, was Nemasia. She has been with us for around three years. Her half brother tied her to the back of his truck on a sled and sped down the hill. Unfortunately, she hit a bump in the road and was thrown from the sled. She landed half way down the side of the canyon. She succumbed to her injuries and the cold before he could reach her," Thomas explained.

"Oh that poor baby," Pearl wept. "I hope the boy wasn't held responsible?"

"I'm afraid he was. He admitted to the police that he tied her up and took her on that road deliberately. He wanted her out of their lives. His Dad had married her Mum and he didn't like having to share," Thomas replied. "He's been in prison ever since. Eight years if I remember correctly."

"Oh dear," Luna whispered as she watched Nemasia glide away and through the door.

"Shall we continue?" Thomas asked his guests.

"I guess," Jhordan replied. He looked down at the floor and raised his hand. "I'll go next."

"Actually, I will," Aura stated. "You can wait until last." She gave a sly smile, walked to the centre of the room and looked around at the people who had gathered to watch the proceedings. "As you are all here, it will give me great pleasure to see your faces when Jhordan here, is claimed by the evil within the mirror. I know the correct mirror, and that will be the one that I choose." Aura waited for the applause from Sylvester and Bruce, but when nothing was heard, she scolded them, "how can you not be pleased? It will mean that we are rid of him! I thought that was what you both wanted?"

"Aura, if you would like to select your mirror before Jhordan than please, be my guest," Thomas told her. He moved back towards the door and gestured for her to choose her mirror.

Aura sauntered over to the mirror that Luna had been eyeing up all night. She turned, smiled at everyone and picked it up, but she didn't look into it straight away. Instead, she walked with it the window and looked out over the rear of the house. "It's such a lovely garden. It's a shame this will be the last time I ever see it."

"Aura, look into the mirror," Thomas told her. "You wanted your turn and now you have it. You have everyone's attention."

"I do don't I?" She smiled. She turned the mirror over and looked into it.

Everyone shielded their eyes as a blinding light filled the room. There was a deep rumbling noise coming from deep within the house. As the rumble edged closer, Pearl grabbed Luna and Monique and hid under the dressing table. Donna and Savannah rugby tackled Jhordan to the floor, and Bruce pulled Sylvester away from the centre of the room just before a huge crack opened up. Aura stayed exactly where she was. A look of terror covered her face. Her eyes were wide and wildly looking for some sort of cover. She dropped the mirror and cowered under the large window.

From the crack in the floor, a dark mist began to emerge. It hissed and crackled as flames whipped up from the floor. As the crack grew wider, a pair of hands emerged, pulling whatever was connected to them up through the floor. A pair of the fieriest red eyes swept the room, bypassing Luna and her family, sweeping over Jhordan and the two detectives and rushing over Bruce and Sylvester. When it finally stopped searching, its eyes rested on Aura as she shielded herself from its glare. Its arms stretched out in front of it, grabbing at Aura until it finally connected with her feet. She screamed with all her breath.

"Get it off me!" She howled. "Stop it! Let me go! Bruce, Sylvester, help me!"

Thomas watched as the houses' evil entity dragged Aura from her hiding place and towards the widened crack in the floor. She tried so hard to stop the pulling force, even grabbed at the dressing table hiding Luna and her family. Pearl hauled them out of the way before Aura could drag the table away.

"What's happening?" Jhordan whispered.

"I don't know honey," Donna replied.

As quickly as the crack had appeared, Aura had been dragged down and the floor had closed up. It was as if nothing had happened. Everyone sat in stunned silence.

"What was that?" Luna asked as she broke away from Pearls grip.

"That was the evil. It doesn't have a name. It's just evil," Thomas replied. "Aura had been watching you the whole time Luna and she believed the mirror you set your eyes on earlier today was the correct one. How did you know it wasn't?"

Luna thought hard before she answered. "Judith. She told me she couldn't tell me the correct one, but she could show me one that it most certainly was NOT."

"Judith is a very wise woman. I have heard a lot about her but sadly, have never met her. The entity that guards the house never allowed her to visit, whether in spirit or human form," Thomas told her. He turned to reassure everyone that it was safe to re-emerge from their safe havens. "The evil has taken Aura. I guess she was right about not seeing the gardens again."

"Won't she see them? Even if she is trapped here?" Jhordan asked, clearly puzzled.

"Sadly not. The evil keeps the mirror choosers away from the windows, He says it attracts the wrong kind of people," Thomas told him. "Are you ready for your turn?"

Jhordan hung his head. He thought he would be OK with just releasing any spirit, but he really wanted to be able to live for real again.

He nodded quickly, "let's get it done."

Everyone stood together and watched as Jhordan walked to the first mirror that caught his eye. He lifted it from its place on the wall and walked to the centre of the room. He looked down at what had been the gigantic crack in the floor and sighed audibly. "At least I know I won't be going down there!" He tried to laugh. He looked at Luna. She looked back at him and smiled.

"I've loved getting to know you Luna. You are a lovely girl," Jhordan said as he turned the mirror over and peered inside. There was a breeze, and a puff of smoke clouded his view. As he lowered the mirror, he looked around. Nothing had changed but Luna and Pearl were looking towards the door.

"Did I do it?" Jhordan asked. He really wanted to be able to live forever, at least long enough to get to know Luna more.

"I'm afraid not young Jhordan," Thomas whispered.

"Who was that?" Luna asked as she pointed towards the door.

"That was Maddox. He's been here for, well, over twelve years if I remember correctly," Thomas replied. "Maddox was orphaned. His parents were tragically killed in a car accident. After he was passed between foster homes he got lost in the system and no one ever checked on him. When his grandparents came from Turkey to find him and take him home, the authorities had no idea where he had been placed. He was, eventually, found under the wing of the local cartel group. They had taken him in after finding him on the streets and, for want of a nicer way of explaining, used him to carry for them. When his grandparents asked the police to get involved, the cartel kingpin made him swallow up to three bags of cocaine and attempted to smuggle him off to Columbia." Thomas stopped for a moment and looked across at Savannah.

Everyone looked in her direction. She had tears streaming down her face. She didn't even make a move to cover her face. Bruce stepped towards her but she stepped back.

"Please, don't," Savannah said as she held her hands up in front of her. "I don't want pity or sympathy."

"You knew him," Thomas said.

Savannah nodded. "Yes. I didn't know him personally, but I was one of the lead officers before it was handed over. I found him."

"Found him where?" Donna asked. She walked over to Savannah and leaned against the wall next to her.

"A plane landed in Colombia. I was working there on an internship. I was on the tarmac waiting for the plane. My partner, rest his soul, confronted the pilot whilst I searched the plane. We didn't find anything in the main body of the plane, all the seats were empty," Savannah began to explain. Luna walked to her and touched her hand. Everything came to her in a rush;

"There's nothing here," Savannah announced. "I'm going to check the baggage hold."

"What makes you think anything will be there, they knew we would be waiting, probably dumped it as they flew," Marc replied.

"Well, I'm going to check, just in case," Savannah shouted as Marc walked away.

As she opened the cargo door, she flicked her torch on and swept it over the empty hold, 'exactly what Marc had predicted, empty,' she thought, but as she swept one last time, she noticed a bundle on the far side of the plane. She ducked down and walked over to it, preparing herself for an ambush. She rolled the bundle over and screamed.

Luna quickly let go of her hands and threw her arms around Savannah's neck. Savannah sobbed into Luna's hair.

"From the reaction I can tell that it was bad. Savannah, there is no need to continue," Thomas told her.

As Luna pulled back from Savannahs grip, she too had tears falling from her eyes. "You were not to blame. He doesn't blame you."

"Are you sure?" Savannah asked. "I blame myself. He had only been gone a matter of minutes. If I had thought to look in there first, I could have saved him."

Luna shook her head. "He told me the bags had burst more than ten minutes before they had landed. He felt it. He said he knew he was going to die, but he hoped he could have been reunited with his parents. Instead he was brought here and trapped."

"Oh Luna. If you can, please tell him that I am sorry," Savannah said.

"He can hear you," Luna whispered.

Savannah smiled through her tears. She thought back to the years of sleepless nights and arguments with Christian. She felt like a weight had been lifted from her shoulders.

"Where's Jhordan?" Thomas asked.

No-one had noticed Jhordan slip away from the room.

Chapter 43

Jhordan began a slow walk back to his temporary house and waited for the spell to wear off. He knew it wouldn't be long and he didn't want Luna to witness him fading away. She had had so much happen to her over the past few hours and days, that she didn't deserve that. He let himself in through the back door and made his way up to his makeshift room. He laid on the bed and stared out of the skylight. The sky was cloudless and the stars twinkled above him. He didn't know if he had a faith or believed in any type of God but he silently wished he could have more time. He closed his eyes and let sleep claim him. He felt rested. He felt like he had accomplished something, even if it wasn't releasing Edith.

"Where could he have gone?" Thomas asked. "I didn't see him go anywhere."

"I think we were a little too engrossed in Savannahs' recollections to notice anything," Monique replied.

"We have to find him. He will be scared," Luna said with a panic. "Bruce, where would he go?"

Bruce was still shocked about what had happened to Aura. He hadn't spoken a word since. "Erm, I guess he would have gone back to the house. I don't know any other place he would go."

"Then we start there. What do we do when we find him?" Pearl asked Thomas.

Thomas looked at Monique and smiled but uttered no words. She nodded her head once. She knew what she would have to do when she found him.

"Bruce, take us there?" Luna asked.

Bruce nodded and led them out of the room and back out into the night. Sylvester hung behind the group. He felt like he didn't belong with them. He had been so nasty to Jhordan before, he wanted to apologise but feared he would be rejected.

"Syl, you OK?" Bruce asked.

"Yeah. I just don't feel like I should be one looking for him, y'know? I was horrible to him after Aura brought him back. I didn't mean to be," Sylvester replied.

"Look, Jhordan is a clued up kid. I'm sure he didn't take any offence, and even if he did, I'm pretty sure he would have forgiven you by now. Especially after you helped us with Aura tonight," Bruce told him.

"Maybe Bruce, but I feel for the kid. I mean, he was trying to do right by Aura, but I think, he kinda likes the girl," Sylvester said.

"I think you're right. He wants to get to know her, but he knows his time is nearly up," Bruce said as he hung his head. "I wish there was something we could do."

Bruce walked side by side with Sylvester as they made their way back to the house Aura had taken over.

"What was that all about back there?" Pearl asked Monique.

"What was what?" She replied.

"The look between you and Thomas," Pearl said.

"Nothing really. Well, it's something but I can't say, not yet anyway," Monique told her. "Let's find him first and worry about the rest later."

Pearl didn't ask any more questions, she watched as Luna looked around the estate. She didn't recognise any of it.

"Are you OK sweetheart?" Pearl called.

"Yes. I just feel sorry for Jhordan. He will go back to being lonely. Aura really was nasty to him," Luna replied. She didn't look back at her mother or grandmother but Pearl knew she was hurting.

"It's number 46, the blue door," Bruce told Donna and Savannah who had been walking a little bit ahead.

"I see it. Do you think he would have come back here, of all places?" Donna asked.

"It's the only place he knows," Bruce replied.

"It's certainly too far away from where he died," Savannah commented.

"Yeah I can see your point. It would be the obvious place though. Either that or he didn't think we would come looking for him," Monique said.

Bruce and Sylvester took the back door, whilst the others tried the front door, sadly it was locked.

"Look," Luna whispered, pointing to the open window. "Boost me up and I'll climb through."

"Be careful," Monique told her.

Pearl and Monique both hoisted her up and she slid through with ease.

Luna stood in a small room, no bigger than a wardrobe. She felt around for a handle of some sort. Upon finding it, she gently opened the door and almost frightened Bruce.

"Sorry," she whispered.

Bruce smiled at her and pointed up the stairs. At the top, there was a small sliver of light coming from under one of the doors.

"It's from the skylight in Jhordans' room, I think it might be better if you go up," Bruce said.

Luna nodded and began to make her way up the stairs but she turned around half way up and asked Bruce to let everyone else in at the front door. He nodded and went to the door.

"Jhordan, can I come in?" Luna whispered as she lightly tapped on the door.

"I guess so," Jhordan replied.

Luna opened the door slowly as Jhordan sat up on his bed. He gestured for her to sit with him.

"Are you OK?" She asked as she sat on the edge of the bed.

"I don't really know. I wanted to be able to live forever. I wanted to be able to be a boy again, to be able to finish school. I wanted to get to know you better," he told her.

"It would be nice to get to know you too. I know we didn't get off to the best of starts, and I, now, know that you were only trying to help someone you thought was a friend. I was horrible to you at times and I'm sorry," Luna told him. She let her hand lay gently on top of his.

"What happens now?" Jhordan asked. "Does Bruce know how long the spell will last?"

"I don't know. Why don't we go downstairs and ask him? Everyone is here. Well, everyone except Thomas. He can't leave Flowerly Hall, but I'm sure he'd love it if you came back with us. We have few things to fix up there before everything is complete," Luna said.

Jhordan thought for a moment. He tried to remember what Aura had told him about the spell, but he couldn't remember anything. He was sure she mentioned how long it would last. He stood up and offered his hand to Luna. "Shall we?"

Luna smiled at him and nodded. They walked out of the door and down the stairs. Bruce was sat in the only lone chair in the room, right under the window. Sylvester was sat at the dining table with Savannah and Donna and Monique and Pearl had the sofa. There was idle chatter going on, but Aura's name was mentioned more than once.

"So that's it? She's gone?" Sylvester asked. "What happens to us?"

"I don't know yet mate. We just have to wait and see," Bruce replied. He was staring at the floor.

Luna cleared her throat as they entered the room and everyone stood to greet Jhordan.

"You OK lad?" Bruce asked him.

Jhordan nodded. "I think so. Bruce, do you know how long this spell will last before I'm sent back?"

"I couldn't say lad," Bruce said, shaking his head. "We are as much in the dark on that as you are."

"I wish I knew how long I had left. Do you think Thomas would know?" Jhordan asked Monique.

"We can always head back and ask him, if you really want to know," Monique replied. "That's up to you though."

"Can we? I need to know. I have to make time for everyone before I go," Jhordan told them all. "Can we go now?"

Pearl linked arms with Jhordan and looked him deep in the eyes, "let's go. Who knows what he might say."

"Thank you," Jhordan replied.

They walked out together, arm in arm. Monique held on to Luna tightly. "You did well baby," she told her.

"Thanks Mum. I really like him. I just wish I hadn't been so nasty to him before," Luna replied.

"Let's not think about that now. Let's focus on getting him some answers and then we can work out the rest," Monique said.

Everyone began to make their way back to Flowerly Hall. It had gradually gotten darker since they left, so they were more conscious of their surroundings. Every little noise made Savannah jump.

"Not familiarized yourself with the city noises yet 'Vannah?" Donna laughed.

"That is not funny," Savannah smiled. "It will take me a while."

"So are you staying up here now?" Donna asked, clearly surprised by what Savannah had said.

"Christian and I have decided to stay here. It seems a better place than where we were to raise a family," Savannah replied, placing her hand across her stomach.

"What! Since when?" Donna almost screamed.

"I'm only a few weeks gone at the moment. Christian is over the moon," Savannah smiled.

"I bet he is! And how do you feel about it?" Donna asked.

"I feel good. Maybe coming back here was meant to be?" Savannah said. She looked ahead of her and watched as Pearl and Jhordan walked together. "I believe they may be lifelong friends!"

Donna smiled, "Pearl is one of a kind."

As Donna spoke the words, her phone rang. She plucked it from her jacket pocket. "It's Martha."

"Hey!" Donna answered.

"Hey, listen I just thought I'd let you know. I've decided to put the deposit down on that house we looked at," Martha said.

"Oh yeah. How come?" Donna replied. Her eyebrows furrowing as she spoke.

"Well, I just got home and there was a message on the answer machine from the adoption agency. They have a baby for us," Martha squealed.

"Wait what! Why has so much good news happened in one night?" Donna exclaimed.

"What else has happened? Did you crack the case?" Martha asked.

"Kind of, we are just tying up loose ends now, but Savannah is pregnant!" Donna said.

"Oh that's fantastic news! Tell her I'm so happy for her and Christian," Martha replied.

"I will. Look I gotta go, I shouldn't be too late tonight, but if I'm not home by twelve, go to bed. I'll be quiet when I come in," Donna told her, and with that she ended the call.

"Wow, so much great news," Jhordan said to Pearl. "It seems everyone has their life on track. I wish it was that easy for me."

"The night is young. Let's see what Thomas has to say. If you have time, you can come back to mine and I will make sure you and Luna have the time you need to get to know one another," Pearl smiled.

"Thank you. I wish I had known my grandmother like how Luna knows you," Jhordan replied.

As they arrived at the gates of Flowerly Hall, its exterior had changed. Gone were the rusty gates, gone were the weeds covering the garden. It was a mass of freshly blooming flowers.

Chapter 44

Thomas watched as the crowd below admired his handy work. He wished that the evil had allowed him to do this before. It would have been great for the reputation of the house. People wouldn't cross the street to avoid it gates. There has been a stigma surrounding this house every since the last owners, maybe now, people will come to love it once more.

As Thomas turned back to face the room, he noticed something written on the large mirror over the fireplace.

'I will take my leave from this house.

The spirits residing here are yours to command or free as you see fit.

Aura will remain with me for eternity.'

Thomas was confused. The evil has never given up occupancy of the house under any circumstances. What could have made it leave so suddenly? He looked for more clues. He searched the chest of drawers. The dressing table, even under the bed but nothing sprang to life. He would need to be very cautious, just in case the evil returned.

He could hear voices from the main entranceway. He walked briskly towards the overhanging balcony.

"Come up! Come up! How do you like the new decor?" Thomas announced.

"It's beautiful. I've never seen it so stunning," Pearl replied.

"I'm glad you approve Mrs Heart. Luna, everyone, please, join me in the Eastern Wing. We have work to do," Thomas smiled.

They looked around at each others, hoping someone knew what he meant, but everyone looked as confused as everyone else. They began their ascent to the upper floors. The staircase had been rebuilt and the paintwork was stunning. The spiral floor tiles had been polished to a brilliant shine. It was as if the house had been brought to life once more.

"I think I may just come back and visit this house once in a while," Luna whispered.

"You would be more than welcome my child. Now, to the Eastern Wing," Thomas commanded.

Everyone followed him as he led the way. It was so different to the Western Wing, like the polar opposite. The Western Wing had been dark and menacing. It had a thick atmosphere, as if everything that lurked in there was evil. The Eastern Wing, however, was full of light and energy. There were bright coloured walls, fairy lights around every dressing table mirror and airy rooms. The atmosphere here was somewhere you would want to stay.

"Please, this room," Thomas gestured to a large room at the end of a pastel yellow hallway.

As everyone entered, Thomas closed the door behind them. The room was large enough to hold a school disco. It had soft baby blue walls and a large window, which, had it been daytime, would have let in an abundance of sunlight, which probably explained why the flowers in there were so tall.

Luna looked around. She looked out of the window, hoping to see more of the grounds, but with it being well past ten p.m, she couldn't see anything. Next she went to the dressing table on the far wall. It had lights that circled the mirror and the contents were well organised. As she lifted her hand to touch the brush, her inner voice told her not to, these were not hers to handle so she slowly lowered her hand.

"What is going to happen in here?" Jhordan asked nervously.

"Nothing bad, that much I can say," Thomas replied. "Please, if you could, all gather in the centre of the room."

Luna rose from the seat in from of the mirror and stood next to Jhordan. She linked her fingers with his and smiled at him. "I'm sure it will all be fine," she told him.

He hoped so.

"I know you have all returned for various reasons and I hope I will be able to answer any questions you have regarding the events of this evening. Where shall we start?" Thomas asked.

"Do you know how long we have left before Aura's spell wears off?" Sylvester asked.

"That was on my list of things to cover but it was a little further down the list. I will get to that," Thomas answered.

"Will Aura be coming back?" Luna asked.

"That is a simple answer and its no. The evil has taken her for eternity, so there will be no chance for her to return, which means, essentially, you are all rid of her," Thomas told them.

"What does that mean for those left behind?" Pearl asked.

Monique stepped forward, "I believe it's time for my speech?" She asked Thomas.

"The floor is yours," Thomas said as he stepped back.

"With Aura gone, the magic she placed upon those left behind will, eventually wear off. The time limit for that is unknown. It, now, comes down to choices. You each have a choice, Bruce, Sylvester and Jhordan. You can decide to allow the spell to wear off in its own time and, inevitably, go back to your spirit form, or, and you must think logically before you make this decision, you can choose to stay in human form. Now, before you jump to your choice," she said as Jhordan painted a smile across his face, "you must remember that you will eventually die. Now, you all know how this feels so you will, no doubt, be prepared, but you will eventually go back to the other side."

Bruce was shocked. Never had he been given such a choice. He looked at Sylvester who, for once, had a sincere smile on his face. He was, Bruce believed, happy.

"We will ask each of you for your answers soon. This gives you time to decide truly what you want," Thomas told them.

"How long do we have?" Bruce asked.

"However long you need, or at least until sun-up," Thomas smiled. "I understand it is a tough choice to make, especially considering how long you have been gone."

Bruce nodded and walked towards the far side of the room. Sylvester joined him.

"Have any idea what you're gonna do?" Sylvester asked as he sat on the floor at Bruce's feet.

"I don't know. I'd love to be able to live. Watch Jhordan live out his childhood at least, if he decides to," Bruce replied looking over at Jhordan who had promptly plonked onto the floor next to Luna.

Jhordan had his head in his hands. It hurt to think so much. He'd never had to before, not this hard anyway.

"Do you need some time alone to think?" Luna asked him. "I can leave you to think."

"Please stay with me," he replied.

"OK, I'll stay, but I won't make your choice for you," Luna laughed.

"Is this what the glance was about earlier?" Pearl asked Monique.

"I'm sorry I couldn't say anything," Monique replied. "We had to get Jhordan back here, otherwise this wouldn't have worked."

"I fully understand," Pearl replied. "It will be hard on Luna if he decides to leave."

"I don't think he will," Monique said. "What's happened today has been hard on him. He has never wanted any harm to come to Luna and when he figured out what was happening, he tried to stop it, or at the very least he tried to get help. I think, he will stay for certain."

"What about the other two?" Pearl asked as they looked over at Bruce and Sylvester.

"Sylvester, well, he's been gone for a fair few years now, sixty to be exact. It wouldn't surprise me in the slightest if he chose not to stay. I overheard him talking to Bruce. He feels guilty that he never treated the boy well," Monique told her. "Bruce, well, I think he has a soft sop for Jhordan, so I think he might just stay if Jhordan does."

"You think he will step up?" Pearl asked.

"I could almost guarantee it," Monique replied.

Thomas had stepped away from the madness that had descended upon the room and watched the living at work. He wished so hard that he had survived and been able to save Penelope, but he had failed. He noticed how protective Monique and Pearl were with Luna and wondered where her father was. He would never pry; only listen if anyone wanted to tell.

"How are things going?" A voice asked from beside him.

"Ah Maximilian! Lovely to see you again!" Thomas exclaimed. "How are you?"

"I'm good. I just wanted to drop in quickly. Any chance Judith could visit Edith? Even if it's just once?" Max asked.

"Give me some time to finish up here and we'll talk. The evil has relocated. I have some other things to do before the end of play here. Why don't you stick around?" Thomas offered.

"I might just do that. She can't see me right?" Max asked.

"Not unless you show yourself or want to be seen," Thomas laughed.

"Then I'll stick around for a while, maybe just glide about the room," Max giggled.

"Make sure Pearl and Luna don't give you away!" Thomas warned him.

"I'm sure I can trust them," Max replied. He glided over to where Monique stood with Pearl and placed his finger over his lips. Pearl's eyes understood the instruction. He did the same with Luna. Luna tried not to smile but it reached her mouth before she could stop it.

"What's got you?" Donna asked as she sat next to her and Jhordan on the floor.

"I just thought of something funny," Luna lied. "it was something my Dad used to say to me."

"You wanna share it?" Donna asked.

"Well, he used to help Mum with the crosswords in the morning, you know, before he died, and he would always get the answer before we did, even if it was hard. He said that it's always good to know a lot of words, even if you don't know the meaning. It makes you seem smart; you just have to hope the other person doesn't know what you're saying," Luna shrugged. "Sometimes I think he was right, other times I think he just wanted us to think he was smart." Luna laughed.

"Your Dad sounds like quite the guy," Donna replied.

"He is. He really is a great guy," Jhordan told her. "He misses Luna a lot."

"Well, I'll leave you both to talk for a while," Donna said as she began to stand up.

"Is it true that you and your wife are adopting a baby?" Luna asked. "Sorry, I heard you on the phone earlier."

"That's right we are. I hope to be able to bring them up to enjoy the world and not be scared," Donna told her.

"My Mum says that. She never wants me to be scared of anything but you can't protect them from everything. Make sure they know what the real world is like too," Luna told her.

"I certainly will," Donna smiled.

As she stood up, she felt a cold breeze past her face. She looked towards the window but saw that it was still closed. She then remembered where she was, this house was filled with spirits.

"So, what are you thinking?" Luna asked Jhordan.

"I really want to stay, but, how would that make you feel?" Jhordan asked her.

Luna looked at him. "This isn't about me. This is about you."

Bruce snapped away from watching Jhordan when Sylvester called him.

"Bruce, I have an idea. Maybe something that will make the pair of them happy," he said.

"What is that?" Bruce asked.

"I want to check it will work first," Sylvester replied. "Wait here."

Sylvester approached Thomas slowly. "Can I ask a brief question about our decision?"

"Go ahead. I'll answer if I can," Thomas replied.

"Hypothetically speaking, if one of us wanted to gift our choice to someone, would it be allowed?" Sylvester asked.

"Who do you have in mind?" Thomas asked.

"Well, I've had my time. Nothing would be the same for me if I came back, but young Luna there," Sylvester glanced her way. "She could do with someone a little more special back in her life."

"You would be willing to give up a life to bring someone back for her?" Thomas said.

"Yes. I would. Would it be allowed?" Sylvester asked.

"I don't see why not. Something as noble as that deserves something good in return," Thomas stated. "What would you wish?"

Sylvester was stumped. He hadn't thought it would be rewarded. "Can I get back to you on that one?"

"I have to know by the time I ask for your answers," Thomas told him. "Go off and have a think."

Sylvester turned from Thomas and walked back to Bruce. He sat down on the floor with his back against the wall.

"So, what's the deal?" Bruce asked.

"What reward do you think I should ask for?" Sylvester countered.

"Reward for what?" Bruce said sounding confused.

"I've decided. I'm not going to take the offer to live," Sylvester replied. "But I'm not telling you anything else."

Bruce was stunned. He had expected Sylvester to jump at the chance of staying alive, but he watched Sylvester rise from his seated position on the floor and walk over to the large window. He hoped his friend had made the right decision.

Savannah had been watching the action from her seat on the bed. She didn't want to throw herself in the mix. She didn't really feel part of it all, nothing phenomenal had happened to her throughout this whole ordeal. She felt like she was riding the strangest rollercoaster ever built.

"Ms Shepherd?" Thomas asked softly so as not to frighten her.

"Yes, sorry, I was daydreaming," Savannah smiled. "How can I help you?"

"May I?" Thomas gestured to the bed.

"Absolutely," she replied.

Thomas sat beside her and watched from her vantage point. "It does seem so different from the other side of things, doesn't it?"

"It certainly does. I don't feel I have been back here long enough to make myself fully involved. I left a few years back and moved south with my husband," Savannah told him.

"Indeed you did. You once had a home here with your parents, but spent most of you time with your grandparents, Mollie and Edward Robertson," Thomas said.

"How did you know that?" Savannah asked him. She was visibly shocked that he knew her grandparents.

"I didn't mean to startle you my dear. In fact, your grandparents visit your parents' house regularly. Where other spirits cannot visit here, I make it my duty to visit the cemetery once or twice a week. Mollie is very proud of you," Thomas smiled.

"I always wanted to make her proud. She was a hard woman to please," Savannah laughed. "Thank you, for visiting them. I feel bad that I haven't been back there yet. I'll make sometime soon. I'm sure they'll want to hear about this little one," she said, placing her hand over her tummy.

"Ahh, indeed they will. Take care Ms Shepherd," Thomas said as he bowed his head and left her to sit.

Thomas walked back to his place and cleared his throat. "Gentlemen, have you all made a decision?"

Jhordan looked over at Bruce and Sylvester. They all nodded.

"Very well, if we could all gather in the centre of the room," Thomas said. "Before we begin, Sylvester, if I might have a short word with you?"

Sylvester walked up to Thomas and whispered something in his ear. Thomas nodded in agreement and Sylvester walked back to his place next to Bruce.

"If anyone would like to volunteer their answer, it would save me embarrassing someone," Thomas laughed.

"I'll go first, if that's OK with you both?" Bruce said.

"Go ahead," Jhordan replied. "I'm a little nervous if I'm honest."

Bruce squeezed his shoulder and smiled at him. "I'd like to remain in the living form. I feel I have some more to give back to this world before I'm gone again."

"Duly noted Mr Stanley, please wait on my left," Thomas gestured.

Jhordan stepped forward. "Can I say something?"

"Absolutely. You hold the audience in your hands young man," Thomas said as he stepped back to allow Jhordan to take centre stage.

"I made this decision based on a special set of people. One of whom I'd really like to get to know better. I was silly in my past life. I know, now, not to mess with spirits. I'd love to be able to continue living and be a great friend to Luna and her family, who have all accepted me even when I was working against them," Jhordan said.

"Wise words Master Bell, please, join Bruce to my left," Thomas told him.

All eyes fell on Sylvester. He had thought long and hard about his choice and he was going to stick to it. He owed it to them. They had helped him see the error of his ways and had given him a chance to fix what he had done wrong.

"Sylvester Whittleford, please, step forward," Thomas asked.

Sylvester held his head high and stepped forward. He kept his eyes on Thomas the whole time.

"Your answer, if you don't mind," Thomas said.

"I would like to bypass the gift of life and pass this onto another, if I may," Sylvester replied.

There was a collective gasp which radiated around the room.

"And to whom may I ask do you wish to bestow this gift?" Thomas asked.

"I wish to pass this on to Spencer Heart. I have lived my life and been gone sixty years. There is nothing left for me here. I have watched my children grow and I don't wish for any man to miss his children's lives. Therefore,

if it is at all possible, I want to pass this on to him,"
Sylvester replied as he looked from Luna, to Monique
and to Pearl.

"Very well. Please, stand to my right," Thomas told
him. "Each participant has made their choice. All that is
left is to grant those desires. Monique, if you will,"
Thomas said.

Monique stepped forward and hugged Sylvester. "Thank
you. You have no idea how much this means to us," she
whispered.

"I think I do," Sylvester replied. "Do what you need to
do."

"Sylvester has, as his reward for his noble gift, requested
to be buried next to his wife. He is currently in a grave
about eight rows east of her," Thomas said.

"That can be arranged," Donna said from the back of the
room. "Leave that one with me."

Thomas nodded.

"Are you both ready?" Monique asked Jhordan and
Bruce.

They looked at each other and over to Sylvester. Jhordan
took a step forward and stretched out his hand.

"That was a really kind thing to do for Luna and her family. Thank you," he said.

Sylvester shook Jhordans hand. "Make sure you take care of them and him," he said, pointing at Bruce.

Jhordan smiled and covered his laugh with a cough, "I will."

"Can you do me first?" Sylvester asked. "I'd like to rest."

"Sure. Close your eyes," Monique whispered. She kissed him on the cheek, closed her eyes and whispered, "Take this soul and rest him well. Allow him peace and quiet. Protect him and remember him."

There was a flash of light, which illuminated the room and lasted mere seconds before everyone unshielded their eyes and Sylvester was gone. Jhordan allowed a solitary tear to race down his cheek.

"Don't worry young man, you will see him again soon," Thomas said as he placed his hand on Jhordans shoulder. "Not too soon though. You need to live for a while first."

Chapter 45

Max was stunned. Donna and Martha were going to adopt a baby. It was the last thing he expected Donna to do. He remembered when she was younger, probably around sixteen or seventeen; she swore she was never having children. That was when she openly told him and their father that she was gay. Max hadn't fully believed her. He flew into a rage about how it was wrong and that she just hadn't found a decent guy yet. He never fully accepted who she was, until after he died. He watched her from the other side as she lived out her life and married Martha.

He watched as she promised to carry out the request of Sylvester Whittleford. She had grown up and become a woman. She was now about to become a mother to someone else's child.

He was proud of her.

Luna felt someone's eyes on the back of her head. She turned her head slightly and spotted Max standing at the back of the room. She smiled at him and he glided towards her.

"I need you to tell Donna something," Max said to her.

Luna nodded.

"I need you tell her how proud I am of her and that I'm sorry I never approved of her before I died," he said.

Luna nodded again.

"Thank you," Max said as he glided to the back of the room once more.

"Are you OK sweetie?" Pearl asked Luna.

"I'm fine. A little tired but I'm fine," Luna replied.

"And Max?" Pearl asked.

"He wants me to pass on a message to Donna. I'll do it after Mum is finished here," Luna told her. She focused her attention back on Jhordan and Bruce.

They stood shoulder to shoulder as if waiting for instructions in the Army.

"Relax guys," Monique laughed. "It won't be anywhere near as bright as that!"

Jhordan smiled but he couldn't bring himself to laugh.

"Honey, are you OK?" Monique asked him.

"Not really," he replied.

"Talk me through the last time this happened," Monique asked. She stood next to him and let him speak. She didn't interrupt him at all.

"It felt weird. Like something was being forced down on me. I felt pressure here," he said, pointing to his chest. "Like someone pushing down on me. I didn't like it, and I know I said I really want to stay alive, I hope it doesn't feel like that again."

Bruce felt horrible. He knew how Aura had done it to Jhordan. It wasn't the same as when she did it to him and Sylvester. She was rougher with Jhordan.

"I know how she did it. It wasn't the same as with me and Syl. She made it feel worse for Jhordan, but I figured out why. Jhordan was so eager to please her that he wouldn't say a bad word against her, not at first anyway," Bruce began to explain.

Luna could see Jhordan getting upset so she stepped forward to comfort him but was stopped by Thomas. She looked up at him with a questioning look.

"For him to experience real life, he has to understand real emotions," Thomas told her. "He knows you are here for him."

"I don't like seeing people upset," Luna whispered.

"I know you don't but sometimes we have to let people show their emotions for them to understand what happened to them. You just being nearby will be enough to comfort him," Thomas replied.

Luna stepped back but made sure Jhordan could see her face. He needed to know she was there. She needed him to know.

"How did it work with you Bruce?" Monique asked.

"It was such a long time ago, but I do remember it. She had somehow perfected a spell that her mother had taught her, one where she could bring the dead back to life. She already had our bodies, us and Monty," Bruce began.

"You mean that evil spirit was once an associate of hers?" Monique asked.

"Far from an associate. Monty would always speak his mind. Aura believed she was the leader of this little company, as she called it, but Monty would always voice his opinion. One day he went too far and she buried him alive. That's when she took Jhordans spirit," Bruce told her. "Monty must have gotten angry in the afterlife and been sent here, but when he knew it was Aura, I think he fed her power because he knew she would over step and mess up, then he knew he could take her and get his own revenge."

"I think you might just be right," Thomas boomed from his standing place next to Luna.

"Do you still want to do this Jhordan? It will be nothing like it was with Aura," Monique asked.

Jhordan nodded. "Yes, I still want to do this."

Monique smiled and stepped back. "So, if you both would like to close your eyes. I can assure you that this will not hurt a bit."

Bruce grabbed Jhordans hand. "I won't let go until it's over. I'm going to be there for you, every day going forward."

Jhordan smiled at him and closed his eyes. He didn't trust his voice to not crack when he spoke.

Luna watched on as her mother spread her arms wide. A pair of white wings emerged from her back. Luna was shocked. She didn't know her Mum had wings.

Monique took a deep breath in and closed her eyes. She whispered in one breath, "Pass the right to life to the two before me and bless them with friends and family."

Her wings flapped twice and the room filled with feathers. She plucked two from the air and handed one each to Jhordan and Bruce. As they took the feather from her, they felt a rush of wind pass over them.

Jhordan was the first to open his eyes. He looked at Monique's wings and was stunned. "I didn't know you were an angel," he said.

"Oh I wish I was an angel, they have a lot more power," she laughed. "I'm known as a Giver. We give to people more than we take."

Bruce opened his eyes when he heard Jhordan speak. "I don't feel any different, are you sure it worked?"

Monique laughed harder this time. "I'm more than certain that it has worked. If it didn't, I wouldn't be here. I'd be up in front of the High Priest and being demoted."

"Does this mean I'm fully alive? That it won't wear off?" Jhordan asked.

"Absolutely. You will live until it is your time to die. Both of you," Monique told them.

Jhordan hugged Bruce hard. "We finally get to live!"

Bruce smiled. He had never smiled so much before. "Why don't you go and see Luna," he told Jhordan.

"Are you sure?" Jhordan asked.

"I'm sure. I need to talk to Monique for a second," Bruce replied, pushing Jhordan away with a laugh.

"OK," Jhordan laughed. "But no kissing! Her husband will be back soon!"

Bruce laughed as Jhordan ran over to Luna and threw his arms around her; they toppled over on to the floor in a fit of laughter.

"What did you want to talk to me about Bruce?" Monique pulled him back into reality.

"So, going forward. How does all this work?" Bruce asked. "Can I get guardianship; I don't know what I'm doing."

"Don't worry Bruce," Monique said as she laid her hand on his shoulder. "It's all taken care of." Monique produced a rolled up piece of paper and handed it to Bruce. "Jhordan is now your son."

"Just like that?" Bruce asked. He was confused at how that could happen so fast.

"Just like that," Monique mimicked. "Now, go and enjoy your life!"

Bruce thanked her and went to show Jhordan the paperwork.

"You did well sweetheart," Pearl gushed from behind her. "I know we didn't get on well to start with, and I'm sorry for how I've treated you all these years. You really are a Heart!"

"Oh Pearl, stop. You'll have me crying my glitter tears," Monique laughed. She pulled Pearl in for a hug and held on a little tighter.

"Do you think they will be able to bring Spencer back?" Pearl whispered. "I'm fine if they can't."

"I don't know. I guess it's a waiting game for now. Why don't we head off home and see what the future brings?" Monique replied, rubbing her hands on Pearl's back.

Pearl nodded and slowly let go of Monique. She scooped Luna up into the air and invited Jhordan and Bruce for something to eat.

As they left the Eastern Wing, Monique lagged behind.

"What is it?" Thomas whispered. "Something is bothering you."

"I'm sceptical. I don't know if you or anyone can bring Spencer back. It doesn't work the same way as it did for Bruce and Jhordan," Monique confessed.

"It is out of your hands now. Go and be with your family and remember, if it's meant to be then it will happen, but rest for now. You have had a very long day," Thomas told her.

Monique nodded and went to catch up with her family.

Donna and Savannah had left the room a little earlier than the Heart family and were standing by their car. As Luna exited Flowerly Hall, she ran to Donna.

"I have a message for you," Luna whispered. She pulled Donna down to her level and whispered what Max had told her earlier in the night.

Donna was left with tears in her eyes. She had forgotten how many times she had wanted Max to be proud of her. How she had always seeked his approval. Now she had it. She couldn't contain her tears.

"He's finally proud of me. After all this time!" Donna cried.

Savannah knelt down beside Donna. She had come to think of her as a best friend more than a work colleague. Savannah put her arm around Donnas shoulder, lent in and whispered, "I want you both be this little ones godmother?"

Chapter 46

"So what happens now Thomas?" Max asked as he emerged from the shadows.

"Now? Well, I don't know about you but I'm exhausted. How are your energy levels?" Thomas asked.

"Not as good as I wanted. I need to know. Will Monique get her husband back? And if so, how will she explain it to everyone?" Max asked. "It would seem rather strange don't you think?"

Thomas thought for a moment. He hadn't anticipated the repercussions of raising someone from the dead so soon after their death. How would Monique explain things? Would he remember anything about his death?

"These are bridges I will have to look at crossing but right now, I need to rest and restore my depleting energy levels. I suggest you do the same. And Max, if you pass by Judith, encourage her to visit," Thomas said. He then faded away and back into the loneliness.

It wasn't dark and scary where Thomas resided. In fact, it was rather bright and airy, but it was lonely. Thomas craved another spirits company. He had spoken to Edith a few times since she had arrived. They had been placed in separate areas of the house, but now the evil had left, he could roam the house with ease. He went in search of Edith.

"Where are you Edith?" Thomas called out.

There was no reply.

"Edith?" Thomas called again. "Are you here?"

There was a giggle from a room down the corridor from his. He opened the door and listened. He could hear two women talking and laughing. He stood outside the door with a smile across his face.

"I know you're out there Thomas. Come on in!" Edith called.

Thomas smiled to himself and opened the door. "I didn't want to disturb you both. I called out for you."

"We know, we could hear you. Now, come and sit with us, we're catching up," Judith replied. She patted the seat next to her.

Thomas sat down and listened as they spoke about their childhoods. It became emotional, especially when they got to the part about Edith's death.

"I wish I could have done something to save you that day," Judith told her. "I've felt guilty my whole life."

"Oh Judith! There was nothing anyone could do. It was my fate. I know that now," Edith told her as she hugged her tight.

"What do you mean by that?" Judith asked.

"I feel that I was chosen to go. I don't think I had a choice in how I went, and believe me it wasn't pleasant, but I think it was meant to be," Edith said.

The two women pulled out of their embrace to see Thomas smiling.

"What has put a smile on that face of yours?" Edith asked.

"It's just lovely to see you both reconnected again. I tried so hard to be able to get you both together," Thomas replied.

"Well, we are back together now," Judith smiled.

"I'm going to recharge. I'll see you both soon I hope," he said. He rose from his seat, took one last look at the sisters and left the room.

"Are you OK Luna?" Jhordan asked as they got closer to Pearls house.

"No. No, I'm not. I have to go back," she replied, turning on her heel and racing back to Flowerly Hall.

"Luna! Where are you going?" Monique called after her.

"I have to go back! Something isn't right," Luna shouted back. "I won't be long!"

Luna ran as fast as her short legs would allow her. Sadly for her, she had inherited her mothers' short stature, but she ran as fast as she could and within minutes she had arrived back at the gates of Flowerly Hall.

She ran in through the front door and up the spiral staircase, taking two steps at a time.

"Luna, wait up!" Jhordan called. He had followed her, wanting to make sure she was OK.

"Jhordan, you didn't have to come," she told him. "I wouldn't have been long."

"I know, but I needed to make sure you were OK," he replied.

Luna smiled. "Come on, I need to find Thomas."

As soon as the name had left her lips, he appeared before her.

"What appears to be the rush? Couldn't it have waited until tomorrow?" Thomas asked.

"No, I'm sorry. You said that Edith's soul was trapped in a looking glass, but I overheard you tell Max to bring

Judith to see Edith. How would she see her?" Luna questioned.

"I can see that this is something you feel quite strongly about, why don't you come and sit with me whilst I try and explain it a little better," William told her.

He led them both to one of the larger living rooms, complete with a built in library. Luna was amazed by how many books were held on the shelves. She scanned some of the titles; *A Midsummer Night's Dream, The Lion, Witch and The Wardrobe, Prince Caspian, The Pit and The Pendulum.*

Luna was surprised. There were so many more but she didn't have time to read them all. She sat on the sofa that Thomas had gestured to. Thomas walked around a large coffee table that sat at the centre if the room. He sat on a large burgundy chair. He clasped his hands together and closed his eyes.

"The evil locked Edith's looks within one of the mirrors. He never really explained why. Edith's spirit was free to roam the house, but only the one who unlocked her via the mirror could see her true form," Thomas began.

"So, now that the evil has left, she can show her true form?" Jhordan asked.

Thomas nodded. "The evil left the house to me. I don't want the spirits to be trapped here unless they want to remain here."

"Have you spoken to them?" Luna asked.

"Have you seen how many there are here?" Thomas laughed.

"I've not seen them all but I have heard them. Have you thought about holding a meeting? I can gather some up now if you'd like?" Luna suggested.

"How many do you think you could gather in, say, thirty minutes?" Thomas asked.

"I would guess at around fifty? Maybe a little less. Would that be enough?" Luna replied.

Thomas thought for a second. "It will have to be a start; maybe they can spread the word around and get an answer back to me."

Luna nodded her head briskly and headed off out of the room and up towards the rooms she had heard cries from earlier in the night. She paused before entering the room, unsure of what she would find behind the door. She braced herself and turned the handle. She was met with a rush of spirits. They all descended on her in an instant.

"Wait, I can only listen to one at a time, but before I listen to you, I need you to listen to me for a second, please," Luna shouted.

The spirits fell silent. An older spirit stepped forward. "What is it you need to say child?"

"I need you to all follow me, I will listen to your pleas after you have heard what needs to be said, but for now, I need you to follow me," Luna told them.

"That we can do," the older spirit replied.

Luna opened the door again and led them back towards the large room. "Please wait here, I need to collect a few others before we can start."

The spirits settled in the room whilst Luna ran off in search of more, there were around thirty more to find, more if she could.

Jhordan stayed seated the entire time. He saw Luna rushing back and forth but didn't see anything else come with her. He thought back to before this night and realised he was able to see people who weren't visible to normal people, now, he couldn't see anything.

"Thomas, why can't I see any of the so called spirits that Luna is bringing back?" He asked. "Why can I only see you?"

Thomas laughed, "That's because I allow you to see me. The spirits that are here now, they don't really know who you are, so, to them, you are a threat. Maybe when they see that Luna trusts you, they will too."

Jhordan could only hope. He wanted to help these people too.

"Oh where is she?" Monique said as she watched the clock and paced the floor.

"She will be fine. Come and sit down, drink some tea and relax. Jhordan is with her, he won't let anything happen to her," Pearl said as she filled each cup with hot water and let it sit for a few minutes. She laid out some biscuits on a plate and set them on the table.

Monique looked at the clock once more, 11:45pm. She made herself move towards the table and sit in the chair. "I'll drink this then I will go and look for her."

"No you won't," came a voice from behind her.

Monique froze to the spot. Pearl almost dropped the kettle.

"Please tell me I'm hearing things," Monique whispered.

Pearl shook her head. "You're not hearing things sweetie, but I might be hallucinating."

Monique spun around on her seat, coming face to face with Spencer. "You're not hallucinating either Pearl, it's really him!"

Monique jumped up and threw her arms around his neck. "How is this possible?"

"I was told that I was given a second chance, so here I am," Spencer replied.

"Oh Sylvester kept his word," Pearl whispered.

"Remind me to thank him when we see him next," Spencer told her.

"Oh Spencer, you won't see him. There is so much you need to know," Pearl told him.

"Why don't you sit down and we will explain as much as we can for now," Monique said.

Spencer took the seat next to his wife and wrapped his hands around the mug of tea that his mother set in front of him. It was like he had never been away.

Chapter 47

Luna had gathered almost a hundred spirits into the living room. She hadn't managed to gather more, her thirty minutes were up. Thomas was amazed at how many she had managed to gather though. He didn't think she would manage this many in such a short space of time.

"Thank you all for coming. I'm sure most of you are aware of this evenings proceedings. How many of you are aware of the outcome?" Thomas asked.

A few of the spirits raised their hands.

"For those of you who are unaware, the evil has left this house. He shall never return," Thomas told them.

There were murmurs from around the room. Luna listened carefully. She heard whispers. Questions about the house and about the spirits.

"They're worried," Luna told Thomas.

"What are they worried about?" Thomas asked.

"Most of them have only ever known this place and the evil. They are worried about how things will continue from now on," Luna replied.

"Please," Thomas said as he rose from Luna's side. "There is no need to worry. You do have a choice."

The murmurs became softer as a man with pale blue eyes drifted forward. "What choices do we have? This is all we have ever known." He said as he spread his arms wide.

"You can remain here, if that is what you desire. You can come and go as you please. You can also venture back to your original resting places. I can promise that you will never be disturbed again," Thomas swore.

The man drifted back towards the group he had been standing with and they bunched themselves together. A lady with brown curls kept looking over at Luna. It seemed as if she were studying her, looking for clues about the legality of Thomas's claims.

Luna sat next to Jhordan and hung her head.

"What is it?" Jhordan asked. "You seem upset."

"I don't know if they will move on from here or stay put. I don't even know if they believe what Thomas is saying to them," Luna explained. "All they have ever known is this house and its deep rooted evilness."

Jhordan gently placed his arm around Luna's shoulders and held her while she allowed her tears to fall. Thomas bent down in front of her and pulled her head back up.

"Do not allow your emotions to take over young Luna. The spirits, as we both knew, will be hard to persuade," Thomas said.

"I know, but I want them to be happy. I feel that they think they are trapped here," Luna told him.

"Then we have to show them that they are not being held here anymore," Jhordan said. He jumped from his seat next to her and opened the doors and windows wide.

"You may have to help him with this one," Thomas told Luna. "He can't see them anymore."

Luna was shocked. "Why?"

"Now he is in full human form, he can only see them if they trust him enough to show themselves," Thomas told her.

Luna stood up and walked over to where Jhordan stood; she linked her arm with his and looked around at the spirits. She smiled. A smile that reached her eyes and radiated trust.

Jhordan watched as, one by one, the spirits formed in front of his eyes. He was surprised by how many there were.

"When you said you could gather loads, I didn't think there would be this many?" Jhordan whispered.

"You should talk to them," Luna said. "They might listen to you."

Jhordan stepped forward. He looked around at the faces that now stared back at him. "Hi, I'm Jhordan. I know you all probably feel a little uneasy about all this and that is totally understandable. I was once like you. I know how it feels to feel like you have been forgotten, but I can assure you, you haven't. Up until I met Luna here, I felt that darkness. When Thomas and Luna tell you that you have a choice, you can trust them. The house is open for all."

Jhordan stepped back beside Luna and whispered, "I hope that was OK?"

Luna smiled up at him. "You did great."

It took one brave spirit to venture past the window frame. A young girl of around twelve poked her head out of the window and took a deep breath in. "It smells fresh. You have to come and look."

As she backed away from the window, more spirits drifted their way, each trying to smell the fresh air.

"There's always the doors?" Jhordan offered.

The spirits glided their way to the doors and out into the evening air. Thomas watched with pride as the spirits enjoyed their release. Upon turning away from the window, Thomas spotted one lonely spirit tucked away in the corner. He made his way over and stooped down.

"What is it?" Thomas asked.

"I'm scared. Of the outside," the small child replied.

"Why?" Thomas asked.

"So many bad things happened to me there, so many bad things," the child said, her eyes drifting into the distance.

"Would you like me to come with you?" Thomas offered.

"Would you?" The girl's eyes lit up. "I'd feel safer with you. You won't hurt me, will you?"

"Why would I hurt you?" He asked.

"The last man I trusted hurt me. He hurt me lots. That's why I am here," the girl told him.

"Do you want to talk about it? I know a lovely rose bush in the gardens," Thomas said.

"Can she come?" The girl asked, pointing at Luna.

"Maybe we could ask her?" Thomas replied. "Come with me." He held his hand out for her to hold.

She hesitated for a second, then slowly reached into his hand and gripped tight.

"Luna, I'm sorry to interrupt. This is," Thomas began.

"Trixie," Luna whispered.

Trixie nodded.

"Oh Trixie. There's no need to be afraid now. He's not here to hurt you anymore," Luna whispered as she hugged Trixie hard.

"She wondered if you would like to join us. We are going to sit by the rose bush and Trixie wants to talk about what happened," Thomas finished.

"I'd love to. Can Jhordan join us?" Luna asked.

"Do you trust him?" Trixie asked.

"Oh absolutely," Luna replied.

"Then he can come," Trixie said. She held out her hand for Jhordan and he gratefully received it with a smile.

They walked round the house into the gardens and to the bench in front of the rose bush. Trixie and Luna sat on the bench whilst Thomas and Jhordan perched on either arm rest.

"We're ready when you are," Thomas whispered. "Take your time."

"So all that happened? Like actually happened? It felt like a dream," Spencer said after his mother and Monique had explained everything.

"You didn't know you died?" Monique asked.

"I knew I'd died, yes, but it didn't feel real, it was as if I had dreamt the whole thing. It was only when I heard you talking about Luna that I realised it wasn't," Spencer tried to explain. "I know, it doesn't make much sense."

"It will all become clearer as we go forward," Pearl told him. "For now, let's just wait for Luna to come back."

"She's been gone a while. Don't you think we should go and see if everything is OK?" Monique said, looking worried.

Bruce laughed from the corner of the room. "She won't stop until you say yes."

Spencer had missed Bruce sitting there so quietly. "Sorry, can I ask who you are?"

Bruce stood and held his hand out. "Bruce Stanley. I'm Jhordans adopted Dad."

"Well, it's nice to meet you. You know this mysterious Sylvester by any chance?" Spencer asked with a smile.

Bruce smiled. "I do and I did. He was a humble man, in the end, but I'll explain more at a later date."

Pearl gave up. "OK, let's go back to Flowerly Hall and see what's happened."

Monique grabbed her coat and pulled on her boots. She opened the door and led the way.

Spencer watched as his wife and mother almost marched down the road in unison. It made him smile. It seemed they had made friends since he had been away.

The closer they got to the house, the faster their feet walked. Monique was worried. Luna never normally ran off like that, but as she walked through the gates to the house, she could see that, whatever had made Luna rush back had been worth it. Spirits of all ages were touring the gardens, smelling the flowers and touching the grass. It was a safe haven for them. Monique smiled.

As Spencer walked through the gates behind her and Pearl, a few of the spirits became inquisitive. They glided over to them and circled the group.

"Why are we just standing here?" Spencer asked.

It was clear to Pearl and Monique, at this point, that Spencer couldn't see the spirits.

"Let's look inside," Pearl said, pulling on Spencer's arm until he followed her.

As Pearl led Spencer into the house, Monique asked the spirits if they had seen Luna.

"Round the back, she is with young Trixie," one of the young girls said as she pointed towards the back of the house.

"Thank you. Enjoy the rest of your evening," Monique said, and she left them to it.

She circled the house and spotted Luna and Jhordan sat with Thomas and a very young spirit. *'That must be Trixie,'* she thought to herself.

As she approached, she could hear the young girl talking. She held perfect eye contact with Luna. Monique wondered if the girl knew that Thomas was just behind her. When Trixie caught sight on Monique she stopped abruptly.

"I didn't mean to interrupt. I'm Monique, Luna's mother. I was just checking on her," Monique said softly.

Trixie looked at Luna and then back at Monique. "It must be nice to be able to look out for your daughter. I wish my Mum was like you."

"Trixie, your Mum had no idea what happened to you. Not until the police told her," Luna explained.

"I know, but she didn't come looking for me, not like your Mum has," Trixie replied, tears forming in her eyes. "My Mum didn't care. She brought that man into our lives. She didn't watch what he did to me."

"I know sweetheart, and I am so sorry for that. I wish we could do more," Luna whispered.

"There isn't though. He's dead now. He confessed whilst he was in prison for a different offence but then killed himself the same night," Thomas told her. "I heard some people talking about it at the graveyard."

"I'm glad he's dead, but that means he could get me here too?" Trixie said. She became increasingly anxious. Looking from left and right.

Thomas took her hands and forced her to look at him. "No-one will hurt you whilst you are with me."

"Are you sure? My Mum said that she would always protect me and she lied," Trixie sobbed.

"I promise. I don't break promises," Thomas replied.

Trixie looked at him for a few moments and then threw her arms around his neck."I trust you," she whispered.

"Are you both ready to go?" Monique asked Luna and Jhordan.

They nodded, said goodbye to Trixie and Thomas and followed Monique to the front of the house. Just as they rounded the corner, they almost run headfirst into Pearl.

"Any sign?" Pearl asked before she spotted Luna and Jhordan behind Monique. "Thank the Lord she is safe."

Monique was worried about how Luna would take the news of her father coming back, but before she could prepare Luna for his arrival, he scooped her into his arms and swung her around.

"My little Luna bug," Spencer whispered.

"Dad!" Luna squealed. "You're back!"

"I'm right here honey. I'm so sorry that you had to go through all that," Spencer said.

"It's ok. I think I handled everything rather well," Luna boasted.

Everyone laughed and Spencer placed Luna back on her own two feet. He stretched his hand out to Jhordan. "I believe you have been by Luna's side a lot over the past few days?"

"I have," Jhordan replied. His voice shaking as he shook Spencer's hand. "I hope to be by her side for a lot longer."

"Well, it will good to have you around Jhordan," Spencer replied.

"OK, let's get home and eat. I bet you are all starving!" Monique said.

They left the house behind as they walked back home. Luna smiled the whole way back. She finally had her whole family back, but something still didn't sit right with her. She decided not to address it just yet; she would wait for a while.

Chapter 48

Max watched Luna and her family head into their house along with Jhordan and Bruce. He was glad they were back together. They deserved it. He wondered if Donna and Martha would be as happy as this family when their little baby arrived from the adoption agency. He decided to pay his sister a visit.

"So when does she arrive?" Donna asked Martha as they sat down to eat.

Martha had ordered Chinese take-out. She said Donna deserved a treat after all that hard work. They had been talking about the adoption since Donna got home. Martha had told her that there was a baby girl, ready to be housed. She didn't have a name yet, but they were accepted to adopt her.

"She will arrive in the morning. Do you want to choose names?" Martha asked.

"I have a name in mind, but I don't know how you would feel about it," Donna confessed.

"Hit me with it," Martha said as she popped another chicken ball in her mouth.

"Maxine," Donna blurted out.

Martha stopped chewing. She stared at Donna.

"You don't like it do you?" Donna asked.

Martha quickly chewed and swallowed the chicken and squealed with delight. "I love it!"

"So we will call her Maxine," Donna said.

"Absolutely," Martha agreed. "I'm going to order some personalised stuff from the internet, like a blanket, a door plaque, cutlery set."

"Don't go too crazy Martha. She can't even eat solid food yet," Donna laughed. "Hey do you think Savannah would agree to be Maxine's godmother? She asked us and I agreed."

"I'm sure she would love that. I'll send her a text," Martha called as she ran to the bedroom to collect her laptop.

Donna felt a cold breeze down her neck, "Martha, close the window. There's a draft!" She called out.

Martha came back looked confused. "The window isn't open. Are you sure you're not coming down with something?"

"I feel fine. I just felt a cold blast. Must have been from the flap at the top of the window, they are the worst,"

Donna said. She stood up to close the flap but it was already closed.

"Max," she whispered. As she finished the word, the curtain fluttered and then stopped.

"He's here?" Martha asked.

"Was. I think he's gone now. Doesn't mean he won't return. He's like the proverbial bad smell, yes I meant that, if you're still listening," Donna laughed.

Martha slumped onto the sofa and opened her laptop. It was still logged into Donnas email. "Honey, Luna has emailed you."

"Luna? What does she say?" Donna asked.

'Dear Detective Canter,

My Dad is back.

Something doesn't feel right.

It doesn't feel like him.

I know there isn't much you can do as a mortal but I'm scared. Jhordan and Bruce are here, they are staying the night. I think Jhordan feels something too. Any chance you can swing by? I don't think this is really him.

Thank you.

Luna Heart.'

"Something doesn't fit right with that," Martha said. "You best go and check on it."

"Are you sure?" Donna asked.

"Yeah, I'll be fine here. Just leave me your credit card?" Martha asked.

Donna smiled and dug into her purse; she gave the card to Martha and kissed her on the cheek. "I'll try not to be too long."

"Take your time," Martha said as she settled back on the sofa and began shopping. "I'll stay up as long as I can."

Donna grabbed her keys and jacket and left the house. She started the car and almost screamed when she looked in the rear view mirror.

"MAX! What are you doing here?"

"Maxine huh? I like it, but onto something more pressing. Spencer isn't Spencer," Max told her.

"I know. Luna emailed me. She's a good kid," Donna told him.

"She knows her stuff. I'm glad she hasn't let on yet," Max replied. "Can I come along?"

"Sure I guess. Luna said Jhordan feels a difference too. She's scared," Donna told him.

She put the car into gear and drove to Luna's house. She came up with something random as to why she was visiting so late.

Donna walked to the front door and knocked three times.

Monique opened the door. "Detective Canter! What a lovely surprise. What brings you here at this time?"

"Mrs Heart, I was just passing on my way back to the station and wanted to check that you all got home OK. Is Luna around?" Donna asked with a smile.

"Who is it?" Spencer called from the kitchen.

"Detective Canter. She has been with us since your grave was first disturbed," Monique explained.

"I was just wondering if I could have a chat with Luna in private," Donna smiled. She noticed that he was incredibly defensive.

"Sure, Luna why don't you go into the living room. We'll wait in here for you," Monique smiled.

Spencer watched them walk into the living room, his eyes never leaving Donna. She turned and pushed the door closed behind her.

"OK, what's going on?" Donna asked quickly.

"He doesn't seem like my Dad. I mean, he looks like him, but my Dad never called me Luna bug," Luna explained. "Something doesn't feel right."

"OK, other than Jhordan, who else has noticed it," Donna asked.

"I don't know. My Grandma doesn't seem to be as close to him as she once was," Luna said. "Mum, well, she's just smitten that he is back."

"What about Bruce? He is normally a good judge of character, Aura being an exception," Donna said.

"I don't know. They haven't really spoken. Dad just doesn't seem to like him. It's as if he is jealous or something," Luna replied.

Donna thought for a moment. How was she going to prove that Spencer wasn't the real Spencer?

"It's not him," Max whispered.

"Max! You made it too!" Luna exclaimed.

"Shh, you don't want anyone coming in," Max laughed.

"Sorry," Luna whispered. "How do you know it isn't him?"

"There's something about him that just doesn't sit right. The Spencer I knew in the afterlife was bubbly and open, this guy seems off and really defensive," Max replied. "I'll have to go back and see if your Dad is still there."

"How long will that take? This guy scares me," Luna asked.

"I'll be as fast as I can. Donna, you go back home to Martha and I'll come back to Luna when I've found something, then I'll come to you. Prepare Martha just in case," Max said. He faded away to nothing.

Donna opened the door to the living room and waved to everyone in the kitchen. "Bye everyone. Have a great evening!"

Donna left the house and returned to her car. She watched as Luna climbed the stairs and switch her light on in her room. Donna promised to make everything OK for her. On the drive home, Donna detoured past Flowerly Hall. She hesitated before entering. She stood at the foot of the spiral staircase and looked up, she had no idea what brought her here but here she stood.

"Are you OK Detective Canter?" Thomas's voice echoed around her.

"I, err, I don't really know. I could probably use some advice," she replied. She felt stupid. It was as if she were talking to herself.

Thomas materialised before her. "How is it that I can help or advise?"

Donna took a deep breath. "Luna's father returned this evening."

"That's good news, is it not?" Thomas asked.

"It would be, if it were her real father. She says that she doesn't feel a connection to him, something she said was always strong," Donna told him. "She said he scares her."

"Well we can't have that. Please, follow me. Let's see if we can't work this mess out once and for all," Thomas said, he motioned for her to follow him. "Wait, did your brother catch up with you?"

"Yes he did. He has gone back to the afterlife to see if the real Spencer is still there," Donna told him.

"I can also find out what happened. If you just give me a second," Thomas said as he disappeared into oblivion.

Donna was left alone in what seemed like an empty room. She looked around and found a light switch. She quickly switched it on and was surprised by how neat and tidy the room was. It had a white four poster bed with lace curtains, made up with cream satin sheets and ruby red scatter cushions. The carpet was soft under Donna's feet. She looked down to see the cream coloured fabric under her. As she walked around the room, there was a wicker chair in one corner. It held a book and a teddy. She walked towards the chair and reached out for the teddy.

"Please, don't touch it," Thomas said from behind her.

"I'm sorry, I didn't realise it was for show," Donna replied, pulling her hand back.

"It's not for show. This was a young girl's room many, many years ago. She had the most amazing smile and an infectious laugh. I used to watch her read in the sunlight on a summers day, or curled up on the window seat when it was beating with rain," Thomas remembered. "Poppy was a smart girl. It was unfortunate when her parents died and she was taken away. I never saw her again. I don't even know if she is still alive, she would probably be around seventy or eighty by now."

"I'm sorry if that has brought back sad memories. It just looks so sweet. I think Martha and I will set something like this up for Maxine when she gets older," Donna said.

"So the rumours are true?" Thomas asked.

"Yes they are. She arrives in the morning. Did you find out anything?" Donna asked.

"I did and I'm afraid it isn't good news," Thomas admitted. "The spirit that was transferred into Spencer's body is that of a one Michael Trystone."

"*THE* Michael Trystone?" Donna asked. "The one who murdered his wife and kids whilst they slept?"

"One and the same. Now, what do you plan on doing with this information?" Thomas replied.

"I don't know what I can do. I can't just walk in there and arrest him for impersonating a dead man, can I?" Donna questioned herself. "I don't even have any evidence."

Thomas watched her as she threw herself deeper into her thinking. She paced the room, left to right. Right to left. She stopped. Then started again. Thomas had begun to get dizzy. "Will you at least sit down for a second; I can't keep up with your backwards and forwards motions."

Donna planted herself right in the centre of the floor.
She crossed her legs and closed her eyes.

"What are you doing now?" Thomas asked.

"Meditating," Donna replied.

He watched her as she took deep breaths in and slowly
released them; she repeated the same action over and
over again. She seemed to calm right down. Just when
he thought she couldn't surprise him anymore, she
jumped up and stared at him.

"What is it?" Thomas asked, clearly shaken by her
stares.

"He will have to do something. I have to catch him red
handed, but the problem will be proving he isn't
Spencer. I mean, it's OK to tell them it's not him, but I
have to prove it," Donna explained.

"And you plan on doing that how?" Thomas asked.

"I'm working on that one, leave it with me. Thank you
for your help," Donna called as she ran back to her car.

Chapter 49

As the night drew to an end, Jhordan and Bruce made their excuses to leave and head home.

"You could stay the night?" Luna offered.

"I think they would probably want to sleep in their own beds tonight honey," Spencer said to her.

Luna hung her head. "OK. I'll see you at school tomorrow Jhordan!"

Spencer and Luna waved them off before closing the door and heading back into the kitchen where Monique and Pearl were still chatting over another cup of hot chocolate.

"Don't you think you should be heading back too," Spencer said to Pearl.

Pearl looked at the clock. It was gone one. "I guess I should be. You be good Luna," Pearl said as she pulled her coat on and opened the front door.

"I will. See you soon," Luna replied giving her a huge hug.

"Come on now Luna, it's time for bed," Spencer said as he pulled her out of the embrace.

Pearl walked down the driveway and away from the house before she stopped. '*Something wasn't right about that man,'* she thought. She didn't quite know what it was but he didn't seem like the real Spencer. She shook it from her mind and continued to walk home. In the distance she saw a set of headlights shining in her direction. The car stopped alongside her and called her over.

"Detective Canter, what brings you by this way again?" Pearl asked.

"Jump in. I'll explain everything," Donna said as she flung open the door.

Pearl climbed into the passenger seat and buckled up.

Donna turned the car around and headed back towards Pearl's house. As she pulled into the driveway she turned to face Pearl. "Is that really Spencer back there?"

"No dear, I don't believe it is, why do you ask?" Pearl replied.

"I shouldn't really tell you this as its confidential but Luna emailed me earlier this evening. She said this man scares her and that her father never called her Luna bug," Donna told her. "That's why I came over tonight. She said that Jhordan feels something isn't right either."

"I was surprised by how he told me to leave. The real Spencer would have insisted I stay the night, especially as it's so late and dark," Pearl replied. "Where are my manners, why don't you come inside, I'll make some tea."

Donna shut off the engine and climbed out of the car. She followed Pearl into the house and made sure to lock the door behind her.

"Pearl, tell me about Bruce. He was there tonight wasn't he?" Donna asked.

"Oh yes, but he didn't say much. I had a feeling 'Spencer' didn't think much of him," Pearl replied. "Bruce was quiet all night actually. Come to think of it, I almost forgot he was there."

"How was 'Spencer' before he died?" Donna asked.

"He was a loving man, adored his wife and Luna. Never spoke to me the way that man did tonight," Pearl answered as she placed the cup of tea in front of Donna.

Donna wasn't surprised. From what she had read about Michael Trystone, it seemed to fit him perfectly.

"What is it dear?" Pearl interrupted her thoughts. "You seem to have something at the front of your mind."

"I went to see Thomas," Donna confessed. "Straight after coming to see Luna. Max has gone back to the afterlife to see if he can track down the real Spencer. Thomas told me that it isn't Spencer."

"Does he know who this man is?" Pearl asked.

"We believe he is Michael Trystone," Donna revealed. "He murdered his wife and kids almost ten years ago, he was arrested and sent to jail for life. When most of the inmates found out what he did, they cornered him and killed him."

"I remember reading about it. We have to warn Monique and Luna," Pearl said, getting to her feet and heading for the phone.

"We can't," Donna told her. She hated saying it.

"Well, why not?" Pearl demanded.

"We don't have any evidence yet, and even when we do, we can't prove he isn't Spencer. We would also have to work out a way to send him back." Donna explained.

Pearl slumped on the chair next to Donna. "I don't know if I will even sleep tonight knowing there is a murderer in that house. Who's to say he won't try and kill Luna and Monique?"

Donna contemplated telling Pearl about Max. She wondered if it would change her perspective knowing that Max would be there if anything did happen. She decided not to say anything yet, that was until a gentle breeze swept behind her.

"Max, welcome," Pearl whispered.

"Hello Pearl," Max replied. He turned to Donna. "I looked for you at home but you weren't there."

"I went to see Thomas. It's not Spencer," Donna told him.

"I know, Spencer was tied up in one of the back rooms, he couldn't escape. Someone took his place," Max told them.

"Michael Trystone." Donna said.

"He's here?" Max asked. He didn't seem surprised.

"Yep, he has taken Spencer's place. What do we do?" Pearl asked.

Max thought for a second. "Well, I've already seen Luna. She is protected, so is Monique," Max told Pearl.

"How?" Donna asked. "You aren't exactly a magician!"

"I have ways, I know people on the other side too, people who are willing to help," Max told her. "No-one in that house will come to any harm."

"So how do we get rid of him, or switch them over?"
Donna asked.

"It's going to be hard and we are going to need some
help, but we need to talk to Thomas first," Max
explained.

Luna pulled her phone from under her pillow and
opened her messages. She selected Jhordans name and
composed her message;

*'Jhordan, this isn't my Dad. Max just came and told me.
He's a murderer. Max is working to get my real Dad
back.*

See you at school.

Luna x'

She closed the phone down and slid it back under her
pillow just as Spencer opened her door.

"Hey, I was just checking you managed to get off to
sleep OK, seems like it's been one hell of a day for
you," he smiled.

"I'm good. I'm just really tired, plus I have school
tomorrow," Luna replied.

"I'll let you get off to sleep then, goodnight," he said and he closed the door behind him.

Luna didn't normally lock her door but tonight she even considered it, but she didn't. Max had told her she and her mother would be safe. She just hoped he was right. She felt her phone vibrate under her pillow; she quickly pulled it out and checked the screen, turning the brightness down to zero.

'I knew it wasn't him. It didn't feel right.

Stay safe tonight.

See you tomorrow.

Jhordan x'

Luna slid the phone away quickly when she saw the landing light come on, she closed her eyes when she saw the handle turn on her door, but she smelt her mother's perfume so she chanced a peek. Monique stood in the doorway watching Luna.

"Goodnight Princess," she whispered.

Monique closed the door behind her and got herself ready for bed. She felt strange. It had been so long since she shared her bed with Spencer and now that he was home, she wasn't ready for that step just yet. She grabbed a spare pillow and sheet from the airing cupboard and made up the sofa.

"Why aren't you coming to bed?" Spencer asked, trying his hardest to look hurt.

"You wouldn't understand. Why don't you go and get some rest upstairs. I'll see you for breakfast in the morning," Monique smiled.

"Try me, I might just get it," Spencer said as he sat at the dining table.

Monique curled herself up under the sheet on the sofa. "Well, it's been quite a while since I shared my bed with anyone."

"I'm not just anyone though am I? I'm your husband," Spencer replied.

"I know, but it's going to take time to get back to that. I mean, you understand right?" Monique hoped he did.

"Of course I do. Look, I'll sleep down here, why don't you take the bed," Spencer smiled. "I'll be fine here."

"Are you sure?" Monique asked.

"Absolutely. Go," Spencer urged her.

Monique smiled and made her way to the stairs. "Goodnight," she called.

"Goodnight, sleep well," Spencer smiled.

When she was at the top of the stairs, he climbed under the sheet and settled down. He would wait until the early hours to do what he came here to do.

Donna returned home from Pearl's house to find Martha asleep on the sofa with the laptop still on her lap. She gently moved the laptop and placed it on the coffee table before covering Martha with a blanket. She then curled up on the chair opposite and drifted off to sleep. She dreamt of Max being able to meet Maxine, but she knew it could never happen. She dreamt Max had never died and that he had been there for her wedding to Martha. So much of her dream made no sense at all but it put a smile on her face.

She woke the next morning to the smell of strong coffee and bacon. Rising from the chair, she stretched herself tall.

"Morning Sunshine!" Martha beamed from the kitchen. "Long night? How was Luna by the way?"

Donna yawned. "She was right all along. That man is not Spencer Heart. It was confirmed last night by two different sources"

"I'm guessing one was Pearl?" Martha laughed.

"No, actually it was Thomas." Donna replied.

"You went back there?" Martha asked.

"Yeah, I knew something wasn't right when I arrived at the house. I went there to get his advice and he found out exactly whose spirit had taken over Spencer's body. It's Michael Trystone," Donna told her.

Martha almost dropped her cup. "Tell me you're joking?"

Donna shook her head. "I wish I was. Thomas confirmed it was him and Max went back into the afterlife and found the real Spencer tied up in the back room."

"But Donna, he murdered his wife and kids! And you left him with Luna and Monique overnight?" Martha screamed.

"Max told me they were protected, he said someone he knew from the other side was helping," Donna explained. "What time is Maxine arriving?"

"Not until eleven, why?" Martha answered.

"I'm going over to Luna's school, she is back in today and then I'll know for certain if Max was right," Donna explained. "I will be back here by ten-thirty."

She quickly grabbed her coat, pulled on her boots and ran out the door. She hoped and prayed that Luna had been OK overnight.

Chapter 50

Luna awoke early the next morning. She climbed from her bed and padded to the bathroom. She could hear water running from inside. She knocked on the door and waited for an answer. To her surprise, Spencer opened the door.

"Morning Luna bug! Sorry I took so long. Bathroom is all yours!" He smiled.

"Thanks," Luna replied and she ran in the bathroom and locked the door behind her.

"I'll see you downstairs for breakfast," Spencer called through the door.

Luna didn't reply. She ran the shower and climbed under the water. She had hoped it had been a dream about this man coming back into their lives. Clearly it wasn't. She tried to take her time before going down for breakfast and tried to miss it all together but she knew that would look suspicious.

After brushing and tying up her hear, Luna joined her parents in the kitchen for breakfast.

"So, what subjects do you have today?" Spencer asked. "I hope you have still been getting high grades."

Luna smiled at him, "I have Maths first thing, then Science and English. After lunch I've got History and IT. My grades are still predicted A's and B's, so nothing has really changed."

Spencer laughed. "My death obviously didn't affect you that much then?"

Luna tried to laugh but she didn't find it funny. Her grades had slipped since her Dad died. Her real one anyway. She had been solid A student until that moment. She was, now, just barely reaching a B.

"You need someone to walk to school with you?" Spencer asked.

"I'm fine. I'm meeting Jhordan at the gates," Luna said before draining her juice and rushing off. "See you both after school!"

"Bye love. Enjoy your day!" Monique called from behind the breakfast bar.

Luna closed the door behind her and almost ran to school. She needed to get away from that house and that man.

Jhordan was already at the gate when Luna arrived. She was panting. Jhordan handed her a bottle of water.

"Did you run here?" He asked.

"I had to get out of there. He's not my Dad," Luna said in between breaths.

"You said that on text last night but you didn't say much else. You had me worried, but Bruce told me that you would be OK and that I should sleep. He said if you weren't at school today then I had to tell him and he would find out what was going on," Jhordan replied. He quickly sent a message to Bruce to tell him that Luna was at school.

"Max came back last night. He told me my real Dad had been tied up and some other guy had taken his place. He said someone on the other side was protecting me and my Mum and that we would be fine. He didn't tell me who it was though," Luna told Jhordan.

"Why don't we get to class? I think we would probably be safer there," Jhordan said. He grabbed his bag and collected Luna's too. She linked her arm with his for stability; she didn't trust her legs to carry her weight.

Jhordan was worried. She had been left alone over night with her mother and some random person. Anything could have happened to her or her mother.

Just as they reached the main entrance, Jhordan spotted Donna at reception. He waved when she looked over and pointed to Luna. Donna rushed out and grabbed hold of her.

"Hey," Donna said, trying to hold Luna's head up.

When she finally managed to get Luna to focus in her, Donna asked her what happened last night.

"We just went to bed. He came to my room not long after I text Jhordan, to see if I managed to get to sleep, but after that I didn't hear anything all night. I guess everyone went to sleep," Luna replied. "Donna, who is he?"

Donna wondered if she should tell Luna the truth worrying that it would trouble her whilst she was at school, but she decided that Luna had been through enough already without having someone else lie to her too.

"It's a man named Michael Trystone. He is known to police. I don't want to tell you about him but I will, and only because I don't think you deserve to be lied to anymore. He killed his wife and kids whilst they slept," Donna said.

"And you let them stay in that house alone with him last night?" Jhordan tried not to shout.

"I only did it because Max said they would be safe," Donna explained. "Look, Max said we can get your real Dad back, but we need help. We need to talk to Thomas."

"Let's go after school. I'll come with you," Luna cried. "I have to get away from him."

"I'll meet you both here at three-thirty. Now, I have to run. We are accepting our baby this morning," Donna smiled.

"Congratulations and good luck. See you later," Jhordan said.

He watched Donna jog from the building and then turned to help Luna to class. Luckily there was still ten minutes before the class started. They sat down and got ready for the lesson. Jhordan was glad that Luna was no longer out of breath. It meant the teacher wouldn't ask questions.

Donna arrived home with plenty of time to have a quick shower before the people from the adoption agency brought the baby over. She smartened herself up, applied a very small amount of make-up and waited nervously by the window.

"Will you calm down?" Martha laughed. "You're making me nervous! Did you see Luna?"

"Yeah, she's OK, but we are going to Flowerly Hall after school. We need to talk to Thomas about all of this. Max said we need his help. You don't mind do you?" Donna asked.

"Of course not. I can take the time to bond with Maxine until you get back. Remember, you're on leave for three weeks after today. No work," Martha teased.

"I'll be on my best behaviour," Donna said as she looked out of the window for the fifth time in as many minutes. "They're here!"

Martha and Donna straightened themselves up and waited for the doorbell to chime. Martha opened the door and welcomed them in. She guided them through to the living room and introduced Donna.

"It's nice to meet you," Donna said as she shook both of their hands. "Please, take a seat."

The two people from the adoption agency sat down and set the car seat they were carrying down next to their feet.

"As I'm sure you know, this little one doesn't have a name yet, so that part will be down to yourselves," the lady stated.

"We already have a name that we like," Martha told them both.

"May I ask what that would be?" The man asked. He had a serious face and very short, stubbly hair. His eyes were very dark.

"Maxine, after my brother Max," Donna told him.

The lady noted that down on the paperwork she was filling out as they spoke.

"I understand you are both police officers?" She asked.

"Yes we are," Donna replied. "Is that an issue?"

"Of course not, we just like to have all the details for Maxine's record. Will there be times where you will all be able to bond together?" She asked.

"Donna and I have three weeks off beginning tomorrow. We plan to spend each day getting to know Maxine and bonding with her. We have both cut hours where we don't need to be at work," Martha explained.

"That's great, it seems you have prioritised well," the man said.

Donna was not happy with his comments and she didn't like the way he spoke to them. He sounded just like Max had when she'd first told him she was gay.

"Can I ask you a question?" Donna said to him.

"Absolutely," he replied.

"Do you have an issue with us being a gay married couple?" Donna asked.

"Donna! I'm so sorry," Martha apologised. "I don't know what brought that on."

"It's simple. He doesn't seem happy about the fact Maxine has been placed with us," Donna replied. "So please, answer the question."

"I'll be blunt. I am sceptical that you can give this baby the love that two parents can give a baby. I am not, however, prejudice towards you. I want to see this work," he replied.

"Then maybe you could start treating us with the same respect you would a mix gender couple?" Donna stated.

The man nodded his head curtly and grasped his hands in his lap.

The lady smiled, "now that's cleared up. Why don't you give little Maxine a tour of the house. I assume she has a nursery set up?"

"It's this way; would you like to follow me?" Martha said as she led the lady up the stairs to the nursery they had painted in a pale yellow.

"I'm sorry you felt that I was against you both," the man said softly. "I didn't mean to come across that way."

"So why be like it?" Donna asked.

"In my line of work, as I'm sure it is similar in yours too, we have to make sure there is an understanding of the safeguarding of the people we work with and for," he began to explain. "But also, I have seen many adoptions fail that involved gay couples. Mainly due to one half of the couple feeling abandoned?"

"I know what you mean. Martha and I have had our problems at work but in the end we stood our ground and here we still are almost twelve years later. We have spoken about adoption for so long, we have taken courses on parenting, had chats with therapists to talk about deeply hidden worries, and we got it all out in the open. That's why we cut our hours and why we are so dedicated to making this work," Donna told him. "Just give us a chance."

"You have my blessing," he smiled and signed the paperwork. "Please, keep us informed of her development?"

"Absolutely," Donna said and she took the paperwork and shook his hand.

Martha came back into the room holding Maxine with the lady following closely behind.

"I've signed the necessary paperwork. It's now up to you. She will need you. Both of you," the man said, before grabbing his coat, bag and following the lady out of the door.

As Donna locked the door behind them, she wished Max could have been alive to see this. She walked back into the living room and looked at Martha and Maxine sitting on the sofa. Maxine had the deepest blue eyes and a mass of blonde curls. She gurgled as Donna lifted her from Martha's arms and cradled her in her arms.

"We're going to have a lot of fun over the years. I promise you that. Whatever you want to do in life, me and Mummy are going to be right there by your side, no matter what," Donna whispered to her. She kissed her on the head and handed her back to Martha. "I'll be as quick as I can."

"Take your time. I'm sure Maxine and I can do without you for a while," Martha smiled.

Donna tried not to laugh but a grin appeared on her face. She grabbed her keys and jacket and opened the front door. She climbed in the car and switched the engine on. As she drove towards Luna's school, she noticed she was being followed by someone in a dark green car. She decided to take a detour; she didn't want whoever it was to follow her to the school, so she took the next left and then a sharp right. The car followed suit. Using her hands free, she quickly dialled Martha.

"Hey honey, miss us already?" Martha answered.

"I've got a tail. I was driving to the school and this car is following my every move. Can you trace the reg? I don't want to call the station; it will be hard to explain why I'm still in contact with Luna," Donna said.

"Sure, go ahead," Martha replied.

Donna read of the registration number and waited for Martha to look it up.

"OK, looks like it registered to Spencer Heart. Purchased earlier today. Honey, why would he be following you?" Martha told her.

"He seemed really off with me last night when I went to see Luna, like really defensive," Donna replied. "I'm going to head to Monique's, see if he follows me back there," Donna said.

"OK, just be careful. Remember, Maxine and I expect you home by seven," Martha said.

They ended the call and Donna made a left turn. She followed the road ahead and turned left again. She watched as the car behind followed her, but as she turned into Monique's street, the car roared past her and cut her off at the junction. Donna screeched to a halt and climbed out of the car, she was now face to face with Spencer Heart.

"Can I help you detective? You seem to be hanging around my family a lot recently. I thought the whole thing was over with now?" Spencer growled.

"There are still a few loose ends to tie up Mr Heart. We have to offer therapy to those involved. That includes your wife, mother and Luna," Donna said, remaining as calm as she could.

"Luna doesn't need any therapy, none of my family do, so you can just leave us alone," Spencer shouted.

Donna climbed back into her car, and before Spencer could start his engine, she sped off down the street, taking the first turnings she could. She quickly parked in between two cars and ducked down just as Spencer sped past her. She checked in her mirror before pulling back onto the street and taking the back way to Luna's school.

When she pulled up outside, Luna and Jhordan were already waiting.

"Sorry I took so long," Donna apologised.

"It's OK. Having a new baby must be demanding," Jhordan laughed.

"I wish it was that that kept me," Donna laughed. "But actually it was your Dad Luna."

"My real Dad or that thing in my house?" Luna asked.

"The second one. He chased me around the streets and then cut me off when I tried to get onto your street. Told me to stay away from you all," Donna explained. "Now listen, we have to meet Max at Flowerly Hall. I don't know much more than that."

"I'm ready," Luna said. She buckled her seat belt and leaned back in the seat.

Donna worried that this might be a bad idea, but she had promised so she would keep that promise.

Chapter 51

Max had emerged at Flowerly Hall hours before Donna was due to arrive. He had taken Thomas aside and explained what had to happen.

"I don't know if she will be up for that Max. She's a hurting young girl," Thomas explained.

"I know, and if there was another way, I would take it, but her mother said this is the only way for it to work," Max told him. "Look, Donna is bringing Luna with her. Maybe she will talk to her?"

Thomas thought for a moment. "It's possible. We will just have to wait until they arrive."

Max watched out of the window and waited for Donna to arrive. He hoped she would come soon. He needed this to work for Luna's sake. He didn't know how much longer she could take staying in the same house as that man and Max knew there was only so much protection his friend on the other side could give. As he looked out towards the gate once more, he could see Donnas' car approaching. He was surprised to see another car following her.

Donna had spotted Spencer's car as they pulled away from the school gates. She had told Luna and Jhordan to keep their heads down; she couldn't risk Luna getting hurt.

She took a different route to Flowerly Hall but Spencer stayed right on her tail, so her next best trick was to bring him with her. She knew the sorts of trouble some of the spirits could cause. She sped through the gates and demanded Luna and Jhordan run into the house and up the stairs, find any room and hide in there. Luna and Jhordan did as they were told.

"Luna, you stop this second. We're going home," Spencer shouted."Don't make me come in there."

Donna climbed from her car and stood in Spencer's way. "She won't come out. She has friends in there."

"No she doesn't. They just use her to talk to the living! None of them are friends," Spencer growled.

"Why don't you come in with me and find out," Donna asked.

"Fine, but I bet I'm right," Spencer spat.

Donna rolled her eyes and led the way into the house. She wished for Max to make an appearance. She could use his help.

"Luna, where are you?" Donna called.

"Usual room," Luna shouted back.

"What's the usual room? You come here with her often?" Spencer asked.

"No, but I know where she is," Donna replied.

Spencer shook his head and followed Donna up the spiral staircase and along the thin corridor. The wallpaper was hanging off the walls and the paintings were all lopsided.

'This wasn't like this earlier,' Donna thought.

As Donna walked past the never ending doors, she hoped what they were about to do would work. This man, this person who took the place of Spencer was unimaginably horrible. His tone of voice was rude and accusing. She wasn't a religious person, but she prayed this would work.

Just as Martha laid Maxine down for her nap, there was a vibrating sound coming from the sofa. She moved cushions around and finally found Donnas phone.

"Hello?" She answered.

"Oh, I'm sorry, I was looking for Detective Canter," a light female voice replied.

"I've afraid she has left her phone behind by mistake, can I take a message?" Martha replied.

"If you wouldn't mind. This is Monique Heart. I was just wondering if she had seen or heard from Luna today. She hasn't returned home from school and, well, I'm quite worried," Monique explained.

"I know where they are. I don't know if I was supposed to say anything or not, but I feel you should really know. The person claiming to be Spencer isn't," Martha tried to explain.

"What do you mean?" Monique asked, her voice becoming very shaky.

Martha sat on the sofa. "Donna explained to me that Luna didn't feel like that man was her father. In fact she sent Donna an email about it. She said Spencer has never called her Luna bug?"

Monique went quiet. "She's right. Spencer used to call her his shining light. Who is this man?"

Martha toyed with whether to tell her the truth or not, but she thought she had a right to know. "His name is Michael Trystone."

Monique gasped. "As in..."

"Yes, the same. I don't really know much of what's happened over the past few days, but I know Donna has been visited by her dead brother and he has confirmed it. Spencer is, technically, still dead." Martha told her.

Monique was quiet on the phone. "We were alone with him last night. What if he had tried something?" She whispered.

"I don't know what happened last night, but Donna said you were safe and I trust her," Martha replied. "Look, I've just put Maxine down to nap, but I can put her in the pram and come over? Donna has the car but a walk will be good for her."

"Oh would you?" Monique asked. "I really don't want to be alone right now and Spencer, well, Michael, he went out earlier and hasn't come back."

"I'll be about twenty minutes," Martha said. She ended the call and got Maxine ready to go out. She locked the door behind her and made her way down the street.

After Monique had hung up the phone, she ran to lock the doors and windows, she didn't want to risk Michael coming back and trying something whilst she was here alone. She paced the living room. Back and forth. Back and forth. By the time Martha arrived, Monique had done this lap almost thirty times. She ran to the door, unbolted the lock and threw the door open.

"I got here as fast as I could," Martha said to her.

Monique threw her arms around her. "I'm so sorry. I'm so scared."

"I understand. I don't really know everything, just what Donna has told me, but I believe her when she says that you are both safe," Martha told her.

Monique released Martha and helped her park the pram in the living room. Maxine was sound asleep.

"She's beautiful," Monique cooed over her.

"She really is. She arrived today so I'm still practicing," Martha laughed.

Monique led Martha to the kitchen and switched the kettle on as Martha sat at the breakfast bar.

"So tell me, what do we know about this guy and why he swapped places with my Spencer?" Monique asked.

"We don't know why he did it, well, at least I don't. I know about Michael's story," Martha began to explain.

There was a shrill ringing coming from the hallway. Monique quickly ran to answer the phone. Martha took over making the tea and had everything on the table just as Monique came back.

"I'm sorry about that. My mother in law. She worries a lot," Monique smiled.

"Did you tell her about Luna?" Martha asked.

"Oh no, she would be round here like a shot. No, she's had enough excitement for now," Monique replied.

"Wouldn't it be good for you to have some added support?" Martha asked.

"I don't know. I would like her here, but I know she would make things worse," Monique replied.

As soon as she finished her sentence, there was a knock at the door. Both women stared at each other. Monique crept towards the door and peeped out of the side window. She let out a sigh of relief and opened the door quickly. Pearl had arrived.

"I could sense something wasn't right on the phone, tell me," she said as she slammed the door behind her.

At that instant Maxine woke with a scream.

"Oh," Pearl exclaimed. "I didn't realise you had company. I'm so sorry."

"It's OK. I'll try and settle her," Martha said as she came out of the kitchen.

Monique pulled Pearl into the kitchen and sat her down. She didn't want to worry her but seeing as she was here she had to tell her what was happening.

"Luna hasn't come home from school. I was worried and I called Detective Canter's phone and her wife answered. She said she thinks Luna is with Detective Canter," Monique began to explain.

"Because Spencer isn't Spencer?" Pearl asked.

"How did you know?" Monique asked.

Pearl closed her eyes for a brief second. "After Spencer told me to go home last night, Detective Canter spotted me walking home, she gave me a lift and I told her that

Spencer just didn't seem the same. My Spencer wouldn't have kicked me out so late at night."

"I thought that too, but then I dismissed it and thought that maybe he just wanted to get to bed and rest. I don't really know what came over me last night," Monique said, her head falling into her hands.

"OK, I've managed to settle Maxine," Martha whispered when she came back into the kitchen.

"I'm sorry dear. I had no idea there was a little one here," Pearl apologised.

"It's perfectly fine. I'm still getting used to her myself," Martha laughed.

"So you knew Spencer wasn't Spencer?" Monique asked.

"Oh, something didn't sit right and Luna felt it too. I know that's why Donna came round last night," Pearl replied.

"I think I know where they are, but I don't think it will be good if we all storm in there, I have a feeling Spencer will be there too," Martha told them. "I'd hate to palm Maxine off so early onto someone, but I trust you both. Would you mind her whilst I go and check?"

"You go right ahead dear. We've both done this baby stuff before. Keep us informed?" Pearl replied. She rose from her seat and wandered over to the pram. "Oh she's a beauty." Pearl bent down and scooped Maxine into her arms. She walked with her to the window overlooking the garden and sang to her. Maxine didn't stir an inch.

Martha took a last look at Maxine and threw the front door open. She stepped out and looked towards Flowerly Hall. She had never been through those gates. Something had stopped her every time she tried. She didn't know what it was but something would make her feet stop just before she walked through. She held her head high and pushed the gate open. Looking up at the roof of the house, she willed her feet to move but they wouldn't. Something frightened her about this house. She turned back but, still, her feet wouldn't move. She stood for a moment, rooted to the spot. She could only turn in a circle. After turning left and right, she stared head on at the house.

"Whatever or whoever it is stopping me from walking through these gates better get out of my way, I'm coming in whether you like it or not," she shouted.

And with that, her feet moved, walking her to the front door of the house and in the door. She looked up at the spiral staircase and began climbing. She had no idea where her feet were taking her so she let them do them walking. As she climbed she looked around at the house. It was in a reasonable condition considering how long it had stood empty.

'Maybe the rumours were true. Maybe Edith did keep the house clean,' she thought.

She came to a halt at the door of the third room along the first corridor. The door opened by itself. Her feet took her inside and over to a tall chest of drawers. The top drawer was slightly open, so she pulled it open some more. She reached inside at the photo lying alone inside. When she held it up in front of her face and nearly fainted. In the photo stood a man and a woman with two children in front of them. The young girl looked very much like herself. She placed the photo on top of the chest and walked away from it, her feet taking her to another part of the room. The wardrobe in the far corner swung open and in it hung a dress, much like the one the girl in the picture was wearing. Without missing a beat, Martha pulled on the dress. Something seemed to have taken over her body; she twirled in front of the mirror. Keeping the dress on, her feet walked her out of the door and towards the end of the corridor. Another door flew open. Inside she could hear soft cries. As she peered through the door, she saw nobody, but the cries were still there.

"Oh Penelope, I wish I could have saved you," she heard.

Martha thought for a second. She had heard her parents talk about a distant, long lost relative called Penelope, but surely, this couldn't have anything to do with her.

"Hello? Is there anyone here?" She called out. She walked inside the room and the door slammed behind her.

Martha looked around the room as it slowly got darker. As she huddled in the corner of the room, her breath became more hurried. Her heart was beating so fast, she felt like she had been running a marathon. She tried to slow her breathing down but nothing worked. Her eyes fluttered shut and the room went dark.

"Penelope, is that you?" She heard a voice ask.

"No, my name is Martha. Who are you?" She asked back.

As she narrowed her eyes against the dark, she could just make out a figure walking towards her.

"Stay back," she called, trying to sound anything but scared, but her voice shook like a magnitude nine earthquake.

"You asked who I was. I'm showing you," came a deep voice from the dark.

"Step forward, slowly," Martha said.

From the shadows came a man, his face still wet from his tears and his eyes as red as rubies. He looked at her and his breath caught in his throat. "You look so much like her."

"Like who?" Martha asked.

"My Penelope. I'm being rude, I'm sorry," he said. He extended his hand, "I'm Thomas. Penelope was my daughter."

Martha was stunned. This was the man from the photo in the first bedroom. He looked very familiar. The eyes were kind and looked a lot like her late grandfathers.

"Do I know you? You look really familiar," she asked.

"As do you my dear. Henry did well," Thomas replied.

Martha's eyes flew open.

"Great Great GrandDad Thomas?"

Chapter 52

Donna led Spencer along the corridor that turned left at the top of the second set of stairs. She came to a stop at the very last door on the right.

"Here it is!" Donna called.

"How can you be so sure? There are so many rooms in this house," Spencer replied. He had dropped back a little.

"Trust me, I was here earlier, I know this house like the back of my hand," Donna shrugged. "At least, I *think* it's this one. It could be the one of the left. Let me check."

Spencer pushed her aside, "I'll check it out."

Donna stepped aside and let him open the door. He pushed it wide and stepped inside. "I don't see her."

"Are you sure?" Donna asked popping her head through the doorway. "Ah, I see what you mean. Must have been the left door then."

"If you are trying to distract me, it isn't going to work," Spencer hissed.

"Who said anything about distracting you? All these doors look the same right?" Donna laughed.

Spencer shook his head as Donna turned round to the door behind her. She opened the door and peeked inside. "That's odd. I'm sure it was this one."

"Where is my daughter?" Spencer shouted.

From behind them a door opened. "I'm right here," Luna replied.

"Oh it was *that* door!" Donna rolled her eyes. "All the doors..."

Spencer was getting angrier by the second. He grabbed Luna by the arm and attempted to drag her away but he couldn't move her. He looked behind her but saw no one. "What? Why aren't you moving?"

"I don't know, maybe I'm going to be stuck here forever," Luna cried. "Someone help me."

Spencer turned to Donna. "You have to help her, she can't move."

Donna pulled on Luna's left arm whilst Spencer pulled on her right, between them, Luna still wouldn't budge.

"I have an idea," Donna said. "I'll go behind her and push her, you get ready to catch her," she told Spencer.

He nodded and held his arms out wide.

As Donna squeezed past Luna, she smiled and winked at her. Luna knew the plan.

"Ready?" Donna called.

"Ready," Spencer shouted back.

"3, 2, 1," Donna called and pulled Luna back into the room and slammed the door shut, throwing the bolt across the door.

Spencer kicked and pounded on the door.

"What do we do now?" Luna asked.

"Through here?" Jhordan called from a little door way in the far wall. "I found another room."

Donna and Luna followed him through the doorway and out into a pastel blue room.

"Wow, where in the house is this?" Donna asked.

"I don't know. I was too scared to open that door," Jhordan said as he pointed at a rather ominous looking door. It hard gargoyles engraved in the main body of the door and the handle was the shape of the devil's tail.

"I don't like the look of it," Donna recoiled from it.

"How do we get back?" Luna asked. She was pointing at the space where the door they came through had been. It was now gone.

"Oh boy. You know, I was starting to like this house, now, I'm not too sure," Donna replied. She sunk down to the floor leaning her back against the wall.

Luna traced her hands across the wall, hoping to find a way out. "How did you manage to get back Jhordan?"

"I left the door open. I think that's where we went wrong. We closed the door to prevent Spencer following us and now, we're stuck," Jhordan replied.

Donna looked at Luna. "Is there anyone or anything in here with us?"

Luna shook her head. "No, this room is, for want of a better word, dead. Nothing has touched this room since the death of a young boy called Jeremiah. He died in this house, in the basement."

"OK. I don't need to hear anymore about that," Donna said.

Luna shrugged. "He would be the only one who could get us out."

"What?" Donna cried. "You could have started with that!"

Luna giggled. "I'm sorry. I can try and contact him. The basement is under this room.

Luna lay on the floor with her ear to the floor. She took a breath to speak and call out for Jeremiah but instead she gasped.

"What is it?" Jhordan said, scrambling to her side. He lay on the floor next to her and followed her gaze. He then jumped to his feet and slid the bed across the floor with a high pitched screech.

Donna was amazed. There, on the floor, was a trapdoor. She tugged at the handle but nothing happened. She tried again and it pulled up a little only for it to slam back down again. Donna tried again. This time it stayed shut.

"Pointless," she exclaimed. She looked back at Luna to find her sitting, cross legged on the floor.

Jhordan pressed his finger to his lips and pointed at Luna.

"You don't want any visitors?" Luna whispered. She nodded her head. "I'm sorry if we disturbed you. We really need to get out of here, can you help?" She nodded again and got to her feet. She walked to the window and bent down. "This one?" She then pulled the panel from under the window sill. "Thank you."

"What...What was that?" Donna asked.

"That was Jeremiah. He wasn't happy about us pulling on the door, but he told me to climb through here and we will end up in the last door in the first corridor. Let's go," Luna explained.

Donna was speechless. This girl was astounding and incredibly calm. She followed Luna through and Jhordan followed her. They crawled through the cramped space, stopping now and then to catch their breath. "How will we know if we make it?" She asked.

At just that second, the wall to the left of Luna fell through and they all tumbled out, landing in a heap next to Martha.

"Oh, hey babe! Where's Maxine?" Donna asked sounding worried.

"She is with Monique and Pearl. Donna something happened in here," Martha whispered.

Donna looked at Martha's clothes. This wasn't what she was wearing earlier. "Yeah, looks like it. Why are you dressed like that?"

Martha looked down at the dress she was wearing. "That's what I have to explain to you."

Just as she finished, the door to the room burst open and Spencer stood in the doorway, huffing and puffing with anger. "Right you little brat," he said, grabbing Luna's arm. "You're coming with me and I will kill anyone who stands in my way."

Donna held Jhordan back. The plan was to hold him here until Max and Thomas arrived. *'Where are they?'* Donna asked herself.

"OK, Mr Heart, there's no need for violence. Put Luna down," Martha said calmly. "You won't get her to do anything if you're acting like that."

Spencer looked Martha up and down and began to laugh. "Do you really think I would take orders from someone who wears that?"

Martha pulled the dress over her head to reveal her black jeans and cream tank underneath. "How about now?" She said flashing her badge.

Spencer placed Luna on the floor but didn't release his grip on her arm. Luna didn't thrash around or try to get free. She stood facing Spencer and stared into his soul. She didn't blink. Her eyes flickered from red to black.

"What's happening to her?" Spencer cried.

"I don't know what you mean. She looks perfectly normal to me," Donna said, looking at Luna.

"Her eyes. They keep changing," Spencer cried, he sounded even more distraught.

Donna walked towards Luna and looked at her face. "I still don't see any problems. Are you sure Spencer?"

"I'm p...positive," he stuttered. He quickly let go of Luna's arm and ran to the other side of the room. He cowered against the wall, visibly shaking.

 As Donna and Martha got closer to Luna, her eyes were still the same dark brown colour they were earlier in the day. Luna walked over to Jhordan and stood by his side. She didn't even acknowledge Spencer. Donna and Martha were puzzled. No one dared go near Spencer. He Mumbled all sorts of inaudible things. Within a few moments, the whole room fell into darkness.

"Luna, are you and Jhordan OK?" Martha called out. She could hardly see her hand in front of her face.

"We're OK," Jhordan replied. "I think. I can't see Luna." He began to panic.

"OK Jhordan, I need you to slow your breathing down for me honey, OK?" Donna called out. "I'll try and find my way to you."

That was harder than she thought it would be. When the room went dark, it also threw their sense of direction off. Being unable to see, Donna walked into the bed and then into the chest of drawers.

"It's no good. I don't even know which way I'm walking," Donna said as she slumped onto the floor, bashing her knee on the dressing table leg.

"Maybe we should just stay put for now," Martha said calmly. "Hey Spencer, you OK?"

Spencer didn't reply, but they could still hear the slightest of Mumblings from him. Donna wondered what he was Mumbling. She wasn't going to risk trying to get closer to him but she wished she knew what he was saying.

"Donna!"

Luna's screams pulled Donna from her thoughts; she looked round just in time to see the door slam shut. She only managed to catch sight of Luna before she was pulled away.

"Luna!" She cried out. Just as she reached out the room lit up with a flash of lightening.

Spencer was gone.

Chapter 53

"I wonder what's taking so long," Pearl said as she walked back from the kitchen with Maxine's bottle.

"I don't know. I don't want to go there again. Not so soon after all that," Monique replied taking the bottle and placing the teat next to Maxine's mouth. She took the bottle well and filled her stomach.

"How are you feeling after all that honey?" Pearl asked as she sat next to Monique on the sofa.

"I feel drained. I've never used my power like that before and I just feel like I could sleep forever," Monique said, closing her eyes briefly.

Pearl took hold of Maxine and settled her on her lap. "Why don't you go and grab some rest? I'll wake you if there is any news."

"Are you sure? I don't feel like I would be any help to anyone like this," Monique replied. She got to her feet and stretched her hands high above her head.

"I'm sure, now go," Pearl laughed. She sat Maxine up and rubbed her back. Seconds later she let out a huge belch. "Well, that's a sign of decent feeding!" Within seconds, Maxine was sound asleep. Pearl slowly stood up and placed her back in her pram and watched Monique walk up the stairs to rest.

"You poor girl. All this happening to you and no one to turn to, well, I'll always be here," she whispered. She looked back into the pram, "I'll be here for you too."

Pearl walked to the bookshelf and pulled out one of the books, sat on the sofa and began reading.

Donna pulled at the door handle and began pounding the door with her fists.

Jhordan stood in the centre of the room shaking his head. "This can't happen. He can't take her, I won't let him!" He shouted. He ran towards the door and kicked it clean off its hinges.

"Well young man, fancy a job?" Donna remarked. "You could break down doors for us on the force!"

The lightening continued to flash. Just as one bolt flashed, Martha waited for the thunder but none came. "Wait," she cried. "Where is the thunder?"

Donna stopped in her tracks, she hadn't thought about that. Her mind was on tracking Luna down and finding out where the hell Max and Thomas were.

Jhordan carried on running; he turned left at the end of the corridor and burst through another door. As he came to a grounding halt; there at the centre of the room sat Spencer, tied to a chair. Jhordan couldn't believe his eyes. Luna stood next to Thomas and she just stared at Spencer.

"Jhordan, what did you...Oh!" Donna called out as she and Martha finally caught up with him. "What the?"

Martha stood next to Donna and they both stared at the scene before then.

"So this is where you've both been? Well, thanks for helping with him," Donna said pointing at Spencer.

"I apologise. I was otherwise engaged for a while," Thomas said, his head hanging down.

"Thomas, what is it?" Jhordan asked, running to his side.

"That's what I was trying to say earlier," Martha whispered.

Donna spun round and looked at her. "What? When you mentioned something happened? What is it?"

Thomas pulled a photo from his pocket and handed it to Donna. "Look at the young girl at the front and then look at your wife," he said.

Donna took the photo and Jhordan looked over her shoulder.

"Oh my," Jhordan gasped. "She looks so much like her. Who is it?"

"That was my daughter, Penelope," Thomas replied. "And that there was Henry, my son." He pointed out the young boy.

"Henry was my great grandfather," Martha said softly. "Thomas is my great great grandfather."

Donna had to hold onto Jhordan to stop herself from falling.

"Babe, are you OK?" Martha held onto Donnas arm.

"I...I'm just stunned, I'll be fine. Don't worry," Donna smiled.

"I bet you're wondering why I gathered you all here today," Max burst into the conversation. "Oh wait, what did I miss?"

"Did you know Martha and Thomas were related?" Donna asked.

"Well, yeah. I thought you knew?" He replied, looking between Martha and Thomas. "You didn't?"

"No they didn't! Maybe you could have let me know?" Donna and Martha said in unison.

"Ah, see that there, that shows you two are meant to be," Max laughed. "I remember Mum always finished Dads' sentences."

Donna smiled at him, "you remember some really useless stuff don't you?"

Max shrugged. "I guess, but it keeps me warm at night."

Donna shook her head, "always the joker!"

Whilst they were laughing, Spencer had tried to untie himself, only for Luna to step towards him and pin him to the chair.

"You're not my father," she told him, staring deep into his eyes. "I don't want you here."

"OK, I think that is our cue to get this over with," Max said as he turned to see Luna staring at Spencer with a hatred he had never seen in anyone before.

Thomas gestured to Donna and Martha to stand back. They pulled Jhordan with them. Watching Max and Thomas work together, Donnas' heart burst with pride. She missed her brother, even if he had been a bit of an idiot before. He had more than made up for it by doing all of this to help Luna.

"Michael Trystone, you can come out now," Max goaded. "We know it's you."

"You know nothing," Spencer growled. "You know absolutely nothing."

Max turned to Thomas. "Looks like we will have to do this the hard way. I mean he could have just come to the surface and left peacefully but...oh well."

Thomas smiled at Max; he knew he was trying to make this less painful for Luna to watch. She missed her father and she was hurt and angry that someone had taken her father's place.

"Here we go then," Thomas said, clapping his hands once. Everyone stared at him. Everyone except Luna. Hey eyes remained fixed on Spencer, flicking from red to black again.

Spencer tried to look away but some unknown force kept his eyes on hers. He squirmed and wriggled, trying to get free, but Luna's grip got tighter and tighter.

"Michael Trystone." Thomas's voice boomed and ricocheted off the walls. "You are summoned to leave this body and return to the deep. You were not granted leave. Either you come willingly or force will have to be taken."

"Like I said to your friend over there," Spencer replied, nodding in Max's direction. "You know nothing about me."

"I know enough to be able to pull your wife and children from their resting places and have them confirm who you are," Thomas told him. "It would take me mere seconds to locate them and bring them here."

"Well, my child is there," Spencer said, looking towards Luna, who had suddenly taken on a new, fierce look. Her eyes bore into Spencer's soul and she had begun to bear her teeth.

"Max," Donna whispered. "Max, come here."

Max glided over to her, "what is it?"

"What the hell have you done to Luna?" She hissed.

"Nothing. Honest. We haven't done anything to her. I don't know why she is behaving like this," Max defended.

Donna was worried.

"Try not to get worked up babe," Martha said as she gently placed her hand on Donnas' arm.

"I've got a bad feeling about this," Jhordan whispered.

Thomas stood over Luna and Spencer and held his hand above Spencer's head. "You have three seconds to disperse from this shell and return to where you belong."

"And if I don't," Spencer smiled. It was an evil smile. One Donna wouldn't forget in a hurry. She tried to get the image of him murdering his family out of her head but after seeing that smile she couldn't.

"Well, if you don't," Thomas began.

Luna growled. Her teeth had become sharpened knives, she bared them at him.

"What has she become?" Spencer cried, trying to turn his head away from her.

"Of that we are unsure, but we know it is not of this world or the other. Maybe you are more acquainted with it?" Max asked.

"No, no it can't be. I made a deal," Spencer screamed.

"The deal was broken as soon as you had those thoughts Michael," Luna hissed. "You now have to return."

"But you can't be him," Spencer whispered.

"I am and I can be," Luna hissed again. "Leave the body or suffer the consequences."

Spencer looked around at the people in the room. "If it hadn't been for you being nosey, I would have gone on with this life," he said as he looked at Donna.

"Hey listen, don't blame me. You weren't even supposed to *be* here!" Donna shouted back.

Luna hissed as she got closer to his face, "what is it to be Michael?"

"I'm not leaving. You can't make me. Your power is useless here," Spencer grinned.

"If you say so," Luna smiled.

She arched her back and let out a gut wrenching roar. As she brought her head back down, her eyes were now flaming red. She growled from deep in her throat and grabbed Spencer by the throat. She pulled her head back, ripping his throat from his body. She spat the flesh on the floor and reached her hand deep inside his body.

Donna turned away before she threw up. What had happened to the young girl who had her father stolen from her? To the girl who helped the spirits connect with their living loved ones? She had become a monster.

Jhordan kept his eyes on Luna the whole time she tore at Spencer's body. This wasn't the girl he knew, but he wasn't scared. He had seen worse when he was with Aura.

As Luna withdrew her hand, there was a glowing white orb in her grasp. She held it up and admired its glow. She looked at it from different angles before rising up to the roof and then, with a flash of light, disappearing into the night.

"Where? What? Max, explain," Donna demanded.

"I...Yeah I don't know," Max admitted. "Thomas?"

"The underground boss likes to make deals with the bad souls. It seems he had a deal with Michael, only he broke a rule and that meant the deal was invalid and he would have to return immediately. Michael believed the boss didn't have any power here, but, thanks to yours truly, he is able to take Michael back to where he belongs," Thomas explained.

"Will she come back as Luna?" Jhordan asked quietly.

"Oh young man. Of course she will. Just give her a few minutes," Thomas replied.

"What about her Dad?" Jhordan asked.

"That we have to wait for, but I warn you. It might not happen. If it does, it will take him a while to adjust. They will have to be patient with him," Thomas replied.

Jhordan focused his attention back on the gaping hole in the roof. He pleaded for Luna to come back. He felt like he had been staring forever when he felt the pressure of a hand on his shoulder.

"Jhordan, are you OK?"

Jhordan spun round and came face to face with Luna.

"But, you just..." He began.

"I know. It's hard to explain, but let's go home. I'm real tired," Luna whispered. Her eyes began to flutter closed.

Jhordan swept her up and headed for the door.

"Not so fast," Thomas stopped him. "Let me check her over first."

Jhordan set Luna down on the nearby bed and stepped back, only far enough to allow Thomas to see that she was OK.

"It's OK Jhordan. He won't hurt her," Donna said as she pulled him back a bit further. "I'll watch over him."

Martha took Jhordan from Donnas grip and walked him over to the window. "She will be OK. You know how strong she is."

Jhordan had no words. He kept his gaze on Thomas's back. He didn't want anything to happen to her. He watched every move Thomas made until he finally stepped away from Luna and turned to face him.

"She's OK. She's just very tired," Thomas told him.

"I'll take her home," Jhordan said. He scooped Luna from the bed and headed out the door.

Donna watched from the window as Jhordan carried Luna across the car park and out the gates.

"What happens now?" She asked Max and Thomas.

"We wait and see. There have been no guarantees as to whether Spencer will return or not. It is his choice," Max explained.

Martha stood at Thomas's side. "So where do we go from here?"

"You go home and look after that precious baby. I'll always be here. You can visit, if you'd like," Thomas replied.

Martha nodded. "I'd like that very much."

Donna watched the exchange between Martha and Thomas. She was glad that Martha finally had some real blood family around, especially after her parents had disowned her when she had come out.

Chapter 54

Monique awoke from a restless sleep, jumping out of bed when she heard the front door close. She pulled on her slippers and ran down the stairs, just in time to see Jhordan place Luna on the sofa.

"Oh my, what's wrong with her?" Monique cried as she rushed to her daughter's side.

"Nothing, she is fine, just very tired. I will explain more, but can I use your bathroom?" Jhordan replied.

"Of course, it's at the top of the stairs," Monique told him.

Whilst Jhordan used the bathroom, Monique covered Luna in a chunky knit blanket. Pearl had drifted off to sleep in the corner chair with a book resting on her chest and Maxine was still sound asleep in her pram. Monique went to the kitchen and switched on the kettle. She placed two cups on the side and spooned heaps of hot chocolate into them. Jhordan ventured into the room just as the kettle finished boiling. He had his phone to his ear.

"I'm fine, I promise. I'm at Luna's house now," he said. "I'll be home soon."

After he had placed the phone in his pocket he looked over at Monique who stood with a full cup in her hand. She passed it to him and gestured for him to sit at the breakfast bar.

"Bruce?" She asked.

"Yes, he has been worried but he said he had a feeling he knew where I would be," Jhordan replied. "Is that normal for parents?"

Monique laughed, "oh absolutely. Sometimes we can sense where our children will be, but tonight was different. I thought all this was over with until detective Canter's wife explained everything to me."

"I'm so sorry you have had to endure all of this. I feel partly responsible," Jhordan told her. He hung his head low.

There was a sudden rapping at the door. Monique sat perfectly still. She still wasn't fully trusting.

"I'll get it," Jhordan said as he stood up. He quickly peeked out of the side window. Spotting Bruce he opened the door and let him in.

"I thought I'd come over and check on everyone. Where's Mrs Heart?" Bruce asked, pulling Jhordan in for a brief hug.

"Which one?" Jhordan laughed.

Bruce realised what he had said and a grin formed across his face. "Monique, where is she?"

"Oh, in the kitchen. I'm just going to check on Luna," Jhordan said, pointing towards the kitchen door where Monique randomly appeared.

"Come through Bruce, tea?" Monique asked.

Bruce nodded and followed her into the kitchen. Jhordan snuck into the living room and gently brushed a piece of hair away from Luna's eyes.

"She's a tough one isn't she?" Pearl whispered from the chair in the corner.

"Oh, Mrs Heart, you made me jump," Jhordan said as he spun his head round to where she was sitting.

"I'm sorry son. Is she going to be OK?" Pearl asked.

Jhordan nodded. "Thomas said she would be, but she is just tired. She was a different being back there. I think it scared everyone,"

Jhordan explained to Pearl what had happened in Flowerly Hall. She wasn't surprised by anything he said. Even when he explained that she became this evil monster.

"It is normal for someone with Luna's gift to be taken over by someone or something from the spirit world, it is something you will have to learn to live with young man," Pearl winked.

As Pearl finished speaking, Luna stirred. She woke up slowly, holding her head in her hands.

"Luna, are you OK?" Jhordan whispered.

"Can you get me some water please?" Luna said, her voice sounding rough.

Jhordan ran to the kitchen and grabbed a glass of water.

"Is Luna awake?" Monique asked as he filled the glass.

"Yes," Jhordan replied. He took the water back to Luna and told her to sip it.

She obeyed and, gradually, her voice returned to normal.

"Oh sweetie," Monique cooed as she ran to Luna's side.

"I'm fine Mum. I don't know what is going to happen with Dad," Luna said softly. "I don't know if he will come back or not."

"We will have to wait and see," Monique told her.

Bruce watched from the doorway and was startled when Maxine awoke in the pram next to him. He reached in and gently picked her up. "Well, aren't you a cute little bundle."

"I almost forgot about her, she was so quiet," Pearl exclaimed. "Oh, she doesn't smell too nice." Pearl giggled and stood to take over.

"I can do it, if you'd like?" Bruce said.

"Are you sure?" Pearl questioned.

"Absolutely. Changing bag?" He asked.

Pearl pointed to the yellow and white striped bag hanging off the handle of the pram.

"Thanks, I'll take her to the bathroom," Bruce said grabbing the bag and humming a tune to Maxine who gurgled at him.

"I didn't expect him to be a dab hand with babies," Pearl whispered to Monique.

"He had children before he died. He knows what he is doing," Jhordan laughed.

Monique smiled. *'Bruce is a nice guy,'* she thought to herself. *'Not bad looking either.'* She laughed to herself. What was she thinking?

Martha and Donna walked back to the Hearts' home to collect Maxine. They hadn't said a word to each other since they left Flowerly Hall. They held hands but said nothing. Arriving at Monique's door, Martha knocked twice and the door swung open.

"Oh, hi," Bruce welcomed them with Maxine in his arms.

"Well, this is a surprise," Donna giggled, plucking Maxine from his arms. "Didn't have you down as a baby man."

"I did have children you know," Bruce laughed. "I took over night feeds."

As the two women entered the living room, Luna stood up and walked to Martha. She hugged her hard.

"Thomas is a good man. You're lucky to have him in your life. He misses his family." Luna whispered.

"Thank you Luna. I'm sure he can visit his family's grave though, can't he?" Martha asked.

Luna shook her head. "His family are buried very far south. The evil took him from his grave and placed him in charge of Flowerly Hall. He can't travel that far. You are now his closest relative."

Martha sunk to the sofa. She wished she had known more about her family. She had the chance, now, to get to know the background of her life. "I will make time to visit Thomas often."

"He would like that," Luna replied.

Donna watched the interaction and smiled. She had her family now. She felt a vibration in her pocket. Pulling her phone out whilst balancing Maxine in her arms, she noticed it was Savannah.

"Hey 'Vannah, what's up?" She answered.

"Hey, I, erm, I've had some bad news," Savannah replied, there was a muffling sound just after she finished talking.

"What's happened?" Donna asked, quickly passing Maxine to Monique and walking to the kitchen for some privacy.

"After I left Flowerly Hall, I drove back towards the station. I was going to catch up on some paperwork. I pulled into the car park and my phone was ringing. I parked up and answered it. It was Christian's sister. Christian was involved in a car accident earlier today. He's dead," Savannah cried.

"Oh 'Vannah! I'm so sorry. Do you want me to come to you?" Donna said softly.

"Could you come over tomorrow? I'm going to Beverly's house tonight," Savannah replied.

"Absolutely, call me if you need anything," Donna said and she ended the call. When she walked back into the living room, Bruce now held Maxine and Martha was looking at something on Luna's laptop.

"Is everything OK babe?" Martha asked when she saw the look on Donnas' face.

Donna relayed everything Savannah had just told her. Everyone in the room was silent. Luna tilted her head slightly and smiled.

"Can you call Savannah back please, I have a message for her," Luna asked Donna.

Donna pulled her phone out and dialled Savannah. "Luna has a message for you."

"Mrs Shepherd. Mr Shepherd says you and Precious are going to be fine. He is watching over you both," Luna told her.

"Precious?" Savannah asked.

"You are carrying a girl Mrs Shepherd. You will call her Precious," Luna told her. "Goodbye Mrs Shepherd."

Donna had tears in her eyes. She let the tears fall as she placed the phone back in her pocket.

Martha stood to embrace Donna and Bruce brought Maxine to them. "I think you need a family hug." He said.

Monique and Pearl watched how gentle Bruce was with Maxine. He always seemed to know the perfect words to say. He walked towards them with a solemn smile.

"I feel for them all," he said.

"Such a tragedy. Savannah is going to be a wonderful mother, and we will all be here to support her," Pearl replied.

Monique studied Bruce closely. He wasn't bad to look at and she had never looked at another man since Spencer. He had a kind face.

Bruce turned to look at her. "If I'm overstepping the mark here, please tell me, but I'd like to take you to dinner sometime?"

"Oh, erm, I, well," Monique stuttered.

'You deserve to be happy my love. Take him up on his offer, he is a kind man. I won't be returning, but I will watch you from here. I will always love you,' she heard Spencer's voice.

She turned back to Bruce. "I would love to. Could we, perhaps, take things slowly?"

"We will go at your pace," Bruce said.

He then leant over and kissed her on the cheek.

Luna watched her mother with Bruce. She turned to Jhordan and linked with his arm laying her head on his shoulder. "My Dad isn't coming home." She said sadly. "Will you stay with me?"

"Always," Jhordan replied. "I won't leave you."

He bent his head slightly and kissed her on the head. He never imagined how much she would come to mean to him. From the first day up to now, she had become more than a target for Aura's evil plan. She had become his best friend and he hoped, with time, she could become more.

Pearl watched as her family began to piece itself back together again. She took a deep breath and smiled. "Oh William. I wish I knew where you had gone, look how much you have missed out on."

'I've not gone far my sweet, but you know I'm not coming home. I'm always by your side. Forever and for always. We will see each other again. I love you.'

Pearl smiled at the sound of William's voice. She settled back into the chair and fell fast asleep.

The End

9 781068 681332